STANDING STRONG

THERESA LINDEN

Copyright © 2017 by Theresa A. Linden

All rights reserved. This book or any portion thereof may not be reproduced or used in any manner whatsoever without the express written permission of the publisher except for the use of brief quotations in a book review.

This is a work of fiction. Names, characters, businesses, places, events, and incidents are either the products of the author's imagination or are used in a fictitious manner. Any resemblance to actual persons, living or dead, or actual events or locales is purely coincidental.

Scripture quotations are from The Revised Standard Version of the Bible: Catholic Edition, copyright © 1965, 1966 the Division of Christian Education of the National Council of the Churches of Christ in the United States of America. Used by permission. All rights reserved.

http://theresalinden.com

Library of Congress Control Number: 2017909653

ISBN-13: 978-0-9976747-2-9

First Edition Silver Fire Publishing, October 2017

Cover: Theresa Linden

Editor: Lisa Mayer

PRAISE FOR *STANDING STRONG*

"Another chapter in Theresa Linden's masterfully-developed series for teens that will resonate with everyone who has struggled to find his place in the world, been tempted to take the easy way out, or doubted the work of God's hand in his life."
~Carolyn Astfalk, author of coming-of-age romance *Rightfully Ours*

"Theresa Linden is an amazing talent in Catholic teen fiction. The ease with which she draws the reader into each scene, with outstanding descriptions and her ability to capture the heart and soul of the tough Jarret West, make *Standing Strong* her most powerful and gripping book yet."
~Leslea Wahl, author of award-winning YA fiction, *The Perfect Blindside*

"It's not easy to reinvent yourself while you're still in high school, Jarret West discovers as he seeks a way to turn his life around after an intense spiritual experience. His twin brother couldn't be more different: Keefe contemplates joining the Franciscan friars. Theresa Linden recounts twin spiritual quests in her newest novel, *Standing Strong.*"
~Barb Szyszkiewicz, editor at CatholicMom.com

"Linden is a master at getting inside the heads of today's teenagers, and her own deep faith and love of God shine through and inspire on every page. After reading *Standing Strong*, your own spiritual life cannot but be strengthened, making you also want to stand strong for God. Highly recommended!"
~Susan Peek, author of *St. Magnus, The Last Viking*

"*Standing Strong* is a beautiful testament to how God works—in the whispers, in the quiet moments, in the gentle guidance of our hearts. It's a reminder that Jesus is with us in ways we may never understand, and that, if we allow it, the Holy Spirit will give us the strength to stand strong for God!"
~Lisa Mayer, author of The Aletheian Journeys Series

BOOKS BY THERESA LINDEN

CHASING LIBERTY TRILOGY

Chasing Liberty
Testing Liberty
Fight for Liberty

WEST BROTHERS SERIES

Roland West, Loner
Life-Changing Love
Battle for His Soul
Standing Strong

SHORT STORIES

"Bound to Find Freedom"
"A Symbol of Hope"
"Made for Love" (in the anthology *Image and Likeness: Literary Reflections on the Theology of the Body*)
"Full Reversal" (in the anthology *Image and Likeness: Literary Reflections on the Theology of the Body*)

DEDICATION

This book is dedicated to my teenage boys, Joseph, Justin, and Cisco. You might not always feel the presence of God but know that He is with you and He has a plan for your life that will give you far greater happiness than you can ever imagine. Trust and surrender.

ACKNOWLEDGMENTS

I am grateful for the assistance I have received from several talented authors: Carolyn Astfalk, Virginia Bliss, Susan Peek, and my editor Lisa Mayer. These authors have helped me to grow as a writer and have encouraged and supported me through this project. I also wish to express my gratitude to Barb Szyszkiewicz for reading an advanced copy of this story even with all her new obligations. Last but not least, I will always be thankful for the love and support of my husband and three boys; I wouldn't be able to write my stories without them.

"Be strong and of good courage...
for it is the Lord your God who goes with you;
He will not fail you or forsake you."
~Deuteronomy 31:6

"Do not be conformed to this world
but be transformed by the renewal of your mind,
that you may prove what is the will of God,
what is good and acceptable and perfect."
~Romans 12:2

CHAPTER 1

Heart racing out of control, seventeen-year-old Jarret West swung open the door to the confessional with a sweaty hand and stumbled out. Eyes to the floor but not really seeing, he staggered to the front of the quiet church and slid into a pew. He lowered the kneeler, dropped to his knees, and slumped over. A bead of sweat dripped down the back of his neck. Too exhausted to care, he let it trace a path to the neckline of his shirt.

"Hail Mary, full of grace..." He moved his lips as he prayed his penance, his voice less than a whisper. The weight of the sins of his past had lifted as Father had spoken the words of absolution, transporting him to the clouds. The effect was similar to the first time he'd confessed them, back in Arizona, after piling up more sins than he should've for a kid his age.

Now he couldn't think straight. But he had to. He needed to plan.

Jarret opened his eyes and caught sight of his hands trembling, dangling over the pew in front of him. He clasped them together and lifted his gaze to the tabernacle. His teary eyes and the spotlight shining on the tabernacle's gold finish made a starburst.

"I know You're in there. Won't You speak to me?" he whispered, hoping vainly for a reply, a feeling, a holy thought popping into his mind. Anything.

Whispers came from the back of the church. And footfalls. Someone coming down the aisle to do their penance, no doubt.

Not wanting to meet up with anyone he knew, he pushed himself up and dashed out the side door of the church. The air cooled his sweaty neck and invigorated him a bit. Squinting against the setting sun, he jogged around the church and glimpsed his red Chrysler 300 on the far side of the parish parking lot. Sun drenched the old blacktop with faded parking stripes. He counted several cars but no people.

As he hustled across it, he dug his keys from his pocket. He pressed "unlock" on the key fob several times, though the headlights had flashed at his first touch, telling him he'd unlocked it. He yanked the car door open. A pungent odor assaulted him.

Irritation and foul thoughts threatening to disrupt his calm, he collapsed into the seat and shoved the key into the ignition. He peeled out of the parking lot with a hand to the window controls, lowering all four windows.

Doggone thing still reeks of Limburger cheese.

He'd discovered the smell three weeks ago, the day he, Papa, and his younger brother, Roland, had returned from Arizona. He'd offered to pick up pizza for their live-in maid and caretaker, Nanny. He'd opened his car for the first time in weeks and gagged. Breathing through their shirts, he and his twin brother, Keefe, dug through the car until they found the source of the smell: a huge block of spoiled Limburger cheese under a seat.

Immediately suspecting Roland's friend Peter, Jarret's anger had propelled him toward the house. Peter was always messing with Jarret, taunting him, and Jarret was tired of him getting away with it. To his irritation, Keefe had stopped him in his tracks and told him to let it go. It took a massive amount of self-control, but he did let it go. At least for that moment. Keefe sprayed air freshener in the car, and they rode with the windows down. The next day, Jarret paid to have the interior cleaned and detailed.

Doggone thing still reeked, especially when closed up for more than an hour.

Jarret turned onto a main road. He hadn't seen Peter since. He'd just confessed indulging in feelings of hate and revenge—and visualizing his fist removing the smug smile from Peter's face—along with everything he'd confessed to the priest in Arizona. That had been his first real confession in years, probably since he'd made his first confession in grade school. Back when Mama was still alive. "Once you've sincerely confessed," Father Carston, their white-haired, forty-something parish priest, had said today, "it's forgiven. You can let it go. And work on forgiving yourself and others."

Easier said than done. But he'd only confessed it all again because he figured if Father Carston was going to be his spiritual director, he should know the real Jarret.

Spiritual director... Jarret shook his head and sighed. Had he lost his mind? The priest in Arizona told him he should get one. Jarret had been going to Mass on Sundays since then, but he'd put off finding a spiritual director. Until today.

Squinting at the sunlight that reflected off the road, Jarret took a deep breath and exhaled. He willed himself to relax, to come down from the emotional state his confession had left him in.

In the canyon in southern Arizona, he'd promised himself he'd make up for his sins, especially for the way he'd treated his younger brother, Roland. He didn't feel the commitment as zealously now. But he still intended to do it. Having a spiritual director would help. And not seeking revenge on Peter was a good first step. He'd work on actual forgiveness later.

Please, God, don't let us cross paths for a while.

Jarret sped past the high school and toward the outskirts of town. On one side of the road, puffy white clouds floated in a blue sky over distant hills. Well-spaced houses sat back far from the road with a few clusters of trees, granite outcroppings, and long stretches of grassy land. Peaceful surroundings that didn't overwhelm the senses. A long drive might help him pull himself together.

Hot wind blew through the open car windows, ruffling Jarret's shirt and bringing in fresh air. He pulled the band from his ponytail and let his hair go wild, curly dark locks slapping his face and neck.

Jarret zoned out, thinking of nothing for a while, just pressing the pedal to the metal and steering the Chrysler 300 around curves. The road wound a lot more out this way, twisting and turning like his mood. As he drove further, the landscape developed character: more hills and evergreen trees, a log cabin or ranch here and there.

Warm wind on his face, hair flapping around his head, noonday sun in his eyes...

Fifteen or twenty minutes from town, Jarret realized with a hint of pride that he'd put himself back together. He tried to think of what road he'd cross next, so he could turn around. But without warning, his heart betrayed him.

Emotions erupted, stinging and rattling him to the core. The grace of forgiveness and a clean soul sent his spirit soaring to the clouds, but the weight of his weakness dragged him back down. How would he find the strength, the power to remain on the right path?

Anguish brought tears to his eyes and blurred his vision. He stepped on the brakes and eased the Chrysler off the road, to the only section of grass he could find that would accommodate his car. Skinny evergreens lined the road, most growing close together. A granite outcropping, low on one side and high on the other, like a split-level house, rose up a stone's throw away. He wouldn't ordinarily park so close to a road, but his emotional state left him no choice.

Jarret glanced over his shoulder, fortunately having enough sense to check for cars, then he jumped out of the Chrysler and dashed to the split-level outcropping. Anguish driving him onward, he staggered around behind it to where he couldn't be seen from the road. Shrinking and helpless against a wave of emotion, he rested a hand on the warm granite and fell to his knees.

"Jesus," he whispered, collapsing to wild grass and hard-packed earth. How could he return to his old life, to school and his friends, and stay on the right path? What would keep him from picking up his old ways? Weak and alone, he longed to experience Jesus' presence again, the way he had in the canyon. But he didn't deserve it, so he didn't dare ask.

The canyon... He tried to call it to mind: the dark, the fear, the chill in the air and in his soul, the exhaustion from having poured out his sins, then the Lord drawing near. His wounded hands. His burning heart.

The memory, fuzzy around the edges, drifted to a distant corner of his mind.

"No." Jarret dug his fingers into clumps of weeds and grass. The memory slipped even further, resisting his efforts to reclaim it. Would he lose it forever?

"Where do I go from here?"

CHAPTER 2

"God enriches the soul which empties itself of everything."
~Saint Pio of Pietrelcina

Keefe leaned his weight into the dresser and pushed, struggling to slide it across the hardwood floor. He'd managed to pull it away from the wall on one side, but now he needed to keep it at an angle so he could maneuver it around his bed. He'd put t-shirts under the feet, thinking it would move more easily across the hardwood floor. Didn't seem to help. Maybe he should rest and wait for Jarret to get home. Meanwhile, he could take care of that email he'd been putting off.

Turning his head, he glimpsed his laptop out of the corner of his eye. No. He wasn't ready for that.

Keefe renewed his efforts and shoved again, grunting as he slid the dresser several feet. He probably should've removed the drawers, but he hadn't wanted to make extra work. It had taken long enough to clear all his new books off the top.

Not new. Old. But new to him. He'd spent the last few weeks searching for anything on St. Francis of Assisi that he could get his hands on. His favorite was the 2000-page Omnibus of Sources. The readings really spoke to him, took him back in time to the little town of Assisi and the sandaled, brown-robed saint.

Sweat dripped down his back, between his shoulder blades. Halfway to the adjacent wall, he stopped pushing, scratched his back furiously, and wiped his sweaty hands on his sweatpants. Then he lifted the hem of his rock-band t-shirt and wiped his face. If Jarret were home, this would go much quicker. It had taken him half an hour to box up all the junk on the old entertainment center. Then another ten minutes to move the awkward thing out into the hallway. Moving one of the two armchairs out hadn't taken much time, but boxing up his old toys and moving his desk had. He'd be glad to finish.

As Keefe leaned into the dresser again, Papa's bedroom door creaked open.

Papa clomped out into the hallway. For years, the distinctive sound of his old cowboy boots had served as a warning when he and Jarret had been up to no good.

"What'cha doing in here?" His father stopped in the doorway, rested a shoulder on the doorframe, and adjusted his Stetson.

Keefe wiped his forehead with his arm. "Oh, just rearranging. Getting rid of a few things." They both looked at the clutter of boxes and furniture in the hallway. "Can I borrow the car to drop that stuff at the thrift shop?"

Papa's brows drew together. Squinting at the pile, he rubbed the back of his neck. "Naw. Let's hold onto it. You boys are nearly grown. You might want it when you move out."

"Uh..." Keefe wasn't going to want it when he moved out. He wasn't going to want anything. The desire to give it all away grew inside him daily. He wanted to be like St. Francis. But he couldn't tell Papa that. Papa had grown up in a tiny ranch house. They'd never had money to spare. He'd struggled to make college happen. Then he struggled to find work as an archeologist. Years later, his determination and hard work paid off. But it had turned around only after a series of fortunate events that had little to do with hard work or determination and everything to do with the generosity and blessings of God. Papa was a poor man in a rich man's house, a cowboy in a mansion. He wouldn't want to go back.

"Sure, okay," Keefe said, resigned. "What'll I do with it then?"

Papa lifted the flap of one of the boxes. He pulled out an action figure, The Doctor, and smiled. "Getting rid of everything, huh?"

Keefe shifted, the heat of embarrassment warming his neck and cheeks. "Well, it's not like I play with that stuff anymore."

"You told me they'd be collectibles one day."

Keefe shrugged. "Maybe they are."

Papa dropped it back in the box. "Put it all in the basement, behind my field gear."

"Okay."

"Maybe you can get Jarret to help you." Papa glanced at Jarret's closed bedroom door. "He home?"

"Uh, no. He went out this morning."

"Where to?"

"Uh..." Years of making excuses for Jarret had him struggling to think of an answer that Papa might like. Better to go with the truth. "He didn't tell me. I saw him with his keys around nine or ten. He said he had things to do, that he'd be back before lunch."

Papa gave a single nod. "Hmm."

"We'll probably take the horses out later. Roland's too."

"That's good. No reason that Roland can't clean out the water troughs and feed buckets." With a final nod, Papa moseyed down the hall and thumped down the steps.

Keefe turned back to his room and the mess he'd created. Books sat stacked against the wall by his desk, a broom and dustpan by the window, a pile of dirty laundry between the closet and bedroom doors. He might need to move the pile to get the dresser past. He sighed. Simplifying was hard work.

Unintentionally, his gaze turned to his laptop, his thoughts to the email that he should've responded to. Would his delay make the Franciscans doubt his sincerity? He wouldn't be able to go there without permission. Maybe he should mention it to Papa first and see what he thought. Was Papa open to one of his boys becoming a Franciscan Brother?

Lord, what should I do?

Waiting for the answer, he made himself aware of the presence of the Lord. At the same time, he kicked the laundry pile aside, shoved the dresser the rest of the way to the wall, and eased it toward the desk in the corner.

Still waiting for an answer, Keefe stripped the sheets off the bed, tossed them into the dirty laundry pile, and slid the mattress off the bed and onto its side. He wanted his bed against the wall with the door so he could have plenty of space for a prayer area by the window. Wrestling with the mattress, trying to walk it toward a wall, he stumbled on the sneakers he'd kicked off earlier. He lost his grip on the mattress and his balance, and he tumbled to the hardwood floor. The mattress fell over him at an angle, landing partially on the bed and partially on his legs.

Lying on his back, Keefe caught his breath and stared at the satiny blue mattress balanced a few inches above him. He should've waited for Jarret to help him. Jarret wouldn't have wanted him to rearrange his room in the first place, but he would've wanted to help if Keefe was determined to do it anyway. Keefe considered crawling out from under the mattress and leaving his room in its present state of chaos until Jarret returned home.

Keefe chuckled, imagining how his twin brother would react. Then he thought of what Jarret would say, questions laced with curse words. Keefe laughed harder. Jarret would think he'd gone off the deep end. Then he'd get distracted by the boxes in the hall, his sentimental side not wanting Keefe to give away anything. His control-freak side wouldn't like that Keefe had started this without consulting him first. But his new "struggling to do the right thing" side would try to let it go.

Keefe's laughter bordered on hysteria now. Tears dripped from the corners of his eyes and his chest hurt. He took a deep breath to force himself to calm down, and then he slid out from under the mattress.

Not wanting to put Jarret to the test, he decided to move the bed and carry the boxes and unwanted furniture to the basement himself. Jarret had really been trying. He didn't need the extra trial.

As Keefe grabbed a corner of the mattress and prepared to heft it, his thoughts returned to the email. He needed to reply. And he should stop putting it off.

He dropped the mattress and stepped to his desk. After wiping his hands on his sweatpants, he opened his inbox and reread the message from Brother Lawrence.

Hey Keefe,

Just sending a quick note. Our new monastery in Arizona is keeping us all busy and coming together slowly, but all in God's time. Would love for you to come down one day and check it out.

For now, thought you might be interested in a discernment retreat. You can learn a lot about our community and the Franciscan way of life. The retreat is in the middle of September and it's in Minnesota, which is much closer for you than Arizona.

If you can't make it, don't worry. Remember the steps of discernment I told you about in a previous email.

Keep in touch.

Pax et Bonum,
Brother Lawrence

Hesitancy overtaking him, Keefe rested his elbow on the desk and combed his fingers through his hair. He'd put off replying for so long; maybe he'd missed the registration date. Maybe they'd have another one in a few months and he could catch that one. It would give him time to talk to Papa.

In the meantime...

Keefe clicked through emails until he found the steps of discernment that Brother Lawrence had sent. The first step had inspired him to simplify his room and set up a prayer corner.

Step one: be quiet

Moved to rest in the presence of the Lord, Keefe closed the laptop and shuffled to the area that he planned to turn into a prayer corner.

CHAPTER 3

A siren blipped nearby. Jarret lifted his forehead from the hard ground and pushed himself up from clumps of weeds and dirt. He brushed gritty dirt from his hands and then wiped his hands on his jeans. His skin crawled at the sounds he heard, the hum of a car's engine, tires rolling off the road and crunching onto the uneven ground, a car door slamming…then a voice announcing Jarret's license plate numbers.

Jarret stepped out from behind the granite outcropping, his gaze snapping to the police officer at the rear of his red Chrysler. The officer had parked his vehicle behind Jarret's.

The police officer's gaze snapped to him at the same instant. He squinted. Then he gave Jarret a crooked smile that creased one side of his face. "What seems to be the problem here?"

"Uh." Jarret strode toward him, forcing himself to walk straight. Praying face-down on the ground had left him shaken. He stopped a few feet from the passenger side of his car. "No problem."

"Had a bit of alcohol?" the officer asked, stuffing a notebook into his chest pocket. "Kind of early in the day for that. How old are you?"

Jarret felt his face scrunching up with his disbelief. "No, I haven't been drinking." He hadn't meant to sound irritated, but he couldn't keep it from his voice. "What is it, like 1:00 p.m.?"

The officer stepped closer, peering at Jarret, hands moving to his hips. "Drugs?"

Eyes narrowing and jaw set, Jarret shook his head. "No drugs. I wasn't feeling well, so I pulled over. That's all."

"Hmm." Not looking convinced, he came even closer. A breeze ruffled his short dark hair, making a few tufts stand on end and emphasizing his widow's peak. His pink complexion and the sprinkling of white whiskers in an otherwise dark, scruffy beard reminded Jarret of the officer who'd given him a speeding ticket a month or so ago.

The officer glanced inside Jarret's car and then turned to Jarret. "I'll need to see your license, proof of insurance, and registration."

Jarret's stomach flipped, certain now that he recognized him. Just his luck; it was the same officer. "Yeah, okay." He shoved a hand in his back pocket, going for his wallet.

"Are you sick or something?" His gaze remained fixed on Jarret as he took the license and insurance card.

"No, I don't know. I just needed to pull over. I'm fine now." Jarret opened the passenger side door and grabbed the registration from the glove compartment.

"I've seen you in my neighborhood. Mostly at the Jenkins' house."

"Oh." *Great.* His friend Kyle Jenkins lived on the same street as the cop. Jarret tried to recall his visit last week. They'd sat out back with a few other kids. Jarret hadn't stayed long. He sure hadn't noticed the officer.

The officer returned to his car, and Jarret leaned against his Chrysler. Was it against the law to park on the side of the road? He should've just gone home.

A few minutes later, the officer sauntered back to him. "You feel good enough to get home?"

"Uh, yeah."

"Okay, then. Stay out of trouble. Drive safe."

A weight lifted. No ticket. Not even a warning. "Yeah, thanks." *You too,* he almost said. But that could've come across as sarcastic.

Jarret dropped into the driver seat, slammed the door, and shoved the key in the ignition. He pulled onto the road and made a U-turn under the police officer's watchful eye. A glance in the rearview mirror showed the officer following him, probably wanting to make sure he wasn't high or drunk.

Gaze flicking between the speedometer, rearview mirror, and the road, Jarret headed back to town.

Fifteen minutes never felt so long. Once he reached the outskirts, he stopped glancing back at the officer's car and paid less attention to his speed. A few minutes later, he glimpsed a bookstore to the left. The bookstore! Remembering what Father Carston had told him to do, he slammed on the brakes and made a hard turn across an empty road, tires squealing as he pulled into the parking lot. As the car decelerated, his heart leaped into his throat. He glanced in the rearview mirror and over his shoulder. Seeing an empty road and no police car, he let out a breath.

Jarret drove to the back of the little parking lot, not wanting to park too close to the other cars. He hated how careless other drivers were, how they'd open their car doors without paying attention and ruin the finish on someone else's car.

He gave his heart a moment to calm down and then strutted into the store. Yanking open the door, little bells chimed, and a nostalgic mood struck him. The smell of old and new books, the few slow-moving customers, the rows and rows of bookshelves... When was the last time he'd visited a bookstore? He couldn't remember. He usually bought stuff online and rarely bought books.

A table with a display of children's books stood off to the left, angled to invite customers to a larger, carpeted area of kids' books.

A solar system mobile hung from the ceiling. Two small children sat with books on the floor, their mother nearby.

Mama used to read to him, Keefe, and Roland several times a day and always before bed. He could hear Mama's sweet voice telling the story of a pig making friends with a spider. Then she died... how he missed hearing her read. He'd never wanted Nanny or their tutors to read to him.

Sucking in a breath to push back the memory, Jarret scanned the rest of the store. Bookshelves lined every wall and formed rows off to the right. A freestanding table with a display of some sort—journals and diaries?—stood in the middle of an open area. He wanted to check it out, if not for the customer browsing there: a blond girl about his age in a denim skirt that showed off her legs.

He bristled at the thought of anyone he knew seeing him shop for a journal. Granted, guys bought journals too. And it wasn't the same thing as a diary, was it? The word "diary" made him think of preteen girls giggling and painting their toe nails.

Moving toward a row of books, Jarret scanned a few titles, momentarily wanting to pick up the reading habit. He pulled a Western from the shelf and smiled. Louis L'Amour. Papa must've owned every Louis L'Amour book available, and Jarret had read most of them out of boredom. Some of them twice. Okay, maybe it wasn't out of boredom. Papa always had that cowboy image, so the books made Jarret curious. Maybe Jarret would get a set of Louis L'Amour books of his own someday.

Strolling down one row and another, Jarret ended up in a nonfiction section with cooking and gardening books. Further down the row, he glimpsed a book with the word "Cyclist" on the spine. Hoping it referred to motorcycling, he pulled it from the shelf. The cover showed a lanky man hunched over a racing bicycle. He flipped through the book, glanced at the pictures, then returned it to the shelf. He strolled to the end of the row and found himself back at the journal display. The girl had gone.

Jarret stepped out, scanning for the girl but not finding her. Maybe she'd left. A box of pens at the end of the table caught his eye. He picked up a silver one with a red stripe and clicked it. A notepad lay on the table, so he scribbled on it, liking the smooth feel of the pen.

After another sweeping glance and not finding any customers nearby, Jarret stepped around the table to browse the journals. Several rugged, manly journals lay among the ones with flowers and butterflies. A leather one with a cord wrapped around it caught his eye. He picked it up, undid the cord, and flipped it open. As he lifted the open journal to his nose—to smell the off-white lined paper—the hair on the back of his neck twitched.

Someone else had come to the table.

A strong temptation to drop the journal, move on, and order one online struck him. But he resisted. He didn't want to wait for it to come in the mail.

Jarret set the brown one down and grabbed a black one. He glanced to the side as he picked it up. A hint of mortification stirred in his chest. It was her.

She shifted her gaze from the table to him, a smile in her aqua blue eyes but not on her lips. Full lips. Long wavy blond hair falling around a shapely face. Pretty. She didn't look familiar but, guessing her age, chances were she went to River Run High.

Jarret tilted his chin and gave that look he couldn't help but give to a pretty girl. Then he snapped his attention back to the journals. Maybe she'd think he was shopping for a girlfriend.

"Do I know you?"

He waited a second before looking up. "Do you go to River Run High?" He asked it in a cocky way, as if she should know him simply because they went to the same school. He'd put a lot of effort into making a name for himself. Every kid in school must know him.

She scanned his face, then looked him up and down. "That's my school."

Her answer stung. She went to his school and didn't know him. On impulse, he grabbed her arm and clicked his pen. She didn't pull away so he wrote his phone number on the underside of her forearm. "You'll know me soon enough."

Giving her a sly smile, he dropped her arm, grabbed the leather journal, and headed for the checkout.

CHAPTER 4

Psyching himself up, Keefe curled and stretched his fingers, then he shook his arms as he strode toward the front hallway. He was going to do it. He was gonna talk to Papa. Mama had had strong faith—she'd taught them the Catechism, turned the walk-in closet off the veranda into a prayer room, and celebrated a gazillion saint days every year. Maybe her faith had drawn Papa from the start. Maybe that's what he'd loved most about her. If so, he shouldn't have a problem with Keefe joining a religious order.

Keefe turned down the front hallway and slowed his pace. His socks silenced his steps. Besides, going on a discernment retreat didn't mean he absolutely would become a Franciscan friar. It only meant he'd find out more about it. He'd have to emphasize that point.

Light seeped from Papa's study and onto the shiny hardwood floor in the hallway. Papa's low voice traveled, his words unclear through the half open door.

Palms sweating and pulse kicking up, Keefe crept to the doorway and flattened his back against the wall. He'd stood outside the door to Papa's study in years past, waiting and listening, always at Jarret's command. Jarret often sent him to spy out a situation. But he just needed to calm himself for a second now. He just wanted to appear relaxed, didn't mean to eavesdro—

"No, really I can't. Sounds like a job I'd like though, so I'm mighty thankful you kept me in mind. You've always been a man I can tie to." Papa paused but his chair squeaked and something tapped, maybe a pen against the desktop.

Keefe pressed his lips together, curious. What job had Papa turned down and why? He didn't seem to have any real commitments lately. That was odd for him. He always liked to keep busy.

"Naw, you're all down but nine." Papa's way of saying someone was clueless. "But it's not something I care to discuss. Let's just say I'm laying low for a year or two."

Keefe jerked back. Laying low for a year or two?

"Yup. Okay, glad to hear it. Take it easy." The old phone clattered as Papa hung it up. His chair squeaked again.

Keefe took a breath. He could do this. It was time. He swung into the room. "Hey, Papa."

Papa stood staring out the tall window by his desk, sunlight turning him into the silhouette of a cowboy. One hand shooting to the brim of his Stetson, he turned and cleared his throat. "Howdy, Keefe. Get your room squared away?"

"Yeah. Mr. Digby helped me move the furniture to the basement. We put it back where you told me."

Papa nodded, looking satisfied. "Jarret home yet?"

"Uh... don't think so."

Papa's eyes narrowed. His lip twitched. "He needs to let me know before he runs off."

Keefe nodded. Papa had spent so much time away from home over the years, and Jarret had always resented having to report to Nanny in his absence. Taking off at will had become a habit for him.

"What's on your mind?" Papa shuffled to his desk, pushed a little globe on a brass stand aside, and sat on the corner of the desk.

"I..." Keefe stepped further into the room and shoved his hands into the front pockets of his jeans. The question bounced around in his mind: "Hey, mind if I go to a retreat?" But he couldn't get it past his lips. He could imagine Papa's silent response, the squint of his eyes that Keefe could never interpret. Did it mean the question irritated him or that he needed a moment to think?

What would he think of Keefe's request? After Mama's death, Papa had stopped going to Mass. Now that Keefe, Jarret, and Roland had made a comeback, Papa had given it a try a time or two. But he never went up for Holy Communion. At home, he rarely mentioned faith and God. Maybe he blamed God for Mama's death. How would he feel about one of his sons joining a religious order? Would he think of it as God taking another loved one?

"Cat got your tongue?" Papa smiled and shifted on the corner of the desk, stretching a leg out.

"No, I..." Keefe ran a hand over his hair. "I kind of wanted to talk to you about something."

"I figured that." Papa gave a crooked grin. "So spit it out."

The question slipped from his mind. How had he planned to ask? Keefe lifted a hand, trying to bring the words together. "So... remember those Franciscan Friars that stayed at the Brandts'?" Heat seemed to radiate from his body, and his gaze slid to the half-open window.

"Sure."

"Well, I've been emailing them."

Papa nodded, not looking fazed. "How's their work coming along? They were forming a new community in Arizona, right?"

Keefe took a breath and released it, wanting to relax. "Right. It's a lot of work, I guess, but going good."

"Wish you'd gone out there this summer?"

Keefe's temperature spiked, overwhelming him with heat. "Uh..." Did Papa already know?

"It'd be quite an experience. I thought about it myself. I never did catch the details. Were they moving into an existing building or were they gonna build from scratch?"

A tingling sensation ran through him. Papa hadn't guessed Keefe's interest in the religious order. He only saw the construction side of it. "Both, I guess. They found a suitable building, an old school that they converted. They've got a temporary chapel. But they'll be building a better one soon."

Papa folded his arms and nodded. "It'd be an honor to help them out. A lot of work, no pay, but an honor."

"Yeah." Keefe dropped his gaze. Didn't seem like Papa would mind him heading out there to volunteer his time. Any way that could happen? He'd end up missing the beginning of the school year, but Papa had never seemed concerned about that. He'd pulled them all out of school once last year—Keefe and Jarret twice—to accompany him on one trip or another.

Keefe's mood lifted with a glimmer of hope.

"What kind of help are they looking for? What time frame?"

"Oh, uh..." He couldn't make something up, couldn't lie about it. "They didn't ask for my help. I was just wondering, I don't know." Knowing for certain that he could not have this talk now, he shook his head.

"Well, find out. Let me know." He glanced at his watch and at the antique pendulum clock on the opposite wall, then he straightened and reached into a pocket. "Hey, uh..." He drew his keys out and offered them to Keefe. "Mind picking up Roland?"

He tossed them before Keefe could answer.

Keefe caught them, but they started to slip through his fingers. "Yeah, sure."

"He's at the Brandts'. Said he needed to be picked up at one or two."

Glancing at the array of keys on Papa's 30-30 Winchester bullet keyring, he backed to the door.

"Oh, hey, Keefe?" Papa put one hand on his hip and talked to the floor. "You know the arrangement I had with Jarret for getting his car, right?" He glanced.

"Yes. He did some work for the Finns and you matched the money he had saved, right?"

Papa nodded. "Well, that offer stands for you too. If the Franciscans will have you, that'll be a right good way to do it. Otherwise, we can come up with something else. There's no reason you shouldn't have your own wheels."

A mix of emotions struck Keefe, none of them the ones a seventeen-year-old should feel at that offer. But Keefe gave the biggest smile he could muster. "Thanks, Papa. I appreciate it."

And he turned to go.

~ ~ ~

Gripping the steering wheel and glancing at the speedometer, Keefe drove down the long winding driveway toward Forest Road. He liked driving Papa's silver Lexus, but he didn't want a car of his own. He didn't want anything. He wanted to get rid of things. He wanted to follow in the footsteps of Saint Francis and give it all up.

He'd just read a story about Brother Bernard's decision to join Saint Francis. Wealthy and successful, Bernard was so touched by the saint's faith and sincerity that he longed to relinquish his worldly goods. To know for certain that God willed it, Bernard met with St. Francis and they opened the Bible randomly.

Keefe's mind paused on the thought. That was it! He would do the same! As soon as he got back from the Brandts' house. Or maybe at the Brandts' house. Bernard and Francis had prayed first. Maybe he should ask Peter and Roland to pray with him. Then he could open the Bible randomly and find God's answer. If the verse convinced him that this was God's will, he would make himself talk to Papa about his desire to join the Franciscans, and get permission to go on the retreat. If this was God's will, he had no reason to worry.

"Lord," he shouted, excited with the idea, "please give me a sign and show me what You want."

As he snapped from his thoughts, he found himself barreling toward Forest Road. He slammed on the brakes. A car zoomed past. Keefe's heart raced, whether from almost pulling into traffic or from the hope that he would find his answer, he didn't know.

A few seconds later, he reached the Forest Gateway Bed & Breakfast and pulled in the driveway on the Brandts' side of the odd-shaped house. They'd converted a bungalow or something into a bed and breakfast by adding a long addition of guestrooms.

Keefe shut off the engine and jumped out of the car. A campfire scent carried on a warm breeze. Women's voices traveled from the kitchen through the screen door as he stomped up the porch steps. He knocked on the door frame.

Laughter erupted. Then a feminine voice. "Oh, hi, Keefe, come on in."

Keefe swung open the screen door and stepped inside, the aroma of baked bread welcoming him.

Mrs. Brandt approached, wiping her hands on a dishtowel. Her smile always made Keefe feel as if he were special to her, but he knew she gave everyone the same smile.

"Good to see you, Keefe. Are you hungry?" She glanced behind him, probably wondering if Jarret had come too. But Jarret's dislike of Peter had him avoiding their house.

"No thanks. Just came to get Roland."

"Oh, okay." She glanced at the living room.

A stack of folded laundry sat on the arm of the couch. Peter's ten-year-old brother, Toby, stood facing the TV. He rocked back and forth as he flipped through scenes of a cartoon. He hit play and the cartoon voices drowned out the pleasant white noise from the dryer down the hall.

Keefe liked visiting the Brandts, maybe because he'd learned about the friars here. But he also liked the family. They were good people, generous, welcoming, and always willing to help anyone in need. He felt at home with them.

Mrs. Brandt led him to the dining room where two strangers sat at a booth. "The boys are out back goofing off." She peered through the glass doors that separated the family's side of the house from the guest side. "How's your summer been going? Glad to have Jarret back?"

"Yeah, glad to have him back. Summer's been slow. The way I like it."

"Not in a hurry for the new school year to begin, huh? You'll be a senior this year, right?"

"Yeah." He knew what question came next, and he didn't want to answer it, so he stepped toward the glass door and looked through the breezeway to the backyard.

But as she slid open the door for him, she asked it anyways. "Any idea what you want to do after high school?"

He sucked in a breath and met her questioning gaze. "Not sure. I'm praying about it."

She nodded and gave that motherly smile. "That's the best way to figure it out."

Keefe's attention snapped to two figures in the middle of the spacious backyard, one in sweatpants and a big leg cast, the other with a stocky, backwoodsman build. Wearing fencing face masks but no other safety gear, Roland and Peter crossed swords. Wait— What were they wielding? Not a metal foil or saber. They resembled walking sticks.

Using both hands to wield his sword, Peter swung like an uncivilized Orc. Roland parried and made a counter attack, his movements smooth and precise despite his long-leg cast. He also used both hands but he stood in one place, his weight on his good leg and his crutches sprawled in the grass.

The wooden *tap tap tap* carried.

Keefe couldn't help but smile as he neared. He loved fencing with his brothers.

Roland, ever aware of his surroundings, swiveled his masked face to Keefe. He took one more swing and lifted a hand to Peter, signaling for a time out. Peter and Roland slid off their face masks. Peter dropped his to the grass and wiped his forearm over his dirty blond hair.

Keefe raised a hand in greeting. "Hey."

"Finally!" Peter rolled his shoulders and struck a pose, raising his wooden sword and gripping it with both hands. "Some competition. Roland's too feeble to offer any real fight."

Eyes narrowed but with the hint of a grin, Roland muttered something to Peter that Keefe didn't catch.

"I thought you had somewhere to go." As Keefe drew near, Roland flipped his sword and offered Keefe the handle. Keefe grabbed the smooth handle, finding the sword sturdy and of a good weight and feel.

"Eh. I'm supposed to go with my dad to clean up some fire damage. It's near the campsites. But that can wait." Peter spun the sword to the left, then the right. "Care to spar?"

"What is this, bamboo?"

"Yeah." He beamed with pride as if he'd made them himself. "They're *shinai*. That's Japanese for sword. I'm trying to teach Roland *kendo*. When he gets that lousy cast off, maybe we can play for real."

"Here, you'll need this." Roland handed Keefe his face mask, a black steel net mesh. "Peter's pretty rough around the edges."

As Keefe took the mask, he pushed thoughts about asking them to pray with him to the back of his mind. He hadn't decided if he wanted to spar or not, but he found himself lifting the mask to his head. The thought of a good fight thrilled him.

Roland limped over and retrieved one of his crutches.

Gripping the handle with both hands, Keefe stepped back and sliced the air on either side. He liked the feel of the bamboo sword, though it didn't compare to metal foils or sabers or the one-handed grip he'd always used. "What do you know about kendo?"

"A lot. You can learn plenty on the Internet. You've got your cuts to the head." Peter demonstrated, raising the stick overhead and coming down fast, then slowing as he neared Roland's uncovered head.

Leaning his weight on a single crutch, Roland rolled his eyes and sighed. A breeze blew wavy black locks out of place and over his forehead.

"And your cut to the wrist..." Peter raised the shinai again. "Hold your hands out like we're fighting," he said to Roland, sounding impatient.

"No." Roland shifted his weight and adjusted the crutch under his arm.

"Well, I'll show you once we get started." Peter stooped for his face mask. "You can strike your opponent in the gut or throat too. Plus, if Roland wasn't so lame..." He grinned and waved his brows at Roland. "I'd be able to knock him down. So body slams are fair game."

"Body slams, huh?" Egged-on by Peter's challenging tone, Keefe whipped the shinai through the air in a series of dramatic moves.

Peter froze, his mouth hanging open. Then he grinned again, pulled the face mask on, and gave a nod. "Ready?" He sidestepped away from Roland, staying lined up with Keefe. Then he bowed and held his bamboo stick out, angling it toward Keefe.

Keefe swung his weapon up and imitated Peter's hold. He'd only ever fought one-handed and with a foil, but he could adjust.

A split second later, Peter hopped forward, whipped the bamboo sword up and sliced downward. Keefe slipped to a one-handed hold and blocked the overhead attack.

"Two hands, man, two hands." Peter laughed. "Lemme show you. Hold your sword out."

Keefe did as told.

Peter showed him the basic moves, tapping him on the head and wrist, then slicing toward his abdomen. "And don't forget about body slams." He sounded happy about that. Eager.

"Got it," Keefe said.

"Okay, let's roll." Peter bowed again. Keefe imitated. Then they began.

They clacked their bamboo weapons together with speed, Peter hopping like a boxer, Keefe moving like a fencer. The intensity of Peter's blows reminded Keefe of Jarret. Granted, Jarret's moves reflected a higher level of skill, but they shared the same over-confident energy.

The bamboo swords cracked together. This time Peter moved in closer, sliding his shinai along Keefe's. Before Keefe realized his strategy, Peter slammed his shoulder into Keefe's.

Keefe stumbled back.

Peter swung the shinai out, Keefe's abdomen his target.

Fencing moves flipping through his mind, Keefe blocked, pivoted, and prepared a counterattack. He pictured his foot moving behind Peter's, knowing he could catch him off guard. But he avoided the step and risked Peter's next blow.

As he beat off Peter's attack, his weak choice convicted him. Why hadn't he made the move? He'd have scored for sure. How often had he avoided similar opportunities with Jarret and sometimes with Roland? Didn't he have that same drive to win? Or had he always worried about the other's pride or seemingly urgent need for victory? Always stepped aside so someone else could win?

In one swift move, Peter swung his bamboo sword upward and then—Bam! Keefe had prepared to block his head, but Peter had twisted the sword suddenly and caught him in the side. In the next second, he lunged into Keefe's space, slammed his shoulder into Keefe's chest, and they both went down.

Blue sky showed through the net mesh of the face mask, then the tree line at the edge of the Brandts' yard, and finally grass. Momentarily disoriented, shoulder aching, and heart pounding, Keefe lay still. Two seconds later, fearing an attack while he was down, he scrambled to sit up.

"All right, Peter, you won." Roland jabbed his crutch into the grass and swung his injured leg forward, taking a step toward Keefe. "I gotta go. Or actually..." He looked at Peter. "Don't you have to go?"

Peter peeled off his face mask and glanced over his shoulder at the house. He sighed as he got to his feet. "I guess so, but first..." He gave Keefe a strange look, the hint of a challenge in his quirky smile. "Fire Starters meet again in September. You gonna officially join us this year?"

The Catholic youth group had taken the name Fire Starters last year, around the same time membership had soared. Though it typically began and ended with the school year, several members continued to meet over the summer, praying and playing together.

"I went to a few meetings and events last year." Keefe handed the bamboo sword back and ran a hand through his hair, fixing what the face mask had flattened. "Doesn't that make me a member?"

"Eh." Peter's eyes swiveled to Roland. Roland squinted back, showing he questioned whether he'd approve of whatever Peter would say next.

Peter took the face mask from Keefe, a look of challenge in his eyes. "You always seem so divided, like you're half in and half out. You gotta be all in."

Roland rolled his eyes and shook his head. Nope. He didn't approve of Peter's game, whatever it was.

Keefe laughed, but he didn't like the accusation. He wasn't divided, was he?

"There's more to joining Fire Starters than just coming to a meeting or activity here or there. If you want to be a member of our radical prayer group, you've got to be all in and you've got to prove it."

"What are you talking about?" Roland tilted his head with that annoyed look he got more often lately, ever since the cast.

"Everyone in the prayer group—" Peter spared a glance for Roland but remained otherwise focused on Keefe. "We're like the Green Berets or the Seals, the few who dare to go deeper. If you want that, you've got to be initiated."

"Father Carston's not going to like that," Roland said. "He's responsible for the group."

"Father Carston doesn't need to know." Peter slapped Roland's arm with the back of his hand.

"So what does initiation consist of?" Keefe asked, still shifting inside from the accusation, fearing that Peter was right. He was divided. Maybe that was what kept him from asking for permission to go on the retreat.

"Good. You're open." Peter gave Roland a "so there" look. "Everyone's different. But for you, what I think you need to do is go alone into the woods and pray for a few days, like over the weekend."

"Oh yeah?" Keefe smiled, wanting to show he knew Peter was kidding. But the idea did appeal to him.

"Yeah. And you take nothing with you. You're like one of those desert monks."

"Or Saint Francis?" Keefe's voice came out just above a whisper.

"Yeah."

"He can't go back there with nothing for a few days." Roland, the voice of reason.

"Okay, so how about forty hours? And he brings a water bottle, which he can refill in the river. And a loaf of bread or some granola bars or something. But that's it."

"Yeah? And where does he sleep?" Roland said. "Don't you always warn about wild animals?"

"Okay, right." Peter paced a few feet. "So he can build a fire to keep them away or..." He stopped and raised an index finger. "Better yet... he can go back in the cave behind the waterfall. It's safe and dry back there."

"And sleep on the cold, hard floor of the cave?"

"Well, it's not supposed to be a pleasure trip. It's initiation. Yeah, there's a bit of discomfort involved."

Roland pointed a finger at his friend. "Could *you* do it?"

"Of course I could. But we can't all do it together, or it defeats the purpose."

"I don't like it." Roland leaned on the crutch.

"I do." Keefe's soul stirred at the thought of the challenge.

Peter and Roland snapped their faces to Keefe.

He'd made up his mind. Peter could see it as initiation into Fire Starters, but Keefe had other reasons. He'd fast, pray, and find his answers. He'd push for the victory. He'd go all in. He'd find out for certain if God wanted him to join the Franciscans, then he'd talk to Papa with no hesitation.

He nodded, a grin stretching across his face while concern colored Roland's expression and approval showed on Peter's. "I like the idea. I'll do it this weekend."

CHAPTER 5

Regret pulsing through him, Jarret tucked the bag from the bookstore under his arm and stepped from the garage through the mud room and into the quiet house. Why had he given that girl his number? He knew nothing about her, not even her name. He'd have to start thinking up a few excuses for when she called. Maybe she'd just text and he could ignore it for a while. Not even two months had passed since Zoe had the baby, and since she'd dumped him. He wasn't ready for a relationship.

Jarret glanced down the dim hallway to his right. All the doors were closed. Dim light from the failing sun traveled from the windows flanking the front door, which was practically on the opposite side of their huge house, and gave a dusty sheen to the hardwood floor on the far end of the hallway. Would Papa be in his study?

Not wanting to cross paths, Jarret strode toward the back of the house. Feeble beams of light streamed in between half-drawn drapes in the family room, obscuring the suit of armor in the corner and other antiques on the tables and shelves. It made the couch and recliner appear inviting though. He could easily curl up with the journal and examine his thoughts, write a few of them down. But someone might see him.

He pushed open the swinging doors to the dark great room. No one ever bothered opening those drapes.

As he rounded the corner, Nanny's voice came from the kitchen. "…something loose to get around that cast and, besides, you're still growing. You should start the school year with new clothes."

"No, I—" Roland clipped off his answer. "The cast comes off soon. There's no point in buying things to fit over it."

"Well, what can you possibly wear to school besides sweat pants? Have you tried your old clothes on like I suggested?"

"No, I… I wear the stuff all the time. I've cut a few things. I have enough that fits."

Nanny groaned. "Well, I'll pick up a few things anyway. Maybe some polo shirts. You like those, right?"

Roland whined, then let out a weary, "Sure, thanks."

Jarret laughed to himself. If Nanny picked up black or other dark colors, Roland would wear it. But otherwise…

Roland's aluminum crutch tapped the floor, then a footfall. Jarret stopped, turned, and descended the steps as Roland emerged from the kitchen.

"Hey," Roland said with a grumpy glance. He had a pile of clothes tucked under one arm and a single crutch under the other.

"Hey, yourself. Need help with that?" Jarret reached for the clothes.

"Na, I'm fine." Roland turned red, the way he always did lately when Jarret tried to help him.

"It's no big deal. I'm going upstairs too, and I don't have a cast."

"Ahh. School starts soon and I'll still have the cast for a week, so I need to learn to get by."

"Nanny bugging you about new clothes?" Jarret suppressed a grin.

"Yeah." Roland lifted the crutch and his lame leg to the first step. "Why doesn't she bother you and Keefe about clothes?"

Jarret kept pace with Roland, taking it a step at a time. "I let her get me things. And Keefe convinced her that he's got enough."

"*I* have enough."

"Ah, you're the baby. She's gotta hold onto that."

Roland shook his head. He reached the top step and gave Jarret a long look. "Are you going camping this year?"

Jarret winced as if struck. He couldn't think of camping without thinking of Zoe and what he'd done that he shouldn't have. And now he'd started something with that blond at the bookstore. Was he strong enough to date a girl and respect her?

He took a breath. "No." He exhaled. "No camping for me." He changed the subject. "You sure you're gonna be okay once school starts, lugging books around and using crutches?"

The gray of Roland's eyes seemed to shift in the shadows. He nodded. "Thanks. I'll be fine. I can wear a backpack." Another long look. "I appreciate the offer."

Jarret shrugged. "What are brothers for?" He meant it, but it felt insincere after how harshly he'd treated Roland over the years. He wanted to make up for it, needed to make up for it. But if Roland didn't want his help, he'd back off a bit. No point in making him uncomfortable.

Roland's single crutch clunked as he moved down the dark hallway to his bedroom.

Jarret swung open his bedroom door to a semi-dark room and flipped on the light. He'd always liked the red, gold, and purple accents, but today they annoyed him, seemed too cheerful. Jarret closed the door behind him and dumped the contents of the bag onto his bed: a leather-bound journal, a pack of gum, and the silver pen.

Reluctant to begin and still irritated by all the colors in his room, he tossed the decorative pillows from his bed, kicked his sneakers off, and sat down. Leaning back against the headboard, Jarret placed the journal on his lap and clicked the pen.

The priest in Arizona had encouraged him to talk to his parish priest, once he got back home, and ask for spiritual direction. Whatever that meant. Jarret had put it off until today. Now he'd be seeing Father Carston forever. "I'd like to see you regularly," Father Carston had said after Jarret's confession. "But we can schedule a time and meet in the rectory instead. Okay? There's always a line of people waiting for confession, and spiritual direction takes time."

As he'd been pouring out his sins, Jarret hadn't thought about all the others standing in line waiting to confess. "Yeah, sure," Jarret had answered, wanting to say no. But he'd unloaded so much humiliating failure that he felt entirely vulnerable and would've agreed to anything.

Then Father had given him homework: start a journal. He wanted Jarret to write down the crossroads he faced during the day, the choices he made, and what he thought God might be telling him. Or whatever else he wanted to write. He wouldn't have to share it with anyone, not even Father Carston.

So how was this going to help him?

Jarret ran a hand down the front of the journal, then untied the cord and opened it. No point in putting it off. If he delayed, he'd probably never do it. He'd wind up thinking about it on Sundays while Father gave his homily and forgetting once he got home.

Not sure what to write, Jarret drummed the page with the pen. What if someone found his journal? His muscles tightened at the thought. Peter's face flashed in his mind. Jarret narrowed his eyes and clicked the pen.

"Read this and die," he wrote on the first page in big angry letters. "This means you!"

Taking a breath to rid himself of the paranoid thoughts, Jarret thought back on the day since he'd fled the church. Did he want to write how his emotional state had him pulling off the road and throwing himself face down on the ground behind a granite outcropping? What would be the point? What was the point of any of this? Maybe he'd start from the bookstore and the crossroads he'd faced there.

Jarret positioned the pen and wrote:

Went to the bookstore today to get this journal. Trying to do what Father told me to do. And there's this babe there, standing at the very display I was looking for. I did my best to avoid her. Not because I was worried about talking to her, and where that might lead—which maybe I should've been—but because I didn't want her thinking I was buying a diary. Didn't want to tarnish my cool image, I guess. But there I was talking to her anyway. And man was she—

Jarret stopped writing and glanced upward. Maybe he shouldn't be putting those kinds of details in his journal. He drew a line through the uncompleted sentence and started a new one.

Guess it shocked me, wounded my ego, that she hadn't heard of me, since we go to the same school. Then before I could stop myself, I'm writing my phone number on her arm.

Jarret's cellphone rang. Glad to stop writing, he tossed the pen onto the bed and yanked the phone from the back pocket of his jeans. He hesitated before glancing at the caller ID. It wouldn't be her, would it? So soon? What would he tell her?

He glanced, relieved to see Kyle's name, and accepted the call.

"What's up, man?" Jarret leaned against the headboard and stretched an arm overhead.

"Hey, dude. Haven't seen you in like forever."

"Ain't been that long." He'd been over at Kyle's house once last week, but Kyle was right. They hadn't done much together since Jarret got back from Arizona.

"Why don't you come over tonight? We can get pizza and play Zombie Island or something."

"Eh, I dunno." All he could think of was the police officer who lived on Kyle's street. He had no desire to see him so soon. Or ever again.

"We gotta do something before school starts back up. It's our senior year, man. Party starts now and goes all the way to graduation."

Jarret laughed. A strange sensation in his mind made him reluctant to commit to anything; it felt almost like he'd forgotten to do something. But he only felt that way around Kyle, and only lately.

"Seriously, dude. We're having a bash this weekend, all weekend long. You gotta come. Or better yet, let's have it at your most awesome house. What'dya say?"

"I dunno." It would give him an excuse if the blond girl wanted to get together with him. And give him something to do. And just because his friends cussed and drank and "kicked up a row," as Papa would say, didn't mean he would. He could resist that temptation easily. "I guess we can. Not tonight though."

"Okay, how 'bout Friday? You open your house and we'll bring the games and food. And girls?"

"No. Just guys. My father will be home. I don't want him thinking he needs to babysit us."

"Fine with me. We have more fun anyway."

A noise outside his bedroom door snagged his attention: Keefe thumping up the stairs in his sandals. He could easily identify everyone in the house by the sound of their footfalls. Papa clomped and scuffed in his cowboy boots. Nanny hurried everywhere she went, her footfalls soft and quick. Mr. Digby shuffled along, in no hurry to get anywhere; kind of amazing how much he got done in one day. And now Roland had the distinctive thud of a single crutch and an occasional footfall. He used to walk undetected through the house.

Kyle was still talking but Jarret had stopped listening. "Look, I gotta go."

Keefe knocked on Jarret's bedroom door with the same beat he always used, but the intensity of it signaled that he had something on his mind.

"Come on in," Jarret hollered, stuffing his phone in his back pocket.

The door flung open. Keefe, wearing jeans and a Christian rock-band t-shirt, stepped in and closed the door behind him. "Hey, what's up?" His gaze traveled from Jarret to the journal on the bed.

Jarret leaned forward and flipped it shut. His neck warmed with embarrassment. Keefe wouldn't care one way or another and Jarret had never worried about his image with him. Why should it bother him?

"Nothing," Jarret answered, grinning, knowing he'd been caught and would have to explain.

Keefe smiled too and approached the bed. "You want to go for a ride, take two horses out?"

Relieved that Keefe didn't bring up the journal, Jarret scooted off the bed and picked it up. "Gotta find someplace for this first."

"I'll tell you where I put mine."

"You've got one?"

"Sure." Keefe went to the dresser and slid a drawer out. "Sometimes I hide it in there. It fits okay if you press it against the back, right between the wood slats that the drawer rests against." Bending over, he peered into the dark cubbyhole. "But I'm usually fine with hiding it between the mattress and the box spring." He shoved the drawer back in place and straightened.

"Works for me." Jarret lifted the edge of the bedspread and hid the journal. Maybe having it there would remind him to write in it. He'd think of it every time he lay down.

Jarret grabbed his knee-high brown leather riding boots from the walk-in closet and followed Keefe to his bedroom. "So what do you write in yours?" He figured Keefe wrote deep, spiritual things, especially since his "God moment" in Italy. Keefe had told Jarret a bit about it, but Jarret knew he'd held some things back. As much as he hated them growing apart, Jarret had made it happen when he rejected Keefe last year because of his new faith. They'd moved past that now, but some distance remained between them.

"Oh, nothing important." Keefe swung open his bedroom door. "Just thoughts and prayers I make up."

"You make up prayers?" Jarret followed Keefe two paces into his bedroom and stopped, stunned. The bed was in the wrong place, against the wall with the door. The dresser and desk were in the complete opposite corner of the room. And what happened to the old entertainment center? And something else was missing. A chair? What else?

"Well, it's not poetry or anything." Keefe strolled through his half-empty bedroom. Then he spoke from inside the closet. "It's just what I want to say to God, or what I want to ask Him. Sometimes I look back and see how He answered my prayers."

Jarret sat on Keefe's bed and shoved a foot into one of his riding boots. His gaze drifted to a stack of books, some new but others seriously old, on the otherwise uncluttered dresser. They'd once had their rooms arranged the same but with different color schemes: Jarret bold purple, gold, and red, Keefe with shades of green and blue.

"What's up with your room? Hired a re-decorator?"

Bent over and stuffing one foot into a riding boot, Keefe poked his head from his closet. "Oh. Yeah. I was going to ask you to help me, but it actually wasn't so bad. Where'd you go this morning?"

Jarret laughed to himself, amused by Keefe's diversionary tactic. Keefe had gotten rid of the TV, TV table... and all his electronic games? He'd kept one chair. A Bible lay in it now.

Over the past few months, he'd given away toys and decorations that he'd held onto since childhood. Jarret had snagged a few items that had sentimental value. He'd felt a stab to his heart, watching Keefe give away the rest. But Keefe could do what he wanted with his life and his stuff. Jarret would support him. No more trying to control him. Just because they were twins didn't mean they had to do everything the same.

Jarret tucked his jeans into his boots and zipped them up. Then he stood and looked himself over in the mirror, above the dresser on the wrong wall. Having forgotten to tie his hair back up, he dug a hair band from a front pocket and pulled his hair into a ponytail.

Keefe scuffed from the closet to the dresser in old black riding boots and stood beside Jarret. They stared at each other's reflections in the mirror. They looked less identical today than ever: Keefe with his cropped hair, glasses, and casual clothes, Jarret with his long curly hair—pulled back now—contacts and designer shirt.

"Ready?" Keefe smiled but his eyes spoke of trouble.

After that night in the canyon, I felt your love,

the love of my Lord,

Wrapped around me like a blanket keeping me safe,

Like a shroud hiding me from temptation.

For many days after, I simply had to sit still

and think about it.

And it all flooded back.

The sound of the wind whistling around the canyon,

The scent of the dusty desert air,

the call of a distant coyote,

The rustle of dry vegetation

from the rim of the canyon wall.

I was right back there, experiencing it all again.

I remembered the breeze cooling the heat of my anger and

the fear of helplessness.

More than all that, I saw You again in my mind.

Your glance stirred me to the depths of my soul

as it had that night.

I felt your love.

CHAPTER 6

In the cool shade of the stable, Keefe adjusted the cinch strap of an old leather saddle on Roland's jet-black horse, Bueno. The aroma of horse sweat, manure, and hay took Keefe back... Some of his fondest memories came from the leisurely rides the family had taken years ago, before Mama left them for heaven. But most of the time, he and Jarret had gone riding without anyone else.

His thoughts stirred up wistful yearnings for the past. Sometimes they set out for adventure, not keeping to the regular paths and making frequent stops to explore. They often sorted out their muddled thoughts and emotions on the trail. Jarret especially. It seemed easier for him to have a deep conversation from the saddle than anywhere else.

"Ready, girl?" Keefe rubbed Bueno's neck and led her from the stable.

Late afternoon shadows covered all but the turrets and battlements of their castle-like house, giving it a story-book quality that deepened Keefe's nostalgic mood. He shoved a boot into the stirrup, forced himself up with one arm and leg, and mounted with a grunt.

"Let's go find Jarret," he said to Bueno, getting her moving with a gentle squeeze of his thighs.

Jarret had already led Desert toward the trail behind the stables. With a nudge to Bueno's sides, Keefe worked on catching up. As much as he wanted to share his tangled thoughts with Jarret, he wasn't sure he should. How would Jarret feel about him taking off for the Franciscans' three-day retreat? How did Jarret honestly feel about Keefe wanting to join the Franciscans for life?

Bueno snorted as she trotted up alongside Desert. Desert lifted his head and turned his ears, welcoming Bueno with a soft nicker. The horses knew each other inside and out, the way Keefe and Jarret knew each other.

Could Keefe really just leave one day, head out to wherever God sent him and not look back? Keefe had always felt like Jarret needed him. Growing up, Jarret had always come up with wild ideas and never seemed to know either his own limits or Papa's. Once he got an idea stuck in his head, he had a hard time letting it go. Over the years, Keefe had turned him away from more than a few bad ideas. But Keefe mostly had to settle with damage control.

Then the Italy trip had put some distance between them. Despite the pain that distance had caused Keefe, he wouldn't trade that trip for anything. He'd found himself there, and he wanted to believe that God had planted the seed of his calling there. Keefe sighed. If only he knew for certain.

Jarret cast a long look at Keefe. "What's eating ya? Gonna tell me? Or are you gonna keep stewing about it, like the dork you've become." Jarret had been calling him a dork ever since he'd come home from Italy with the haircut.

Keefe snapped out of his thoughts and shot Jarret a narrow-eyed look, but he couldn't hide his smile completely. Jarret had things on his mind too—Keefe could tell—but he was letting Keefe go first. Whatever'd happened in Arizona, Jarret had changed for the good, though he still seemed vulnerable. He'd told Keefe a bit about it, how he'd never felt anger as strong as he had then, how he'd never felt repentance as deep, how he'd never felt the Lord's love so real and personal. And he'd struggled to share that last part, so Keefe hadn't asked any questions. He figured Jarret would share what he needed to. The rest he'd keep as a treasure. And he should.

"You sure *I'm* the dork?" Keefe stalled for time, still not sure what to admit to Jarret even though he was dying to share his thoughts with someone.

"It sure ain't me." Jarret grinned, a challenge ever-present in his eyes.

Their horses trotted a few more yards down the well-worn, shady trail before Keefe felt ready to talk. Finding a way to ease into his concerns, he said, "Have you noticed anything strange about the way Papa's been acting lately?"

"Strange?" Jarret rode a few paces to the sound of the hoofbeats. "Nah, he's just home more. We ain't used to that."

"Right. But why do you think he's home more?"

"No work."

They both knew Papa's work came in spurts. All the same, he'd always found other things to do, people to help with their work. An archaeological dig here. Mining work there. He liked to keep busy and on location.

"I heard him turn down a job today," Keefe said.

Jarret faced him, the curl of his lip showing admiration, the look in his eyes doubt; he apparently couldn't believe that Keefe had eavesdropped. The old Jarret always wanted to know everyone's business. Keefe had hated spying for him and never did it without Jarret forcing him to.

"I was on my way to ask him something," Keefe explained, "when I overheard him."

"What'd you ask him?"

"Well, I wanted to ask him to go somewhere. The Franciscans have a retreat coming up, a discernment retreat." There he said it. If only he'd said it to Papa, but he could count this as practice.

"So what'd he say?" A grumpy expression flitted across his face, but it vanished behind a more disinterested look.

"I didn't end up asking him. He misunderstood me."

Jarret stared ahead, riding loose and relaxed as if he didn't care.

Keefe studied him, trying to read his mood. This past summer, Jarret had tried hard to turn Keefe away from the thought of joining. Did he really no longer care? Did he feel ready to give up Keefe and walk alone? Did he still need Keefe?

"How long?" Jarret finally said.

"Three days."

"So tell Papa and go." Jarret had never liked wishy-washy behavior. Whatever he set his mind to, he did. And he admired that in others, whether or not he agreed with what they did.

"Really? I'm just going to leave you?"

"You did before. And for a lot longer than three days."

Catching the hurt in Jarret's words, Keefe opened his mouth for a quick reply, but he wasn't sure how to take him and didn't know what to say.

Jarret smiled, letting Keefe know he could chill. "When is the thing?"

"Just after school starts." Keefe shrugged. "I probably won't be allowed, but I'd only have to miss one or two days."

"Eh, Papa don't care about school the way other parents do. He won't mind. Just tell him and go."

"I haven't even told him I'm interested in the Franciscans, you know, as a vocation."

Jarret took a breath and breathed out loudly. "Gotta tell him sooner or later."

"Yeah. But I'm not sure about anything. So I'm going to do something stupid first. Maybe I can get some discernment on my own."

Jarret shot him a crooked grin. "Something stupid? Count me in."

Keefe smiled. "You wouldn't like it. I'll be roughing it out in the woods, praying and fasting. Besides, I have to do this alone."

"Roughing it? Why?"

"Well, it started as a challenge but I really want to do it now."

"Challenge from who?"

"Peter." Keefe ignored the sour look that came to Jarret's face at the name. "He had other reasons for the challenge, but I have my own. And I like the idea." He'd read about Saint Francis' forty-day fast. One lent, Francis had gone out alone to a deserted island with nothing more than two loaves of bread. God had spoken to him then, even sent an angel to mark him with the wounds of Christ. Not that Keefe wanted anything like that to happen. But maybe he'd get a definite answer to the question of his vocation. He'd find out God's will and ask Papa with confidence to go on the retreat.

"You know I hate that kid, right? I wouldn't do anything he suggested."

"You can't hate a person, Jarret. That's wrong."

"Hate's a feeling. I thought feelings weren't wrong. And it's not like I'm doing anything with my hate. I just avoid that kid like the plague. And I sure wouldn't do what he told me, challenge or no challenge."

Keefe sighed. "Still. Why can't you just dislike a few things about him and leave hate to the devil?"

"Why can't I dislike everything about him instead?"

Keefe groaned, then threw a grin that said he knew he wouldn't win this one.

Jarret returned the grin, his gaze shifting. "So when are you doing that, Peter's challenge? I was thinking of having some friends over Friday, just for something to do."

"Oh, that's when I'm doing it. Who're you inviting over?"

"Eh, Kyle and the gang."

Keefe grunted, knowing that "the gang" included a few wild kids that trouble followed. "I'm sure Papa's gonna be home."

"Yeah?" he said in a "what are you hinting at?" tone.

Not wanting to provoke Jarret, Keefe only shrugged.

"I'm just trying to stay busy. I met this girl and I..." Jarret shook his head for a whole second, his face coloring with conflicting expressions. "Just trying to stay busy. How do you do it?"

"Do what?" Keefe smiled inside, suspecting that Jarret wanted to avoid trouble.

"Since you found God across the sea in Italy, you haven't been the same. How's that working out for you?"

"Uh, fine."

"Don't you ever get tempted?"

"Sure. All the time."

"So how do you..." His head bobbed from side to side. He had no idea how to talk about spiritual things. Even when he'd told Keefe about his experience in Arizona, he'd struggled to explain and had left most of it to Keefe's imagination.

"I don't know. You just do. You try not to do every little thing you're tempted to do. You do the right thing. And everyone thinks you're strange. But you do it anyways."

Jarret sighed and squirmed a bit in the saddle.

"Keeping a journal's a good idea." Keefe wondered if he should've brought it up. Jarret had seemed uncomfortable with Keefe knowing he had one. "Then you can think about how the day went."

"And where you messed up," Jarret said.

"Yeah, and sometimes I figure out that God's been trying to tell me something. Which reminds me..." Maybe he had something that could stay with Jarret, help him when Keefe couldn't. Keefe transferred the reins to one hand, reached inside the neckline of his shirt, and grabbed the brown cord of his scapular. He yanked it off over his head. "Here, wear this."

Rather than take it from Keefe, Jarret squinted suspiciously at it.

"It's a brown scapular. It's something that helps me stay on track. Mama gave them to us when we were little. Remember? Made us wear them for years." Keefe continued to hold it out, anxious for Jarret to take it.

"Yeah, I sorta remember." He finally swung a hand out and grabbed it. "Is that why you wear it? Reminds you of Mama?"

"No, I wear it for the promises attached to it, you know, the heavenly help."

"So it's like a good luck charm?"

Keefe bristled. "No, it's not at all like a good luck charm. It's like asking the Blessed Mother to help you. Saying you belong to her." While he'd worn it as a child, he'd learned about the scapular for himself just recently. Maybe he could explain it in words that Jarret would understand. "It's like a weapon in the spiritual battle. Wear the scapular. Go weapons hot."

Jarret laughed. "It's just a cord and cloth. Isn't that kid stuff?"

Having no idea how to explain it better, Keefe shrugged. "We're supposed to become like little children before God, right?"

Jarret stuffed the scapular in the pocket of his jeans. "Thanks."

Then he said, "Who could that be?" and pulled his phone from his back pocket, its low vibrating sound becoming audible. He stared at the screen for a few seconds and tucked the phone away.

"Who was that?" Keefe said.

"Eh, girl I met at the bookstore today."

"You met her today, and you gave her your number?"

Jarret waved his brows, but his eyes showed something less cocky. "Yeah, I don't know why. I just did it. Kind of regret it now.

I'm not ready for a girlfriend. But it doesn't matter. She's not ready for me."

"What'd her message say?"

"Changed my mind. Not interested." He sneered.

Keefe hid a smile. Apparently, she'd hurt his ego a bit, but he seemed more relieved than anything.

"I'm cool with it."

They rode on at an easy pace with only a comment now and then, trotting down the trail that led toward the river and Forest Road. Leaves stirred in a breeze, making sunlight and shadows flicker on the dirt path. Keefe turned his thoughts inward. How could he even entertain the idea of leaving Jarret now? Jarret wanted to do the right thing, but he needed direction. He needed Keefe as a mentor, not a monk. They had one more year of high school. Would that be long enough?

Lord, give me answers. Show me the way over my forty hours in the woods.

CHAPTER 7

Papa sat at the head of the long dinner table, hunched over a plate of roast beef and scalloped potatoes. He glanced up for the fifth time, his gaze traveling over Jarret and Keefe, who sat to his right, and the Digbys on the far end of the table. He gazed for a full second at Roland's empty chair, the one on his left. Did he have something to say? What kept him from just saying it?

Jarret reached for the serving fork for the roast beef and turned to his right to see if Keefe had noticed Papa's pensive mood.

Staring at the huge framed hunting painting on the wall across from him, Keefe held an empty fork and chewed and chewed and chewed. What, forty-seven times? Nanny made a good roast beef, not the least bit chewy. In fact, she could probably beat any of those cooking show chefs with anything she'd made for them these past few weeks. While she kept meals simple, boring even, when Papa was off on assignments, she went all out when he ate at home. Which was every day now.

Mr. Digby mumbled something to Nanny, who mumbled something back, and they laughed. He'd always been a soup and sandwich man, but he did seem to like the menu upgrade.

Jarret slopped more roast beef and gravy onto his plate and grabbed another dinner roll, putting off the question he should've asked sooner.

Papa cleaned his plate and leaned back, his gaze shifting again to Roland's empty chair. "So where's Roland tonight?" He looked down the table at Nanny for the answer.

Jarret and Keefe exchanged glances. Papa had been home almost every night, but he still struggled to keep tabs on them.

Nanny stopped in the middle of cutting a piece of pie for her husband. "He's at the Brandts' house."

Mr. Digby's fingers twitched, then he took the knife from his wife and finished the job.

"He moving in over there or what?" Papa sounded miffed.

"He's staying the night, remember?" Nanny cocked her head to the side. Was that a look of pity she just gave Papa? "He asked you yesterday at breakfast."

"Oh, thought he was staying last night."

"No, he's staying tonight." Nanny cut another piece of pie and slid the plate toward Keefe.

A whole thirty seconds later, Papa squinted at Nanny again. "Where was he last night?"

"At the Brandts'. But he came home in the evening. You were in your study, I believe."

Papa nodded, his gaze sliding to Keefe now. "Did you say you were going somewhere?"

Always the polite one, Keefe swallowed his mouthful and used his napkin before answering. "Yeah, if that's okay. I'm going camping. Primitive style."

The squint of his father's eyes said he remembered. "Camping. Right."

Keefe slid two plates of pie down the table, one for Papa and one for Jarret. None for himself. Something must've still been eating at him. He rarely passed up dessert.

Papa took one plate, picked up his fork, and rested his forearms on the table. "Now, this isn't that big annual camping trip, right?"

"No. Right. I'm going alone." When Papa turned his attention to his pie, Keefe threw a worried look to Jarret, eyebrows slanted and eyes open wide. He'd told Jarret how Papa had responded to his request, all the questions he'd asked. Keefe had thought he had Papa convinced and he was allowed to go.

Jarret snuck a slight head shake back, communicating that everything would work out. They were seventeen. Papa shouldn't really mind.

"Why are you camping all alone, anyways?" Papa said. "Why not with Jarret or one of your friends?"

"Uh..." Keefe's face fell as if he really didn't want to explain this to Papa, at least not yet. "Just something to do. Besides, Jarret has other plans." Then Keefe gave Jarret another look.

Jarret's stomach clenched. He knew the look. Keefe wanted to remind him that he too had a question for Papa. He dropped his half-eaten roll into the gravy on his plate, took a breath, and turned to Papa. "Uh, hey, you don't care if some friends come over tonight, do you?" He hadn't had anyone over in a long time. Papa wouldn't have any reason to say no. But he still should've asked sooner.

"What friends and how many?"

"I don't know. Four or five. Kyle, Nate, C.W. Those guys."

"Any girls?"

An unintentional sneer flashed on Jarret's face. Papa couldn't trust him yet. He was probably imagining a rerun of what had happened with Zoe. Not that he blamed him. But there was no way in... Well, there was no way he would let what happened with Zoe happen again. Never. He'd learned his lesson. He had changed.

"No." Jarret did his best to keep the irritation from his tone. "Just dudes."

Papa scraped the last traces of pie from his plate. "S'pose that's fine. I don't want them here to 4:00 a.m. though."

"How about 3:00 a.m.?" Jarret said, joking.

Papa narrowed his eyes. Not joking. "How about midnight. That's late enough."

"It's summer vacation. How about 1:00 a.m. at the latest?"

Papa held Jarret's gaze for a few long seconds. "Fine. I'll be in my study. No alcohol."

A burst of indignation had Jarret huffing and lifting his hands. Sure he'd made a few mistakes in his past but—

Papa grinned.

Oh, so he'd meant it as a joke. Relieved and annoyed at the same time, Jarret shook his head and got up to take his dirty plate to the kitchen.

Keefe scraped his chair back too and reached for Nanny's and Mr. Digby's dirty plates.

"Hold it there, you two."

Not liking the tone of Papa's voice, Jarret hesitated in the doorway. He braced himself for whatever Papa wanted to say, then he turned around.

Keefe stood by his chair, dishes in hand, and eyes on Papa.

Looking uncharacteristically out of sorts, Papa twisted his mouth to one side. His chest rose and fell with a deep breath. "I've, uh, taken a teaching job."

"What?" Jarret and Keefe said together. Papa had always told them he'd never take a teaching job. He wanted to work out in the field, wouldn't balk at an occasional job as an adviser, might give a talk or two here or there. But he'd sooner herd cats for a living than be roped into a desk or teaching job.

"At River Run High?" Jarret could've kicked himself for the pathetic, whispery voice that came out of him. But he didn't want his father working at his school. He could only imagine what that would do to his image.

Papa's lip curled, amusement flickering in his piercing blue eyes. "No. This school's online."

Jarret exhaled, slumping forward unintentionally. "Well, what are you doing that for?"

Papa shrugged. "Change of pace." He scooted his chair back and withdrew his pipe from the chest pocket of his shirt, signaling the end of the conversation. "We can talk about it later." Puffing on his empty pipe, he left the room.

Jarret stood frozen until the sound of Papa's boots in the hallway trailed off.

"Wow, that was weird." Keefe finally moved, turning from the table to Jarret.

Nanny and Mr. Digby mumbled back and forth, probably discussing Papa's revelation, saying aloud the questions that Keefe and Jarret only thought.

Keefe followed Jarret into the kitchen, silverware clanking against the stack of plates he carried. "Hey, can you give me a ride?" He set the dirty dishes on the bar counter while Jarret walked around to the sink.

"A ride to where?" Jarret ran water over his plate and slid the other dirty ones closer. Ever since returning from Arizona, he'd been forcing himself to help with dishes. Every night he felt less inclined.

"The Brandts'. I'll head out to the woods from there." Keefe played with the clutter on the counter: a napkin holder, a dirty knife, and a cutting board.

"Yeah, I guess I can." Jarret opened the dishwasher, releasing the odor of citrus detergent and fishy minerals.

"You can see me off, walk back there with me."

Jarret glanced, wondering if Keefe was serious. "No thanks. You know how I love to be around Peter Brandt."

"Aw, come on. He hasn't done anything to you lately."

"It wasn't that long ago. Every time I get in my car and the odor of Limburger cheese hits me, I smell the need for revenge." If felt weird admitting weakness. But he still entertained the idea of pummeling Peter as payback. So he needed to keep a healthy distance. What would he do once school started and he saw him in the hall? Any chance he'd have true forgiveness by then?

"Besides." Jarret ran water over a messy fork. "I got Kyle and them coming over."

"Yeah, okay." Keefe spun the napkin dispenser in a circle. "I just need a jacket and I'm ready to go."

"Don't you need to pack anything?"

"Just bringing that." He nodded to indicate a little canvas tote bag hanging from a hook near the pantry.

"What's in it?" Jarret dropped the last of the silverware into the dishwasher and closed it.

"Water bottle and a loaf of bread."

"For forty hours? You're gonna be hungry."

"That's the point. I'm keeping it simple, praying for discernment. Can't hurt to fast too, right?"

Jarret shrugged, not seeing the point of fasting or of a lot of other things Keefe did lately. Stopping at the cupboard on the wall across from the kitchen island, he searched behind the emergency candles on an upper shelf. "At least take this." He slapped a flashlight into Keefe's hand.

Keefe stared at it, as if deciding.

"If you don't take it, I won't give you a ride."

Keefe huffed but he said, "Fine."

Jarret dug his keys from the front pocket of his jeans. "I want to pick up a few things from the store anyway."

CHAPTER 8

A spark of excitement flared inside Keefe as he strode behind Roland and Peter to his lonely destination. A peaceful blue sky stretched out above, peeking through lush green leaves and branches of ponderosa pines. At least he could count on perfect weather. The rude *beep, beep, beep* of a red breasted nuthatch rose above the soft trills of the other birds, the tanagers, warblers, and juncos that Keefe had often seen in these woods. Why had God made all of this—every plant, animal, and bird—so unique?

"So you've got nothing to worry about as long as you stay near the waterfall after dark, or better yet, sleep in the cave." Peter had been blabbing instructions, guidelines, and warnings ever since they set off down the trail behind his house. With a forest ranger for a father, he probably knew his stuff.

Distracted by the excitement buzzing inside, Keefe tried paying attention, but he wasn't exactly clueless when it came to hiking alone or camping in the wilderness. His family had plenty of wilderness adventures over the years, some intentional, others accidental.

Keefe readjusted the canvas bag he carried over his shoulder. His stomach was his biggest worry. He'd never liked skipping a meal, but he'd intentionally eaten a light dinner and passed up dessert. Now he'd have a single loaf of bread to stretch over the next forty hours. Saint Francis went forty days, eating only half a loaf. He could last forty hours.

"You'll find a couple of lighters inside the cave. And you know those candles are in there. But you might want to build a fire out on the riverbank. Not in the cave, of course. You'd be smoked out..."

Roland threw Keefe a concerned glance. Or maybe Peter's babbling was annoying him. He'd been plodding along with the crutches at a good clip, thumping the crutches down and swinging his body forward, fast enough to win a contest. Thump, swing, thump, swing.

"Make sure you go back into the cave where the water falls intermittently."

"What?" Keefe tuned in to Peter's ramblings, thinking that last detail might matter.

"You'll see. Rain last week made the waterfall heavier than usual for this time of year. But you'll barely get wet if you go back where I'm telling you. You'll have to be careful because the cave entrance isn't exactly there, where less water comes down. That just gets you behind the waterfall. Then you have to take a few steps to the left. Understand?"

Keefe tried to process and store the information, but just as Peter glanced at him, he'd opened his mouth for a question that never materialized.

Peter dropped back and slapped his arm. "You'll be fine. If you go in at the wrong point, you'll just get a little wet.

"Did you bring your phone?" Roland slowed and waited for Keefe and Peter to walk alongside him. The path was wide enough here to walk three across.

"He can't bring a phone," Peter whined. "But you should have a watch so you know when to come back." He swung his arm up and gazed at his bulky outdoor watch with a brown leather band, a birthday gift from his father. It had an altimeter, barometer, compass, thermometer, and whatever else. "He's got forty hours out here, so this time tomorrow is twenty-four and then you just gotta make it through another night. So at like nine on Sunday morning you can head back."

"You should have a phone." Roland glanced between Keefe and the path ahead, his gray eyes heavy with worry. "You can take mine."

"I can't have a phone, Roland. I'll be tempted to play games or call someone when I'm bored." He tried giving Roland a reassuring smile. "No, I'm doing this without a phone. And, no, I don't have a watch. I can tell when it's nine o'clock. I like to go riding at that time every morning." Worry flickering through him, he turned away from Roland and stared wide-eyed at the trail ahead. Who would exercise his horse while he was gone? He hadn't asked Mr. Digby or Jarret, and Roland couldn't do it.

"Don't worry about your horse." Roland must've read his mind. "I'll take care of it."

Keefe looked at him, ready to ask how.

Roland shrugged. "Well, not personally. I'll get Jarret or Mr. Digby to do it." Then he said through gritted teeth, "Can't wait until this cast comes off."

Keefe took a breath and exhaled to relax. Jarret still felt guilty for the mishap in Arizona that had led to Roland breaking his leg. So he was still doing everything Roland asked. He'd take care of the horse.

"So this is as far as we go." Peter stopped in his tracks, grabbing Roland's arm.

Roland kept going for a step, following through after planting his crutches. "We can go farther. Are you turning back because of me? I told you my leg feels fine, doesn't bother me at all. It's just that this cast is awkward to walk in." He averted his gaze and mumbled again, "Can't *wait* to get it off."

Walking a few paces behind them, Keefe stopped too. They'd been walking three wide when the path allowed but it narrowed up here.

"No, it's the time." Peter pointed to his watch and then locked gazes with Keefe. "Your forty hours starts now. You're on your own. You and God. If you can survive this—no food other than the bread, no place to lay your head other than what mother nature provides, no one to talk to but God—then you become one of us. The few, the proud, the... uh..." His gaze slid to Roland. "What do you think? The pyromaniacs?"

"Huh? No. How does that work?"

"I don't know. We're the Fire Starters, right? So the few that go the extra mile need a stronger name. So pyromaniacs."

Roland shook his head, turning to Keefe now. "You sure you want to do this?"

"Of course. I'll be fine."

"Come on." Peter whacked Roland's arm. "Let's get back to the house. I'm hungry for dessert. Mom made three kinds of pies and a coffee cake."

"Why would you say that in front of him? He's got a loaf of bread for the next two days."

Peter laughed. "He'll be fine. He's tough." He started walking backwards, back the way they came. "Right, Keefe?"

Keefe shrugged, but he knew he could last forty hours out here. It wasn't a big deal. And watching Peter backing up, knowing Roland would soon join him and he'd be left alone, a great feeling of comfort came over him. His private retreat began now. He was ready for this. He would find answers. God would lead him to knowledge. And whatever the answer, Keefe was ready to go all in. Nothing by halves. Nothing held back. He would talk to Papa about becoming a Franciscan or he would give the idea up, content to mentor Jarret for however long Jarret needed it.

A verse came to mind as he turned away from Roland and Peter. *Jesus said to him: No one who puts his hand to the plough and looks back is fit for the kingdom of God.*

Keefe strolled away without looking back.

Peter's voice faded. The warblers continued to sing and leaves rustled in a comfortable breeze. A squirrel scampered through underbrush somewhere out of view. And the rocky trail welcomed him to his journey.

CHAPTER 9

With the driver-side window open, one arm hanging out, and barely tapping the gas pedal, Jarret drove at ease down the long winding driveway toward home. He'd picked up some pop, pretzels, and chips and would get home in plenty of time before his friends came over. The warm breeze ruffled through his hair and made the sleeve of his t-shirt flap. The tension in his chest—a result of seeing Peter step outside onto the front porch when he'd dropped off Keefe—had almost left him.

"Stay safe," he'd said as Keefe got out of the car. But Keefe was always cautious, so Jarret had no real worry.

The Wests' castle-like house inched into view. Fluffy white clouds and a rich blue sky formed a backdrop, accenting the stone battlements and two turrets. He loved their house inside and out. Never wanted to move.

As Jarret rounded the last curve, his breath caught. Cars and kids came into view, four cars in the circular drive and about fifteen kids on the porch and in the yard.

"Fifteen?" Jarret blew a breath out his mouth, regret creeping in. What would Papa have to say about this?

Half of the kids turned as Jarret pulled into the circular drive. Kyle threw his arms overhead and waved. Everyone flocked toward the car.

"Hey," Jarret called, his eyes on Kyle but meaning for everyone to listen. "Jump back in your cars and pull around to the garage. Park side by side in the grass next to the driveway. I'll let you in through the veranda."

"Did he say veranda?" Sherman Maher said, playing with his hair. It framed his face and stuck up in thick dark tufts with blond streaks. He must've spent hours styling and staring at it.

"What's a veranda?" another kid said.

"I'll show you. Get in the car," Kyle replied.

Jarret cringed at the noise they made getting back in and starting their cars. The window to Papa's study was closed so maybe he wouldn't hear it, but he'd probably seen the cars drive by.

Jarret parked out front, grabbed the grocery bags, and stomped up the porch steps to the heavy front door. He strode down the front hallway, sneakers thumping along the hardwood floor. The door to Papa's study was ajar. He could busy himself in there for hours, and hopefully he would. Maybe he taught an evening class. On Friday? Probably not.

Halfway down the hall, Nanny emerged from her suite at the far end. "Oh, there you are." She scurried toward him waving her hands, a motherly expression on her face. "I thought it would be nice to make a few snacks for your friends."

"Nah, don't bother." Jarret lifted one bag. "I picked up some snacks. Besides, we're just gonna hang out."

"It's no bother. I've already made little sandwiches and put some jalapeno poppers in the oven." She hurried past him, in her element with all the food preparations lately. "I'll go check on those and bring them..." Her voice trailed off as she rounded the corner.

Jarret strode to the veranda. Kyle stood on the other side of the door, mouthing something through the window. As soon as Jarret unlocked and opened the door, everyone pushed into the house, some giving a greeting as they passed but others just plowing their way in. Several carried grocery bags. Had they brought snacks too? Cool, they'd be eating good tonight.

Two kids went to a table at the back of the long veranda. Jocks that had little zeal for football, probably the worst on the team. What were their names? Oh yeah, Trent and Konner. Granted, the veranda had enough tables for everyone and it had a lot of class, what with the windows stretching across one wall and the fancy patio tables and chairs. The slant of the evening light cast long blue shadows across everything. But Jarret had planned on everyone playing pool or darts in the rec room. Of course, he hadn't planned on fifteen guys raiding his house.

"Party's in here," Jarret hollered to Trent and Konner.

Konner had already placed a deck of cards and a pile of coins on the table. "Aw, man. Can't we sit out here?"

Trent laughed and threw his hands in the air. "Really, Bro, you can trust us. I need to school Konner here at poker."

"You school me?" Konner leaned back, tapped his chest, and flung his arms out. "That some kind of joke?"

Trent, Konner, and C.W. did everything together. The three of them had inferiority complexes and spent half their days trying to prove themselves to each other or to anyone that paid attention. The rest of the time they worked at making others look small. It was strange that C.W. had gone inside with everyone else, instead of staying out here with Konner and Trent.

Jarret rolled his eyes and left them, following the last of his guests toward the living room.

The scent of lemon wood polish hung in the air. Open drapes on the back wall brought in enough light to make a person curious about the decor. Dust-free, artistically-placed antiques sat on polished shelves and tables all around the long family room. Most gave a feel for medieval Europe or ancient Rome, Papa's favorite places and time periods. Jarret, Keefe, and Roland usually favored the far side of the room, watching TV or lounging around. They rarely set foot in the museum-like side.

Sherman sat cross-legged on the floor a few feet from the TV, which he'd already turned on. The TV flipped from program to program and then to a blue screen. Three other kids stood by the suit of armor in the far corner, one of them messing with the face mask.

"Hey," Jarret shouted, all four of them looking. "Don't mess with that."

Jarret checked the rec room, hoping the rest of the gang had gone in there and not somewhere else in the house. A few kids stood around the pool table, racking balls and boasting about their summers. One messed with the sound system in the corner. And Kyle sat on the old couch against the far wall, a paper bag between his feet and a brand-new pack of menthol cigarettes in his hand. He'd never been much of a smoker, even when Jarret had been, and he looked awkward as he opened the pack.

Was this everyone? Jarret counted fifteen dudes and five plastic grocery bags.

"Hey, Bro." Kyle grinned at Jarret. The overhead lighting made his red hair match his freckles. "Cigarette?" He tapped one out an inch and offered it to Jarret.

On impulse, Jarret licked his lips. The cigarette called to him, but he shook his head. He hadn't had one in a month. No point in starting back up now.

"Thought you had a fridge in here." Kyle lit the cigarette and set the pack and lighter on the arm of the couch.

"No fridge." Should he tell Kyle not to smoke in the house? What were the chances Papa would come back here? It's not like Jarret was smoking, but Papa still wouldn't want teens smoking in his house. Smoking wouldn't be as bad as... "What's in the bags?"

"Can't have a party without beverages." A devious glint to his eyes, Kyle stuffed his hand in the bag at his feet and lifted out a six-pack.

A wave of heat rushed over Jarret. "You brought beer into my house without asking?"

"Like you're gonna say no? You know you want one." Chuckling, he wrestled a can from the plastic ring. He cracked it open, the sound of pressure releasing and striking Jarret somewhere inside.

"Yeah, I'm gonna say no. You know my father's home, right?"

"No." Kyle's hazel eyes opened wide, drawing attention to his thick, pale eyelashes. He took a swig of beer and stood. "Hey, bros, don't bring the beer out in the open. Wait till I get back."

"Back from where?" Jarret asked, concern growing.

"You'll see." Kyle handed his lit cigarette to a friend and strutted from the room.

Bouncy music came on, soft, the way Roland listened to it; then it rose in volume to an ear-thrashing level.

"Don't blare it." Jarret stomped back to the family room.

The TV still showed a blue screen. Two kids now sat on the floor, Sherman and C.W. fiddling with remotes. C.W. must've chosen video games over his buddies Trent and Konner. The other kids had moved behind the couch that divided the extra-long family room. Their raised voices said they disagreed about something. They inched toward and away from each other in the yellow light of the lamps they'd turned on without asking.

Jarret marched to the kids on the floor to help get their video game started. On his way, he glimpsed two things at the same time, both stirring up his ire. The medieval sword no longer hung over the fireplace, and his father would have a fit if he saw two of the five video games on the coffee table. Jarret considered saying something about it, but fear of ruining his image kept his mouth shut. He could find another way to take care of it.

"Gimme the remote." Jarret dropped down on one knee behind Sherman. He pressed a few buttons and got the game on in seconds, some old monster game. Aside from stylized gore, it wasn't too bad. As he straightened, he snatched the games his father wouldn't want to see and stuffed them behind the back cushion of the couch.

He turned his attention to the arguing kids on the other side of the family room. "Get the sword back on the wall. Don't touch the antiques."

"Aw, come on, bro," Jaxson said, swinging his arm out from behind him and brandishing the sword. His over-sized basketball shirt swished with his adept movements. He'd probably kick butt in a sword fight, and if the party were outside, Jarret would suggest it. He loved fencing and relished the idea of showing up every one of these guys. Most of them would need instruction though, which he'd find more annoying than fun. Most seemed to lack coordination.

"Your crib be phat," Jaxson said, relinquishing the sword to Jarret. "Where'd your peeps get all these old things?"

"Eh, my father collects," Jarret said as if it were no big deal, though it gave him a sense of pride.

"Nice."

"Problem solved," Kyle shouted as he backed through the swinging doors that separated the family room from the great room. Walking with a confident air, he carried a bottle of juice, a two-liter of clear pop, a stack of plastic cups, and a plate of jalapeno poppers, all on one tray. A fried food aroma accompanied him. He set the tray on the sofa table and took something from a front pocket of his jeans.

"What problem is that?" Jarret said with sarcasm.

Grinning, Kyle slipped the top cup off the stack and darted into the rec room. He returned, pouring beer into the cup.

"Watch." With dramatic flair, he set the can down, produced a little bottle of red food color and squeezed a couple of drops into the beer. "Walla! I'm drinking punch." He proceeded to bring the cup to his lips and chug his new creation.

Doubting that would deceive Papa, Jarret shook his head and blew out a breath.

A heartbeat later, a line formed next to Kyle and wrapped around the couch. Colt handed cans of beer to Kyle, who then poured them into cups and added red food coloring.

Jarret backed away, bumped an end table, and flopped onto a couch. Every time a can cracked open, he winced. He wished the sound of the gaming music, explosions, and bleeps covered it. The faintest image of Jesus hovered in his mind, but not the way he'd seen him in the canyon. Now his hands were bound to a pillar, his bleeding back exposed. Every time a can opened, the whip cracked again.

Someone plopped down next to Jarret on the couch, jarring him from thought.

"So who's this, your mom?" C.W. held an old framed picture of Mama and Papa.

Not interested in dialog, Jarret snatched it from him and placed it with care on the sofa table behind the couch.

"So I see the Mexican in you and Keefe, what with your swarthy skin. That's what your mom was, right? Mexican? So what happened with Roland?" C.W. tapped the screen of his cellphone. "That boy is *white*." He emphasized the last word.

Jarret sighed and shook his head. Another can cracked open.

"Hey, dude, check this out." C.W. shoved his cellphone in front of Jarret's face. "I saw this babe at the county fair. She didn't even know I took her picture. Check her out. Didn't know anyone was watching. Got some other pics on here too."

Growing numb to his surroundings, Jarret glanced at C.W. and his greasy blond hair parted down the middle, his stained jeans that he probably wore while changing the oil in his car, and then the phone in his hand. And the image of the girl that had no idea he'd taken her picture.

Jarret snatched the phone and deleted the picture. Then he tossed the phone to the couch and got up.

"What'd you do that for?" C.W. whined.

He should've said it aloud, but his answer remained in his mind. *Don't take pictures like that of girls.*

Laughter, cigarette smoke, thumping music, and loud taunting voices spewed from the rec room. Kyle no longer served beer from the sofa table, but a few full glasses sat between a lamp and the almost-empty plate of poppers. Pool balls cracked as Jarret stepped into the rec room. If Papa came around, he'd be ticked off. Jarret needed to make everyone leave. The words rolled around Jarret's mind but disappeared like pool balls sinking into pockets.

Colt stared at his beer in the light of the fluorescent bar sign. Another kid shouted obscenities at him, offended about something... seeming like he needed anger management. Kyle leaned over the table for a shot.

Disgusted with himself and not wanting to even see Kyle, Jarret snatched the pack of cigarettes and lighter from the arm of the couch and left the room.

In the living room, Sherman and another kid flipped through games, probably looking for the ones Jarret had hidden. Someone had taken the sword off the wall again, and the shield too. Papa had had the shield custom made with their family logo on it.

Jarret strode past the shouting and laughter, the gamers and fighters, and out through the veranda. The door closed with a click behind him.

Standing on the cement steps, he gazed out toward the stables, the row of trees behind them, and the orange tinged clouds in the darkening sky. His ears still rang from the music and voices inside. He tapped a cigarette from the pack, surprised to see his hands trembling.

Then his mind tried to wrap around a thought, but it flitted away. He'd forgotten something. But what?

Steadying his hands, he lit the cigarette and took a long drag off it. The fresh, minty menthol taste surprised him. He shouldn't be starting up the bad habit again. No, he just needed one cigarette. He'd never touch them again after this. Finding a comfortable position on the steps, he exhaled the pungent smoke and peered through it at the line of trees that ran behind the stables.

A warm breeze carried his thoughts back to the canyon in Arizona. The cigarette smoke kept him from smelling the fresh air. Not that it mattered. The scent of the green woods around him didn't compare to the arid desert scent, wouldn't help him go back there in his mind, wouldn't get him any closer to remembering.

Jarret rubbed a hand up his chest and rested it on his opposite shoulder. *Jesus, come back.*

Desperate for a connection to that life-changing moment, Jarret closed his eyes and tried bringing images to his mind. The darkening sky. The high canyon walls. The dry creek down the middle of the canyon and rough rocks everywhere. He'd slipped trying to walk over them, trying to run after he'd heard Roland's desperate call.

Jarret's stomach twisted. Roland had lain there in such pain, his leg broken and bleeding, his face drained of color. The harsh words that Jarret had spoken replayed in his mind. His cruel confession of everything he'd ever done against him.

"I don't care," Roland had said. "I still forgive you."

The thought of Roland's unswerving mercy struck Jarret with a little stabbing pain in his heart. Jarret had caved in then, and repented. And then He came... the Lord.

Jarret sifted through images in his mind, struggling to bring the memory back. The ache, the longing in his heart magnified, but he couldn't regain any of it. He'd felt it so vividly for two weeks after it had happened. He should've gone to Father Carston as soon as he'd returned home from Arizona, just as the priest had told him to do. He'd put it off for three weeks. Maybe that explained why the memory had faded.

Or maybe he just didn't deserve it.

He'd promised then to change. He'd wanted it with every cell and fiber of his being. If the feelings of mercy, forgiveness, and love faded, and the feelings of the closeness of the Lord left him, how could he remain faithful?

A horse whinnied, maybe even Jarret's horse.

He heard Papa's deep voice in his mind. "Cowboy up, Jarret."

Jarret took another drag off the cigarette and gazed out at the trees. A single cricket chirped. The trees swayed in a silent breeze. Yeah, with or without consolation, he'd just have to cowboy up. He could do this. He had to do this.

For days I remembered every one of Your words
And the sound of Your voice,
how it had reverberated through me.
Your love and mercy overwhelmed me,
Dropping me again to my knees
Whenever my mind took me back to that night.
You love me and accept me through and through,
Personally and individually,
despite my failings.

CHAPTER 10

"Blessed is he who takes no offense at me."

The verse came unbidden, and Keefe's mood sank a level. Before Jarret had given him a ride to Peter's, he'd said a prayer, opened the Bible, and dropped a finger to the page. It had landed on that verse, Luke 7:23. Maybe he hadn't done it right. When Saint Francis and Bernard had done it, they'd gone to Mass first and then had the priest open the Bible.

This message didn't seem to apply to his situation. In fact, it bothered him and he wished he could shake it from his mind and pull up another one. With all the Bible reading he'd done lately, he had several memorized. Why had it opened to that verse? Was he just being superstitious by expecting God to answer him that way? Nah, the Bible was God's word. Why wouldn't He answer Keefe through it?

Though he strolled at a leisurely pace, he soon emerged from the canopy of branches and reached the riverbank. The sky, half shrouded with puffy white clouds—the lower edges tinted orange—had turned a richer blue and colored the trees on the opposite side of the river in soothing shades of green. Rippling waves moved past, gentle and mesmerizing. So beautiful.

Kicking an occasional rock and letting his canvas bag swing at his side, Keefe walked along the bank, heading in the direction of the waterfall. His mind returned to the story about how St. Francis spent forty entire days on a deserted island with nothing more to eat than a bit of bread. He'd found a hiding place between shrubs and trees. And there he'd prayed and contemplated heavenly things.

Keefe regarded the trees on the opposite side of the river again, turning his heart to God. The wispy leaves of a willow tree hung in the river, swaying with the current. The lime green leaves of an aspen fluttered in the breeze. A bushier tree with darker leaves had a sprinkling of yellow already, probably not turning yet, though summer would soon end. The trees would soon become an artist's palette of colors, some turning orange and yellow right away, others clinging to their green leaves for as long as possible.

Keefe wanted to cling to nothing of his own ideas or goals. He wanted to let go and let God. Let God transform him from the ordinary into something he could not even imagine. He wanted to dry up his own desires and live for God alone, going through the world as the Franciscans do, as pilgrims and strangers, taking nothing with him but Christ crucified.

Sometime later, a dirt ridge rose to his right and the sound of rushing water grew louder with every step. Pink now colored the sky ahead, while purplish blue hung above.

Keefe stopped and picked up two branches in his path. He'd need them and a lot more to get a fire started.

Several minutes later, the rushing white waterfall came into view. Awed by the beauty, Keefe gazed at it as he strolled closer with his armful of branches. Then he found a smooth area on the riverbank and set the branches near it. The canvas bag slid off his shoulder, so he placed it beside the woodpile. Grabbing fist-sized and larger rocks, he made a circular border for the campfire he'd build later tonight. He'd need to gather more firewood and kindling before sundown.

~ ~ ~

The door swung open and Dillon stepped outside, worry showing on his dark face and the slant of his thin black brows. "Yo, bro, we got us an emergency." He never spoke above a whisper, not even now, but his tone said this was serious.

Jarret crushed out his second cigarette and tossed it behind a bush. "What happened?"

"Don't know, bro. Something's wrong with Nate. First I thought he had a bad case of acne."

Not sure if he should worry, Jarret jumped up and followed Dillon back into the house through the veranda. "Yeah, he's always kind of..." Jarret didn't bother finishing the sentence. He'd been lucky to have nothing more than a zit here or there. Nate hadn't had that luck.

"Right. But those suckers started springing up everywhere." He gestured rhythmically with both hands, indicating his arms and neck.

"You mean like hives?"

"Don't know man. I'm thinking we should call 9-1-1."

Amidst blaring music and air hazy with cigarette smoke, everyone stood around the couch that divided the living room in two. Why hadn't anyone done anything? Several kids looked at Jarret as he neared, panic and confusion in their eyes. He'd always acted like he knew everything, so now they expected him to know what to do.

"Sherman, take Nate out to my car. Now. I'm parked out front." Jarret pointed to the swinging doors that led to the great room and the hallway that ran to the front door. "And you..." He turned to Dillon, the only kid here he'd trust in a crisis. "...get everyone to clean up and go home. Don't leave beer cans behind."

Dillon gave what looked like a confident nod.

As Sherman helped Nate to his feet, Jarret's heart kicked into high gear and his mouth went dry.

Angry red hives covered Nate's face like a bad burn.

"Itches, man." Nate hugged himself and winced. "I think—I think—my throat's closing up." His voice came out strained.

"You'll be okay." Jarret patted his shoulder. "Try to relax. We'll get you to the emergency room."

~ ~ ~

Drained from the surge of adrenaline he'd experienced as he sped to the hospital, Jarret slumped in the driver's seat of his Chrysler and gazed at the lighted ER entrance. He had dropped Nate and Sherman off at the door and parked across the street. He'd go inside—as soon as he calmed down.

He hated all this. Since returning from Arizona, his days had been peaceful. He should never have invited his friends over. Like him, they couldn't stay out of trouble. Had Dillon gotten everyone out of the house? What about all the beer? Had Papa seen anything? Staying in his study like that, seemed like he wanted to trust Jarret.

A jolt of self-recrimination had him slamming the steering wheel. Man, he'd blown it. Again.

Jarret took a breath.

Lights flashed in his peripheral vision, an ambulance racing toward the hospital. Should Jarret have called an ambulance? Nah. Nate would be fine. They probably had him checked in already and had given him some Benadryl or a shot of steroids by now. Probably wouldn't discharge him for hours though. Maybe his parents—

Oh, yeah. Jarret stuffed a hand into his back pocket and retrieved his phone. He'd told Nate he'd call his parents. Unable to speak above a whisper, Nate had kept shaking his head and waving his hand. But his parents had to know, and he was in no condition to call them.

Two seconds of scrolling and Jarret found the number. With a sigh, he pressed "call." While the phone rang, he lowered the driver's side window and rested his arm on the frame.

Voices traveled from across the street, from a couple walking toward the glowing ER door. Bugs swarmed around a nearby streetlight.

A woman answered. "Hello?"

"Mrs. Lynch?"

"Yes?"

"Uh, hey..." Jarret shifted in his seat, uneasiness rattling him. He'd never met Nate's parents. Never even seen them. Had Nate ever mentioned Jarret's name to them? "This is Jarret West, Nate's friend. We're, uh, at the hospital."

"Who's up at the hospital?" Her curious tone transformed to one of hard concern.

"Nate. We took him to the ER. He had some kind of reaction, broke out in hives. I'm sure he'll be okay but—"

"Who is this again?" Now she sounded skeptical, as if she couldn't believe this had anything to do with her son.

"Jarret. Jarret West." He switched his phone from one sweaty hand to the other. "I just dropped Nate off at the ER. Sherman's with him and I'm on my way inside. Just wanted to call you first."

"No, Nate went to Kyle's house tonight."

Did she think he had her son confused with some other kid? "Yeah, well, they came over to my house. Kyle too."

"But Nate's not allowed over at your house."

Jarret jerked back, bumping his head on the headrest. So she had heard of him. Was his reputation so bad that kids weren't allowed over to his house? What had she heard? Had to have been about the Halloween party last October. Maybe it had to do with his and Keefe's sword fight. Or maybe she knew about Zoe and didn't want her son hanging out with a bad influence.

Jarret rubbed his forehead. "Well, I just wanted to let you know. I'm going in now to see how he's doing." He raised his window and waited a second for a reply. A man and woman spoke in the background but nothing he could make out.

Before he ended the call, his phone buzzed, receiving a text. Couldn't be Keefe because he hadn't taken his phone. He probably should've. What if something went wrong?

One hand to the door handle, he glanced at the message and his stomach clenched.

Hi. It's me. The girl from the bookstore.

Two heartbeats later, another message. My name's Chantelle. How r u?

Jarret sucked in a breath and lifted his gaze to the dark parking lot. Chantelle? How do you even pronounce that?

He exhaled as he stuffed the phone away and got out of the car. The girl—Chantelle—had said she wasn't interested, so he thought he'd dodged that bullet.

With the slightest glance down the road in each direction, Jarret strode across the street. He just wouldn't reply to her. She'd think he was a jerk. They'd see each other in school and she'd say something to him about it, something snide. He'd come back with a rude, flirtatious remark. Then something would start between them. What could he do to avoid it? He needed a do-over. He never should've given her his number. Never should've invited Kyle and the gang over; he knew they'd cause trouble.

Jarret stepped through the sliding doors of the ER and into the crowded waiting area. He had no strength to resist this stuff. He needed to feel the presence of the Lord again.

CHAPTER 11

Stomach rumbling and a headache threatening, Keefe headed back from his third trip for firewood. He'd gone so far that he could no longer hear the waterfall. *No, wait...*

A soft sound of rushing water rose above other night noises. He'd kept the river in view the whole time, remaining close to it as he'd searched for fallen branches at the edge of the woods.

Sticking to the river to avoid getting lost made him think of the wisdom of staying close to the Blessed Mother. She wouldn't let him stray from the truth, from Jesus. As he'd walked along, the thought inspired him to pray the Rosary, though he hadn't brought his black beads. Didn't even have his scapular. He hadn't brought anything. But he had ten fingers, so he'd counted off the ten Hail Marys on them. Ten, eleven, or twelve. With an armful of branches, it proved a challenge.

Keefe shifted his load. Branches dug into his hands and even his arms through the jacket. He'd gathered more on this trip than on the first two, but the air had grown cooler as the sun set, and he didn't want to shiver all night. Would the cave be warmer? Probably not. He didn't like the idea of sleeping in there anyway. Too dark. But he would have to go in for the lighter. He should get the fire started soon.

The trees parted and gave way to the riverbank. Keefe emerged from the woods at the top of a steep slope, his fire ring and pile of branches not too far below. He stood taking in the view for a moment. Shadows had shrouded almost everything in the woods, leaving only a few slivers of light, but he hadn't expected to find the sky this dark when he left the woods.

Tired of walking and heart pounding from all his hard work, Keefe decided to take his chances and climb down the slope. He looked for a good place to descend, then took a cautious step. *Good, so far.* His next step didn't work out so well. He tipped forward and took two more steps to keep from falling. The momentum forced him to jog the rest of the way down, his feet tingling with every step.

As he reached the rocky riverbank, his load of branches lurched, several sticks escaping his grip. He carried the rest to his woodpile. Instead of placing them on the pile, as he had with the other loads, he opened his arms and let them clatter onto the pile and tumble to the ground. Catching his breath, he brushed his hands on his jeans. His gaze locked onto the canvas sack—his bread and water. His stomach growled and mouth watered just looking at it. But he needed to get the fire going first.

Stars twinkled overhead in a sky just shy of midnight blue. He couldn't find the moon—clouds might have hidden it. And the waterfall, so pretty and blue in the evening light... He glanced at the crude stack of branches, then back at the rushing water. He'd better get in there and find Peter's lighter before he lost the last trace of sunlight.

Feeling a measure of urgency, he wrestled the flashlight from his bag and jogged the few yards to the point of the riverbank closest to the fall. He studied the stepping stones jutting from the river, waves lapping over them. He could get to the waterfall in a few steps. He had nothing to worry about; the river was shallow most of the way. Lifting his gaze, he tried locating the thinnest section of the waterfall. Peter had said the water fell sporadically at one point.

A section of water, between two thicker downpours, fell with a rhythmic pattern. *That must be it.*

Keefe sucked in a breath and took a step. The first few rocks felt firm under his sneaker. The next rock wobbled. And the next—he misjudged the distance or the size of the rock. His sneaker splashed down, his heart leaping to his throat, and his arms flying out.

The flashlight sailed from his hand.

He jerked his leg back up and made a futile glance at the turbulent water, knowing he would not see his flashlight. Then he strained to glimpse the next rock, but the falls agitated the dark water, disguising the rocks as waves.

About to lose his balance, he sent up a prayer and took a chance. His foot landed on something solid. Two more steps, two more chances, and he found himself pelted by stray drops of water. Out of the corner of his eye—he couldn't risk turning his head—he glimpsed a section of water falling in spurts. So he reached a leg out and found rock, good solid rock. Timing it right, he lunged forward between sheets of water. Shuddering a sigh of relief, he reached out and touched the wall of rock. Then he shuffled along a narrow ledge until darkness deepened before him and his hands slipped off the rock and to nothingness. He'd found the opening of the cave.

Sucking in air too quickly, he stumbled into the dark cave. A shiver ran through him, ending in a groan that he couldn't control. One hand to the cold wall, he shuffled to the back of the cave. The waterfall formed a loud blue-gray wall behind him, providing hazy light that revealed little more than odd shapes he couldn't identify. He couldn't see the rock table or the two tree stumps that Peter used as chairs. Peter had probably left the lighter on the table.

Keefe squinted into the darkness. Even his depth perception felt off. He wished he were back on the riverbank, but he'd have to go through the waterfall again to get there. And try to make out the stepping stones again.

Goosebumps popped out on his arms and the hair on his arms stood up. With hands cold as ice, Keefe zipped his hooded sweat jacket up to this neck. He should've worn something warmer. How would he make it through the night? A campfire would help. He needed that lighter.

Renewed in his mission, Keefe shuffled along the perimeter, one frozen hand to the rough wall, the other waving in front of him. He bumped something loose on the wall. Hoping to identify it, he reached out to touch it.

It crashed at his feet with the sound of breaking glass that the roar of the waterfall soon swallowed. Must've been one of the candle holders.

He continued, his next step crunching on broken glass. A few steps later, the toe of his shoe slammed into something, and he lost his balance. He planted his foot forward to steady himself and cracked his leg into something. A jolt of pain shot up his leg and dropped him to his knees. One knee bumped something—the log stump? *Thank God.*

The thought that he could offer up his pain—unite it to the cross of Christ—flitted through his mind, but he just wanted that lighter.

Feeling around, reaching gingerly this time, he identified the stump and sat on it, then he found the rock table. He slid his hands across the cold gritty surface until he found something smooth and rectangular. The lighter! And another one too. He stuffed them both into his jeans front pocket and got up to leave. The darkness in the cave had him looking over his shoulder.

Still not trusting his depth perception and afraid of falling in the pool behind the waterfall, he put a hand to the cave wall again. His fingertips smarted from scraping along its rough surface by the time he reached the ledge. Drawing near to the icy gray curtain, he put up his hood, sucked in a few breaths, and prepared to push through.

Wait! Not here. He had to leave the cave first and move a few steps to where the water fell in spurts.

He took another breath and rested his hands on the edge of the cave wall. Drops of water hit his face and made him blink. He'd stayed relatively dry so far. He could do this.

Clinging to the wall, he shuffled out of the cave and around the corner. Head turned, he glimpsed the thinner water falling in sheets, two heartbeats between them. He turned a bit so he could find the stepping stones. Should've been right there. No? His gaze snapped to various points in the river, his heart rate quickening. He couldn't see them.

Wait... The water didn't move the same in one spot two feet away from him. Had to be the first stepping stone. And the other stones were spaced one long stretch apart, except for a few. Which ones?

Keefe glanced at the starry sky, the silhouettes of trees on either side of the river, and the shore which appeared dark mottled blue. The sooner he did this, the sooner he could get a fire going and warm up.

Tentatively, Keefe reached out with his foot. He exhaled. He'd found the first stone. A tingling sensation rushed through him as he shifted his weight to his foot on the stone.

He sized up the waves, guessing at the distance of the next stone. Finding an odd shadow, he took a chance. Found the next stone. Relief shuddered through him. Transferring his weight again, he searched for the next one.

Four stepping-stones later, rather than land on something solid, his sneaker went down, down, down. Ugh! Panic rose inside. The world shifted. Stomach leaping up, Keefe sailed down. Icy water engulfed him.

~ ~ ~

Jarret followed Nate and his parents from the ER, keeping his distance. Nate's parents had arrived twenty minutes after Jarret had gone inside. They'd spotted him and Sherman in the waiting room but hadn't come up to them. After piercing Jarret with a sharp glare, they'd gone to a nurse and then straight back through the doors. When they'd reemerged two hours later, Mrs. Lynch had stabbed Jarret with another icy glare. He'd waited all that time and no one had told him a thing. Nate must've confessed to the beer.

Oh well. Nate walked out on his own, so he must've been fine.

Sherman hadn't stuck around. Soon after the Lynches arrived, he'd stood up and messed with his spiky hair while staring at his reflection in a dark window. Gaze flicking to the doors, he'd leaned towards Jarret. "His parents are here, so I'm taking off."

"Walking?" Irked by Sherman's lack of concern, Jarret had cocked a brow to challenge him. He had no intention of leaving until he knew Nate was fine.

"No, Kyle's coming to get me. I'll wait outside."

Jarret unlocked his car remotely as he strode across the street. His cherry red Chrysler 300 waited under a streetlight. It had always soothed him to see it shining in the light.

Taking the last steps to his car, he sucked in a breath of cool late summer air and wished for another cigarette. As he reached for the door handle, he froze and his eyes bugged.

The pack of cigarettes! He'd left them on the steps outside of the veranda.

He breathed, willing himself to chill. Papa would have no reason to go out that way tonight. Jarret could get them as soon as he got home. He wished he could call Keefe to get them, but Keefe was camping. Too bad Keefe hadn't brought his phone. Jarret needed to talk.

Jarret dropped into the driver's seat and cranked the engine to life. Maybe he could trek into the woods and find Keefe. He'd said something about camping near that waterfall with the cave. A gravel service road ran along the river. Mr. Brandt had driven a truck down it before. Granted he was the park ranger, but who would care if Jarret used it?

CHAPTER 12

Stooped over and splashing through ice cold failure, Keefe bumbled through shallow water to the riverbank. When he'd taken that false step, he'd thrown himself off kilter and flopped face down into knee-high water. If he'd only kept his balance, he'd have a wet pant leg or two at the worst. But now he didn't have a dry spot on him.

Keefe hugged himself, convulsing from the cold, and peered at the shadowy line of trees ahead to orient himself. Now what? The weather forecast predicted low sixties tonight. Not a bad temperature for spending the night in the woods. Unless a person was wearing soaking wet clothes.

Wet jeans restricting his movements, he trudged along the dark bank and peered at shadows to find the woodpile he'd made. He couldn't even see the ground beneath his feet, much less anything in the distance. He needed a fire. Could he possibly warm himself enough with it?

Keefe's heart plummeted. Even a roaring fire wouldn't dry his drenched clothes. He'd have to give up. Saint Francis had survived in the wilderness during forty cold days of Lent, and he couldn't even last a few hours.

Too bad he'd lost the flashlight. He'd have to find his way back to the Brandts' house. The thought of the door opening to Peter and Roland made his heart sink. Was this God's way of saying no?

With his next jerky step, something sharp jabbed into his shin. He'd found his wood pile. Shivering and undone, strung out from the cold and wet, Keefe fell to his knees and lay curled up on the ground. He should've returned to the waterfall sooner, before sunset, instead of gathering so many sticks. He'd gone camping enough times in his life. He should've known better. Feeling like a fool, he hugged himself tighter.

Maybe he shouldn't have come out here at all. He should've just talked to Papa about what he wanted. Why had he avoided it? Somewhere inside, he doubted he'd ever felt called. He knew he couldn't follow through with such a profound life commitment. He'd never followed through on anything. He never pursued the victory. He gave it up every time. Why?

"My God and my all," he whispered, thinking of Saint Francis' prayer.

The trembling increased until his entire body convulsed. When it passed he lifted his head and looked at the sloppy pile of sticks. A few twigs lay apart. A few more stuck out from between bigger sticks.

Keefe pushed himself up and gathered the smaller sticks and twigs. Clutching them, he scooted toward the fire ring. With shaking hands, he arranged them into a little tepee. Leaning back, every move an effort, he stuffed a hand into his cold wet pocket and wrapped his frozen fingers around the two lighters. Water wouldn't have damaged them, would it?

He dropped one lighter aside and flicked the other once, twice, before a flame appeared. Another wave of cold shuddering through him, his hand shook violently as he tried to hold the flame to the twigs.

"Light. Light!" he demanded. The flame burnt his thumb and he dropped the lighter, a cuss word coming to mind but not passing his lips.

A sound caught his attention. Wheels crunching over natural terrain? The sound grew louder.

Two points of light appeared in the distance on the service road that ran parallel to the river. Headlights? Why would a car come out here at this hour? Wouldn't be a park ranger. Maybe kids looking for a good time. Hopefully not anyone he knew from school. The rumors surrounding his family never bothered him much last year, but this felt too personal.

The car came within ten feet and stopped.

Keefe brought an arm up to shield his eyes from the glaring headlights. Lowering his arm, he squinted to identify the car. A Chrysler 300? Jarret?

Relief weaved in between the shivering. He wanted to sit up and greet his brother, but he slumped back down on the ground and hugged himself. Had Jarret sensed trouble? All their lives they'd sensed things about each other.

The car door opened and closed. Footfalls came near.

"What the..." Jarret squatted beside him, looking him over. "What the heck happened? You're soaking wet."

Keefe forced himself to sit up. "F-fell in the... r-river." His teeth chattered.

"Good thing I came. You should've brought your phone."

"H-help m-make f-f-fire." His chattering teeth kept him from saying more. He pulled his arm away from his side—cool air striking him at once—and pointed at the little pile of twigs.

"You're kidding." Jarret straightened and adopted a wide-legged stance, showing his unyielding attitude. "Get up. I guess I'm gonna have to sacrifice my car, get the passenger seat all wet. Not that it matters. Thing reeks anyway."

"No. I have to do this." Keefe felt a glimmer of hope. Forty hours. If he could dry off, he could do it.

"Yeah, right. Looks like it's *game over* for you. You'll die of hypothermia if you don't get home."

"I'm not gonna die. Get me some clothes." Misery kept him from asking the way he normally would, with a few logical suggestions that led up to a polite request.

Jarret shook his head, the darkness hiding his expression.

A long couple of seconds stretched out.

"All right. Fine." Jarret unzipped his leather bomber, his favorite designer jacket. He shrugged out of it and unbuttoned his shirt. "Strip your wet stuff off. I'll run home and grab a few things."

"Thanks." Shivering beyond control, Keefe climbed to his feet and fumbled with the zipper of his soaking wet sweat jacket.

Jarret dropped onto one knee by the fire ring and rearranged a few twigs. A flame caught in seconds. He continued building the fire while Keefe peeled off his wet clothes.

The fire reflected off Jarret's bare chest covered in goosebumps, shadows emphasizing the muscular physique he'd worked so hard for on the weight set in the basement. Keefe had a similar build but less muscular, getting most of his exercise from things like grooming the horses and yard work. While Jarret looked more impressive, Keefe probably had more stamina.

Helpless to control the shaking of his body, he stuffed an arm into Jarret's shirt. Frozen fingers made buttoning the shirt nearly impossible.

"You lose your food too?" Jarret straightened and turned away from the fire. Acting like it was no big deal, he buttoned Keefe's shirt.

"No, it's in the bag." He tipped his chin to indicate it. Once Jarret finished with the last button, Keefe grabbed the jacket.

Jarret stepped back. "Keep up with the fire and I'll be back."

He'd left before Keefe had a chance to ask why he came. Had he sensed trouble? Or did he have trouble of his own?

~ ~ ~

Jacket zipped and hands in his pockets, Keefe gazed at the snapping, twisting flames. The fire had grown to a good size. The shivering had stopped, though he still wished he could get warmer. He sat with his knees up and his bare feet close to the warmth. Thankfulness wrestled with humiliation inside him. Even if he made it through the rest of the forty hours, he'd failed. If not for Jarret's unexpected appearance, he'd be on his way to the Brandts' house by now. And he'd have to admit everything.

If he made it through the forty hours, would he have to tell Peter and Roland about this mishap?

A story from the *Little Flowers of St. Francis* popped into his head. St. Francis sent Brother Bernard to Bologna. When he got there, the children assumed by his poor clothing that he was a madman, and they laughed at and mocked him. Instead of letting this bother him—it would've humiliated Keefe—Bernard embraced it and set off for the market place so more people could see him and make fun of him. They pushed him around, threw stones and dirt at him, and shouted mean things. Brother Bernard responded only with silence, the joy evident on his face. And he went back every day for more, until one man recognized that his behavior was only possible for a great saint. After this, everyone loved and honored him, and so he asked St. Francis if he could leave that town.

Keefe thought for a moment, his gaze fixed on a little blue flame between bigger, brighter ones in the campfire. Could he ever do that? He had an opportunity for humility now, because of his failure.

Pressing his cold lips together, he decided. Yes. He would tell Peter and Roland in detail how he'd blown it and almost had to give up. If he lasted the forty hours, he'd explain how they shouldn't count it because he'd messed up and needed help. He wasn't alone the entire time.

The headlights of Jarret's Chrysler 300 appeared in the distance, along with the sounds of music and of tires crunching closer. Jarret parked in the same spot and jumped out, this time shutting off the headlights. The light from the roaring campfire must've satisfied him. He cruised around the front of the car to the passenger side and brought out a duffel bag—which he slung over his shoulder. Then a sleeping bag, blanket, and pillow—which he stuffed under one arm, and a case of bottled water.

"What's all that about?" Keefe stood up. "I just wanted dry clothes."

Jarret dropped the case of water near Keefe's canvas bag and let the strap of the duffel bag fall off his shoulder. "What, are you gonna drink—river water? Who knows what's in it?"

Keefe took the duffel bag and squatted as he unzipped it. "Well, I don't need the sleeping bag. I can be uncomfortable for two nights." He pulled a clean pair of jeans from the bottom of the bag.

"Why?" Jarret undid the ties and flopped the sleeping bag out on the ground near the campfire. He tossed the pillow and folded blanket onto it and then stood hands on hips, staring at Keefe for the answer.

"It's the challenge of it. I'm supposed to be out here for forty hours with nothing but the clothes on my back and a loaf of bread."

"Whatever." Jarret made himself comfortable on the sleeping bag, stretching out on his side and propping his head up with his hand.

"Thanks for the clothes anyway. You sure got back here fast," Keefe said, wanting to lift Jarret's mood. Did it bother Jarret that Keefe wouldn't go home or accept all his help?

"Yeah, I was barreling down the road, praying Officer O'Brien wasn't on duty."

"You know police officers by name?"

"Just him. He gave me my first ticket two months ago. Then I met up with him last week."

"I didn't know that. Another ticket?"

Jarret shook his head. "Thank God. I don't need any more points on my license."

Feeling almost back to normal in dry clothes, Keefe sat on the ground and dug through the bag for his socks. In addition to jeans, Jarret had grabbed a t-shirt, a sweatshirt, his warmest jacket, hiking boots, and the old white socks with the little holes in the heels.

"So why'd you come out here anyway? Thought you'd still have friends over." Keefe wrestled a sock onto his foot, hoping that Jarret wouldn't know how to answer that question, or that Jarret would say that he'd sensed something. Keefe could take that as a sign of sorts, couldn't he? Maybe God had sent Jarret out here to rescue him.

If Jarret had a real reason for the unexpected visit, it would most likely mean that Jarret had found himself in some desperate situation where he needed Keefe's advice. That would tell Keefe that Jarret, with his new and weak faith, still needed him, that God wanted Keefe to mentor him for as long as it took for Jarret to stand on his own. That maybe he wasn't called to the life of a Franciscan. At least not yet.

Jarret gazed at the fire as he answered. "I messed up."

Disappointment crept into Keefe's soul. He sighed and yanked the ties of his hiking boot.

"Had to take Nate to the hospital."

"What?" That didn't sound good. "Party get wild?" Keefe finished tying his other boot.

Jarret grabbed the folded blanket and tossed it to Keefe. Then he fidgeted with his ponytail fastener, let his hair loose, and dropped his head onto the pillow. "You could say that." Then he proceeded to spell out all the details, more kids coming over than expected, all of them taking over the house, blaring the music, messing with the antiques, smoking... and the beer.

"You ever think you should find new friends?"

Jarret made an effort to look at Keefe, one brow raised. "Why?"

"I don't know. Bad company corrupts good character." He'd read that saying somewhere, maybe in the Bible.

"Theirs or mine?" He grinned and laid his head back down. "I just won't invite them over anymore. We can party at one of their houses."

"So you think Nate's allergic to red food coloring? I'm surprised Papa didn't drive him to the hospital." He unfolded the blanket—an old wool one that Papa favored—and draped it around his shoulders, appreciating the cozy feel and extra warmth.

"Papa doesn't know." Jarret twisted a lock of hair on the top of his head. "Well, maybe he knows now. I didn't see him when I fetched your clothes. I made a point of avoiding him." He grinned, giving his same old sneaky look. "So I don't know if he came around while everyone was leaving. I hope they cleaned up. Bet they didn't."

"You should tell him."

Jarret stared at the sky. "Yeaaaah, I know, but I'm sure he knows by now."

"Let him hear it from you anyway. Call him."

"You mean now?"

"Why not?"

Twisting to one side, Jarret drew his phone from his pocket. Then he sat up and rested an arm on his raised knee. "Here goes nothing," he said, putting the phone to his ear. "Pick up, old man." He sighed and glanced at Keefe. "He's not picking up. See?" He turned the phone so Keefe could hear Papa's recorded message, though Keefe couldn't really make out the words.

"So leave a message."

Jarret narrowed one eye to show his reluctance.

Keefe motioned for him to do it.

As if resigning himself to the consequences of his actions, Jarret took a breath. "So hey, Papa. You probably already know that the party broke up. I know it wasn't supposed to be a party, just a few friends coming over. But it turned out to be a few more friends than I expected, like, uh, fifteen to twenty, and one of my friends had an allergic reaction to... well, food coloring, I guess. So I took him to the hospital. He's fine. His parents took him home. I told everyone else to leave. Not sure if they did. But..." He dipped his head and shoved a hand into his hair. "But they brought beer and I don't know what else." He paused, not sure what to say next. "Sorry. I messed up." He ended the call and tossed the phone onto the sleeping bag.

Keefe smiled, proud of Jarret. "So are you wearing the scapular I gave you?"

A guilty-looking grin stretched across Jarret's face. "No, but it's in my pocket." He stuffed a hand into a front pocket of his jeans.

"Why don't you wear it?"

"Maybe you need it more than I do tonight." He tossed it to Keefe.

He'd wanted to encourage Jarret to put it on, but a feeling of comfort overwhelmed him at the touch of the brown cloth. Past promises to Jesus and Mary flitted through his mind, so he put the scapular on over his head and stuffed it into his shirt. "For now. But you should wear one too. It can remind you of who you want to be and that God is always there to help, especially through His mother."

"So I wear it and like magic I'm going to do the right thing."

Keefe swooshed his hand at Jarret, unwilling to reply to his lame response. Jarret didn't understand yet. Maybe he could find something online to explain it better. For now, he appreciated having it with him for his forty hours.

"So that girl texted me."

"What girl? The one from the bookstore?"

He nodded.

"What'd she want this time?"

"Told me her name. But I didn't text back."

"Going to?" Keefe hoped he'd say no. Had he straightened himself out and healed from the mess with his last girlfriend?

"Nah." With a sigh, Jarret got to his feet and stuffed his phone back into his pocket. "She goes to River Run High, so I'll see her soon enough. She can tell me to my face what she thinks of me for ignoring her message." He grabbed the pillow. "Sure you don't want the sleeping bag or pillow?"

"I'm sure." Blanket sliding from his shoulders, Keefe got up and stuffed his wet clothes into the duffel bag while Jarret rolled up the sleeping bag. "Thanks for the help. I know I kind of blew it—"

"Yeah, like three hours in."

Keefe shrugged, taking Jarret's teasing in stride. "But I want to finish the forty hours. And thanks to you, I can."

"Want my phone?" Jarret stuffed the sleeping bag and pillow through the open passenger side window.

"No. I'll be fine. I won't do anything stupid." Keefe pushed the duffel bag through the open window.

"Okay, see ya back at the fort." Jarret got in behind the wheel and slammed the door. Music came on as he started the car, something with a hard beat, but it sounded to Keefe like a Christian song.

Keefe watched him drive off, determination growing inside him. He could've easily given up, taken a ride home with Jarret. He could've easily accepted the comforts. But he was claiming this victory for himself. Forty hours. He could do this.

CHAPTER 13

The beams from the Chrysler's headlights cut through the dark. They illuminated a long stretch of road, the weeds and blades of grass that edged it, and a few trees further back.

Thoughts and images scrolled through Jarret's mind like a social media feed, not in order of importance or chronologically, and none of them getting a "like": Nate moaning and rocking in the front passenger seat of Jarret's car, Kyle cracking open a beer can, Trent and Konner playing cards on the veranda, a trail of smoke rising off the cigarette Jarret puffed outside, Keefe shivering on the ground by a stack of firewood...

Jarret wiped his forehead and ran his hand over his hair. Nate would be fine. He'd walked out of the hospital. Maybe he wouldn't get too much heat for being at Jarret's house.

Jarret's eyes narrowed and his grip tightened on the steering wheel. So, Nate wasn't even allowed to come over? How many other kids weren't allowed over? He wasn't that bad. Granted, tonight was a mess. But the beer wasn't his idea. Neither was the food coloring. He'd just wanted to play pool and hang out, to do *something* before school started. Maybe they should've gone out instead.

"So hey, Papa. You probably already know the party broke up..." The message Jarret had left Papa played in his mind and made his stomach clench in knots. Part of him wished he hadn't left a

message. But he'd need to tell him anyway. Was Papa still up? Maybe he'd gone to bed early and hadn't even heard the message. They could talk about it in the morning.

A wave of exhaustion passed over Jarret, and he yawned. How would Keefe handle camping all alone under the stars? Jarret would've liked to have stayed with him. They could've talked themselves silly until the sun came up, like in the good old days.

But he knew Keefe wanted—maybe needed—to go it alone. Maybe everyone reached that point as they grew up. A man had to make his own decisions, decide the type of person he wanted to be and where he wanted to go in life, and figure out how to get there. Would he need to blaze his own trail or take a familiar path?

Jarret turned down Forest Road, where he could drive on auto pilot, and let his vision blur. Where was he headed? He should start thinking about life after high school. Did he want to go to college or learn a trade? What would he go to college for? What trade? Nothing called to him.

Keefe seemed to have an idea for his future: join the Franciscans. And if he got his answer from God, he seemed more than willing to go all in. Jarret tried picturing Keefe in a long brown robe.

What if God wanted that of him too?

Jarret's breath caught. Panic flashed in his mind and faded. *Get real.* God knew he wasn't cut out for that. But how open was he to God's will? Was he ready, willing, or able to make the changes needed to stay on the right path? What would he have to change? He didn't want to give up his friends or his reputation. Maybe he could change his friends, help them see that there was more to life than parties, girls, and games. Nah. He couldn't see himself talking about anything deep with them. He'd only gotten his toe wet in all this faith stuff. He knew little to nothing.

Maybe Father Carston could help him with all this.

Jarret eased off the accelerator. *Oh, yeah...* He had an appointment tomorrow. He was supposed to meet Father Carston for spiritual direction. What was he going to tell Father? A week had passed since his last confession, and he had too much to talk about already. Is that what spiritual direction was about? Telling on yourself like in confession? There had to be more. Maybe Father could give him advice about what he needed to do to stand strong.

Jarret turned down the long gravel driveway that led home, palmed the steering wheel, and let his mind rest.

A moment later, he rounded a bend. The dark trees opened to their castle-like house. Floodlights made it glow and emphasized the rough stone exterior and jagged battlements. No light shown from the windows. No cars in the circular drive or near the garage.

He exhaled, relieved that all his friends had left. But as he pulled up to the garage, he glimpsed something in his peripheral vision. And his heart skipped a beat.

A porchlight illuminated a lone figure on the veranda steps. *Papa.* He sat slouched, with one leg stretched and the other bent, his Stetson hiding his face, and a trail of tobacco smoke rising from his pipe.

Rather than park in the garage, Jarret pulled up to it, shut the Chrysler's engine off, and got out. He shoved his keys into a pocket and inhaled a deep breath on his way over, psyching himself up. Papa must've gotten his message.

"Hey, Papa." Jarret stopped where the grass met the concrete and stuck his thumbs in his belt loops. "Got my message?"

As Papa lifted his head, he tapped his cowboy hat up and squinted at Jarret, his expression unreadable. "Yup."

Jarret shifted, his heart hammering in his chest. "I, uh, I honestly didn't expect so many kids to come over. Wasn't planning on having a party, just a few friends playing games in the rec room."

Yeah, work that angle. He could throw the blame on all of them. He could pretend he didn't know —

"Don't try to pass the buck, son."

"What? I..." The imaginary knots in his gut tightened. Lies and excuses always popped into his mind, but he wanted to be honest. Besides, he liked the peace in the house since they'd returned from Arizona and the feeling of Papa being proud of him. He wanted that back. "Okay, I – I guess I shoulda made everyone leave when I saw they'd brought beer. Shouldn't have let them drink it over here." Jarret toed the edge of the concrete, his heart still pounding. "You're probably pretty ticked off, huh?"

"Who's the kid you took to the hospital?"

"Oh. Nate. He's fine. His parents came up, but I stayed until they let him go." He debated for a second whether he should tell him what else he did. Then he just blurted it out. "Then I went out to see Keefe."

Papa gave a nod and took a puff off his pipe. "How's Keefe?"

"Uh, fine." He decided against mentioning Keefe's mishap in the stream. Keefe was safe now.

Papa's gaze shifted to some point in the distance. Smoke swirled from his mouth, and the silence stretched out. A man of few words, he was probably planning what he'd say next, trying to figure out what to do about it.

"So..." The knots in his gut twisted. He'd let Papa down, and he wished he could make it right. He wasn't letting him down again. Jarret stopped toeing the concrete and planted his foot. "I'm ready for my consequences. I bet there's a mess inside that I should clean up."

"Nanny took care of most of it, throwing away evidence." Papa cracked a smile.

"Oh."

"All but the rec room. You can clean that up."

"Yeah, sure. I'll pull my car into the garage and get started." He took a step. He'd clean it up before bed instead of waiting—

"Hold up."

"Yeah?"

"I hope you don't have plans for the weekend. I don't want you going anywhere."

"Uh..." Jarret crossed his arms over his chest and snorted. "What, like I'm grounded?"

"Yup." Papa didn't quite smile, but his eyes lit up. "Just like you're grounded."

"But I..." Okay, he wanted to make things right, so he needed to accept this without an attitude. But what about his appointment with Father Carston tomorrow? Did he want to tell Papa about that? *No way.* He'd have to reschedule. And what about Mass on Sunday? Nah, Papa wouldn't keep him from that.

"You start school on Monday, but I don't want you going anywhere else."

"What?!" His face twitched and eyes bugged. How old did Papa think he was? "For how long?"

"Eh, one week, I s'pose." Papa stood and stretched, one hand cradling his pipe. "Look, Jarret, I know you're trying. But you know that tonight put a spoke in the wheel. Maybe you oughta find better friends to tie to."

"I..." Anger and indignation rising inside, Jarret bit his tongue. If he said something now, it wouldn't be nice. Besides, he deserved it. He could handle this. "Whatever." He turned and stomped away.

CHAPTER 14

A masked figure in a black robe and gloves knelt in the shadows before Keefe, collecting himself for the fight. A warrior. He rested one hand on his knee and held a bamboo sword in the other, the shinai.

Not ready for this, Keefe's skin crawled and his heart pounded. Terror rose inside him. A glance to either side revealed impenetrable cold, darkness all around him. Then he looked down and gasped. He too held a bamboo sword. Must've been a mistake. He'd told no one he was a warrior.

The warrior stood and bowed, the gesture indicating his desire for victory but also to pay respect to his opponent before the fight. Then he moved forward, his long robe making him seem to glide rather than walk. As he neared, he swung the sword out in front and grabbed it with both hands.

Though he knew he ought to do the same, move forward and ready his sword, Keefe wanted to shrink back. He wanted to bolt. He didn't want his identity known. Didn't want to fight.

As if unaware of Keefe's hesitancy, the warrior sidestepped around Keefe, gripping his bamboo sword and holding it high.

Panic flooding him, Keefe lifted his own sword and turned to keep his face to the warrior. The blackness behind and around the warrior drew Keefe's gaze. Faces appeared, moving in and out of focus. Familiar faces. Papa, Jarret, Roland, Peter, and every kid he knew from school. They saw. They would soon know his heart. And they would see him fail.

Heart racing, eyes searching, Keefe racked his brain for a way out. Finding none, fear flowed through his veins.

At once the warrior called his intended strike, Keefe's head, and moved. Like lightning falling from the sky, his sword ripped through the air with a whoosh.

Moving on impulse, Keefe swung upward and blocked the attack. The swords met with a hollow clack and bounced back. The warrior pressed on, locking his sword against Keefe's, the two of them shuffling together, each seeking to score. Each seeking the victory.

Victory or defeat. The desires clashed inside Keefe. To take the victory for himself was to give defeat to his opponent. To allow defeat was to fail. He could not choose.

Moving with great agility and perfect form, the warrior pivoted and slid his sword across Keefe's. He called it and struck Keefe on the forearm. A score for the warrior.

Keefe took steps back. The warrior moved in. Their swords crossed, clacking together, and crossed again repeatedly with intricate movements, quick and intense, as they each attempted a score. Heart pounding and alive with the fight, Keefe lunged and struck, missed, and pushed himself against his opponent, a winning maneuver playing out in his mind. A simple shove, and a jump back, and he could strike the warrior's trunk.

His opponent lifted his sword. Keefe jumped back... he'd delayed and missed his opportunity. Had he done it on purpose? Had he sealed his own fate? Forfeited? Guaranteeing the warrior's victory and his loss?

As the warrior called his strike zone, Keefe lunged and blocked his black-clad arms with his own arms, their swords moving together overhead. One more point and the warrior would win.

Hunger for victory. Fear of being exposed. Fear of failure. Fear of going all in. Keefe swung again and called his intended strike, dipping his sword down for his opponent's abdomen, ready to make his attack.

The warrior twisted out of the way, but Keefe had expected the move. He had simply now to follow through with a counterattack and claim the victory. But he hesitated. And the warrior's voice rang out his final strike as his sword swung round to Keefe's head.

The strike stung and rattled through Keefe, filling him with grief. He fell back, down, down, down into ice cold failure, the faces fading in and out. Watching everything. Knowing.

"Blessed is he who takes no offense at me."

Something poked his shoulder, making it smart. Not the warrior's sword. The fight had ended with Keefe's defeat.

Keefe inhaled a whiff of something burning. His ears tuned in to a white noise that sounded like the rush of water or a strong wind through leaves. Then something nearby cracked and popped.

Awareness broke through. Reality sucked Keefe from his dream, cords of regret and heartfelt pain clinging to him, not shaking loose.

Keefe blinked his eyes open and pushed himself up, a stick from the woodpile scraping his shoulder as he moved. The blanket fell off his chest, and cool air hit his sweaty neck.

Night surrounded him. The campfire had burned down to glowing orange embers and a few stubborn branches.

How long had he slept? Sometime after Jarret had taken off for home, sleep had overwhelmed him. He'd slept heavily too, even out under the stars and on the cold, hard ground. If that weird dream hadn't woken him, he'd still be asleep.

A shiver ran through Keefe, urging him to action. He grabbed a branch, then several more, and arranged them on the embers. A few gentle puffs of his breath ignited them.

Eyes heavy with sleep, Keefe built the campfire to a good size that should last him an hour or so. Then he stretched out on the ground and covered himself with the blanket. He was glad he hadn't realized, at first, that Jarret had left it. Wanting the complete experience, he would've made Jarret take it home. But he appreciated it now that the night air had grown cool. How would he have slept without it?

Keefe's eyes closed and his mind settled.

...the masked warrior swung again, his move fierce, his weapon a blur.

Sword slipping from his sweaty hands, fingers tingling, Keefe dodged and rolled onto the cold, hard ground.

"Oof." He grunted and sat bolt upright. A shock of cool air to his sweat-drenched neck snapped him to full consciousness.

Embers glowed white and orange nearby. A dark blue sky overhead. Waterfall roaring in the distance.

Heart pounding, Keefe gulped breaths of campfire-scented air. The last breath burnt the back of his throat, and he doubled over coughing.

The dream had woken him yet again. Same one haunting him over and over. He lost again to the Japanese warrior. And each time he knew that if he had fought harder, he could've won.

Keefe's stomach lurched. It sickened him to know he'd forfeited the victory intentionally.

~ ~ ~

Dream waking him again, Keefe rolled over, draped his arm over his eyes, and groaned. A melody rose above the white noise of the waterfall, robins singing in the treetops.

Birds up already? Keefe lowered his arm and eased open his eyes. A blue early-morning sky stretched out above him.

With a long sigh, he abandoned hope for more sleep. "Morning, Lord," he prayed aloud as he pushed himself up. "Guess I might as well start the day, huh? We have a lot to talk about."

After a few moments of disjointed prayer, and after neatly folding his blanket, he shuffled to the stream and splashed cold water on his face. As he straightened, he stumbled on an old dry branch by the river's edge.

"Perfect for firewood!" He snatched it up and scanned for more, deciding to gather sticks for the night. He'd be more prepared this time.

A load of branches in his arms, Keefe strolled through the woods, toward his campsite. His stomach grumbled loud enough to hear, but he wanted to put off eating for as long as possible. Saint Francis had done it. He could too.

Two hours later, Keefe staggered along the riverbank, branches falling from his armful of firewood. His head had grown light. And his stomach was turning, between grumbling and growling. "You need to eat. You have no energy," a voice in his head said. "Especially after falling in the river last night. If you don't eat soon, you'll get sick, maybe die of starvation."

Get a grip, he tried telling himself.

Keefe stacked the firewood on the pile, his head even more woozy.

"Okay, I give in." Recognizing that he was no Saint Francis, he dropped to his knees by the canvas tote bag and dug out a loaf of bread. His mouth watered as he opened the plastic wrapper, bowed his head, and blessed his food. At the word "Amen," he ripped off a chunk and shoved it into his mouth.

After devouring two slices, he slowed his pace. For the rest of his meal, he ate thoughtfully and disciplined. Still, he polished off a third of the loaf and drank two bottles of water. Satisfied, he turned his heart to prayer and appreciated the beauty of creation.

The day continued in much the same way, slow and peaceful, with his stomach reminding him of his weakness and his mind cycling through thoughts: lamenting his faults, begging for a sign, and praising God for His goodness.

The next morning, at the end of his forty hours, he strolled to Peter Brandt's house filled with peace. But he still had no answer to his prayer. Was God calling him or not?

CHAPTER 15

First day of school.

Dressed in Levis and a slim-fit Hugo Boss button-down shirt, Jarret stood in the middle of intersecting hallways with his books hanging at his side. Kids rushed past him, nerds, jocks, preps, emo, and thugs. He recognized many, their faces if not their names. A few greeted him with things like, "Hey," "What's up?" and "Yo." He nodded in reply and shifted his gaze, not wanting to talk to anyone. Even Dominic the Gossip had said, "Hola, Vato," as he zipped by. The freshmen—none of whom he knew—stood out with that lost "this school is big, wish I had a GPS" look in their eyes. But it really wasn't a big school, just big compared to middle school.

Jarret had come to the intersecting hallways looking for Keefe. He'd seen Keefe down a hall, but Keefe waved him on. He must've had something to do. Jarret hadn't moved from the intersection though because a wistful, reflective mood had struck him. Something about kids on every side, chattering to each other and rushing past him, had brought it on.

A group of freshmen moved down the middle of the hallway, coming towards him. One by one they glimpsed him standing there and their eyes flickered, filling with something resembling awe. Then they went around him, giving him a wide berth.

Jarret's chest swelled with satisfaction.

Before he could exhale, a body slammed into him from behind, and he stumbled forward and dropped his books.

"Oh, sorry." A girl in a long skirt stooped for his books, her messy red locks tumbling over her face.

The girl with her said, "Come on. Let's go," in a strained voice. Then she looked at Jarret. "She's sorry. She wasn't looking. I tried to tell her." She backed away with small steps, holding up her palm as if trying to push the incident away. A dozen bracelets dangled from her wrist.

Jarret bit back a rude reply. He glared at the girl who awkwardly gathered his books, impatience flaring.

She stood and lifted her head, shoving the books at him.

Recognizing her, he sighed. Of course it was Roland's friend Caitlyn. Clumsiest girl he'd ever known.

She and her friend speed-walked off.

Hoping no one had noticed him drop his books, Jarret returned to his zone and strutted down the hall.

He'd had tutors all his life until last year, his first year in a brick-and-mortar school. He'd loved it. From the first day of school, he'd had an image. Kids here, especially Dominic the Gossip, spread a lot of rumors, and the West boys had been the hot topic at the beginning of last school year. With Keefe by his side, it hadn't taken much effort for Jarret to mold his image the way he wanted it. Guys feared and admired him. Girls liked him. Living up to his image had gotten him in some trouble—he forced thoughts of Zoe from his mind—but he had strengthened it too. Even when he and Keefe had grown distant, hostile even, Jarret had maintained his image, maybe even amped it up with his bad attitude.

The look in kids' eyes as they passed him today showed that the long summer hadn't weakened his reputation in the least. He had no need to start over. Was it wrong for him to like the way others saw him?

"Hi, Jarret," came a feminine voice.

Not ready for this, for her—was it her?—Jarret's heart skipped a beat. Then he found the girl who spoke: Kelli, a petite girl with short straight hair and a killer smile. The onslaught of tension slipped away on an exhale.

"Hey, Kelli." He gave her a flirtatious grin, though he shifted his gaze away from her.

Sooner or later he'd bump into Chantelle. How did she even pronounce her name? "Ch" like in "chill" or "sh" like in "chef"? Maybe he'd hear someone say her name before he attempted it.

What was he going to say to her? She'd wonder why he hadn't messaged her back. Was he ready to get into a relationship with a girl? Did he have the ability to master himself? Would he lose control so that his next girlfriend ended up—

A shudder ran through him, and he clenched his jaw. No, that wouldn't happen. He'd changed. That wasn't him anymore. He could do this. Besides, he was a senior now. He had plenty besides girls to keep him busy. He'd have tons of schoolwork. This year he wouldn't beg, threaten, or bribe Keefe to do any of it for him. He'd do it all himself.

Jarret's gaze caught something that made him wince. A lone figure halfway down the hall to the right moved out of sync with everyone else, head bobbing up and down to a jerky rhythm. Roland on his crutches.

Struck with a familiar surge of arrogance and fear of humiliation, Jarret tensed and glanced away. During his entire junior year he'd been annoyed by Roland's shyness and awkwardness, and had felt the need to strengthen his own reputation. As a senior, he shouldn't have to worry about that. His reputation was solid and couldn't be touched by little things.

Jarret's gaze slid to the hallway on his left. A part of him wanted to dart down it before Roland reached him. As he glanced back, his gaze connected with Roland's, and his heart melted. He couldn't abandon him no matter what anyone thought.

A few more awkward steps brought Roland face to face with Jarret, the two of them now in the middle of intersecting hallways, the center of attention for all who passed. Face paler than usual, distress flickering in Roland's gray eyes, something bothered him. Maybe getting around with crutches and a load of books was tougher than he'd expected.

"Hey, Jarret. How's it going?"

"What's up, Roland?"

With a dip of his head, Roland glanced over his shoulder. Then he looked back at Jarret and took a breath through his mouth. "I don't know who, but someone's following me."

Jarret peered behind Roland to humor him. "Uh, yeah, I think about thirty kids are following you."

Roland glanced over his shoulder and then back with a weary look that said he didn't appreciate Jarret's humor.

"Rough getting around with crutches, huh? Sure you don't want my help?"

"I'm sure." He bit his lip, seeming hesitant to go on. "Someone's messing with me. He yanked my backpack, almost knocked me over."

Jarret inhaled a breath that made his chest heave. He threw furtive glances to each side and then indicated with a tilt of his chin for Roland to follow him. Before he took a step, he noticed Roland's backpack slung over one arm, the strap digging into his shoulder from the weight of his books.

"Lemme take that." Jarret grabbed the strap and helped Roland maneuver his crutch out of the way. Then he lugged the backpack over his own shoulder. The weight made him think that Roland carried every book to every class.

Weaving past kids, Jarret led Roland a few yards down the least traveled hallway. He lowered the backpack to the floor and leaned against a yellow brick wall. "So who's messing with you?"

"Not sure." Roland gathered both crutches in one hand and leaned against the wall too, favoring his injured leg. He wore the dark green button-front that Nanny had gotten him, a satiny thing with a pattern of tiny tan w's, not something that Roland would've chosen on his own. But it looked good on him. Despite the jeans split up the leg to accommodate the cast.

"The halls are crowded. Someone probably bumped into you." He debated telling him about Caitlyn bumping him and knocking his books to the floor.

"No. I saw a kid following me. I think. Then someone yanked my backpack. On purpose. And then I heard my name and thought I saw someone following me again."

"Eh, you're just being paranoid. Lighten up." Jarret tapped Roland's shoulder with his fist. He wished he could help Roland out of his shyness, but how could a person change that?

"I'm not being paranoid. Someone yanked my backpack." Roland's expression fell and he turned away.

"So what do you want me to do about it, beat him up?" Jarret grinned at the idea, knowing Roland would never want that no matter what.

"No. I-I don't know. I guess I don't want you to do anything." He still looked away, likely embarrassed and frustrated. He probably hadn't counted on the attention he'd get with the crutches or the struggle he'd have trying to get around school.

Moved with a hint of compassion, Jarret wished he had something to offer. Maybe some brotherly advice. "Listen, Roland, the world's not out to get you. And you don't need to hide in the shadows. This is high school."

Roland still stared off in the distance. "I hate high school."

"I know. Get through it." Adjusting his own books at his side, Jarret pushed off the wall. "So you want me to help you with this?" He lifted Roland's backpack off the floor. "Where you headed? Bell's gonna ring in a minute or two."

"Nah, I'm just down the hall." Roland leaned his crutches against the wall, keeping them in place with his foot, then he shrugged his backpack onto his back.

"Sure? 'Cuz I don't mind being late."

Roland rolled his eyes, seeming pretty sick of Jarret's help. "Thanks, though. Appreciate the offer."

"Yeah, right." Jarret grinned just as his phone buzzed in his back pocket, notifying him of a new text. He watched Roland hobble off, a bit relieved that he didn't want help. His old conceit and arrogance pushed hard to regain their footing. The attitude appealed to him, called to him, but he didn't want that. Maybe he could walk a line between the old and new. Keep his image but make better choices.

Drawing his phone from a pocket, he checked the message. *Heard about Nate. Totally your fault.*

The words stung a bit, then made him angry. Who would blame him for that? His gaze shifted to the previous message: *Changed my mind. Not interested.*

Chantelle?

"Wait." Jarret checked the last message she'd sent him, the one where she'd given her name. It came from a different number. So who was this one from?

"Hey, there you are." Kyle strutted toward him and raised a hand in greeting. He always wore the worst colors for a freckled redhead. Today he had on a fluorescent orange t-shirt.

Jarret reached up, gave a hi-five, and turned to walk with him.

"You're in my World Lit class, right?" Kyle checked his schedule.

"Yup." Jarret had only needed to check his schedule once. Now he had it all committed to memory.

"You really missed out over the weekend. We had a blast at Sherman's house." Kyle laughed. "That boy can par-tae. Then at the park downtown, and one night we snuck onto the Hossen's farmland. You probably heard the rumors already. So the Hossen's got that barn back there..."

Gazing down the hallway at nothing in particular, letting his vision blur, Jarret tuned Kyle out. Afraid of messing up, he'd ignored his friends' calls and messages. A bit of ire built inside, making his eyes narrow up. He had missed out, and for what reason? He didn't need to avoid his friends entirely just to stay on the straight and narrow, did he? Was he that weak? Maybe he was being scrupulous.

"Yo, check her out," Kyle said as they neared the classroom. "She's got her eyes on you already? Know her?"

Jarret looked to see and a burst of heat struck him. He had to force himself to not break his stride.

Chantelle stood outside the open classroom door, leaning her shoulder against a locker and hugging her books, her hip sticking out, emphasizing her curves. And yeah, her eyes were on him.

He held her gaze and maintained his stride as he closed the distance between them. What would he tell her? What excuse could he give? He could've lost his phone or broken it. Maybe the battery died. The thought of lying stood like a door that he'd have to swing open if he really planned to do it.

Maybe he shouldn't lie. But he couldn't tell the truth. Any chance the bell would ring and he wouldn't have to tell her anything? He reached for his back pocket to check the time on his phone but stopped. He didn't want to remind her of it and the text she'd sent.

"Hey, you're the girl from the bookstore, right?" He stopped two feet from her, closer than he should've stood, but her sulky expression drew him.

She huffed and straightened, readjusting her books. "The *girl* from the bookstore." She shook her head, looking disgusted. A lock of blond hair fell over one eye. "My name's Chantelle."

Chantelle with a "sh" sound, like in chic, chiffon, champagne... Jarret swallowed hard, coming to his senses. "Sh" as in chaperone. Which is what he'd need if he dated her.

"Hey, Chantelle. How's it going?" Jarret leaned his forearm up on the lockers now, looking her over and flirting like nobody's business. He needed to knock it off and get in the classroom. Ring, bell.

"Didn't you get my text? Or was that really your number you wrote on my arm?" Her thick lashes fluttered as her gaze bounced around his face.

Her attention made his lips burn. "I got it."

She arched a brow and huffed again, offended. "Oh."

He laughed. Then smiled. Then touched a lock of hair that draped over her shoulder. *Hands to yourself. What are you thinking?* He shifted his books to his right hand. "So you really go to the same school as me. I don't remember you from last year."

She glanced, the look in her eyes saying that she didn't know whether or not to trust him. "We just moved here."

He didn't even get to say "Oh" before the bell rang and they both winced. Seemed like they stood directly under it. She swung into the room without another glance.

Relieved, yet disappointed, he exhaled and followed. When she veered toward the front of the classroom, he turned in the opposite direction, toward Kyle who sat in the middle row in the back.

"You know her, huh?" Kyle waved his pale brows.

"I will." Jarret regretted the overconfident attitude, but he couldn't help it.

~ ~ ~

Later in the day, the bell rang and Jarret shot out of Physics before everyone else. Mr. Weiss hadn't finished giving the assignment, but Jarret could get it from Keefe. Too bad he and Keefe had nothing except lunch and study hall together. Jarret wanted to talk to him. Teachers probably did that on purpose, not wanting them together because they were twins.

Jarret walked with attitude in his step. First day of school hadn't been too bad. One more class and he could go home. Next semester, he and Keefe would get to cut out two periods early.

Turning toward the main hallway, Jarret started the long journey to his locker as kids emerged from classrooms and the hallway filled up. Should he grab all the books he needed to take home or just take a notebook to his last class? He didn't want to go back to his locker after Art Appreciation, but he didn't want to carry all his books to class either. Every teacher had assigned homework today, and he'd only finished one subject in study hall. Guess it wouldn't matter if he blew out of school a few minutes later than he'd like. If Roland wanted a ride home, he'd have to wait for him anyway. At least he didn't have to wait for the bus.

His thoughts turned to his Chrysler 300, the way it looked in the sun after a wash, the way it felt cruising down a lonely stretch of road with the window down. Then his thoughts soured, turning to the smell that he couldn't get out. Eyes narrowing, Jarret scanned the hallway for Peter. Thank God, they hadn't crossed paths today. He could still see himself slamming Peter against a row of lockers and making him pay in one way or another. He couldn't see himself avoiding it.

A hallway branched off to one side. Jerky movement at the end of it and loud voices made him look twice. A commotion drew a few observers in the otherwise empty corridor. Maybe a fight or a freshman hazing. Jarret turned his attention back to his destination, his locker a few yards away. Then a familiar sound rose above the chatter and the lockers slamming shut, the squeaking sneakers and stomping footfalls. Jarret froze.

Somewhere down that hallway, aluminum crutches clattered to the floor.

Backing up his steps, he considered for half a second whether he should keep his cool and walk to check it out or tear down the hall like a madman. Could something else have made that sound? Something other than Roland's crutches?

Heart rate accelerating, Jarret cast cool to the side and bolted down the hall toward the gathering crowd. Two girls in his way forced him to slow. He weaved around them and other slow-moving students. Could Roland have fallen? The cast would protect his leg, right?

He'd gone halfway down the hall when three teen boys raced out of the farthest classroom, one of them laughing but none of them close enough for Jarret to identify. Panic pushed Jarret harder and he sprinted to the classroom.

Stomach turning in expectation and fearing the worst, he thumped into the shady room.

Roland stood hunched over and facing the far wall, wiping his eyes or something. Crying? His crutches lay at odd angles on the floor between them, one partially under a desk.

"Roland?" Jarret set his books down. A tingling sensation started in his chest as he stepped closer. "You okay?"

Roland lifted the bottom of his shirt to his face and wiped it again. He stood on his own two legs, even with the cast and no crutches, and didn't seem hurt. What could've happened?

"My eyes sting." Breaking from his wiping efforts, he turned his head an inch to one side. "Are there a lot of people in the hall?"

"Uh, yeah. What happened?" Jarret came up behind him, reached for his upper arm, and hesitated. Then he grabbed him and turned him around.

Jarret jerked back, the tingling sensation spreading to his neck and face.

Dropping his chin, Roland looked up at him and opened his mouth as if wanting to say something. His entire face had been sprayed orange or tan or something, a sloppy, uneven job. His shirt hung half open, one button hanging by a thread, and they'd gotten his chest and neck too.

Flames flared inside Jarret and shot out his eyes. "Who did this?" he growled, anger making it hard to speak, guilt slamming through him. He should've listened to Roland this morning. Why hadn't he taken him seriously?

Dropping his gaze to some point behind Jarret, Roland shifted his weight. "I need to get to the bathroom, try to wash it off." He lifted his arm in slow motion and pointed. "Could you get my crutches?"

Jarret sucked in a sharp breath. He stepped backwards and leaned for the crutches. An orange bottle of spray tan lay a yard away. "Who did this?" he demanded again. "You'd better tell me."

"Na, I'm sure it'll wash off." He stared at the crutches in Jarret's hands.

"That's not gonna wash off." Closer inspection of Roland's face inflamed Jarret's rage and had his mind shifting through possible suspects. Someone had recently said something to Jarret about Roland's pale skin. Jarret flipped through memories, stopping at the party at his house. C.W. had plopped down on the couch next to him, yammering on about whatever. But he'd also talked about Roland. "That boy is *white*," C.W. had said.

Now he knew the identity of the three dudes he'd seen running from the room: Trent, Konner, and C.W.

Jarret handed Roland the crutches and backed toward the door.

Roland stuffed the crutches under his arms. Then he met Jarret's gaze and flinched as if reading Jarret's mind. "Let it go."

Too angry to speak, Jarret shook his head and bolted from the classroom. He could not let this go.

C.W. hazed his brother, made a laughing-stock of him, a kid on crutches. He was gonna pay.

Jarret's boots pounded the floor. With hands balled into fists and jaw clenched, he stormed down the hall. His destination: C.W.'s locker. His purpose: retaliation. C.W. would learn a lesson he'd never forget. Nobody messes with a West boy.

Kids stumbled out of his way, eyes wide with shock. A girl shrieked and then giggled to her friends.

Then he glimpsed something strange... A figure appeared in his peripheral vision, someone familiar, someone who cared about him. Golden light surrounded the figure. A migraine aura?

No, not a migraine. But something felt so familiar. Something... What was it? Maybe he'd forgotten something important. But what?

Jarret rounded the corner, and the questions slipped away.

His gaze snapped to C.W., who stood reaching into his locker a few yards down the hall. In a hurry to get to class before the bell rang? Running late because of the time it took to torment Roland?

Without giving a warning or explanation, Jarret grabbed the back of his shirt with both hands and yanked him.

C.W. staggered back, cussing, and turned to Jarret. He smiled, but the blush of guilt crept to his face too.

Angry and wound so tightly he could've snapped, Jarret spit out questions. "Did you do that to my brother? Huh? Think it was funny? He's getting around on crutches, and the three of you gang up on him?"

C.W.'s eyes opened wider than seemed possible, the whites showing all around his irises. He shuffled back a few steps from Jarret.

Unable to stop himself, Jarret moved in, an imaginary band drawing them together.

"I don't know what you're talking about, bro." C.W.'s hands went up in a gesture of innocence. His eyes darted back and forth.

Jarret's gaze clicked to C.W.'s elevated arm and his right hand. And the orange stain on his index finger.

Words no longer seemed necessary. Or possible. A surge of adrenaline kicked him into action. Jarret pulled his fist back and—

Before he let fly... a warning flashed in his mind. It was as if he stood before a closed door, with a choice. He could leave the door closed and walk away, or he could open it and obey the heat of his passion. But he would need to intentionally open it before he could throw that first punch.

Another image flashed in his mind, swallowing up the warning. C.W. had orange paint on his finger. He did that to Roland.

With a burst of fury, Jarret willed open the door in his mind, the thing holding him back. And his fist met its target.

C.W.'s body jerked to one side under the impact.

Rage controlling his actions, Jarret swung at him again, but C.W. jumped out of the way. Unwilling to let C.W. get away, Jarret lunged for him.

The rest unfolded as an electrically-charged blur, Jarret throwing punches and grabbing C.W. to control him, C.W. dodging, squirming, and wrestling to get away. Within seconds, the fight went down to the floor with Jarret on top.

But as Jarret made a move to pin C.W. to the floor, muscular arms snaked around his chest from behind.

Not ready to stop his attack, Jarret resisted for a moment and continued trying to pin C.W.'s arms. Thinking better of it, he yielded to whoever had grabbed him.

He was yanked to his feet and shoved down the hallway.

Hot white anger still flashing in his vision, Jarret glimpsed a few faces. Apparently, kids had gathered to watch the fight. No one followed as Jarret's escort led him down a breezy hallway and to a room across from the principal's office.

"Wait in here." Jarret's escort—a young male teacher, new to River Run High—held open a door and motioned Jarret inside. He didn't seem angry. Just businesslike. He probably wanted to take care of C.W. or hunt down the principal. Or call the police.

Jarret obeyed, and the door closed behind him.

Pulse racing, body still tense, he stood alone in a little room with a long table and no windows. The old fluorescent lights hummed and turned the walls a sickly grayish yellow.

Jarret took a deep breath, wanting to calm down. He could hear his heart thumping in his ears. He scraped a chair away from the table, pushed it against the wall, and sat down. The knuckles of his right hand hurt, his arms ached, and his cheek smarted. He sucked in a few deep breaths. After shaking his hand out, he slumped forward and rested his arms on his thighs. His heartrate slowed to a sickening thud.

Had he hurt C.W. badly?

He buried his head in his hands, and his thoughts tangled in his mind.

Several minutes later, the door swung open and Jarret sat up.

The principal, Mr. Freeman, a short man in jeans and a dress shirt, marched into the room. "Jarret West." He directed a stern look to Jarret as he sat at the head of the long table. "You're a senior, right? Last year was your first year with us? I seem to remember you causing some trouble last year too."

Jarret remained expressionless and stared at a choppy smiley-face carved into the tabletop. The fight had drained him and everything ached.

Mr. Freeman rambled on about school policy, ending with, "So why did you do it?"

Jarret met his gaze. "Did you see my brother? See what C.W. did to him?"

His eyes drooped and mouth fell open. "Uh..." He pushed his chair out. "You stay here. I'll be back."

Jarret yanked the band from his ponytail, slouched in his chair, and pulled his hair over his face. How should he feel about what he'd done?

~ ~ ~

Keefe slumped over his desk. He'd made it to his last class of the day: Spanish. Mr. Segura, a tall suave man in his fifties with a melodic voice, rattled on in Spanish, directing the class's attention to an image on the screen in the front of the classroom.

Drawn blinds, low lights, and the warm, stuffy air made Keefe's eyelids droop. He struggled to stay awake. The forty sleepless hours in the woods were taking their toll. But he didn't want to doze off at school. Whenever he closed his eyes, he still faced that Japanese warrior. And his failure moved to the forefront of his mind.

Keefe's head bobbed. He jerked to attention and snapped his eyes wide open. He couldn't wait to get home. First thing he was doing: crashing on his bed. But then he'd have that dream again. Why the dream? Why the verse? Why not an answer? Did the dream mean something?

"Hey, Keefe." Sherman Maher slumped forward in his seat, his head of blond-streaked spiky hair resting on his arm outstretched across his desk. "Is it past your bedtime?" He gave a quirky grin and stifled a laugh.

Keefe wiped his sweaty face and took a deep breath.

"So Jarret showed C.W. who's boss, huh?" Sherman still lay with his head resting on his arm, looking at Keefe with amusement in his eyes. "Sometimes that kid's a big jerkwad anyways. C.W. Not your brother."

Not sure what Sherman referred to, Keefe squinted and shook his head.

"You know what your brother just did, don't you? Like right before class?"

Worry removing all traces of drowsiness, Keefe shook his head again.

"Out in the hallway after last period? Yeah, Jarret gave C.W. the smack-down. C.W. threw a few punches of his own, but that boy was wrecked."

"What?" Warning bells went off in Keefe's head. He glanced at the door, anxious to go. What had Jarret done? Had he been taken to the principal's office? Probably. And they'd have called Papa.

"After what C.W. did to Roland, who could blame him?"

Keefe snapped his gaze back to Sherman, his stomach rolling. "What'd he do to Roland?"

Sherman sat up and ran a hand over the back of his hair, disbelief on his face. "You don't know?"

"Tell me," he commanded, fear ripping through him.

"Uh..." Sherman pressed his lips together as if hesitant to explain. "Apparently, C.W. and... I can't say who else. But they decided your brother's a little too white and they decided to do something about it."

Keefe shook his head, irritated and not understanding. "What did they do about it?"

"They cornered him and got him with spray tan." Sherman remained straight-faced, but one corner of his mouth flickered for a split second. "It's not just Roland, though. They've been hazing freshman too."

"They did what?" Keefe didn't really want him to repeat it. He'd heard enough. And he knew Jarret. Jarret didn't take nicely to anyone messing with his family, and he still struggled with self-control. So of course he beat C.W. to a pulp.

Keefe slouched back, the sting of failure striking intensely. Like the swing of the Japanese warrior's blade.

Finally understanding, he dragged in a breath. He understood the meaning of the dream. He couldn't abandon Jarret to pursue a vocation. He'd only gone away for the weekend and Jarret had gotten in a ton of trouble.

He had to lose this fight. He'd asked for a sign and he'd gotten more than a few: the verse, the dream, even Jarret's trouble. Everything pointed to an answer of "no." No, he didn't need to go on the retreat. Because, no, he wasn't called to be a Franciscan, at least not now. He needed to step back and switch gears, forgo the move that would get him closer to victory. He needed to take a fall.

The thought sat like lead in the pit of his stomach. He couldn't digest it. Tension in his chest drew the lead from his stomach to his heart. He couldn't accept it.

It was just an excuse.

The Lord wouldn't want him to hold back out of fear for what another might do.

He'd put off talking with Papa about his potential calling for one reason. Fear of judgment. He feared that Papa's lack of faith would make him hostile to Keefe's calling. He was afraid that Papa would stand in the way, and make Keefe have to fight for it. He didn't want to fight against Papa. He didn't want Papa to feel the pain of losing someone for any reason.

Even with the Fire Starters, among kids who shared his faith, he'd kept his calling a secret, afraid half the time that Peter might say something. Peter probably suspected. He'd known about

Keefe's interest in the Franciscan Friars that had stayed at his family's bed and breakfast last fall.

Why did he care if the Fire Starters knew anyway? He wore a cross every day, the only symbol he could get away with at school since the dress code forbade graphic t-shirts. Did he fear exposing his deepest desires to the world, his longing to wear the brown robe of a mendicant order? Did he fear others knowing that he didn't aspire to the same things they did? That he wanted to give up everything and embrace the Franciscan way of life?

Did he fear that he'd pursue a vocation only to find out that God didn't want him? That this wasn't really his calling? Then what?

How badly did he want this? Would he fight for it?

Determination sparked in his heart. He bowed to the warrior in his dreams and lifted his sword. He wanted this. Whether he ended up flat on his face and exposed to the world, he wouldn't back down. He would take every chance that presented itself. He would claim the victory.

The bell rang, signaling the end of the school day.

Keefe grabbed his books and bolted from the classroom to find Jarret.

CHAPTER 17

The door swung open and two men strode into the small, windowless room.

Recognizing the sound of Papa's boots, Jarret swallowed hard and pushed locks of hair off his face.

Mr. Freeman grabbed the chair at the head of the table and motioned for Papa to take a seat across from Jarret, who still sat against the wall.

Papa glanced at Jarret and tugged the rim of his cowboy hat in greeting. Once he sat down, he breathed and exhaled loudly. He probably hated coming up for trouble on the first day of school.

Jarret straightened in his chair and redid his ponytail.

Mr. Freeman clasped his hands and rested them on the table. "So, Jarret, I spoke with your father, and we're going to be sending you home."

Jarret considered glancing at his watch. The bell for the end of the day would ring soon. Everyone would be going home, not just him. He wouldn't get off that easy. There had to be more.

"Now, I don't want to come down too hard. I understand you were retaliating on behalf of your younger brother, but we don't tolerate violence in our school." He rambled on more about school policy, anger management, and alternative ways of handling things. "So, we have to suspend you for a week."

Jarret remained expressionless, not looking at anyone. He didn't care.

After an uncomfortable stretch of silence, the principal said, "Do you understand?"

Jarret glanced. He understood but he couldn't get himself to reply, so a bit more silent tension developed.

Papa broke the cold war. "What about schoolwork?"

Mr. Freeman took a breath and tugged the cuff of his sleeve. "Make sure he takes all his books home. His teachers can call or email with assignments."

After a few more exchanges between the adults, the bell rang, and Mr. Freeman ushered them from the room.

"We'll talk at home." Papa turned and clomped toward the sunny entranceway, his blue eyes maintaining their typical unreadable look.

~ ~ ~

Still in a fog, Jarret trudged up the dark staircase to his bedroom. Papa had left school before Jarret had been dismissed. He'd given Keefe and Roland a ride and beat Jarret home. Fortunately, Jarret had spotted no one when he'd come in through the garage. For half a second, he'd considered going to Papa's study; Papa would want to talk about this. But Jarret couldn't get himself to do it.

One sore hand to the handrail, he reached the top step. Slivers of light crept from under the doors on one side of the dark hallway. The sound of the shower blasting traveled through the closed bathroom door on the other side of the hallway: probably Roland trying to wash off the tan.

Jarret curled and uncurled his hands. He'd wanted to wash them in the bathroom. They hurt. He should've used one of the downstairs bathrooms, but he wouldn't bother with it now. They could ache for a bit more. He deserved it.

Two steps from his bedroom door, a doorknob rattled and Keefe's bedroom door swung open with a burst of natural light. As Keefe stepped into the hallway, the light from his bedroom fell on his short hair and glasses and a face riddled with concern.

Before Keefe could utter a word, Jarret cast a weary look and shook his head. "Not now." He grabbed the knob to his own bedroom door.

"Okay, but I'm here when you need me."

Face to his bedroom door, Jarret nodded. He pushed the door open wide enough to get into the room and closed it behind him. Half drawn drapes let in too much light for his mood. Red and purple pillows and gold decorations taunted him.

Deep regret and a sense of failure rushed him. Jarret flung himself face down on his bed and hugged a purple pillow to his chest. He'd lost it, totally lost it this time. He shouldn't have thrashed C.W. like that.

That first punch and the look of shock in C.W.'s eyes...

He'd never pummeled a kid like that. Jarret clutched the pillow tighter and groaned. What a failure. And he'd been given an internal warning too. Two of them even.

Jarret opened his eyes, trying to sort out the details. It took effort to remember the first thing he'd done after leaving Roland in the classroom. He'd stormed to C.W's locker. On the way, a thought had flitted through his mind like a butterfly he couldn't catch. He'd forgotten something important.

Still hugging the pillow, Jarret rolled onto his side and squinted at the sunny window. *Oh, yeah...* He'd seen a strange light that had disturbed him to the core. What was that? *Whatever.* He'd ignored it once he'd seen C.W.

Then just before he'd thrown the first punch, a concrete warning flashed in his mind. He could back down and find another way to handle this mess, but he'd made a conscious choice to unleash his violence.

He'd done it deliberately. Maybe that explained why guilt weighed so heavily now.

Needing a better grasp of all this, Jarret scooted off the bed, lifted the edge of the bedspread, and stuffed his hand between the mattress and the box spring to find his journal. He slid his hand left and right across the cool mattress. Where was it?

He stopped breathing. What if someone had taken it? Who would know he kept it here? Who even knew he had a journal?

Fear creeping in, he made a wider swipe and bumped something. His journal! Taking a breath and aware of his thumping heart, he slid it out.

Journal in hand, he slid to the floor and leaned against the bed, facing the window.

He unwrapped the leather cord, took the pen he'd stuffed in between the pages and immediately set to writing.

God, I'm such a failure. But I didn't know the right thing to do. Still don't. He did that to my brother. Do I let him get away with it and do nothing? He'll just do it again someday. Or something worse. Sorry, Lord, but I had to do something. If there's a better way, I don't know it. Show me. I want to understand. Show me.

His hand ached from writing—no, from having slugged C.W. a few too many times. Jarret tossed the journal aside and slumped back. He was supposed to have met with Father Carston this past Saturday. Did he want to talk to Father about this? His first meeting had drained him. And now with all this...

His mind veered back to the fight, to the rage he'd felt and the uncontrollable need to keep punching.

The light from his bedroom window overwhelming him, Jarret rubbed his face with both hands and dropped his chin to his chest. Who was he kidding? His impulses ruled him. As much as he hated the person he'd been, he had no power to behave any differently. At least not in some situations. Like this one.

Why couldn't he bring back that night in the canyon? The intensity of Jesus' love for him, the words He had spoken, the repentance and longing to give his life over to God. It all felt so vague now.

Jarret's cellphone buzzed in his back pocket, notifying him of a text.

His hand snapped to it. Would C.W. have something to say? One of his other friends? One of their mothers? Irritated at his impulsiveness, he hesitated before drawing it out. But he did draw it out, he couldn't *not* draw it out, and his gaze snapped to the message notification. Chantelle.

Jarret tossed the phone onto the journal. He didn't need to talk to her. Didn't need any of his friends. Was Kyle in on it too? Nah, probably just the three stooges: C.W., Trent, and Konner. They worked at making others look small. He should've pounded all three of them. They deserved —

On impulse, Jarret lunged and snatched his phone. He did need friends. Certainly God didn't intend for a person to have no friends just because they messed up a few times.

Sitting with his knees up and his back to the bed, he tapped the screen until Chantelle's message appeared.

Heard what happened. You okay?

He stared at the phone. What could she have heard? Jarret had had the upper hand the entire time. Anyone standing around would've seen that. She must've known he was okay. Physically at least. He shifted his gaze. Maybe she meant emotionally. Maybe she figured he felt bad about it, that he wasn't really a monster.

Jarret tapped out his reply. *Yeah, fine.*

A second later: *Heard what C.W. did to your brother.*

Jarret tapped out a bad name and a curse for C.W. Then he took a breath and deleted it, typing instead, "I'm suspended from school."

Two seconds for her reply this time. *Oh. I'll miss you.*

Her message touched somewhere deep inside, comforting and thrilling him at the same time. He liked when girls looked at him, flirted with him, gave him attention. Was he ready for a girlfriend? What should he text back? If he told her he'd miss her too, he'd seal it. They'd be more than friends. He could text back something vague and noncommittal like, "Yeah sure," or "See you in a week."

Jarret's thumbs hovered over the keypad. He moved to strike a letter when a knock sounded on his bedroom door. Papa's knock.

Pulse kicking up, Jarret stuffed his phone in his back pocket. He snatched the journal, squeezed it between the mattress and the box spring, and jumped to his feet.

"Come in," he said as the doorknob turned.

Jarret stood ready for the talk he knew Papa had to give him. He'd let Papa down. Let himself down. Again. Since when did he start caring so much about Papa's opinion of him? But he did.

Staring at the floor, Papa scuffed into Jarret's room in his cowboy boots. He stopped at the foot of the bed and squinted at Jarret, who stood in the open area between the bed and the window. The two of them could sit in the armchairs and talk, but Papa didn't look like he wanted to sit. His graying hair, flattened on the sides, held the impression of his cowboy hat. His mouth curled up, and his blue eyes flickered with a look of contemplation.

Papa might've been thinking about their last talk and wondering if Jarret's good streak had ended. Maybe he was wondering what level of heat he needed to bring to this conversation. If he got angry enough, he'd be spitting out his cowboy slang. He'd tell Jarret he was too hell-fired outta control, or ask if he was studying to be a half-wit or off his mental reservation.

Sucking in a breath and readying himself, Jarret stood taller and waited.

Papa's mouth twitched. Words had never come easy for him. He often confessed that he missed having Mama around because she always knew the right thing to say.

"Saw that kid you beat up."

Jarret winced and turned away, then back. "Yeah, I messed up." That was an understatement, but he decided against making excuses. "He gonna be okay?"

Papa shrugged. "S'pose so." He shifted his weight to one leg and stuffed his thumbs in his belt loops. "You don't really need me to tell you that violence ain't the answer, now do you? That there are better ways of handling things?" He paused. "I mean, you've made the choice to go to Mass lately, since Arizona, so I s'pose you ought to be thinking more about turning the other cheek. Right?"

Jarret nodded. Papa was right, but he had no idea how to live that commandment. Maybe if C.W. had done something to him instead of his brother... Nah, that wouldn't have mattered. He didn't have "turn the other cheek" in him.

"Been thinking 'bout if I were in your shoes and a kid had done that to my brother, if'n I had a brother." He paused. "Can't say I'da done much different than what you did."

Jarret's jaw dropped.

"Even now as a grown man..." His jaw tightened. "That boy's lucky I didn't see him do it."

Stunned, Jarret let out a chuckle. "Uh, what would you've done?"

Papa's eyes twitched. "Roland's not like other kids. He's kind of vulnerable. And not just because of the cast. He's too..." He squinted even more, searching for the right word. "Forgiving."

Knowing that more than anyone, Jarret nodded.

"I know you've been trying, Jarret. Don't let this get you down. You're already grounded for the week, so now you'll do schoolwork at home. Big deal, right?"

A lump in his throat kept Jarret from answering.

Papa scuffed back to the door and stopped. "Suspended the first week of school. That's gotta be a record."

As Papa left the room and closed the door, Jarret's phone signaled another message. Assuming it came from Chantelle and wanting to share his renewed spirit with someone, he grabbed his phone.

A glance at the message put a sudden stop to his slightly elated mood and shifted him back down a few gears. It came from the stranger who'd sent the other cruel messages.

What happened to Roland today—totally your fault.

Jarret typed a message back without thinking. *Who are you?*

The reply came a few seconds later.

Someone who knows your kind.

JARRET'S JOURNAL

Since returning home from Arizona, the memory has faded.

I struggle now to remember.

Some days I can't remember much of that night at all.

I only remember that it had happened.

And the general order of things,

How I'd confessed to Roland without meaning it,

And how Roland had forgiven me

for all I confessed and more.

How his act of forgiveness

had brought me crashing to my knees.

I'd repented then, for the first time.

Repented of it all, wished I'd never done any of it,

wished I could erase it.

Then You came.

I remember what I saw but only in an impersonal way

As if it hadn't happened to me.

CHAPTER 18

The combination of warm afternoon sun streaming through his bedroom window and a pile of homework he didn't want to do had dropped Keefe like a felled tree to his bed. The replay of the warrior dream had him clawing his way back to consciousness.

Keefe sat on the edge of his bed, easing out of a stupor. His conscience ruffled him. Same as it had ever since he'd decided to stop at nothing short of victory.

He'd better go talk to Papa about the retreat. Get it over with. He'd say yes or he'd say no. And Keefe could handle it.

Taking a deep breath and stretching, Keefe left his bedroom, passed Jarret's closed door, and padded down the hallway in his socks. He'd had every intention of asking for permission earlier in the week. But then Jarret had gotten suspended and Roland came home with an orange-streaked complexion. And for two days after, Papa seemed out of sorts. He couldn't look at Roland for more than a second without his jaw clenching. And he seemed to think he needed to say or do something more to keep track of Jarret.

They'd had some pretty cold dinner conversations. Papa said things like, "Teachers send you schoolwork?"

Jarret never answered right away. His eyes narrowed and his gaze shifted to Papa. "Yeah."

"You get it done?"

Jarret shrugged. "What do you think I've been doing all day?"

Papa often twitched at the rude replies, but then he'd bite his tongue and take a breath.

Sometimes a hint of remorse had colored Jarret's expression and he'd given Papa a bit more information, telling him about one assignment or another. Papa had nodded and looked satisfied.

Keefe strolled past the kitchen, inhaling a savory chicken aroma and glimpsing Nanny hunched over the little kitchen table. He'd avoided asking on Wednesday because Papa had taken Roland for a doctor visit, a final x-ray to make sure he'd healed right. Roland had been begging to get the cast off and trying to get Papa to insist. He'd even threatened to do it himself. He'd seen a video online and thought he could figure it out. Fortunately, the doctor said it could come off Friday, so Roland agreed to let him handle it.

As Keefe neared the front hallway, he squinted at the light streaming through the window beside the front door. Then movement came from the little sitting room off the foyer. And mumbling.

Keefe peeked his head into the room.

Dressed in cut-off sweatpants and a long-sleeved gray t-shirt and resting his weight on his good leg, Roland stood facing the antique oval floor mirror in the corner. He lifted his head from the index cards in his hands and glimpsed Keefe through the mirror. Then he tipped his head with a shy look and turned around, pivoting on his good leg.

"Hey, Roland, what's up?" Keefe said.

"Speech class." Roland lifted the cards. "I don't think I can do it."

Keefe laughed. "Sure you can. Keep practicing." Keefe guessed that Roland had been practicing all week. He'd heard him mumbling in his bedroom almost every night.

He left Roland to his business and headed down the front hallway, his eyes locking onto the half-open door of Papa's office.

Voices came from Papa's study, one feminine and the other Papa's rough voice, their words becoming clear as Keefe drew near.

Not wanting to walk in on a conversation, Keefe slowed his pace. The quality of the woman's voice told him it came through the speaker phone, and it sounded like Miss Anna Meadows.

Keefe had met her a few months ago on one of Papa's digs in Mississippi. He'd known Papa liked her. Did they talk often?

"Sorry, I can't, Anna. I told you about my teaching job."

She laughed. "It's online, Ignatius, and you know we've got Internet. We might dig up bones and stone tools, but we don't work with them."

"Yeah, yeah."

"Don't 'yeah' me. You know I could use your help. What's your real reason for not wanting to see me?"

Papa groaned. "Now don't start that. You know I'd give anything to see you. I was just fixin' to stay holed up at the home front for a spell."

Keefe stopped near the doorway, not wanting Papa to see him yet. Papa's switch to cowboy talk meant he was getting agitated.

"And why's that? It's not in your blood to stay 'holed up at the home front.' " Her tone held an edge.

"Con sarn it, Anna." A chair squeaked and Papa's boots thudded to the floor. He'd probably had them propped up on the desk. "You know the reason why. Don't make me talk about it again, least not on the phone. You want to talk about it, why don't you light a shuck and get on over here." His voice softened. "Take a break from your work. I'd like to see you."

"Are you inviting me over?" Her voice softened too.

"Sure, if you want. We've got the room."

"Is this for a day or a few days?"

"Long as you like."

"Hmm. I'll check my schedule and let you know. I gotta run, cowboy."

"All right then. Talk to you soon."

A pause and then she said, "I miss you."

A longer pause before Papa's reply. "Miss you too, Anna." His voice hitched when he spoke her name.

Keefe found himself backing up and his senses heightening. If he stepped into his study now, Papa might know he'd heard all that.

Glad he wasn't wearing shoes, he turned and retraced his steps down the hallway. Back toward his bedroom. Something sat funny inside him. First Papa had given up his freelance work and travel. And he'd taken an online teaching job. Now he wouldn't even go visit Miss Meadows. Keefe had never heard Papa raise his voice to a woman, much less Miss Meadows. Something was wrong.

As he mounted the steps, music came on in Jarret's room and traveled through the closed bedroom door, some emotional, contemporary song that Jarret liked to play over and over. Getting suspended the first day of school had probably put him in a mood.

Keefe stopped at his door. Should he talk to Jarret about Papa? Maybe he should get Roland too, and the three of them could talk about it. Keefe didn't want to jump to conclusions. But his mind kept pointing him to one answer.

CHAPTER 19

Feeling fly and ready for the weekend, Jarret dumped frozen onion rings onto a cookie sheet and slid the sheet into the warm oven. He added an extra minute to the time since the oven hadn't warmed up all the way. Then he reached for the box of pizza pockets and his mouth watered. He couldn't wait to eat them. After all, he'd skipped lunch.

He'd been finishing up the last bit of schoolwork the teachers had given him for the week, and he hadn't wanted to stop. He felt good getting it all done on his own, without being told, and without cheating.

In fact, he'd never felt more in control of himself than he did now. He'd decided to stick to the routine he'd adopted last school year: wake up early to work out on his weight set in the basement, shower, eat, and school. While he had wished he were back at school, he liked the option of doing schoolwork at the dining room table, out on the front porch, on the couch in the living room, or stretched out on his bed. Besides, he'd probably needed the time to get over what C.W. had done, so he wouldn't try confronting him again.

Or maybe he'd just needed the week to himself, at home while everyone else went to school. Not that he was exactly alone. He and Papa crossed paths often throughout the day, usually on their way to get something from the kitchen. It was weird having him home so much. And Nanny always seemed to be everywhere at once, cleaning and cooking and mumbling to herself throughout the house.

And he'd been texting Chantelle since the first day of his suspension. She'd sent the first message, saying she'd missed him. He'd debated how to reply, but then Papa's little talk had lifted a weight. Despite Jarret's mess up, Papa hadn't lost all respect for him. Wanting to share his good mood, Jarret had yanked out his phone and messaged Chantelle. *Text me whenever you want.*

She could interpret that any way she wanted, but it didn't commit him.

They'd sent each other messages ten times a day after that. Stupid little messages mostly. He'd ask, "What class are you in now?" and "Who's the teacher?" And he'd tell her what he was up to or "Can't text, working out." And things like that.

Her messages mostly consisted of questions and complaining. "What are you having for lunch?" "How long do you work out?" "This class is sooo boring." And she'd told him a bit about life as a cheerleader.

He'd intentionally avoided asking what she was doing after school or what she was wearing. He didn't want her sending any pictures that he'd have to go to confession over. Nanny shuffled from the dining room and toward the kitchen island, her eyes on the pocket notebook in her hand. "I made extra of everything last night so you boys and your father could just heat things up for dinner tonight." Dressed to go out—a flowered skirt and twenty-year-old pink top—she smoothed her gray curls absentmindedly as she stared at whatever list she'd made.

"No thanks. I can't eat meatloaf two nights in a row." Besides, he was hungry now. Jarret arranged the frozen pizza pockets on a cookie sheet. Then he scanned the box for the oven temperature.

Good, same temperature as the onion rings. "So where are you going all dressed up?"

"Hmm? Oh, we're meeting friends for dinner at a fancy restaurant, then going to their house for a night of cards." She pulled out a barstool and sat down.

He slid the cookie sheet into the oven on the shelf above the onion rings and came around the island to her. "So what's the fancy restaurant?" Attempting to tease her, Jarret leaned into her space and gave her a crooked grin, one arm on the countertop. Her idea of a fancy restaurant and his were likely polar opposites.

She glanced up from her list. "We're going to a steakhouse."

"Mmm. Fancy." He gave her a quick kiss on the forehead. Knowing the gesture would leave her flummoxed, he took off toward the hallway. He'd spent years being nasty and not appreciating her, even resenting her after Mama died, so poor Nanny never knew how to take his recent attempts at kindness. He stopped at the doorway and glanced back.

She sat on the barstool, one hand to her chest, eyes blinking rapidly as she looked at him.

"Have fun tonight," he said, emotion creeping up.

"Thank you... dear. But I... What is that I smell?" She peered at the oven. "I wish you would stop bringing TV dinners into the house."

"I'm not making TV dinners. I'm making pizza pockets and onion rings." He grinned, knowing it would still offend her. She made everything from scratch. Who cared that she served gravy and three carbs with every meal?

"Those things are terrible for you. Don't you know all the preservatives and strange ingredients they put in them? Didn't you hear me say we have leftovers?"

Jarret gave her a smile and waved a brow. "Thanks, but I'm not in the mood for meatloaf." He stepped into the hallway, turning away from her and toward the great room. "I exercise and eat healthy every day. Today, I'm eating junk food."

Two steps down the hallway, sensing his twin brother, Jarret stopped and turned around.

Keefe strolled from the foyer toward him, a stack of textbooks at his side and a package, letters, and junk mail in his hand.

"You're home." Glad to see him, Jarret stuffed his thumbs into the back pockets of his jeans and waited for Keefe to reach him.

"So how's your last day of home school?" With the mail in one hand, Keefe awkwardly shifted the stack of books from his hip to Jarret.

Not expecting them, Jarret almost dropped the thick World Lit book. "Working at home's easy. I'm sure I get done way ahead of you." Then he glanced at the stack of books he now held at his side. "It's Friday. You got homework?"

Keefe nodded as he tucked junk mail and bills under his arm, separating them from the package: a thick orange envelope. "I haven't been getting much done in class." Keefe used to get almost everything done before the class ended.

"Why not?"

"Distracted." He ripped open the package and reached inside. "Good, they're here." He lifted a brown scapular out and dangled it in front of Jarret. It was a heavy-duty scapular with folds still in the cords from the way it had been packed. "This is for you." He lifted it, as if to slip it over Jarret's head.

"Thanks." Jarret jerked back and stuck out a hand. "I think I'll look into it a bit more before I start wearing it."

"Oh." Hurt flickered in his twin's brown eyes.

"I just wanna understand what it's about. Don't want to just go through the motions." Jarret stuffed the scapular into a front pocket of his jeans. Honestly, he just didn't see the point. No matter what Keefe said, the devotion seemed childish and a bit superstitious.

Keefe nodded, a look of acceptance replacing the fleeting stab of hurt. He reached back into the bag. "Roland home yet? I've got one for him too. For everyone: Nanny, Mr. Digby, Papa."

"Nah, Roland's not home yet." Papa had picked Roland up early and taken him to get the cast off. Jarret looked forward to feeling a bit of closure today, since he felt responsible for Roland's broken leg. "Hungry? I'm making onion rings and six pizza pockets. You can have one if you want." Ready to drop Keefe's books, he took the mail from under Keefe's arm and shoved the books toward him.

"You're making six, and I can only have one?" Keefe stuffed the package under his arm and took the books.

Jarret grinned. "Count yourself lucky. I don't feel like sharing." His phone rang while he handed off the books, World Lit almost falling.

Jarret yanked out his phone. A quick glance showed the call came from Papa. "Hey, Papa, what's up? Did Roland get his—"

"Keefe home?" Papa spoke over Jarret's second question.

"Yeah, he's right here." Jarret lifted his gaze to Keefe, who looked curious and stepped forward to listen.

"Good. Stay put. We're on our way home to pick you both up for dinner. Roland's got his cast off and we're going to celebrate."

"We're eating out?" Jarret asked, mildly shocked. While they always ate out when on assignments with Papa, they rarely did otherwise. He couldn't remember the last time they'd gone out in their hometown.

"Wait, no." Roland's troubled voice came over the phone. "I need a shower first."

"You don't need a shower," Papa said.

"Yes, I do. My leg feels gross."

"It's not gonna kill you to go to dinner first. You can take a long hot bath before bed."

"I don't take baths."

Papa's voice came over the phone louder. "See ya in five." Then he ended the call.

Jarret slid his phone into his back pocket and cut a sad glance toward the kitchen.

"Did he say we're going out?" Keefe asked, though he'd stood near enough to hear.

Jarret nodded. "What about my pizza pockets?"

Keefe shrugged. "Turn the oven off and finish them later tonight."

Heart set on the junk food, Jarret sighed.

~ ~ ~

Jarret slumped back in the bench seat and folded his arms across his chest. He'd glimpsed the Digbys at a table by the window as the hostess had led them to their booth. All the way here, he had protested the restaurant choice, a Western steak house. Keefe hadn't cared. And Roland wanted what Papa wanted. Of course. Jarret tried to dismiss the thoughts about Roland being Papa's pet, but he couldn't keep from tossing a sour look in Roland's direction.

Running a hand through his hair and looking out of sorts, Roland sat next to Papa, who sat across from Jarret. Keefe sat beside Jarret and across from Roland. He'd piled a mound of peanuts onto his plate, but he hadn't shelled any of them. He sat with arms folded on the table, leaning toward Roland and looking interested in every detail of the cast removal that Roland shared.

"Still itches like mad." Roland turned his eyes to Papa with an accusing glare. "Wish I could've showered."

Papa either didn't hear or pretended not to. He sat hunched over the table, relaxing with his ice-cold beer. He and about six others in the dimly-lit restaurant, one woman and the rest men, wore cowboy hats. Papa would've won for the most authentic, most weathered. The rest were all hat and no cattle, as Papa liked to say about anyone pretending to be something they weren't.

Papa lifted his steely-blue eyes to Jarret, the hint of a smile coming to his face. "Got your schoolwork done?"

Jarret gave him a cold look. Wasn't this supposed to be a celebration dinner? "Yeah. I do. Ready to go back to school." He added the last line with less attitude, giving Papa the benefit of the doubt. He probably couldn't think of anything else to say.

Papa shifted his attention to Roland. "Now that your cast is off, you ready to get back in the saddle?"

Roland nodded enthusiastically. "I miss riding."

"Maybe we can all ride together, the four of us." Papa cracked a shell and tossed the peanut into his mouth. "Take the trails on our property or take the horses out to the Badlands."

"That's over an hour away." Stomach growling, Jarret straightened and grabbed a handful of peanuts from the tin bucket on the table. He liked the idea of riding out in the prairies, maybe coming across bison or bighorn sheep. But Papa had never seemed interested in anything like this before. *What gives?*

"So we get a horse trailer." Papa tossed more peanuts into his mouth.

"Sounds fun." Keefe bumped Jarret's leg with his own.

Shoving a handful of peanuts into his mouth, Jarret glanced to see what Keefe wanted.

Anyone else would've read contentment on Keefe's face, but Jarret recognized trouble in his eyes. Something bothered him. Something about what Papa said. Papa had been acting strange lately. Keefe had brought it up before, but now Jarret was seeing it for himself.

"Yeah that sounds great," Roland said. "Let me get back to riding first, see how my leg feels. Think we can go there this fall?"

Papa nodded. "Something else I was thinking for the fall... The Brandts sponsor that camping event every year."

Jarret stopped chewing, all senses alert now. Keefe seemed to freeze too.

"Why don't we all go this year?" Papa took a swig of beer.

"Uh..." Keefe jerked forward and back. "I, um, I can't."

Jarret exhaled, relieved that Keefe had spoken first. He didn't have a good excuse to offer yet. He needed a few seconds to come up with something.

"Why's that?" Head down so that his Stetson almost covered his eyes, Papa twisted his beer mug.

"I, uh, have somewhere I need to be." Keefe took a breath and seemed to hold it. He must not have told Papa about that Franciscan retreat yet.

Jarret shifted his gaze to Keefe in warning. Now was not the time to bring it up. They could enjoy a family meal out together and hash out their business at home another time.

Keefe acknowledged Jarret's warning with the slightest nod. And he breathed again. "It's a bad weekend for me, that's all."

"Me too," Jarret said. "I can't go camping." He caught Roland's glance. Roland probably guessed why. The place reminded Jarret of the mistake he'd made with Zoe, and he didn't want to think about that for an entire weekend. Besides, what if Chantelle went too? Or he met some other cute girl? Would he make the same mistake twice? Girls made him crazy, especially one on one, made him say and do things he maybe shouldn't.

Papa played with something in his chest pocket, something with a rectangular outline. A pack of cigarettes? Papa didn't smoke cigarettes. He smoked a pipe. Still with his head down and seeming deep in thought, Papa lifted the pack a bit so that the green metallic wrapper peeked from his pocket.

"You smoke menthol cigarettes?" Jarret blurted out, wishing he hadn't. His memory shoved something to the forefront of his mind. Papa had probably found Kyle's cigarettes out on the veranda steps, right where Jarret had left them. Jarret hadn't mentioned the cigarettes when he'd told on himself the night his friends had come over.

"I do now." Papa grinned, his look saying a lot more than Jarret hoped he'd say aloud. Maybe Papa thought he hadn't come entirely clean.

Jarret took a drink of his Coke. He glanced over his shoulder just as the waitress—young and slender with silky dark hair and a ton of makeup—arrived with their plates. Thank God. Maybe they wouldn't talk more about it.

"Can I get you anything else?" she asked, glancing from face to face.

"Nope." Papa tipped his hat. "Looks mighty fine."

She gave him a flirtatious smile and zipped to the next table.

"Should we pray?" Keefe cast a hesitant glance at everyone, and a longer look at Papa.

Papa held a knife and fork in his hands.

Roland reddened.

Jarret dropped his fork to the table. He'd started praying before meals, with or without the family, but he'd planned on offering the prayer silently.

After a moment of everyone staring at Keefe, Papa said, "Sure, why not?" and they all bowed their heads and mumbled the Prayer Before Meals in voices so low that their guardian angels probably struggled to hear them.

They ate in silence for a few minutes until Roland started the camping conversation back up with Papa, making Jarret throw another ice-cold glare at him. Roland still wanted to go, even if Jarret and Keefe couldn't. Maybe that would satisfy Papa anyway.

"So Fire Starters have their first meeting this Monday," Keefe said to Jarret, leaning a bit so the conversation stayed between the two of them.

"Yeah?" Jarret cut a bite-sized chunk off his steak. It didn't satisfy him like the pizza pocket would've, but he liked it. They'd cooked it just right.

"You wanna come?"

Jarret shot him a look to ask if he was crazy.

"Why not?" Keefe pressed.

Jarret swallowed his bite. "You know why not," he answered coolly. Keefe knew him better than anyone, knew the challenges he'd faced all his life, and knew he'd wanted to do things right from now on. Why would he even ask?

"Because of Peter? He's not the only kid in the group. Just ignore him."

Jarret shook his head and shoved a bite of baked potato into his mouth. If he wanted to stay out of trouble, he had to avoid certain people and places. Peter was one of them. And now C.W. and his friends. And he was *not* going camping. He glanced upward, his thoughts turning in irritation to the Lord. *God, why do you make this so hard? You know I'm trying.*

"So are you going to avoid Kyle and all your other friends too?"

Not getting his point, Jarret stopped chewing and glared. "Why? That doesn't make sense."

"Well, I assume you're avoiding Peter to keep from making a mistake. Don't you think your friends are bad company too?"

He shook his head, a sneer taking over. "No, they're not. They don't tempt me to do anything. I just won't have them over. If I want to see them, I'll go to their houses. Or hang out somewhere else." His voice had risen to where Papa could've heard if he hadn't been absorbed in talking to Roland about camping.

"You know they always end up doing something they shouldn't."

"So? I can hang with them and not do everything they do. I'm not that weak."

Keefe's mouth opened, closed, then he sighed.

"I'll avoid people I want to strangle." Jarret turned back to his plate, signaling the end of the conversation.

Papa set his fork down, took a swig of beer, and sat back, folding his arms across his wide chest. "Let's *hang fire* before we make up our minds about camping, okay?" His piercing blue eyes shifted from Keefe to Jarret.

Hang fire was cowboy talk for wait awhile. Jarret shook his head, unable to come up with an intelligent answer. He couldn't. He wouldn't. He was not going camping.

Keefe's reaction must've communicated the same thing because then Papa set his jaw and his expression turned hard. "You boys are really souring my milk, you know that?"

Dying to get out of his dress shirt and tie, Keefe slid out of Mr. Digby's Crown Victoria. He often sat in the middle of the back seat when riding with the Digbys, so he had to wait for his brothers to exit. With Father Carston's Sunday homily about little daily sacrifices fresh in his mind, he sat in the middle today so that Jarret and Roland could have the more comfortable window seats. He'd had a different reason in the past. Jarret used to pick on Roland, so Keefe had made himself a buffer.

As soon as Keefe closed the car door, Mr. Digby pulled away from the circular drive and pulled around to the garage. He'd gotten in the habit of dropping everyone at the front door so his wife could get going on the food, as if the extra few minutes mattered.

"Well, I'll go get brunch started," Nanny said as she stepped past Jarret, who held the door open for her. "Such a gentleman today." Her slanted brows said she wasn't sure how to take him.

"Just today? What am I on other days?" Jarret grinned and threw a glance to Keefe as he climbed the porch steps. "No, don't answer that." Jarret's silky gray tie hung loose around his neck and he'd already unbuttoned the top two buttons of his royal blue shirt.

Standing off to the side, probably waiting for Keefe and Jarret to go inside first, Roland loosened his tie. Like most Sundays, he wore black on black. Today he could wear his regular dress pants, not the modified ones with the Velcro that Nanny had made to go over his cast.

"After you." Jarret bowed and placed his hand against his chest.

"Uh. Thanks." Roland stepped inside, still favoring his leg a bit.

"You're in a good mood," Keefe said to Jarret.

"Yeah. School tomorrow." Jarret closed the door behind Keefe and untucked his shirt.

"You're excited about school, huh?"

Jarret shrugged. "It's boring around here when everyone else is gone." He took a few steps and stopped, probably because Keefe didn't walk with him. "Supposed to get hot today. I'm gonna throw some shorts on."

"I'll change later. I want to talk to Papa." Keefe tilted his head in the direction of Papa's study, one of three open rooms casting squares of sunlight on the sleepy front hallway. He'd put off doing it during Jarret's week of expulsion, not wanting to add to Papa's headache. But the quote of some Franciscan saint kept nagging him: *"The sun never hides his light for fear of inconveniencing the owls."*

The shifting of Jarret's brown eyes showed he knew what Keefe was thinking. He gave an encouraging nod and walked away.

Stuffing his hands in the pockets of his dress pants, Keefe turned toward his destination and his insides quivered. He would never feel ready to discuss this, but he was determined to do it now anyway.

He walked down the hall, matching the rhythm of his footfalls with the beating of his heart. What did he have to fear?

Keefe's thoughts drifted to a story he'd read from the *Little Flowers of St. Francis* last night and the scene played out in his mind. Leaves rustling in a warm summer breeze. A blue sky above. A wide river rushing past, too wide to cross. Brother Bernard, in bare feet and a brown tunic, strolled along the banks of the great river, searching for a safe place to cross. He'd seen none in the past half hour, but he needed to cross in order to return home.

"God give thee peace, good brother," came a strong but melodious voice.

Delighted to hear the customary greeting of his own country, Brother Bernard had turned to greet the stranger.

A traveler with staff and cloak drew near, handsome to behold and with kindness in his eyes.

"Where do you come from?" Brother Bernard asked.

"I come from the convent where Francis dwells. I wished to speak with him but could not because he was in the forest contemplating divine things, and I would not disturb him. I spoke with others there. Brother Masseo taught me the proper way to knock at the convent gate. But Brother Elias would not answer my questions, so I left. He repented afterward and wanted to speak with me, but it was too late."

Brother Bernard marveled at his words.

"Why do you not cross the river?" the stranger asked, taking in the river with a sweeping gaze.

"Because I fear to perish in the waters. They are very deep."

"Let us cross together." The stranger offered a hand to Bernard. "Fear naught."

Moved by faith, Brother Bernard placed his hand in the stranger's and in an instant they stood on the other side of the river.

Great joy and awe tingled through him. And realization that the stranger was an angel of God.

~ ~ ~

Bringing his thoughts back to the moment, Keefe now stared at the open door to Papa's study. "Let us cross together," he whispered to his guardian angel. Courage crushed the fear and produced a strange sensation like electricity zipping through his body. Ready to reveal his deepest desires, he took a breath and stepped into the room.

Keefe stared at an empty desk. Lamps off, desk tidy…no Papa.

Disappointed, yet relieved, Keefe exhaled and stood at ease. He scratched his head. Okay, Papa had to be somewhere in the house. He wasn't giving up that easily. He'd already put this off for too long.

A quick stroll through the house, and Keefe found Papa watching TV in the family room. He sat alone in the middle of the couch, cowboy hat on the armrest and feet propped up on the coffee table. Odd for him, he wore socks but not his boots. An old Humphrey Bogart movie, *Casablanca,* played on the big screen TV. Mama had loved this one. Did Papa have a reason for watching it now? He'd been acting so strangely lately. Something had to be wrong.

Keefe tried to make some noise as he approached from behind the couch, not wanting to interrupt an emotional moment or anything. He shuffled to the adjacent couch and sat in the middle of it.

Papa's hand shot out for his Stetson but he didn't put it on. "Hey there, Keefe. Back from Mass?"

"Yeah. I wondered if I could talk to you. But maybe now's not a good time." He glanced at the TV.

"Naw, you're fine." Papa grabbed the remote and shut the TV off. "Just watching a movie I've seen a dozen times."

"Yeah, so what made you put that one on?" Keefe stalled, trying to gather his thoughts and regain his courage.

Papa uncrossed his feet and propped them on the edge of the coffee table. "I don't know. Don't care much for newer movies."

The swinging doors that led to the great room moved and Roland came through. His gaze connected with Keefe's and he opened his mouth, but then Jarret came from behind and grabbed him by the back of the shirt. Jarret turned Roland around and gave Keefe a nod, communicating that he'd make sure Keefe had privacy to talk with Papa.

Keefe smiled and dipped his head.

"So what's up?" Papa said, paying no attention to the minor disruption.

"Um... It's about next weekend and why I don't want to go camping."

"Okay. Let's hear it." Papa slid his cowboy hat onto his lap and messed with the rim.

"You know those Franciscan friars we were talking about?"

"Sure."

"Well, they're having a discernment retreat the same weekend as the Brandts' camping trip."

The blue of Papa's eyes seemed to swirl and change hues. "I'm not following you."

"I want to go. I feel like maybe..." Keefe struggled with how to say it and that verse came back to mind: *Blessed is he who takes no offense at me.* So he just blurted it out. "I think God's calling me to join them." He wanted to qualify his statement with things like he wasn't really sure, and maybe it was just a childish dream, but he forced himself to leave it at that.

Staring at his Stetson, Papa made no reaction for two whole minutes. Then he sucked in a breath and bit his bottom lip. "You mean... you... want to join the Franciscans?"

Relief rushed through him. "Yes."

Papa's eyelids flickered. "Wow. That's a commitment."

"Yeah."

Papa nodded slowly and then met his gaze. "So when did you decide this?"

"Well, I haven't decided. That's why I want to go on the retreat. But my interest started sometime last year."

"Italy?"

"Yeah, I guess it started there." His heart stirred. The day he'd stepped into the Romanesque Basilica in Bagno di Romagna had changed his life. Gazing at the Eucharistic miracle, overpowered by the love of Christ, he'd made a promise to always listen to God's voice. And maybe God was calling him to life as a Franciscan.

"Italy made an impression on me too, I suppose." Papa squinted at him. "But you won't find me running off to a monastery. You don't have to leave the world to live right. Maybe you're taking those feelings too far."

Keefe wanted to say something about Papa's Mass attendance, but he pushed the thought back. He'd asked him in Italy if the family could start going again. And when they'd returned home Papa had made everyone go for a while, but that didn't last long. And now everyone went but him.

"Papa, I don't feel satisfied thinking about any other future. Only this one. I want to do what Francis did."

"You ain't gonna strip your clothes off and disown me, are ya?"

It took a second for Keefe to get the joke, but then he laughed.

Papa smiled. Once his smiled faded, he stared at Keefe for a long moment. "My father was a farmer in southern Arizona. His father was a cattle rancher. And you know we've got 49ers in our family, right? Searching for gold but not getting too lucky."

Keefe nodded, wondering at Papa's message in the family history lesson.

"My father wanted me to take over the farm. His untimely death and the Zamoranos taking care of me, changed things. I might've followed in my father's footsteps, but my heart was always somewhere else." Papa leaned his head back and rubbed the front of his neck up to his clean-shaven jaw. "I liked digging things up." He smiled. "My father once told me that his father wanted him to be a cattle rancher too. To be honest, I'd always hoped one of my boys would want to follow in my footsteps as an archaeologist." The side of his mouth curled up in a smile that conveyed a hint of sentimental sadness. "But us Wests have never quite followed our fathers' dreams."

Hope filling him by degrees, Keefe waited with bated breath for Papa to say more.

But Papa shut his mouth and gazed ahead, lost in thoughts maybe. A minute passed. Two minutes. Papa turned to him again. "So where is the retreat? And how long is it?"

"Minnesota, nine hours away. And I'd have to leave on a Thursday and get back late Sunday."

"How do you plan to get there?"

"Um." He hadn't thought of that, but the answer was easy. "I was hoping you'd let me borrow your car or truck, whichever one you won't be needing."

"What about schoolwork for the two days you'll miss?"

"It'll just be one day. Friday's a teachers' day or something. No school. And I'll see if I can do the work for Thursday in advance."

Papa nodded, looking satisfied that Keefe had thought it all through. "S'pose that's fine as long as the school's okay with it."

Relief and a fit of joy had him jumping to his feet, wanting to hug Papa but not sure if he'd welcome that.

A split second later, Papa stood too and opened his arms.

Smiling inside and out, Keefe fell into his father's embrace.

A moment later, Papa pushed him back and returned to his spot on the couch. "You can take the truck. The Lexus needs tires."

"Thanks." Keefe stopped mid-stride, about to walk off. "Hey, I've been meaning to ask you. You always said that you'd never take a teaching job. Why'd you take this one?"

Papa turned the remote over in his hands. "I didn't say I'd *never* take one. Said I'd hate a teaching job."

Not getting the difference, Keefe pressed for more. "Okay, so why'd you take it? Won't you miss working in the field?"

"I'm not giving it up forever. Just for a time." Papa's look held something Keefe didn't understand, but he couldn't get himself to dig further.

CHAPTER 21

Tuesday after school, Jarret sat back on his bed, writing in his journal. Mid-sentence, an image appeared in his mind and he glanced up. Long blond hair, aqua blue eyes, and a pretty face. Clothes that drew attention to her figure. *Chantelle.*

Once Monday had rolled around, she'd found him at school between classes three times. And four today, never seeming uncomfortable around him. In fact, she seemed to understand him. And not judge.

Where did he want their friendship to go? Was he ready for more?

Taking a long breath, he leaned his head on pillows behind him and gazed at the ceiling fan. He'd changed since Zoe. He knew now where to draw the line. And he wanted to stay on the right road. Why shouldn't they see each other? He'd need to make sure their relationship stayed more like friendship than lovers. They'd need to avoid hanging out alone.

With the journal and pen in hand, Jarret scooted off the bed and shuffled to his open bedroom window. He gazed down at the sprawling front yard and the trees behind it, admiring the shades of green created by the late afternoon sunlight. A strong breeze blew, bringing fresh air into his room and making leaves shimmer and show their silvery undersides. They wouldn't turn gold and orange for a couple of weeks yet, though the melancholy mood of autumn had already found his spirit.

He hated letting go of summer, but this one would stand out in his mind forever... because of the night in the canyon. Soon all the trees would let go of their leaves. After a long cold winter of barren branches and frozen ground, spring would bring the green leaves and grass back.

He never wanted back the things he'd let go—his cold heart, total selfishness, and lack of faith—though it still caused a bit of sorrow to leave his old ways behind.

Jarret returned to his bed and sank into the mound of pillows he'd arranged a few minutes earlier, when he'd first sat down to write in his journal. Father Carston had wanted him to write something every day, but he'd only made a few pathetic entries in the past two-and-a-half weeks. Which reminded him...

He should've rescheduled his appointment with Father. Father had wanted to see him once a week. Jarret had thought about at least calling last Saturday. All day long. But he couldn't get himself to do it. Then at Mass Sunday morning, he felt like Father kept looking at him during the homily. Jarret had avoided making eye contact with Father and even skipped out through a side door at the end of Mass.

Maybe he'd schedule for this upcoming Saturday. He should at least make a few more attempts at writing in his journal before then.

Jarret wrote the first thoughts that came to mind:

Finally went back to school after a week of suspension. Got some pretty wild looks from kids and a lot more space in the halls. Everyone probably thinks I've got a short fuse, or that I'm a time bomb, and now they're more afraid of me than ever. Maybe they'll know not to mess with my brothers.

Jarret winced, replaying a single moment from his altercation with C.W., the moment his fist landed on his face. He hated how he'd made the choice to do it, and then lost control of himself.

His phone buzzed, vibrating on the nightstand.

Setting the journal aside, Jarret twisted to reach it. He glanced at the text as he lay back.

If she knew you, she wouldn't like you.

Jarret sat upright. Anger teased him and subsided. Who kept sending him nasty messages? Besides C.W. and Peter, who had a reason to hate him enough to keep bothering him? Maybe he'd offended one of his other friends without realizing it. Or a past friend.

Zoe? His heart lurched.

No, not her. *She'd* broken it off. He'd stayed by her, hadn't wanted to break up, but he accepted it without any hostility. She had no reason to hate him.

Did Chantelle know about Zoe? She had a younger brother who also went to River Run High, Tyrone. Did he know? No one had secrets at River Run High. If she hadn't heard about his relationship with Zoe, how she'd been pregnant with his baby, she would soon. Maybe she wouldn't like him. Maybe she'd want nothing to do with him, thinking he'd want more from her than he really did. He'd have to convince her that he didn't, that he wasn't like that anymore. Would she believe him?

If she didn't, she might tell her friends everything he said about it. He'd lose his image for sure.

He sighed. Oh well. His conscience wasn't going to let him stay the same. The next girl he got that close to would be wearing his ring on her finger. A wedding ring. But he wasn't in any hurry for that.

A knock on the bedroom door snapped him from his thoughts: Papa's knock.

Jarret scrambled off the bed and slid the journal between the mattress and the box spring. "Yeah, what?"

The door creaked open and Papa stepped into the room in hat and boots, holding a book or something at his side. "You sittin' in here twiddling your thumbs?"

Jarret straightened up, brushing the bedspread in place. "Ain't got nothing better to do."

"Keefe and Roland went off with that church group again, right?" Papa squinted. "What do they call themselves?"

"Yeah, the Fire Starters. Don't ask me why they're called that." Keefe had tried explaining it to him. The little group had seen their prayers answered in dramatic ways and wanted to devote themselves to fulfilling Jesus' desire: *I came to cast fire upon the earth; and would that it were already kindled!*

"That's right. Second night in a row with that group, huh?" He adjusted his hat, replacing it on his wavy graying hair, the book still hanging at his side.

No, wait... Jarret's temperature spiked. Not a book. Two video games. "Yeah, I think they had their opening meeting last night. And they're helping clean up vandalism at some girl's house tonight."

"Sounds like a mighty nice thing to do. Why aren't you out there?"

"Eh, don't feel like it." Jarret's leg bounced, anxiety building.

Papa peered out the window, a distant look in tired eyes surrounded by crow's feet. "I reckon I spent too many years doing my own thing. Working with others, for others—now, that builds something lasting. Makes a difference when we help each other out."

"Is that why you took that teaching job?" Jarret immediately regretted his words. He didn't want Papa saying more than he wanted to, or more than Jarret wanted to hear.

"In a roundabout way, I s'pose."

"Hoping to make a difference in your students' lives?"

Papa shrugged. "That's not necessarily my goal, but you never know."

Not sure he could handle the answer, Jarret decided not to ask his true goal. Something bothered Papa lately, and he was bound to spill it sooner or later. Given the choice, he'd rather hear it with Keefe and Roland at his side.

Papa added nothing more, but he didn't seem inclined to leave Jarret's bedroom either. He simply stared out the window. Working himself up to confronting Jarret about the video games? Or maybe he wanted Jarret to bring it up first. Or did he have something else to say?

Tired of waiting for the bomb to drop and irritated at how his pulse had kicked up, Jarret made an obvious glance at the video games. "Whatcha got there?"

Papa lifted a brow, as if not sure what Jarret referred to, then he glowered and swung the games out in front. "This horse crap yours?"

Jarret shook his head, a bit relieved to have it out in the open. Indifferent as to whether or not Papa believed him, he said, "Nah, my friends brought them over. I stuffed them behind a couch cushion so they'd play something else. That where you found them?"

"Yeah. I'm sure they'll be wanting them back." Papa placed them on Jarret's dresser, no longer appearing to care. "Feel like going for a ride?"

"Uh..." Jarret squirmed, uncomfortable that Papa had more to talk to him about. "Car or horse?"

Papa grinned. "Either one."

~ ~ ~

Ten minutes later, they rode side by side under a thick canopy of trees, taking the trail that wrapped around to the back of the property.

Jarret rode Desert, his creamy buckskin Quarter Horse, and Papa his bay Pure Spanish Horse. Papa's horse, a bit shorter than

Jarret's, had a more compact body that gave her a tougher look. And Papa always looked tough on a horse, him with his rugged old Stetson, the same brown as the bay, and his solid cowboy build. He sat tall and relaxed, his gaze fixed ahead of him, one hand holding the reins and the other resting on his thigh. What made the old man tick?

He shot a glance to Jarret. "Something on your mind?"

Feeling stupid for staring, Jarret shook his head, turned face forward, and spit out a quick, "No. Something on yours?"

"Yup."

Jarret looked again but didn't want to ask.

Papa didn't make him wait. "So you don't want to join that youth group. What do you want to do?"

"Uh, I don't know. Why do I have to do something?"

"You're a senior now. What about after graduation?"

"Uh... college I guess."

"Which one?"

"I dunno. Maybe one in Arizona." He hadn't given it any thought. But if he was gonna go out of state, Arizona would be nice. He'd probably try to make his way back to the canyon.

"Northern Arizona U has a good Archeology program."

"Yeah? I'll have to check it out." Worried he'd just committed himself, Jarret threw a furtive glance at Papa. What was his deal, anyway?

Papa smiled. "Let's do that. We can check it out together when we get home."

Before Jarret could think of an excuse to get out of it, Papa did something even more unpredictable. Jarret's mouth fell open, and he could only stare in shock.

"H'ya!" Papa leaned forward and signaled for his horse to pick up speed. The bay took off from a trot and galloped down the trail.

Desert whinnied and lifted his head, watching the Spanish race away.

"All right, let's give chase. Maybe I can figure out my batty old man." Jarret signaled his horse with a click of his tongue. Then he leaned forward to keep his balance as Desert kicked it into gear. Gripping the reins and moving with the horse's rhythmic flow, he couldn't remember the last time he'd let Desert go so fast. He liked it.

Papa galloped toward the cornfield that butted up against their property, elbows out, gripping the reins, and moving with his horse as if glued to the saddle, not looking inclined to slow the bay.

Jarret urged Desert to go faster, squeezing the horse with his thighs and letting his body absorb the movement of the horse. Gaining on Papa.

Walls of six-foot-high corn stalks rose up on either side of them. The rich, sweet green smell of the cornfield and the breeze from the speed gave Jarret a sense of excitement that battled against his worry over Papa. Papa rode half a field ahead of him.

Shaping Desert's movement, directing his energy, Jarret closed the distance. He let the worry slip away and enjoyed the ride, half hoping Papa would turn down the next row so they could keep going.

Nearing the end of the cornfield, one hand to his Stetson, Papa slowed his horse and wheeled her around. He walked the horse a few paces toward Jarret, a look of pure exhilaration on his face.

Jarret leaned back and used his thighs to slow Desert, a smile sneaking onto his face despite the fact that Papa had either lost his mind or had something big troubling him.

"Well, that was fun," Papa said. "Wanna go again?"

CHAPTER 22

Joy buzzed in Keefe's chest and made him smile as he left the office at River Run High, Wednesday afternoon, and joined the rush of students anxious to leave for the day. It was all coming together now. He had permission from Papa and the school. Why had he ever delayed in asking?

Be not afraid. Pope Saint John Paul II had said that. The Lord had said it too. And from now on, Keefe would take it as his motto. Fear had kept him from too much in his life already, fear of hurting someone's feelings or letting someone down, fear of getting caught when doing the wrong thing, fear of the unknown. No more.

In exactly one week, he'd be sitting behind the wheel of Papa's charcoal gray Ford F-150, heading for St. Paul, Minnesota. Heading for the Franciscan discernment retreat and the beginning of his vocation. More and more, he knew it. He wanted to give it all away and follow Christ in the footsteps of St. Francis. And, unless the retreat shed light on obstacles he hadn't considered, he would come home from it knowing that he'd wear the brown cloth of the Franciscans for the rest of his life. He'd abandon his life wholly into the hands of God.

Keefe turned down the hall that led to his and Jarret's lockers and walked against the current. Tomorrow he'd show his permission slip to his teachers and get the assignments for the day he'd miss.

Halfway down the hall, Jarret stood resting one hand on his open locker door, in high flirt posture, his attention on the blond girl in the frilly shirt and turquoise blue pants—which were more like tights—beside him. Chantelle. They'd been hanging out in the hallway all week long.

Warning signals went off in Keefe, as they had all week. But why? Was he jealous of the attention Chantelle stole that Keefe would've gotten? Keefe might only have one more year at home, one year before he abandoned his fate to God. Was he worried that Jarret might repeat old mistakes? Jarret didn't seem too cautious. He seemed drawn to girls that appeared to have little self-respect.

Chantelle laughed, leaning toward Jarret, her blond hair cascading over her shoulder. Jarret's hand shot toward her arm, but he drew it back and put it on his hip. She grabbed his arm, as if she needed support to stand.

As he approached them, Keefe stuffed his permission slip into his pocket. He'd tell Jarret about it later.

Always seeming to sense when Keefe drew near, Jarret glanced over his shoulder. He gave a nod in greeting, then he straightened and dashed the opposite way down the hallway. Roland had come from around a corner.

While Roland and Jarret stood talking, Keefe went to his own locker. "Hey," he said to Chantelle as he unlocked it.

"Bye." She smiled flirtatiously, tossed her hair, and sauntered away.

Keefe sighed and grabbed his books.

A minute later, Roland's voice came to his ears. "But I just joined a group, and they meet right after school." Roland and Jarret strode toward Keefe.

Surprised by that revelation, Keefe slammed his locker shut and turned to see Roland's expression.

Roland peered up at Jarret, sulking.

"You did what? What group?" Jarret sneered, looking both incredulous and disgusted. "Never mind. I'll take you right back up here. Okay? We won't be that long. We just need to talk."

Roland blinked, a worried look passing over his pale face. No matter how nicely Jarret had treated him these past few weeks, years of abuse had taken their toll. Roland tossed an uncertain glance in Keefe's direction as he approached.

"What's up?" Keefe asked.

"Good, we can go." Jarret glanced at Keefe's books, all businesslike. Not even a smile. "We need to talk. The three of us."

"About?" Roland said.

Jarret glanced from one to the other, his look saying they should know. "Papa."

Roland's features softened and concern colored it now. He must've noticed things too. Maybe he'd even noticed more.

The three of them marched for the doors.

~ ~ ~

No one spoke as Jarret drove them to the park across from St. Michael's church, so Keefe allowed his mind to wander. Papa called a family meeting every now and then, when something big bothered him and he thought everyone needed to talk about it. Now Jarret had called one, well, for everyone except Papa. Keefe had found Papa's behavior strange too, but he hadn't worried frantically over it. Did Jarret have more to go on?

Jarret shut off the engine and glanced at Keefe with a somber expression. He peered at Roland in the rearview mirror before cracking his door open. Jarret in the lead and Keefe walking beside Roland, they strolled toward a big granite boulder in the shadiest part of the park. Little kids liked to climb on it and teens would sit on it. As they neared, little hands appeared on the top of the boulder, then a tiny girl's face popped up. She climbed up a bit more, no doubt wanting to sit on top of it. Her big brown eyes flicked to Jarret, Keefe, and then Roland.

Jarret stopped on the opposite side of the boulder. He jerked his thumb to one side and said in a toneless voice, "Beat it, kid."

Her eyes went wide. She dropped back down and took off running.

Roland watched her run away. "Well, that was mean, scaring that little girl away."

Keefe stifled his own comment, satisfied that Roland had made the point.

A pained look crossed Jarret's face. He stuffed his hand into his hair and jerked it back out, a lock of hair coming loose from his ponytail. "Yeah, whoops." Looking genuinely sorry, he peered in the direction in which the girl had run.

"Don't worry about it now." Keefe was proud of Jarret even though he'd made a mistake. At least he cared after the fact. He never would've cared before.

Jarret leaned his butt against the granite boulder and hung his thumbs in his belt loops. "Okay, so something's up with Papa, and we all know it."

Stepping closer, Keefe nodded and folded his arms across his chest. He liked that Jarret had taken the lead, because he hadn't decided if they should discuss it or let Papa keep it private. Maybe Papa was going through a stage. Wasn't he too old for a mid-life crisis?

Hands in the front pockets of his gray jeans, Roland remained at a bit of a distance. "What makes you think that?"

"You haven't noticed?" Jarret pushed off the boulder and strutted up to him, a bit of his old attitude showing.

Roland shrugged and averted his gaze.

"So you don't think nothing about that dinner on Friday?" Jarret said. "And Papa's bucket list?"

"Bucket list?" Keefe stepped up to them, the three of them now in a tight circle. "He just wants to do things with us."

Shaking his head emphatically, Jarret looked from Roland to Keefe. "Yesterday, while you both were out with Fire Starters, he barged into my room to talk."

"What about?" Offended that Jarret hadn't told him sooner, Keefe gave Jarret a shove.

"What? You were praying or something in your room this morning, so I couldn't talk to you."

"If you weren't always with Chantelle between classes, you could've talked to me anytime today."

"Jealous?" Jarret smirked.

Roland angled his body toward Jarret and propped his hands on his hips. "Okay, so why don't you tell us what Papa said?"

Jarret gave him the once-over and grinned. He always seemed to like when Roland did something the slightest bit brave, like standing up to him. "Well, Roland," he said, emphasizing his name, "he wanted to know why I don't belong to the Catholic youth group."

"So why don't you?"

"Really? You've ridden in my car, smelled the fresh air. You really telling me that you don't know?" He turned the challenge back on Roland.

Roland rolled his eyes and shook his head, then he stepped back.

Jarret moved closer, locking eyes with him. "Then Papa wanted to know what I've been up to and what I plan to do with my life."

"So what'd you tell him?" Keefe asked, mostly to get Jarret to back away from Roland.

Redirecting his attention to Keefe, Jarret's expression showed an uncharacteristic look of uncertainty. "I told him college, just to have an answer, maybe Arizona. He said Northern Arizona U has a good Archeology program, as if I'd said I was interested in that. Then later he wanted to look it up on my laptop." Jarret shifted uncomfortably and dropped his gaze to the flowery landscaping near the boulder.

"Together?"

"Yeah, together, side by side, looking it up on my laptop."

"You got things on there you don't want him to see?" Keefe said, not sure he should've asked in front of Roland.

Jarret opened his mouth, his gaze sliding to Roland and back to Keefe. "That's what he said when I protested." He gave a crooked smile, stooped, and picked a purple bloom from among a group of purple, yellow, and orange Chrysanthemums. Roland gave him a disapproving glare. "But no... I ain't got nothing bad on there anymore. I'm reformed."

Keefe took a breath and released it, relieved at his answer. "It's my fault Papa asked you that anyway."

"You?"

"Probably. I finally told him what I wanted to do with my life, that I want to join the Franciscans."

Roland smiled. "You did?"

"Yeah." Keefe smiled back, appreciating that Roland seemed truly pleased. "What about you? What're your plans?"

Roland shrugged, clamming up again. "I'm only in tenth grade. I have plenty of time to figure that out."

"Still, you should have an idea."

"I do have an idea."

"Well, what is it?"

Roland shrugged.

"Come on. *I* told you." He didn't understand Roland's secretiveness. Why couldn't he share his dreams and goals with his brothers?

"Wow, you're a couple of babies." Then Jarret whined, "'You tell me 'cuz I told you.'" And he shook his head, glaring at his brothers. "We got something serious to talk about here."

Jarret paced back and forth, twirling the flower between his fingers. "I didn't even tell you the thing that really has me worried." He stood with his back to them. Then he spun to Keefe. "You tell Roland what you overheard first."

"Okay..." Keefe stared at Roland, wondering what the things he'd heard meant in the long run. "I heard Papa turn down an assignment, said he wasn't planning on going anywhere for a long while. Like years. Another day, I overheard him talking to Miss Meadows. She wanted his help for something, I think. But he said no. He said she could visit if she wanted, but he was staying put."

Roland blinked a few times, probably processing it or comparing it to things only he knew.

"What about you?" Jarret studied Roland's non-verbal response. "You must've noticed things."

"Yeah, I don't know." Roland shifted his weight from one foot to the other. "He's just around all the time now, which I like. But you're right, that's not him. And when did he start smoking cigarettes?"

Jarret threw a glance, looking guilty. "That could be my fault. I'm not really worried about that."

"So what *has* got you worried?" Keefe asked.

Staring into the purple flower, Jarret hesitated. "After he came to talk to me, he wanted to go horseback riding. So we headed toward the back of the property, and Papa went all Buffalo Bill on me, took off galloping straight back through the neighbor's cornfield."

Not knowing what to say, Keefe stared.

Jarret continued. "Papa's weird behavior, adding it all up, I keep coming up with the same answer."

"Which is?" Keefe said, though he'd guessed Jarret's conclusion already.

"Papa's dying."

Roland's eyes watered and he turned away.

Keefe grabbed Jarret's arm. "We don't know that. It could be any number of things. Has he even been to a doctor? I think we'd know. Maybe he's having a midlife crisis or something." His suggestion didn't seem likely, given Papa's behavior, but he wanted some other possibility out there.

"Did you look at those bills you brought in the other day?" Jarret said. "Some of those were doctor bills."

"Probably for Roland," Keefe said.

"How's your leg without the cast anyway?" Jarret said to Roland.

"Good." Roland's sulky look returned, his gray eyes glistening in the light that filtered through the leaves.

"Good." Jarret continued to stare at him.

"So how are we going to find out?" Keefe said, still holding onto hope.

"I dunno. We could wait until he's out or distracted. Or maybe one of us could go horseback riding with him, and then we could dig around in his office."

Keefe huffed, annoyed at the suggestion. "Not a good idea."

"Why?" Jarret said.

"Why don't we just talk to him?" Roland said.

"Okay, you can talk to him," Jarret snapped.

"Me?" Something in his shocked and pouty expression made him look five years younger.

"Why don't we all talk to him?" Keefe said. "Let's do it on the weekend. Saturday morning. Family meeting."

"Deal." Jarret took off, striding toward the little girl he'd scared from the boulder. She sat curled up beside her mother on a bench, probably waiting for them to leave so she could play on the boulder again.

"What's he up to?" Roland said to Keefe.

Jarret handed the purple flower to the girl and mumbled something to her. Then he headed for the parking lot.

Keefe smiled, proud of Jarret. He turned his attention to Roland as they strolled side by side to the car. "So what club did you join?"

"I don't want to say."

Keefe would've pried but other thoughts tangled in his mind. If Papa were dying, would he tell them?

CHAPTER 23

A debate going on his mind, Jarret strutted down the hallway toward his World Literature class. Should he or shouldn't he ask Chantelle out? Since he'd come back to school, they found each other in the halls three times a day, ate lunch together, and sat next to each other in World Literature. She'd been there for him. She was the first person who reached out to him when he got suspended from school. Second person, actually. Keefe was always the first.

A blur of dull blond hair and a familiar goofy laugh caught Jarret's attention. *Peter Brandt.*

All other thoughts receding, he slowed and glanced in the direction of the laugh, down a side hall. He glimpsed Peter standing with Roland, Phoebe, and Caitlyn outside a classroom, but then a kid coming down the hall blocked his view. The kid, a junior on the football team—Chantelle's brother Tyrone?—shifted his gaze to Jarret as he strode past, a hard look in his eyes. Then Brandt was back in Jarret's view.

Jarret's jaw clenched, and he came to a standstill. Lucky for Peter, Jarret hadn't seen him in the halls since school started, well, not since he'd come back from his week of suspension. If they stood closer now, like in the same hallway and not twenty feet apart, this would be a bad day for Peter. But Jarret wouldn't go out of his way for payback. He had more self-control than that. Right? Right.

Jarret took a breath and walked on, proud of his accomplishment, his glimmer of self-control. He crossed paths with C.W. at least once a day, not counting the Spanish class they shared. They gave each other ugly looks as they passed but that was it. C.W.'s bruised nose reminded Jarret of his failure, but he'd never let on that he felt the slightest bit of remorse. Yesterday Jarret had gotten a strange sensation inside, making him think he owed C.W. an apology. Did he? Could he even get himself to apologize?

Jarret steeled his mind, discarding the stray and unreasonable thought. C.W. owed Roland an apology. And anyway, as much as C.W. bothered him, Peter irked him more, mostly because of what he'd done to Jarret's car. How was he ever gonna get over that?

Reality slammed Jarret hard and he stopped paying attention to his surroundings for a moment, his mind sifting through potential scenarios. If he took Chantelle on a date, they'd go in his Chrysler 300.

"What's that horrible smell?" she'd demand, her face crinkling up. What would she think it was? A dead animal? Maybe she'd attribute it to him and say nothing. She'd think he stank. She'd tell her friends.

The possibilities gnawed at him, making his free hand curl into a fist. Jarret would have to explain the odor. He'd have to talk about Peter, and then he'd just want to rip Peter's head off even more than he did now.

Snapping back to the present, Jarret swerved around a group of kids that he noticed at the last minute. His mind drifted back to Chantelle. So was he going to do it? Was he really going to ask her out and get into another relationship with a girl? Was he ready? What was the worst that could happen?

He shuddered. He knew the worst that could happen. He'd be unable to control his impulses. He'd use her. She'd get pregnant.

Maybe she wouldn't even tell him. And if she didn't want the baby… maybe she'd…

He tensed, determined. No way in hell was he going to let that happen. No way in *hell*? What did that saying mean anyway? If he treated her the way he'd treated Zoe, he'd be choosing sin, he'd be cruising down the wide and easy road that led to hell. Father Carston once said that more souls went to hell for "sins of the flesh" than for any other reason.

Jarret turned down the next hall, glimpsed Chantelle, and smiled inside.

Dressed in a flowing pastel pink shirt and dark jeans with jewels down one leg, Chantelle stood in their spot along the lockers outside the World Literature classroom. She wore her hair the same way every day, loose blond curls falling around her shoulders.

Her eyes lit up, and she smiled as he drew near.

"Hey." He stopped and stood squarely in front of her, instead of leaning against the lockers like he usually did.

She narrowed her eyes, giving him a playful, suspicious look. "What's up with you?"

Not ready to ask her yet, he shook his head but couldn't suppress the sly grin that showed he was up to something.

"Did you write your essay?" She tilted her chin in a flirtatious way.

"Of course. We got the assignment last week." Having little else to do, he'd thrown himself into schoolwork, reading chapters, taking quizzes the teachers emailed him, and writing essays. It wasn't as bad as he thought it would be. He actually looked forward to finding out his grades. He hadn't cared last year.

"Oh, rip, that's right." Kyle came up behind Jarret, fumbling through a folder. He looked up, the whites of his eyes showing all around his hazel irises. His freckled face turned a strange shade of pink that didn't jibe with his coppery orange hair. "Essay… I wonder if I can write something real quick." He shuffled past Jarret and into the classroom.

Jarret and Chantelle laughed.

"You finish yours?" Jarret decided to use it as a lead up to asking her out. Butterflies started in his chest. Was he ready for this? There was that wall again too, standing between him and the question. But the question was working its way out, pushing through the wall, and he doubted he could stop it. Why shouldn't he be ready? He knew where to draw the line now, knew how to respect a girl. And himself. He was not going to let things happen that shouldn't. He could handle this.

She brushed a stray lock of hair from her face. "Of course. I finished it in study hall and printed it off in the library."

"Good. And you don't have cheerleader practice, so you're free tonight."

She lowered her books and wiggled her shoulders playfully, leaning towards him. "Free for what?"

Her closeness made his pulse race. He clenched his jaw to keep from trying to kiss her right there in the hallway. He wasn't going to kiss her on their date either... if she'd even go out with him. Of course she'd say yes. He just needed to ask her. What was he waiting for?

He tried to take a deep breath without it being obvious. "Let's do something. Get burgers or pizza. Whatever you want." Why had he suggested burgers or pizza? Maybe it seemed more casual. Less serious.

"Sure." She batted her eyes and gave him a sweet smile. "Is this a date?"

He smiled back, liking how she looked at him. "Do you want it to be?"

"Hmm..." She drew back and tapped her chin. "I'll have to think about it."

A hint of indignation threatened his mood, a dent to his ego. Even though he knew she meant it as a joke, he still replied with, "Don't take too long, or I'll ask someone else."

She opened her mouth as if pretending to be shocked and smacked his arm.

He smiled, pleased with her reaction.

"Actually..." Casting playfulness aside, she bit her lip and her brows crept together. "I'm going for ice cream with the other cheerleaders tonight."

He blinked a few times. Speechless. It had to happen sooner or later, a girl telling him no.

"But I'd..." She batted her eyelashes again, her expression sweetening. "I'd love it if you came too, if you drove me."

"Oh." Would he be the only guy? Him out with a bunch of cheerleaders. He couldn't help but grin, thinking about it.

"Maybe you can take me home after school and we can go up there together. Everyone's meeting at four."

He hesitated. Her house? That could mean trouble. "No, I gotta take my brothers home. I'll pick you up at ten to four."

~ ~ ~

Jarret scooted into the library as the bell rang, earning a scowl from the librarian at the reference desk. He smiled at her anyways. Then he scanned tables of about a dozen kids until he saw his short-haired, glasses-wearing lookalike. Pen in one hand, Keefe sat hunched over an open notebook, alone at the table nearest to the bookshelves.

Still floating like a helium balloon about seeing Chantelle tonight, he dropped into the chair opposite Keefe and slid his books onto the table.

Keefe glanced up and gave Jarret the once-over, probably evaluating his mood.

"So I did it." Jarret grinned. He hadn't told Keefe that he'd planned to ask Chantelle out, but he still didn't feel the need to explain. Keefe always had him figured out. Of course, he might've put two and two together this morning when Jarret had changed his shirt twice and spent extra time slicking up in the bathroom.

Keefe grinned back. "What'd she say?"

Jarret turned a palm up and huffed. "What do you think?"

Keefe dropped his pen and gave Jarret a fist bump, but his eyes showed a hint of reservation. Staring at Jarret, he picked up and played with his pen. "So you really like her, huh?"

A bit of helium seeped from Jarret's mood, reality taking its place. Was Keefe worried about where this would lead?

Jarret shrugged. "It won't get serious."

Keefe's look showed something else now, the slightest nod, a flicker of respect. No one else would pick up on it. No one but Jarret.

Jarret had to shift his gaze before his eyes watered. Keefe believed in him.

Once Keefe had turned back to his studies, Jarret looked at him again. A brown cord peeked out through the v-neck of his shirt. The scapular? Did he wear it every day? Maybe it reminded him, like his haircut did, of the person he wanted to be or the promises he'd made to God.

Keefe had truly changed. Jarret winced, thinking how Keefe had followed and obeyed him for years, most likely ignoring his own conscience. But he'd always leaned toward goodness. So he'd always tried reasoning with Jarret. And he'd swayed him often but not all the time. Now Keefe followed no man. He followed his conscience and God. Keefe would still try reasoning with him, Jarret knew, but he must've sensed that he didn't need to now.

"Hey." An idea popping into his head, Jarret tapped Keefe's notebook with his pen. "Wanna come with me?"

Keefe took a second to reply. "On your date?"

"Yeah. It's not really a date. She's meeting the other cheerleaders for ice cream. We're all just hanging out."

Another second and a crooked grin. "You and all the cheerleaders?"

Jarret shrugged, totally liking the sound of that. "And you. And I don't know who else. Maybe some of their boyfriends."

"I don't know." His grin faded. "You know where my heart is."

"Yeah, I know. And I'm not trying to change that. I just thought..." He didn't know how to finish his sentence. What did he think? He needed a babysitter? A chaperone?

A sound from a nearby bookshelf caught Jarret's attention.

A bulky kid with short sandy hair and bad posture slid a book off the shelf and cracked it open. His oversized jeans had the imprint of a cellphone on the back pocket. He turned a page, then his eyes swiveled to Jarret.

Jarret recognized him even though they'd never met. Chantelle's brother, Tyrone, a junior on the football team.

Tyrone pointed at Jarret and then gestured for him to come over with a jerk of his hand, an insistent, demanding motion.

A smirk slithered onto Jarret's face, recognizing the attitude, but he pushed his chair back and sauntered over. Bookshelves hid them from everyone but Keefe.

"What's up, Tyrone?" Jarret asked in a low voice.

"So you know I'm Chantelle's brother?" Tyrone stood a hair taller than Jarret but the tilt of his big chin exaggerated the difference. Still, he was a much bigger dude than Jarret, more meat than muscle maybe. But the squint of his hazel eyes showed he was ticked off.

Jarret raised his brows and nodded.

"So you're going out with my sister?" While heavy with disapproval, his tone held a note of vulnerability. His sister was older than he was. Jarret was older too. What could he do about it?

"Got a problem with that?" Jarret said in a cool tone, doing his best to appear unfazed though it ruffled him a bit. He knew why Tyrone cared, why any boy would worry about Jarret dating his sister. Everyone knew what had happened to Jarret's last girlfriend.

Eyes locked on Jarret, Tyrone's neck and cheeks flushed. His fingers tightened around the book. He was probably mustering every bit of strength he had to keep himself under control. It would be a different story if they were out in the parking lot. Jarret might not fare so well.

"Look..." Jarret eased the book from Tyrone and placed it on the shelf.

Tyrone sucked in a breath and seemed to hold it.

"I get that you're worried," Jarret said, "but you can chill. I'll respect your sister in every way." He cringed, hearing his father's words come out of his mouth. *"You better be respecting your girlfriend," Papa had told him last year, referring to Zoe.*

"You'd better." Tyrone jabbed Jarret in the chest and kept his finger there.

Jarret forced a level of calm and self-control that he didn't think he had in him.

"Because if I find out that you're..." He pinched his lips together. "If she ends up like your last girlfriend..." He squeezed his lips shut again.

"Message taken." Keeping his own attitude in check, Jarret held his gaze. He deserved this and would not hold it against Tyrone in the least.

Another jab. "If you do anything to her, I'm coming after you."

Wanting to show that he was worth his promise, Jarret raised his hands and tried to look sincere. "I got it."

Tyrone withdrew his finger from Jarret's chest, yanked a book from the shelf, and dropped it. It slammed to the floor at Jarret's feet with a noise that would've made him jump if he hadn't seen it happen.

Jarret watched Tyrone lumber away, then he stooped for the book. The title caught his eye as he returned it to the shelf: *Weapons of War, from the age of hand-to-hand fighting.*

CHAPTER 24

"There. Is that her?" Keefe tapped the front passenger-side window, pointing to the blond on the front porch of a white French colonial. The house sat on a wide, well-manicured lot. Black address numbers hung over a black mailbox, the address Jarret had told Keefe to watch out for.

"Huh?" Jarret slowed his Chrysler and peered out Keefe's window. "Uh, yeah." He stepped on the brakes, Keefe jerking forward, then he backed up and swung into the driveway.

They were late. They'd left the house with just enough time to drive to hers. Keefe had advised Jarret to leave a bit early, but then Jarret decided to change his shirt. Then he changed again. Then he put the shirt he'd worn to school back on. It was an edgy button-front Rock & Republic plaid that looked good on him. He'd probably changed back to avoid appearing overly concerned about his appearance. Even though he was.

They still might've gotten to her house on time. But Jarret had turned the wrong way down her street and hadn't realized it for several blocks. If Keefe hadn't been so lost in thought...

Shifting the Chrysler to park, Jarret glanced at Keefe. "So we're five minutes late, so what?"

Keefe shrugged and swung open the car door.

An old-fashioned wheelbarrow overflowing with flowers sat on one side of the porch, Chantelle on the other. She got up from a green bench. A shadowy figure showed through the half-open drapes, someone pacing in the living room.

Hair pulled back into a loose ponytail, Chantelle bounced down the porch steps. She wore a summer dress with a lacy sweater.

"Hey, Chantelle." Keefe smiled, trying not to show the reservation he felt about this evening. He didn't want any of her cheerleader friends thinking of him as boyfriend material.

Leaving the radio on and car running, Jarret sauntered around the Chrysler a bit too late to be a gentleman. Chantelle already had one hand on the open front passenger door.

"I didn't know you were coming," she said to Keefe over the car door.

"Oh?" Keefe glanced at Jarret.

Jarret shrugged. He probably hadn't thought of it as an issue.

"It's okay, right?" Keefe grabbed the top of the passenger door, ready to close it for her.

"Sure. All you West boys can come. The more the merrier." She slid into the front passenger seat.

Before Keefe closed the door for her, the screen door creaked open and her brother, Tyrone, stepped outside. "Don't be coming home later than you said," he hollered to Chantelle. Then he threw a threatening glare at Jarret and propped a hand on a porch post, flexing his bicep as he did it.

Jarret saluted him with two fingers to his forehead, his expression a mix of amusement and attitude. Then he got back in the Chrysler, and Keefe slid into the backseat.

Cranking the key in the ignition, Jarret threw Keefe a worried glance through the rearview mirror and inhaled. He must've been hoping the "new car smell" air freshener would do the job. They'd picked it up after school, leaving Roland to wait in the car. Right there in the parking lot, they'd sprayed it under the seats—especially where he'd found the Limburger cheese—and in the vents. Roland claimed he couldn't breathe and had insisted that they drive with the windows down. Jarret liked the idea and had left them open ever since.

"You look nice." Jarret shifted into reverse.

"Thanks." She played with a curl that hung free from her ponytail. "Hey, is it okay if we put the windows up?"

Jarret's mouth fell open. He exchanged glances with Keefe in the rearview window, then backed out of the driveway. "I like the wind."

Keefe suppressed a grin. How long before Jarret gets fed up and trades his smelly car in?

"My hair will be all over my face," she said. "Please." She stuck her bottom lip out and batted her eyes. Jarret was a sucker for a pouty face.

~ ~ ~

Keefe played with the peanut butter chocolate ice cream in his cup, his attention given to the girl across from him in the booth: Rachel, Chantelle's best friend and also a cheerleader. She liked horseback riding, though she didn't own a horse. And she belonged to the Junior Shooters club.

"...and if I ever get one of my own, I'd want it to be a Pinto."

"What colors?"

"Well, aren't they always brown and white?"

The shy smile she gave before answering questions appealed to Keefe more than he cared to admit. It stirred something inside him. "No. They can be any colors."

She smiled again, her gaze flitting between him and her ice cream.

He smiled back. Talking with her came easy. They'd started talking with each other immediately after getting their ice cream and sliding across from each other into the booth. First, they'd exchanged little comments about ice cream and basketball, then they

195

moved into more personal topics like what they did over the summer.

"Invite her over for a ride," Jarret whispered, leaning into Keefe. He sat next to Keefe and across from Chantelle, in an outside seat of the booth.

Keefe bumped his leg into Jarret's under the table, warning him.

Jarret smiled and shifted his gaze to the group that had come with them to the ice cream shop. Ten other cheerleaders and two boys sat at other booths and purplish tables, all of them talking over each other and goofing off, acting like they owned the place.

Keefe could tell from his brother's pleasant expression that he was enjoying himself. Maybe it was the ratio of three girls to every boy, or the playful attitude of the group, or the way Chantelle flirted with him. Keefe couldn't remember the last time Jarret had seemed so happy.

"So how do you like being a twin?" Rachel smiled at Keefe.

"Ask me when he's not around," Keefe teased, tossing a glance at Jarret.

Jarret rammed his shoulder into Keefe's. "He loves it. He especially loves the idea of double dating."

Keefe's face burned. Okay, so Jarret was teasing back. *He* probably liked the idea of double dating. It would help him stay out of trouble. But he knew what Keefe wanted. Did he think a pretty girl would have Keefe changing his mind?

Jarret turned his attention back to Chantelle. "You and your friends go out a lot?" Jarret tipped his head in the direction of the loudest group of girls.

"Sort of." Chantelle stirred the melted remains of her rainbow sherbet. "Not always here. Sometimes the coffee shop. Or the park if the weather's good."

"Did someone say park?" a loudmouthed girl said. Keefe had yet to learn all their names.

"Yeah, let's go to the park," another girl said, this one with mousy brown hair and a peppy bounce in her every move. "We can power walk around the trail."

"You think you can work off your ice cream?" another asked with a laugh.

The three of them got into it, laughing and exchanging banter with one another.

Jarret watched them for a moment, looking amused and a bit contemplative.

"Okay, let's do it. To the park." Chantelle grabbed Jarret's and Keefe's ice cream dishes and carried them to the garbage can.

Jarret shifted his attention to Keefe. "Want to?"

Keefe's mind went blank, his gaze sliding to Rachel and back to Jarret. He liked her. He really did. A part of him wanted to keep talking, to talk all night, to get to know her and discover what else they had in common.

His heart beat so hard that he could feel it thumping in his chest. Could a girl change his mind? After thinking all this time that God had been calling him to a vocation, would he give it all up for a girl?

Jarret and Rachel stared at him, waiting for his answer.

Keefe ran a hand through his hair, momentarily remembering when he'd worn it long like Jarret's. "What park, the one across from St. Michael's?"

"Yeah, probably. It's just a couple blocks away."

"Sounds fun, don't you think?" Rachel gave Keefe a shy smile.

Indecision surged through him, his mouth wrapping around the first word of his reply. He shot Jarret a silent plea for help.

"He's got something to do," Jarret said. "Maybe he'll catch up with us."

Slouching back with relief, he nodded. "Yeah, I need to stop by... somewhere."

The flicker of Jarret's eyes said he realized that "somewhere" meant the church. "You walking?" He slid out of the booth.

"Uh. Sure." Expecting a ride, Keefe couldn't stop his face from screwing up.

He and Rachel slid out of the booth next, at the same time.

"See you." Rachel gave him a long look.

"Yeah, see you." He watched her walk away.

While everyone converged on the doors, including Chantelle and Rachel, Jarret and Keefe lagged behind.

"I can take you," Jarret said. "Just thought you'd rather walk. I'm about to offer a ride to whoever wants it. Your girlfriend there might take me up on it."

Keefe sighed, releasing tension. At least Jarret was looking out for him. "Yeah, I'll walk. It's only a couple blocks away."

"Okay, then catch up with us at the park later."

Keefe nodded and caught the glass door before it swung shut.

~ ~ ~

Turning off the main road that the ice cream store was on, Keefe strolled down a residential street with tiny houses and no sidewalks. A gentle breeze blew, comfortable weather that lifted his soul to the fluffy white clouds that filled the evening sky.

He imagined himself walking with Rachel. Holding her hand. If he had gone, they would've probably walked around the park together or stood talking under a tree. They'd get to know each other better. What if he liked her and she liked him?

Two preschoolers played in a front yard, a boy chasing a squealing girl.

Was he really going to give up girls for the rest of his life? He'd never even kissed a girl. Give up marriage and family? He'd never have children. Could he live with that? Did he want that? Was he seeking to close himself off from others, to make his life empty, centered only on himself?

Peace reigned in Keefe's soul as he thought about it. No, he didn't want to close himself off from anyone. He wasn't trying to get away from his family or to avoid girls and marriage. And he didn't see it as giving up anything—girls, marriage, a nice house, career, or car. He saw it as giving it all to God. Not divided. All in. That's what he wanted.

Keefe's pace quickened as he strode down a slope. His heart stirred in its depths. He wanted to love God above all else. He longed for total love, to love with all his heart, soul, and strength. He wanted an undivided love that pours itself out for the beloved, empties itself, giving till it hurts even, giving until death.

But where did God want him? He knew in his heart that in God's will alone would he find happiness.

CHAPTER 25

Jarret had driven four cheerleaders in his Chrysler 300, Chantelle in the front and Rachel and two other girls in the back. They chattered and giggled all the way to the park. Good thing it was only a few blocks. Girls sure could get silly when they got together.

An elderly couple crossed Jarret and Chantelle's path, strolling along the trail that circled around the park. Several people walked dogs. Children's voices traveled from the playground partially visible between trees. Three cheerleaders and one boy moseyed toward a bench, deep in conversation. The rest of the group took off around the trail, speed walking. Or power walking. Whatever they called it.

Jarret and Chantelle strolled through the grass toward an aspen tree with yellow leaves and a white trunk. Their hands bumped once, then again. Chantelle's aqua blue eyes caught a beam of sunlight as she glanced at him. She'd removed the hair fastener and let her blond curls fall freely down her back and shoulders, over her lacy sweater.

"We're all going camping this year, on that annual fall camping trip. Are you?"

Jarret's heart slammed into his throat and landed back in place with a thud. "No. Absolutely not."

"Oh, why not?"

They weaved around trees, slowing their pace.

"Not my thing. I gave it a chance last year." He glanced at St. Michael's Church across the street and rubbed his stubbly jaw, trying not to think about it. "It didn't work out so well." She wouldn't know his real reason, and he had no intention of telling her. She only needed to know he absolutely was not going.

"Oh, that's too bad."

They walked a few minutes in silence, his heart settling down and his thoughts evening out.

"Let's go on a real date."

Jarret's heart moved again, a strange fluttery sensation that came a bit from flattery but more from caution. Did she just ask him out? He couldn't let their relationship move too fast. He needed to set the pace. Not her.

"This isn't a real date?" He bumped her hand on purpose this time, then grabbed it, holding it for the first time. Soft, warm, real... Such a little thing felt like such a big step.

At his touch she came alive, bouncing to a stop and facing him. "A real date means just the two of us."

"Oh." So group outings wouldn't satisfy her? Back at the ice cream shop, he'd been thinking they could get to know each other by hanging out with her friends after school. They'd never be alone, so he'd never get himself into trouble. He could have a girlfriend without crossing lines he shouldn't.

But to her a date meant just the two of them... How could he accommodate that? They absolutely would not, could not, go to each other's houses. Unless one of their parents invited them over, wanting to meet them. Not Jarret's house though. Papa gave him too much space, too much privacy. He could talk to Papa about that. Nah, that'd be a weird conversation.

If he and Chantelle started to get serious, they'd need to set a few rules or something. What about double dating... Or maybe he'd just decide the when and where, and keep it somewhere public like... "Wanna see a movie?"

She swung their hands, smiling up at him. "I'd love to. When?"

"I dunno." He and his brothers planned on talking to Papa this weekend. So not then. Was he ready for this? Yes, he could make this work. He would stay in control. "How about next weekend?"

Her smile turned into a frown, and she squeezed his hand. "But I'm going camping."

"Oh yeah."

"I wish I could talk you into going."

He shook his head slowly, telling her with his eyes that it would never happen. "We'll see a movie the day before you go. Thursday."

"Next Thursday?" She tapped her chin and gazed upward. Then she beamed a smile and swung their hands. "Okay."

~ ~ ~

An hour later, an orange sun sank between groups of trees along the horizon, streetlights blinked on, and shadows spread through the square. The park closed at sunset so everyone except for their group had gone. And now most of their group, including Chantelle, stood together near the parking spaces, talking about school and the upcoming camping trip.

Jarret leaned against a tree, sending a text to Keefe. *We're ready to go. Where are you?*

Chantelle glanced over her shoulder in Jarret's direction, shadows hiding her expression.

Lifting his index finger, he signaled for her to wait.

Keefe's message popped onto Jarret's phone. *Can you drop her off and come back for me?*

Jarret huffed and clenched his jaw. It didn't really matter though, did it? He could just pull up to the driveway and let her out, tell her he had to pick up Keefe next. Or what difference would it make if he walked her to the door and bolted back to his car? She hadn't considered it a real date, so she wouldn't be expecting a kiss. And even if he did kiss her, he could keep it simple.

Jarret messaged back, *Guess so. See you in ten.*

Their group had thinned, leaving Chantelle, two other girls, and one guy standing on the sidewalk. Two cars backed out at the same time, then Chantelle said her goodbyes to the remaining three before bouncing up to Jarret. "Are you taking me home or do I need to hitch a ride?" She propped her hands on her hips and tilted her head.

"I gotcha." He pushed off the tree, grabbed her hand, and led her to the car.

Windows up to keep her hair from blowing in her face, Jarret took the quickest route to her house. The whole way, she talked about the movies she wanted to see, never seeming to notice the smell.

Jarret slowed as he neared the driveway. Drop her at the driveway or walk her to the door? He sighed and stepped on the gas, swinging the car into the driveway. He didn't need to be scrupulous, right? He had more self-control than he gave himself credit for. He'd seen Peter in the hallway and not pummeled him, right? And he'd reacted calmly when Tyrone threatened him in the library. He had this under control.

Leaving the engine running, Jarret swung open the driver-side door. Chantelle got out at the same time. Somewhere inside, he liked the idea of opening a girl's door for her. Did that make him a chauvinist?

She waited for him to come around the car. Then she looped her arm through his, took one step, and glanced over her shoulder at his Chrysler. "Why didn't you shut off your car?"

"I gotta take off." He nudged her forward, toward the porch steps. "I'll see you at school tomorrow."

She stopped at the foot of the porch steps, slipped her arm from his, and faced him. "I thought you could come in for a while."

His heart skipped a beat. "Nah, I gotta run back and pick up Keefe."

"Do you have to get him right away?"

"I—" Did he have to get him right away? *Yes. Yes. Don't even think about it.*

"My parents aren't home."

A flurry of images assailed him, none of them good. For the second time that evening, he forced himself to say no. He smiled and gave her a look that said he appreciated the offer. What exactly was she offering? Would he face this temptation every time he took her out? How long could he resist?

He backed up a few steps, then blurted out, "See ya," and hoofed it to his car.

She was still standing by the porch steps as he tore out of the driveway, shifted into drive, and squealed down the road.

Man, what had he gotten himself into? One invitation from her, and he found his will power crumbling apart.

Jarret raced back to the square and pulled up in front of the wide steps of St. Michael's church. Frustrated with himself, he wrestled his phone from his back pocket and scrolled through phone numbers. He put the phone to his ear and whispered, "Don't answer. Don't answer."

But on the third ring, someone picked up. "This is Father Carston."

Head growing light, Jarret sucked in a breath and exhaled hard. "Uh, hey, Father, it's Jarret."

"Oh, hello, Jarret. Everything okay?"

Jarret should've made this call a long time ago. Father had suggested they meet every week.

"Still there?" Father said.

"Huh? Yeah, I, um, I'm calling to reschedule our appointment. I need to see you."

"Sure, let me check my calendar." He paused. "How does this Saturday sound, say 2:30?"

"This Saturday?" Maybe he could tell Father he was right outside. Maybe Father could see him now. Jarret took a breath. He didn't need to rush it. He'd see Father in two days, almost a week before his date. "Sure, see ya then."

Jarret ended the call and rested his head back, sifting through his plans to make sure that day and time would work. He'd answered without thinking about it.

A pounding on the passenger side window jerked Jarret from his thoughts and made his heart flipflop again.

"Are you going to let me in?" Keefe peeked in the closed window.

CHAPTER 26

Six days before the Franciscan retreat... Anxious to get to the prayer corner in his bedroom, Keefe strode beside Roland from the garage and through the house. Father Carston had said something to the Fire Starters tonight about praying for God's will and Keefe had thought of little else. Father had meant for them to pray about something in particular, something about the weather and the camping trip. A storm headed this way? But Keefe had other intentions in mind and he'd spent the rest of their Friday meeting in a half-distracted state.

"I can't believe Papa's going camping this year. Too bad you can't go," Roland said as they strolled around the corner to the family room.

All the drapes hung open, even though the sun had gone down an hour ago, and lamps reflected their yellowy light on a few dark windows. The TV glowed, an old movie showing on the screen. No one around to watch it.

"Yeah, I missed going last year. And if I join the Franciscans after graduation, I'll miss it next year too."

"This would've been your last chance." Roland gave a lingering look, then his gaze shifted to the old western on the TV. "Everything you do will be for the last time."

"What?" Keefe gave him a funny look, a bit surprised by the sentimental tone.

Roland stopped at the swinging doors to the great room and met his gaze. "If you leave after graduation, this will be your last fall with the family."

"Oh, right." He loved horseback riding in the fall, colorful leaves above them, a carpet of leaves below, a campfire smell in the air. As a friar, would he ever ride a horse again? A sentimental mood now teased Keefe's soul.

"Last Thanksgiving, last Christmas, last everything."

"I never thought of that." It saddened him but also stirred a sense of adventure. Doors would close. Other doors would open.

Roland lifted a hand to the swinging doors and stopped. "Could that be how Papa's feeling about things? I mean if Jarret's right and he's really..." He gave a little head shake, unable to complete the sentence.

Keefe couldn't complete it either. He didn't want it to be true. "Maybe."

Roland finally pushed open the doors. Papa's voice carried from the kitchen. "...that chicken potpie you make and that one salad, uh..."

"You mean with the romaine lettuce, I believe." Nanny's voice. "Very well, I'll put that down for Monday."

As they rounded the corner, Keefe's gaze snapped to the bright kitchen doorway, though he couldn't see Papa and Nanny from the far end of the hallway.

Then a whispered voice snagged his attention. "Hey."

Across from the kitchen doorway, Jarret peeked from the staircase into the hall, his head sticking around the corner. With an agitated jerk of his hand, he motioned them over.

Roland and Keefe exchanged a glance and walked to the stairs, careful to make little noise.

"What's up?" Keefe whispered.

Jarret's gaze flicked to the kitchen, where Papa and Nanny continued to discuss meals. "It's conference time." He stomped up the stairs in his bare feet.

Keefe and Roland thumped after him and followed him into Jarret's bedroom.

Jarret closed the door behind them and paced across his room toward the drawn drapes. Roland approached Jarret's bed, looked like he might sit down, then sank his hands into the front pockets of his jeans instead.

Keefe remained just inside the door, standing near the dresser. He glimpsed the brown scapular he'd given Jarret, his heart sinking a bit, wishing Jarret would wear it. "So, what's the matter?"

Pacing toward him, Jarret placed his hands on his hips. Then he stopped in the middle of the room. "Did you hear Papa down there? He's telling Nanny everything he wants her to cook."

"So?" Keefe said.

"So have you ever known Papa to care what he eats? Nanny always asks him and he says..."

"Whatever you have a mind to make," Jarret and Roland said together.

"So you're thinking what?" Keefe glanced at the scapular again.

Jarret followed his gaze. "Don't worry about the scapular. I haven't looked it up." Then his gaze shot to the ceiling, and he shoved a hand in his hair. "I don't know what I'm thinking. It's like..." A crease formed between his brows as he struggled to complete his thought.

Roland gave Keefe a look. "It's like he wants to enjoy things he might not have for very long."

Jarret threw a hand out in Roland's direction. "Exactly."

"Okay, so let's talk to him," Keefe said. "All of us together."

"When?" Roland tilted his head down and peered up at them, reluctance showing in every way.

"Tomorrow." Jarret folded his arms across his chest. "Right after breakfast."

Roland turned pale. "Maybe before breakfast."

"Nah, not before breakfast." Jarret shook his head. "No one's gonna wanna eat when we're done talking."

"Are we gonna want to eat before?" Roland's stomach was probably in knots already.

Jarret shrugged. "So who's gonna start it? What are we gonna say?"

Keefe took a breath. "I'll start it. I'll say we want to talk. We've noticed some changes in him and we're concerned."

"Yeah." Jarret nodded with vigor, no doubt relieved that Keefe would do the talking.

"And what if it's something bad?" Shoulders slumping, Roland dipped his head even more.

Keefe's heart went out to him. Roland wouldn't be able to handle something bad. Maybe that's why Papa hadn't told them. And Jarret never handled bad news in an appropriate way. How would Keefe handle it? He dropped his gaze, thinking about it. If Papa were dying, it would change all his plans. He wouldn't go on retreat. He'd be incapable of thinking about anything else. He looked up. "Well, we've got to be there for him. Whatever he says."

Roland nodded. Jarret sighed heavily and looked away.

Keefe's heart thumped. *Wait, no...* The thumping came from the other side of the door: boots clomping up the stairs. Papa coming.

Keefe sucked in a breath. Jarret's eyes went wide and his gaze shot around the room, from Roland to Keefe to the door.

"We could talk to him now," Keefe said.

Roland froze but then his mouth fell open. "Not yet."

Lips pressed together, Jarret shook his head. "Tomorrow."

Papa knocked on the door. "Jarret, you got a minute?"

Keefe and Jarret exchanged glances, Keefe getting permission before opening the door, though he knew Jarret would want him to. He swung open the door.

Cowboy hat in one hand, Papa stood running the other hand through his hair. He glanced at each of them. "Good, you're all together. I wanted to talk to you." He glanced at Keefe who stood holding the door. Then one corner of his mouth turned up, an amused look. "May I?" He motioned for Keefe to let him in.

"Oh." Keefe stepped back and finally breathed. Papa wanted to talk to them. Papa wanted to talk now. This was it.

Roland shuffled towards the doorway, the last traces of color draining from his face. "I've got homework."

Papa stood in his way. "This'll just take a sec." He placed his cowboy hat on his head, adjusting it a few times. "I'd be much obliged if you boys hung around the house for the next few days. Ask me before going anywhere."

Roland exhaled. Jarret let out a breathy chuckle. They were both probably relieved that Papa hadn't said something earth-shattering.

Relief washed through Keefe, though a part of him had wished Papa would've confided in them.

"We'll be having company tomorrow." Papa smiled. "Nearly forgot to let you know."

"Company? Who?" Jarret said.

"Miss Meadows. She'll be flying in and staying for a few days. I'll pick her up early tomorrow. I'd like you to be on your best. And like I said, try to stick around."

They exchanged glances. Before anyone else came up with something to say, Papa tipped his hat and left them alone.

CHAPTER 27

The timer rang. Jarret's stomach growled as he slid off the kitchen countertop and snatched an oven mitt. Yanking open the oven, a savory tomato and basil aroma teased his senses. He slid out the cookie sheet of pizza pockets, heat finding his finger through the oven mitt.

"Yeow, ow!" He spun toward the hot pad holder on the marble countertop, the cookie sheet tilting, pizza pockets sliding. As he dropped the scorching sheet, one pocket flew off and took a dive.

Not wanting his bare leg burned, Jarret let out a modified cuss word and jumped back.

The pizza pocket landed on the floor and split open, steam rising from its hot red contents.

He stared at it, irritated at his loss. Now he only had five.

Movement on the opposite side of the kitchen made him look up.

Miss Meadows strolled into the room, hands in the pockets of a long casual skirt, an olive-colored thing that gave her a rugged and relaxed look. Since arriving Saturday morning, she'd worn her sandy hair in a ponytail and either jeans or canvas pants, as well as her white sunhat.

Jarret had worked with her on an archaeological dig in Mississippi last spring, and now that hat was the first thing that came to mind whenever he thought of her. Like Papa with his cowboy hat, she always wore it or kept it nearby. Except for now.

"Something smells good." She smiled as she strolled to the kitchen island, but something seemed off.

"Yeah, want one?" Jarret stood with one foot on either side of the pizza pocket on the floor, deciding to clean it up later. He grabbed a second plate and whisked a pocket onto it, burning his fingertips but not cussing this time. Not in front of her. Something about her made him want to be on his best behavior. And not just because she was easy on the eyes.

Since Saturday, the family had eaten dinners together and sat around a campfire almost every night. Miss Meadows had a nice laugh and she never lacked for conversation, not that she gabbed on and on or anything. She just seemed to know the right thing to say at the right time. And she seemed to understand people, almost like she could read minds.

"Sure." She sat on a barstool as he slid the plate to her.

He grabbed a fork from a drawer in case she wanted it. "Something to drink?" He pulled two glasses from a cupboard.

"Water sounds good."

Deciding against a Coke, Jarret brought two bottles of spring water from the refrigerator and slid one across the countertop to her. "Thought you and Papa were sitting out on the porch." She and Papa had gone horseback riding after dinner and had settled themselves on the front porch afterward.

"We were." She cut into the pizza pocket, giving Jarret a sharp glance. Was she trying to tell him something?

Not understanding the look, Jarret picked up his pizza pocket. A thought came to him and he set it back down. Maybe she was as concerned about Papa's behavior as he, Keefe, and Roland. Too bad they'd had to put off talking to him, but maybe Papa had told *her* something.

"So, hey..." He wrestled with how to word what he wanted to say. "I, uh, I'm glad you're here and all. It's nice. But... we think something's up with Papa."

She stopped chewing and met his gaze, a look of amusement passing over her face. She finished chewing and wiped her mouth with her fingers. "What do you think's up with him?"

"I don't know. Don't you think he's acting strange?"

Sitting straighter, she laughed. "Strange?"

"Well, yeah. He's practically glued to the house lately, taking that online teaching job, turning down his typical on-site freelance work, turning down... Well, you're here when he... he usually goes to you, right?"

"Well, yes, but we've talked about me coming for a visit for a long time."

"I don't have a problem with it. I like that you're here. It's just... I'm worried something's wrong with my old man."

She stuffed the last bite of her hot pocket into her mouth and gazed thoughtfully at her plate while she chewed. Then she lifted her eyes to Jarret. "Maybe your old man simply wants to spend more time with you."

Footfalls in the hallway made them both turn to the doorway; Papa's cowboy boots clomped toward the kitchen.

Papa wouldn't like to see the pizza pocket on the floor. Jarret glanced at Miss Meadows. "I gotta clean something up." He snatched two napkins from the dispenser and dropped to the floor. He tried grabbing the pizza pocket with a napkin but it slipped from his grip, making more of a mess.

"There you are." Papa scuffed into the room.

"Yes, here I am." An edge in Miss Meadows voice?

"Sorry about clamming up. I guess I'm just not ready to talk about that."

With the pocket in his bare hand, Jarret froze. Talk about what?

Silence.

Miss Meadows had probably silenced Papa with a nonverbal signal, informing him of Jarret's presence.

Jarret wiped pizza sauce from the floor and stood with the pizza pocket and dirty napkins in hand.

Papa flinched. "Whatcha doing down there?"

Jarret lifted his hands, showing Papa the mess, then turned toward the trash can. "I dropped something." Anxious to skedaddle, he tossed the remaining three pizza pockets onto the plate with the one he hadn't touched yet and scooted around the bar counter.

Papa snatched a pocket as Jarret passed and gave Jarret a strange look, almost a warning, but the look softened. "Thanks."

Papa and Miss Meadows remained silent while Jarret left the kitchen.

Tempted to sneak down the hall a bit and eavesdrop, Jarret climbed the steps. What wasn't Papa ready to talk about?

Jarret set his plate of food on the corner of the dresser and stood silently in the doorway. No voices traveled. And what if they did? Was he really gonna listen to their private conversation? With a sigh, he closed his bedroom door and grabbed his plate. His finger caught the cord of the brown scapular that he'd placed on the dresser a few days ago. He'd set it next to a picture of Mama and a rough rock of turquoise that she'd collected the year she and Papa married. Jarret dropped the scapular and took his plate to his desk.

So, Miss Meadows had been trying to talk to Papa out on the porch, but he'd clammed up. What could they have been talking about?

Jarret shook his head and bit into one of the pizza pockets. None of his business, right? He and his brothers would talk to Papa soon enough, sometime after Miss Meadows left.

As he chewed, his gaze shifted to a scrap of paper next to his laptop. Honoring Papa's request to stay put, he'd rescheduled his appointment with Father Carston again. Father had given him Friday at three o'clock. Maybe he'd look up the scapular now and take his mind off Papa.

THE BROWN SCAPULAR

What is it? Two squares of brown wool attached by a cord. Words on one square. A dude kneeling before the Blessed Mother on the other. Mary appeared to Saint Simon Stock in 1251 and gave him the scapular as a sign of her favor and protection. Simon must be the kneeling dude. Still, what is it?

Not magic. Not a talisman.
Childish? Yeah, kind of.
Like a little kid carrying a baby blanket around for security?
Maybe.
The Brown Scapular is a silent reminder
that the Blessed Mother is right there with you.
You're not alone.
It's a promise of her prayer for you.
Security in your Heavenly Mother's love.
It's a sacramental, a little way of showing your love for Mary
and trust in her protection. Just wearing it is a prayer.
Just wearing it.
A symbol of devotion. A promise of obedience.
A sign of belonging to Mary and a pledge of her motherly
protection now and in the next life.

"If you had recommended yourself to me, you would not have run into such danger," Mary said to Blessed Alan de la Roche, one of her devoted servants.

CHAPTER 28

Thursday morning, at last. Spirit soaring above him, Christian music blasting on the radio, Keefe cruised down the freeway in Papa's F-150. Clouds hid the sunrise and the smell of rain pumped through the air vents, mixing with the aroma of the coffee he'd picked up before leaving town. Nothing could dampen his mood. He had a full tank of gas and his journey began now.

Keefe glanced at the brown paper bag that held the crumb-topped muffins he'd bought with his coffee. He decided to pace himself and wait until he reached the interstate before eating his breakfast. He had a nine-hour drive ahead of him.

Twenty minutes later, nearing a small town, the traffic picked up and Keefe found himself gripping the steering wheel and glancing in the rearview and side mirrors. He'd never driven far from town, and now he was headed to an entirely different state. Alone.

His heart stirred. Not alone, the Lord reminded him. They made this journey together. Relaxing a bit, Keefe's gaze fixed on a golden sunbeam that stole through heavy clouds and fell on a lonely hill. The sunbeam accompanied him for a few more minutes, until the shifting clouds made it disappear.

The sun rose higher in the sky, at times visible through the clouds as a pale orb, at other times invisible. Traffic increased as Keefe drove through hills and twists toward Rapid City and the interstate. He decided that he preferred sitting high over the road in the full-size truck to sitting low in the Lexus. He felt more in control and aware of his surroundings.

Almost an hour into his trip, he reached the interstate that he would spend the next six hours driving on. His soul stirred again, a tingling sensation running along his arms and to his chest. This was really happening. He set out today, searching for God's will for his life, opening himself to all possibilities, holding nothing back. The road trip itself felt like part of his discernment retreat. How far was he willing to go? What was he willing to give up?

A peaceful mood enveloped him. Cars and trucks whizzed past. Attention half on the road and half on the stirrings in his soul, Keefe drove on.

An hour later, the traffic lessoned, dwindling to a few cars and semi-trucks. Flat land stretched out to gently rolling horizons on both sides. Gray clouds hung low in the sky, threatening rain at any minute. Something foreboding about them. Too bad he wouldn't have a clear blue sky for his trip. But maybe God had a message for him in the gloominess.

Keefe sighed, relaxing with the easy landscape. He took a hand from the steering wheel and grabbed his coffee. A degree warmer than room temperature, it comforted him as he gulped it down. He replaced the coffee cup in the cup holder and reached into a brown paper bag for one of the muffins. His gaze skimmed the other bag of snacks he'd brought and the water bottles in the passenger seat, his black canvas overnight bag on the floor. He wanted to make the nine-hour drive with as few stops as possible.

Two hours later, Christian music still played in the background, just over the hum of the engine, but he couldn't make the song out half the time. Working on his second muffin, the darkest of the gray clouds hung above and ahead, paler skies in the rearview mirror. An empty freeway stretched out before him.

Keefe took a deep breath and sighed. His mood sank with the monotony of the drive and landscape. He hadn't considered the extra time it would take to drive in the rain. What if he arrived late? They'd think he didn't take this seriously. If they knew his past, the way he'd followed Jarret down so many bad roads, they wouldn't take him seriously either. But they didn't need to know all that, did they? He wasn't that person anymore, so why couldn't he shake the feeling that he wasn't worthy of a calling?

The sense of foreboding intensified, sitting like a rock in his stomach. Keefe dropped the half-eaten muffin back into the bag, wiped crumbs from his lap, and tightened his grip on the steering wheel.

An hour later, he passed the last bit of heavy traffic he expected to encounter in South Dakota, crossed into Minnesota, and drove until he found himself alone on the road again. The rambling music grating on his nerves, he shut the radio off and lowered the windows. Warm wind blew his face and hair and created a soothing white noise. He remembered the sensation of wind whipping through his hair when he'd worn it long like Jarret did, before the haircut that signaled the promises he'd made to God and to himself.

Keefe's thoughts turned to God. He didn't need to worry about anything. Everything would work out according to God's will. He could trust God's plan for today and for his life. "Trusting you, Lord," he whispered, not entirely feeling it. He whispered more prayers, thinking of everyone in his family, his thoughts lingering on Papa.

Papa had seemed ten years younger during the five days of Miss Meadows' visit. But he'd seemed restless since she left. Keefe had enjoyed the visit too. Miss Meadows kept them all entertained at family dinners and around a campfire in the backyard. Keefe had even gone horseback riding with them. Like Papa, Miss Meadows had a private side and kept to herself much of the time, either in her room or strolling about outside. Papa had taken her shopping and to dinner a few times too, dressing in new button-down shirts. He'd worn a new cowboy hat for a few hours one day, but it must not have fit right. He'd worn the old one ever since.

Jarret had still wanted to figure out Papa's deal, so when he found Miss Meadows alone in the kitchen, he brought up Papa's online teaching job. "Maybe your old man wants to spend more time with you," she'd said with a smile.

The answer hadn't satisfied him in the least, but Jarret decided that he, Keefe, and Roland should wait until after this weekend, when everyone could talk to him together. Roland and Papa had gone on the annual camping trip, so maybe Roland would have a few answers before then.

Glimpsing a car on the side of the road, Keefe snapped from his thoughts. He glanced in the rearview and side mirrors. Alone on the road, he changed to the far left lane. As he drew near, he saw the problem.

An old blue Toyota with a flat tire sat on the berm. His gaze connected with the driver, a young woman in a white top and a long skirt the color of storm clouds. Her skirt flapped about her legs. She stood with her hands on her hips, staring at the flat, but she turned as he sped past. Strands of hair ripped free from her pony tail and flew around her face. She looked at him. And he at her. A message of heart-wrenching agony passed between them, fleeting but so real it shook him to the core.

Keefe's breath caught and his heart twisted with the sharp pain of sympathy. His thoughts jumped to his forty hours in the woods. *Frozen, coughing, and gasping, blinded by the dark of night, he dragged himself from the river to the bank of failure. He would have to trudge through the woods to Peter's house, shivering in soaking wet clothes, admit defeat and live with it.*

The car shrunk in the side mirror as he drove on. Guilt had him glancing every few seconds. She was alone and needed help. Didn't she have a cellphone? He should've stopped. But he hadn't known that she'd needed help until too late. He couldn't back up on the highway. He could easily cross the strip of grass between east and westbound roads and turn around. Any police cars on the road? How far to the next exit?

Keefe glanced at the clock. He was six hours in on a nine-hour journey. Did he have time to help her? He'd left the house with a half hour to spare. He could change a tire in half an hour. And so what if he were a little late?

A flat horizon and a scattering of trees lined both sides of the road. Not a house in sight. A green highway sign to the side of the road showed he'd reach the next exit in two miles. Two miles to the exit. Sixty miles per hour. Two minutes, plus a minute to cross over the highway and get on in the opposite direction. Then he'd have to backtrack and turn around at the exit just past her. How far away was that exit?

Keefe moaned and slammed the steering wheel, his conscience convicting him. Her look had told him everything he needed to know. She needed help. And for whatever reason, she had no one else to help her.

Ten minutes later, and still not seeing an exit after he'd gotten on the highway in the opposite direction, Keefe hit the brakes and pulled onto the grassy median. Cranking the wheel, he drove the F-150 into and out of a ditch that the grass had hidden.

He'd passed the lady and her Toyota five minutes ago. Keefe stepped on the gas pedal, driving over the speed limit until her car came into view again. He eased off the gas and slowed, then pulled up behind her.

She stood by the open trunk of her car, two cardboard boxes overflowing with junk on the ground and a jack and lug wrench in her hands. The wind still playing with her hair and skirt, she turned as he slammed the door of the truck.

"Need a hand?" He strode toward her, his limbs appreciating the stretch.

About twenty-something and a bit rough around the edges, she seemed like a girl who in normal situations could take care of herself and resented this monkey wrench thrown into her plans. Biting her lip, she looked him over, worry and distrust in her eyes. And something else. Something similar to the hopelessness Keefe had felt down by the river. "I've just never changed a tire before." With a forced smile, she offered him the jack and lug wrench.

"I have." Wanting to ease her anxiety, he smiled and pushed back all the anxious thoughts about how long this would take and making it to the retreat in time. *All in God's hands.* "My father made me practice several times before he let me drive anything of his." He jabbed a thumb over his shoulder. "That's his truck."

She glanced at the truck. "My father would never have trusted me with his car. He..." Her gaze snapped back to him, her eyes distant, then she turned away and a breeze thrust her hair into her face.

"You wanna turn the flashers on and set the parking brake? I'll get something from my truck to block a tire." Keefe set the jack and lug wrench on the ground, his gaze sliding to the boxes. A blow dryer hung out of one, stuffed grocery bags and folded clothes filling the other. Keefe jogged back to the truck for a wheel chock.

As he returned, the Toyota's hazards flashed and the lady got out of the driver side and slammed the door.

Keefe stuffed the wheel chock under the tire opposite of the flat. Not wanting to waste time, he jogged around the car and snatched the lug wrench. A quick glance over his shoulder told him the road was clear. He dropped onto one knee on the gravelly berm, pried off the hubcap, and loosened the lug nuts. One minute, two minutes... He could do this in less than ten.

A few feet away, she stood watching him with folded arms and hair blowing in her face. Still looking hopeless.

Loosening the last lug nut, he glanced up at her. "I forgot to say... my name's Keefe."

"Oh." She unfolded and refolded her arms as if not sure whether she should offer her hand. "Piper."

He nodded, smiling again, though his mind hadn't stopped calculating the time. Then he dropped onto all fours to find a good place on the frame for the jack. Placing the jack, he got back up to one knee and inserted the jack handle. Another minute?

"Do you live around here?" He peered up at her as he cranked the jack handle.

"No, not really. I'm about an hour south. Just passing through on my way to see my dad. He's..." She shut her mouth and shook her head, pain passing over her expression.

"So he lives around here?" He'd only asked to have something to say, but a part of him wished she'd called a friend or relative for help.

"Oh no." Piper waved a hand in the air and stared across the highway. "I've got a while to go. I can't believe I got a flat. But something's always going wrong with this old beater." She watched the flat creep up off the ground. "How long will the spare last?"

"Not sure. Forty or fifty miles? You'll probably want to get your tire fixed as soon as you can." Satisfied he'd gotten the tire far enough off the ground, he set the jack handle down and twisted the lug nuts the rest of the way off. "How far are you going?"

"I've got another hour or so up to Sleepy Eye." They exchanged a glance and a little smile passed her lips. "Ever heard of it?"

He shook his head and dropped the last of the lug nuts in the upside-down hub cap. "Sounds boring."

The comment seemed to have caught her off guard. One hand flew to her mouth, and she let out a loud high laugh, a good sound that made Keefe smile.

"I don't know if it is or not. Dad moved there when I was younger." Her tone softened. "I've never been there."

No longer keeping track of the time but certain he could complete the job within ten minutes, Keefe shoved the hubcap out of the way. He gripped the tire with both hands and yanked the wheel from the lug studs. Then he followed her to the trunk and set the tire flat on the ground.

Keefe reached into the trunk and wrapped his fingers around the spare, his stomach sinking as his fingers sank into the rubber. "Uh oh. Looks like this one's flat too."

She stared as if not believing him, then her eyes turned hard and glassy, a mix of emotion showing on her face.

"So you don't know anyone around here?"

"No." She turned away and shoved one hand into her hair. "Now what?" Her voice broke.

"Do you have roadside assistance?"

Her dead expression and teary eyes answered his question. "And my phone's dead anyways. Can't find my charger."

"Well, I..." Keefe threw a longing glance at his truck, his gaze skittering over the interstate highway and the formidable clouds, wishing he were on the road again. "I guess we could toss the tire in the truck, find a shop, and get it fixed."

She dragged the back of her hand over her eyes, pushing hair off her face and probably drying tears. "You'd do that for me?"

How far could it be to the nearest shop? How long could it possibly take? He'd already used up his spare half hour. How late would it make him? The retreat started at four. So what if he got there by five? He could call and tell the friars he'd be late.

"Sure," Keefe said, hiding all traces of disappointment and anxiety. "I need to get gas and lunch anyways." Keefe lifted the tire to the back of the truck, squeezed his overnight bag, water bottles, and snacks behind the seats, and motioned for Piper to get in. Using his cellphone, he found a tire and auto parts store in the nearest town, fifteen or so minutes away.

A drop of rain splattered on the windshield as Keefe eased onto the interstate. Then the sky let loose.

~ ~ ~

An hour and a half later, Keefe sat across from Piper in a booth in a family restaurant. The dark sky and pouring rain, visible through the slats of the window blinds, made it feel like evening, though it was only around 2:00 p.m. Keefe rubbed the goosebumps on his arm, and a shiver ran through him. Piper sat hunched with her hands stuffed in the opposite sleeves, her stringy wet hair hanging over her shoulders. They'd gotten drenched running from the truck to the auto parts store, back to the truck, and then into the restaurant. The rain had lessened some but hadn't quit.

A family with a toddler and an older kid, maybe eight or nine, sat two tables away. The toddler's voice carried. He wanted to stand on his chair or sit by the windows and see the rain. A half wall that split the dining area in two blocked his view.

"Do you have brothers and sisters?" Piper caught him staring.

He reached for the glass of iced tea that the waitress had brought a few minutes ago and twisted it one way and the other. "Yeah, two brothers. One's two years younger, the other's my twin."

She leaned forward, as if totally enthralled, her eyes glittering in the yellow light from the low-hanging lamp above the booth. "Twins, huh?" She slipped her hands from her sleeves and played with the paper seal on the napkin-wrapped silverware in front of her. "I always wished my younger sister and I were twins. Are you two close?"

"Yeah, pretty close." His thoughts flitted to Jarret. The rain seemed to be heading west. If Jarret went out with Chantelle tonight, they'd probably be caught in it. It would give them an excuse to stay in.

Something moved in Keefe's peripheral vision.

The waitress, dressed in gray and black, sashayed around tables, carrying a tray with two plates and condiments. She set a burger and fries in front of each of them. "Can I get you anything else?" She glanced at their glasses, but neither one of them had touched their cold drinks.

Keefe watched her go, stalling while he considered how to bless his food. He prayed before every meal nowadays, usually aloud, silently at school, but always beginning with the Sign of the Cross. No one ever noticed at school. Or if they did, they never said anything to him about it. Why did he hesitate now? Why should he care what she thought? He didn't even know her, and he'd never see her again. Was he ashamed to let his faith show? What kind of Franciscan would he make?

Piper squirted a mound of ketchup onto her plate and offered the bottle to him.

"Thanks." He set it aside and took the plunge, bowing his head and lifting a hand to his forehead for the Sign of the Cross. He prayed silently, moving his lips, aware of her eyes on him, and struggling to mean the words of the prayer while his deeper prayer went, "Lord, let me not be ashamed of showing my faith in you."

They ate without speaking for a few minutes, the only sounds the whines of the toddler, the indistinct chatter of his parents, and the clanking of forks on china.

Piper dropped a fry back to her plate and looked at Keefe for a few seconds.

Thinking maybe he had ketchup somewhere, he grabbed his napkin and wiped his mouth. "What's up?"

Her gaze flickered from him to her plate to something behind him and back to him. "My dad's in hospice. He's dying."

Pangs of sympathy and grief stabbing him, Keefe set his burger down. "Oh sorry. That stinks."

"Yeah, we found out last month. We didn't even know he was sick, and here he has cancer."

Before Keefe could figure out how her father could be that far along without anyone knowing, she added, "My mom and sister drove up to see him right away." She gave a sad smile. "But I couldn't get myself to go with them. I'm still not sure I want to see him."

Understanding now that her parents lived apart made Keefe even sadder.

"All I can think of..." Eyes downcast, she slumped over her plate and lowered her voice. "...is how he left us ten years ago, left my mom alone with two teens and an eight-year-old." She looked at him. "I was fourteen. I never understood why he left us. I hated him for it. Still hate him. I don't even know why I decided to go today. I guess..." Her voice broke. "They said he was looking real bad, might not make it much longer." Her voice fell to a whisper. "This is my last chance."

Moved by her grief, Keefe slid his hand across the table and touched the back of her hand. Uncomfortable making contact, he pulled away and struggled to think of something to say. "Sorry."

"When my tire went flat, I thought it was a sign. Maybe I shouldn't have taken this trip. I wasn't meant to see him. He'd made his choices. He chose some other woman over us. We all have to live with the consequences of our choices. Or die with them." She lifted her gaze to his. "And then you came along, like a godsend, like a sign I should keep going. Do you think God works like that, sends other people into our path to guide us?"

"Yeah, I'm sure He does." It touched him that she mentioned God. Would she have done it if she hadn't seen a glimmer of faith in him? But her question also sparked a question in him. Did God have a message for both of them in this?

"So maybe now, I'll get there before he—" Her brows drew together. "I feel like... I need to know why he did it. Or maybe I just need to see him one last time. I need to forgive him. For myself, I need to forgive him."

Keefe resisted the urge to reach for her hand again. "I'm glad I came along then," he said, his voice low.

Recomposing herself, she pressed her lips together, shoved a stringy lock of wet hair behind her ear, and nodded. Then she took a deep breath and picked up her hamburger. "Me too."

Keefe picked up his burger too, questioning whether he meant what he'd said. Was he glad he came along? If he hadn't, surely someone else would've, maybe someone who had nothing better to do. He'd most likely arrive at the Franciscans over two hours late. They wouldn't turn him away, would they? Maybe he should see this as a sign from God, finish helping Piper, and go back home. It would be a bit of relief. He'd have his answer, right?

"So I never asked," she said with her mouth full, "what you were out doing today, before you got tangled in my miserable web? Do you live around here?"

Keefe chewed and took a sip of iced tea. "No, I live on the far side of South Dakota, about six hours away."

She dropped her hamburger, smiling. "Really? What-cha doing out here? Joyriding in your father's truck?"

"No, actually I'm on my way to St. Paul."

"That's a long drive. Got family there?"

"Uh, no." He dragged a fry through ketchup, hesitating to admit his destination, partly because he didn't want her to feel bad about him helping her. But also because he suspected she'd think he was strange for wanting to live as a consecrated brother. And besides, God knew he'd come across her today and stop to help. So God knew he'd consider it a sign. If this was His sign, then—

A memory flashed in his mind. A dusty sunbeam illuminated the San Damiano crucifix on the wall in the new prayer corner he'd made in his room. Dazzled by the sight and filled with expectancy, Keefe knelt to pray. He bowed his head and focused on the presence of the Lord before him, beside him, around him, within him. "Please, Lord," he had whispered, filled with peace, "guide me to my vocation. Give me a sign. Let me read it in your Word."

In imitation of Francis and Bernard, who had prayed for discernment this way, he opened his black leather Bible to a random page in the New Testament. He dropped his finger to the page and read aloud, "Blessed is he who takes no offense at me."

Keefe had jerked back as if struck. What kind of message did that have for him?

"So...?"

Keefe snapped from the thought, his eyes focusing on Piper, who waited for an answer. "A group of Franciscan friars live up there. They're offering a discernment retreat."

She stopped chewing and only stared, then she finished chewing and took a sip of her pop. "Wow, so you want to become a priest?"

Heat assailed him, climbing up his neck. He dropped his gaze and wiped his hands on a napkin. "I don't know. I'm not sure. I'm going to learn more about becoming a Franciscan friar. Maybe I'm called."

"Wow, I've never met anyone who, you know."

He dipped his head and grabbed a fry. "Yeah, I know. Neither have I."

"So by 'called' you mean, God calling you? How would you know?"

"I don't know." He smiled. "That's why I'm going to the discernment retreat. But I've felt something inside, in my soul, I guess, like God calling." Keefe sat back and sighed, his thoughts turning inward. No matter how late this unplanned excursion made him, he'd keep going. He'd never live with himself if he turned back now.

CHAPTER 29

Chantelle squeezed Jarret's hand as she dragged him to the top row of the dimly lit auditorium. Movie previews flashed on the screen, the sound too low and then too loud. Overhead spotlights made the squiggly lines and shapes on the carpeted steps glow. Chantelle's perfume and the buttery locker room odor of the auditorium confused Jarret's senses.

"The top row, really?" He scanned the other rows, counting fifteen people. They'd picked a movie that came out a while ago, so everyone else must've seen it already.

"Are you afraid of heights?" Chantelle smiled at him over her shoulder as she sauntered to the seat in the middle of the row.

"No, but the movie screen looks two inches tall from up here."

"Oh well. It's a date. We don't have to watch the movie." Her hair fell over her shoulder as she pushed her seat down. Taking her seat, she smiled up at him, her expression sultry.

Jarret's mouth fell open while he tried to think of a reply. He shook his head, still not coming up with one. Then he just said, "Yeah, we're here to watch the movie." He settled himself, slouching so that his knees almost touched the seatback in front of him and resting his forearms on the armrests. "Sure you don't want popcorn?"

"Are you kidding? I'm stuffed." She rubbed her tummy, making him look.

He redirected his gaze to the movie screen, lacing his fingers together to keep from grabbing her hand. "You hardly ate anything." He'd taken her to the nicest restaurant in town. Not that that was saying much. It was better than the buffet. Maybe better than the steakhouse. But if he really wanted to impress a girl, he should think about driving a bit farther from home. Still, he'd spent too much money for how little she ate of her fancy salmon and wild rice dinner. He'd put a killing on his steak.

"I wasn't that hungry. You should've accepted my offer to cook for you. We could be watching a movie at my house right now."

When he'd gone to pick her up, she'd suggested they have dinner and watch a movie at her house since her parents were gone. Not one to make excuses, he'd simply said, "I don't want to," and jabbed his thumb in the direction of his Chrysler in the driveway.

"You can cook for me some other day," he said, eyes on the movie screen. "When your parents are home."

Chantelle pursed her lips, her eyes narrowing with a look of dissatisfaction. "They'll be home later. They're just shopping, picking up a few things for tomorrow." She twisted in her seat, angling her body towards him. "I wish you'd change your mind about camping. We could have so much fun."

Loving and hating the idea, remembering the "fun" he'd had last year, he dropped his head back and stared at the black ceiling for two seconds before looking at her. "Nope. No camping for me. And no school tomorrow—teacher day or whatever—so after tonight, I'll see you on Monday."

She straightened in her seat and folded her arms across her chest with an attitude. The lights dimmed and the screen went black. A second later, the movie started and Chantelle snapped from her negative mood. She scooted close to the armrest between them.

Thinking she wanted the armrest, he slid his arm off it. Then he focused on the movie.

She draped her arm over the armrest and rested her hand on his leg.

A red flag went up in Jarret's mind, but he left her hand there. It was a harmless gesture, right? But then she moved her hand. His heart hammered in his chest. He sucked in a breath, trying to keep his thoughts from going where they shouldn't. Then he snatched her hand and decided to hold it.

Out of the corner of his eye, he caught her glance, but he kept his eyes glued to the movie screen. They'd come to watch a movie. Not fool around.

A few minutes later, once Jarret had started getting into the movie, Chantelle squeezed his hand and dragged it to her lap.

He drew his hand back and snapped, "Man, just watch the movie." Then he hogged both armrests, lacing his fingers together on his chest again.

Light from the screen illuminated her amused, somewhat puzzled expression. She'd probably never had a guy reject her moves before.

~ ~ ~

Keefe gripped the steering wheel with sweaty palms and squinted at a green highway sign as he drew near. Not his exit yet. He redirected his attention to the car in front of him. He'd never braved a highway with four lanes of traffic, cars and trucks whizzing by on either side. He didn't want to take another wrong exit. Misunderstanding his GPS, he'd done that once today and ended up on a longer route. His GPS assured him he'd still get there, though.

Keefe glanced at the clock. 7:49. He'd spent over three hours with Piper. Didn't seem possible. It had taken forever for the auto shop mechanic to call. He and Piper had finished their lunch, ordered dessert, and were working on coffee. Then Keefe had taken Piper and the repaired tire back to her Toyota, and he'd installed it quickly. She'd wanted his address so she could repay him some day—he'd paid for lunch and the tire—but he wouldn't give it to her. He'd used Papa's charge card. Papa wouldn't care. And if he did, Keefe would pay him back.

Then they'd said goodbye. She kissed him on the cheek and said, "Good luck."

"I hope you get to your father in time. I'll pray for you both," he had said, walking a few steps backwards to his truck.

Her mouth had trembled and curved into a smile. She nodded and climbed into her little blue Toyota.

Headlights glared in the rearview mirror, blinding Keefe and breaking him from his thoughts. He turned the mirror a bit until only black showed. The sun had gone down about an hour ago. He should've arrived at the Franciscans' place in daylight. Now all the new surroundings had an ominous, hostile quality. Everything felt like a negative sign. The Bible verse, running into Piper, the fact that he'd be almost four hours late... Keefe bit his lip and glanced at the next glowing green highway sign.

Before he could make out the words, his cellphone rang.

Keefe glanced at it. He'd propped it in the cup holder that didn't hold his water bottle. Should he pick it up while trying to navigate through this? It rang a few times before he gave in and answered.

"Hey, Keefe, it's Roland."

"Roland, what's up?" His anxiety level jumped up a notch. Roland would never have called without good reason. He would assume that Keefe was on retreat right now and wouldn't want to bother him. Before Roland could respond, wild ideas raced through Keefe's mind. Something bad had happened at home. If Keefe had turned around earlier, he'd be home in time to help. He'd asked God for a sign but hadn't listened when he'd received it. And now others would suffer.

CHAPTER 30

Halfway through the movie, Chantelle shifted in her seat, seeming uncomfortable. Then she turned to Jarret. "Mind if I put this up?" She tugged on the armrest.

He slid his elbow off it.

With a sweet smile, she swung the armrest up and scooted toward him. Then she dragged his hand over her shoulders and leaned her head on his chest. The scent of her shampoo tickled his nose. Did he like the smell? He inhaled again and decided that he liked the musky herbal scent. It seemed familiar and struck him somewhere deep inside.

He hadn't meant for her to realize that he'd checked out her hair, but she turned to him with her dark sultry eyes on his mouth.

He opened his mouth to ask her to back away, but he never got the chance to speak. Her lips found his before he could get out the first syllable. Overwhelmed with the thrill of it, he kissed her back the way he used to kiss Zoe, in a way he shouldn't be kissing any girl he hadn't married first. He'd been fearing this moment ever since he wrote his number on her arm. He'd known it would come to this. He was too weak to resist.

He needed to act. He needed to...

Flailing about for inner strength, Jarret pulled away and sucked in a breath.

She smothered him with another kiss, drawing him back to her web.

He needed to stop this. But her uninhibited actions rendered him powerless.

The movie quieted, the screen throwing off more light that seeped in through his closed eyelids. Then a sound came from his chest pocket, and his eyes snapped open. Despite all the reminders, he'd forgotten to shut his cellphone off.

Fumbling for his phone, he pulled away from her.

Her gaze went to his phone as she drew back.

Jarret silenced the phone and checked the caller id. Keefe? He should've been at the Franciscans by now. Had something gone wrong? Maybe he'd gotten lost or needed information.

"I'll be back." He kissed Chantelle's head, then glimpsed her irritated expression—brows drawn together and a sulky mouth.

Relief and cool air greeted him as he descended the steps and slipped around the corner. He lengthened his stride, anxious to get out of the auditorium and into the hallway. "Lord, thank you, thank you, thank you," he whispered as he pushed open the door. He'd been headed down a bad road with no brake pedal.

Jarret stopped beside a cardboard display for a spy movie and called Keefe.

Keefe answered on the second ring. "Hey, Jarret."

"Hey, you okay? Reach your destination?"

"Huh? Almost there. But I'm calling for Roland. He needs your help."

"Roland?" Jarret pressed the phone to his ear, worry flickering through him. "Why didn't he call me?"

"I don't know. Maybe he thought I'd need to convince you."

Since returning from Arizona, Jarret had helped Roland with everything he could. Why would he be uncomfortable asking? Unless...

"Peter's stranded an hour away."

"No." Jarret had figured it out a split-second before Keefe said the loathsome kid's name. No way was he helping that kid with anything, unless— "Is Roland with him?"

"No, Roland's on his way over to Peter's house, riding his bike. Apparently, Peter has a new battery at home. That's all he needs."

Relief washed through him, knowing that Roland didn't really need him. It was just Peter. And Heaven itself couldn't get him to go out of his way for Peter. Jarret cringed at the thought. Heaven should be a sufficient motivator for anything. But Heaven wasn't asking this of him. Roland was. He would help Roland in anything else but not this.

"I gotta go." Jarret peered at the theater door. "My date's waiting on me."

"Date? You're out with Chantelle? Where at?" Worry tinged Keefe's tone.

"We're seeing a movie. But I don't think it's gonna work out between us."

Keefe exhaled into the phone. "Yeah, good. She's not your type."

Jarret smiled, loving Keefe even more. "What is my type?"

"I don't know. But it's not her. She's too ... um... I don't know. Not your type."

"Yeah, I'm starting to see that."

Silence followed. Was Keefe amazed at the changes in Jarret? Jarret was also amazed, but he was intensely aware that he was one slip from reverting back to his old self. He had to end this date before something happened that he'd regret. The failure would prove he wasn't cut out for this fight between good and evil. Sin was in his blood. Thanks to Adam, that was true. A drop of blood appeared in his mind, falling in slow motion. Falling from what?

"Okay." Keefe interrupted Jarret's thoughts. "I've got to get back on the road. I'm almost there. Why don't you give Roland a call?

Papa's out and Mr. Brandt got called somewhere else. I don't think he knows anyone else who can help."

"All right, maybe. I'll see you. Have fun with the monks." Jarret stuffed his phone into his chest pocket and stepped into the men's bathroom. After splashing water on his face, he gazed at his reflection in the mirror. He admired his facial hair, the stubble he'd left on his upper lip and chin, a faint goatee. And he tapped a curl into place and touched the hair fastener to make sure his ponytail was secure.

He could probably get any girl he wanted. Girls liked him. He simply had to glance in a girl's direction and she'd blush or give him that flirty look. Was there a girl at school who wouldn't go out with him? Maybe he should experiment with that.

No, bad idea. He'd have to break up with most of them, every one that didn't work out. He'd get a reputation of dumping girls and no one would go out with him. He didn't want that reputation. But he had to dump Chantelle.

Or did he? Maybe they could talk more and do things in groups. Like Caitlyn with her courtship rules. He'd mocked it then, but now...

Jarret flexed his biceps and straightened his shirt. He always wore shirts cut for his build, to accentuate the muscles that he had worked so hard to develop. The clothes, hair, the way he walked, his attitude... What kind of girl was he attracting with his image? What kind of girl did he like?

Jarret took a breath and gave himself one last glance in the mirror. As he headed for the door, his phone belted out his ring tone. He snatched it from his pocket. He really needed to silence it before he went back— Roland's name showed on the screen.

Roland was going to ask him himself.

Jarret brought the phone to his ear as he strode from the restroom. "Hey, Roland. Can't talk. I'm on a date right now." Two girls stood outside the women's bathroom, both of them watching as he emerged.

"Yeah, hi, Jarret. I know. And if I could think of any other way, I wouldn't bother you." Roland panted between words, sounding winded.

"What, are you outside taking a jog?"

"A what? No, I'm on my bike. I just stopped to get Keefe's call and, well, to talk to you."

"Yeah, he told me what you wanted and no can do."

"Please, Jarret. I know you've been helping me out with everything lately, and I really appreciate it and don't want to take advantage…"

Jarret sighed. He couldn't talk to Roland without feeling a combination of guilt from the way he'd treated him in the past and thankfulness for Roland's forgiveness.

"…but I don't know what else to do. I don't have friends with cars."

"What about Leo?" Jarret remembered the kid driving Roland and Peter around last year.

"We aren't exactly friends, but when Keefe told me you couldn't do it, I did try to call him."

Jarret's heart sank. True, he'd been helping Roland at every opportunity, but Roland never *asked* him to do anything. And now he'd had to turn to someone else because Jarret wouldn't help him. Okay, so maybe he could do this for Roland without feeling like he was helping Peter. "So what exactly do you need me to do?"

"Really? You'll help?"

"I don't know. Tell me what you need."

"I'm on my way to Peter's. His car broke down an hour north of here, and he just needs the battery in his garage."

"Wait. Peter has a car? He's not even sixteen."

"Yes, he is. He turned sixteen last month."

"Okay, so I'm supposed to drive you and a battery out to Peter? Then I leave?" He knew the answer to the second question. He'd never leave Roland in an unpredictable situation.

"Yeah, then you can leave. Peter can get his car going, no problem. I'll ride home with him."

Staring at the door to the theater, Jarret couldn't get himself to answer. It would save him from the temptations that Chantelle forced on him. But Peter...

"Okay, well, I'm gonna get going," Roland said. "I'm five minutes from Peter's. I'll wait there for ten minutes, but then I'll ask Peter's aunt if she can do it. Or someone. I'll find someone. I shouldn't have bothered you. I knew you were on a date." Without pause Roland said, "Bye."

Jarret ended the call and slid the phone back into his pocket. He yanked open the door to the auditorium and stepped into darkness. Should he let Roland find someone else to take him? No, he couldn't do that. He'd take Chantelle home.

He'd still see her. But from now on, they'd only go out in groups and not to their friends' houses. He'd make sure one of their parents was around and... *Yeah, wow.* This was what Keefe said courtship was like, back when Keefe went out with Caitlyn.

Though no one knew his thoughts or could even see his face in the dark theater, heat rushed to his chest and cheeks as he stomped up the steps to the top row.

Chantelle reached a hand up as he neared his seat. "What was that about?" She grabbed his hand and tugged.

He gripped her hand and tugged back, yanking her to her feet. "I got something I gotta do. I'll take you home first." Squeezing her hand, he led her down the steps.

She was fidgeting with something, maybe her purse, and taking ungraceful steps beside him. Zoe came to mind and her ever-graceful moves. He missed her.

As they rounded the corner to the long dark hallway that led out of the auditorium, Chantelle regained her poise and yanked her hand free. "Jarret, stop."

He kept walking and palmed the door open. Then he leaned against it, holding it for her and watching as she passed from darkness to light.

Angry eyes glared at him. She folded her arms, and her purse strap slipped off her shoulder. With a grunt, she put it back in place. "So what's this about? Some emergency?"

Jarret shrugged. "You could say that." He put a hand on her back, guiding her toward the main lobby. "I'll make it up to you sometime."

"You can at least tell me what the emergency is." She flipped her hair over her shoulder and looked at him.

He debated whether or not to tell her for two seconds. But it wasn't his emergency so he didn't mind sharing. "You know Peter Brandt?"

"Ew. He's in my Environmental Science class. He's such a dork."

They entered the gaudy lobby where fluorescent pink and blue lights hung over movie posters high on the walls. Three grade-school-age boys and a woman stood in line at the concession counter. A group of teens, probably from River Run High, huddled together in the middle of the lobby, laughing and talking. The wall of windows and glass doors showed trouble brewing, heavy gray clouds covering all but a trace of an orange sky. Great. They'd probably be driving in rain.

Jarret pushed open a glass door and nodded for her to go first. "Okay, so Peter's car broke down. He's stranded an hour away. And I'm gonna help him out."

"Why you? I never knew you were friends." Her heels clacked on the sidewalk. She took his hand.

"We're not." Even the thought of it made his stomach flip. Fishing his keys out of a pocket, he led her to the parking lot. He walked with confidence, though he couldn't remember which row he'd parked in and the lot had filled up since they arrived.

"So why are you ruining our date to help him?"

Jarret took a deep breath. He'd been asking himself the same questions. If not for Roland... "My brother asked me to. It's his friend."

"So you'll do anything your brother asks?"

He shrugged again, smirking and liking that he could answer that with a *yes*. "Family. You know."

"No, I don't know. So why can't I go with you?"

"Want to?" He glanced at her and—bonus—glimpsed his cherry red Chrysler 300 behind her in the next row over. Squeezing her hand, he changed direction and headed for the car.

"Sure. We can talk on the way."

"Okay, but you'd better promise to keep your hands to yourself. My brother's going with us." A few raindrops sprinkled his face.

She bounced her next two steps. "I'll try."

~ ~ ~

Jarret slowed as he glimpsed the hot pink neon sign that announced the Forest Gateway B & B attached to Peter Brandt's house. Roland stood under the overhang of the detached garage, out of the rain, a toolbox and battery at his feet and a black jacket in his hand.

"Girls at school tell me that your brother's Goth." Chantelle sized Roland up as they pulled into the driveway. Dressed in faded jeans and a dark gray t-shirt, he stood with one leg bent, looking uncomfortable in his skin.

"No, he's just a dork who likes to wear black." Jarret regretted the comment. He should think before he spoke, rather than let every sarcastic thought fly out.

Not wasting a second, Roland grabbed the toolbox and battery and rushed to the trunk. He would know Jarret wouldn't allow that junk anywhere else. Coming from Peter's garage, it probably had grease all over it. Not that it mattered anymore. What, with the perpetual Limburger cheese stench.

Jarret popped the trunk and glanced at Chantelle. She'd never mentioned the stink in his car. Maybe she couldn't smell it over her perfume.

Chantelle gave a sulky glance back. "An hour away, huh?"

"Need to call your parents?"

Shaking her head, she turned toward the front passenger-side window. "I texted Mom."

Roland slammed the trunk and jumped in the back seat, a sweaty, wet, outdoorsy breeze whooshing into the car with him. "Thanks, Jarret. I really appreciate this."

"Yeah." Jarret couldn't have sounded more disgusted. Not that he'd wanted to come across that way. The tone just came out.

"Hi, Chantelle," Roland said to the back of her head. "Sorry to ruin your date."

Chantelle twisted around to look at him and gave a smile that Jarret suspected was fake. This mission may have irritated her more than him.

Jarret glanced at Roland through the rearview mirror. "I didn't know Peter had a car. What's he driving?" He drove back through town, the rain falling harder.

"It's an old Dodge Durango."

"Oh. Fun," he said with sarcasm. He flipped the wipers up a level.

"*He* thinks it's fun. He wanted something to fix up." Roland leaned forward and squinted out the window. "Did you just pass up that state route?"

"Yeah, I'm not going that way."

"Peter said to take the route that goes north."

"I don't care what Peter said. I know how to get to Rapid City."

"We're going east."

A rush of indignation. "Yeah, so I'm going east to the interstate which goes north. To Rapid City. And I can fly down this road instead of crawl around all the twists and turns on Peter's route."

"With all this rain, maybe you don't want to fly."

Jarret glared through the mirror. "Buckle up, boy, 'cuz I'm flying."

Roland sat back and folded his arms, saying nothing but looking grumpy.

Taking a breath, Jarret regretted snapping at him. Using the nicest tone he could muster, he said, "Peter intentionally bought a beater, huh? So why's he driving a beater all over the state?"

"I don't know. A friend needed a ride."

"What friend? A girl?" Jarret found himself grinning, amused at the thought of Peter having a girlfriend.

Roland hesitated. "Yeah. A girl."

"Who?" Chantelle, who hadn't been paying attention to their conversation before, twisted to see Roland over her shoulder.

Roland hesitated again, longer. "You don't know her."

"Does she go to River Run?"

Roland shrugged.

Adjusting her seatbelt to get some slack, Chantelle turned completely in her seat and draped an arm around the headrest. "So tell me who."

Roland let out a sigh. "Brice."

"Brice Maddox?" Chantelle laughed. "Isn't she the girl whose house just got vandalized?"

"I didn't think she was the dating type," Jarret said, choosing his words. He'd seen her in the halls. That girl's attitude said she had no time for guys. How had Peter made friends with her?

"It's not a date. She needed a ride. She's been helping Peter with the Durango."

Chantelle laughed in that cruel way that only a girl can. "Not helping him enough, obviously, if it broke down an hour from home." She turned back around and adjusted her seatbelt.

Roland stared out the window with a stony expression.

Jarret turned to Chantelle. They had an hour-long drive. They should get to know each other.

"Wanna listen to the radio?" he said, turning it on.

"Sure." She smiled in a sweet way that Jarret could get used to.

"What do you listen to?"

Their conversation went from favorite songs and least favorite classes to favorite foods, pet peeves, and hobbies.

"Watching movies and texting friends ain't hobbies," Jarret said. He'd already told her that he was into horseback riding, fencing, marksmanship, and pool.

"They are the way I do them." Chantelle giggled and beamed a smile at him. "Oh, and I take pictures."

"Now you're talking." If she liked photographing things, she could have a field day on their property. It ran along a river on one side and a cliff on another. Farmer's field in the back. Evergreens scattered everywhere. Cool rock formations closer to the house. Yeah, he could give her the tour one day. Maybe she'd like to take pictures of their horses, too. "So what do you take pictures of?"

"Myself." She took her cellphone from her purse and tapped her thumbs on the screen. "My friends. Sometimes food. Wanna see?"

Jarret's gaze slid from the road to her phone. He glimpsed an image of her in a swimsuit. Pulse shifting to a higher gear, his gaze clicked back to the road. "No. I hate looking at pictures."

"But they're pictures of me."

"I'm driving anyway."

She leaned and whispered in his ear, "I'll show you later."

A shiver ran down his neck from her breath on his skin. He glanced in the rearview mirror.

Roland stared, mouth hanging open and a hint of disgust on his face. "So, Chantelle, do you go to church?" he blurted out. First words he'd spoken since Jarret had questioned him about Peter.

Jarret's guard went up. He didn't want to talk to Chantelle about his faith. It was too personal, deeply personal. Not something he'd ever share with her. Why had Roland asked?

"Me?" Chantelle flipped golden curls off her shoulder and twisted to face him. "No. I... mean... I have. But hardly ever. Why?"

"Are you a Christian?" This from the boy who ran out of speech class because fear took his voice.

Irritated by the shift in conversation, Jarret tried shooting a warning through the rearview mirror but Roland didn't acknowledge it.

"I don't know. I guess so. I mean, I celebrate Christmas. That counts, right?" She giggled and looked at Jarret.

Roland turned back to the window. "Hmm."

Seething inside, Jarret threw hostile glances at Roland through the mirror. Roland caught none of them. Why had he butted into their conversation? Why bring up her faith? Maybe Roland had seen through her right from the start. Maybe Roland thought she wasn't right for Jarret, wasn't his type. What was his type? One of the Fire Starters? What would a faithful Catholic girl see in him? He'd messed up in big ways that everyone knew about.

Clutching the steering wheel with stiff hands, Jarret stared straight ahead and stepped on the accelerator. Rain drops pounded on the windshield and the wipers thumped them away, never fast enough, leaving Jarret with a blurry view of the road and nothing else.

Did he want to date Chantelle knowing that the Lord wasn't high on her priority list? Did he want to date her knowing that her morals were lower than his? He had no intention of giving in, but did he want to put himself to that test every day? How long before he caved? Then where would he be?

The gloominess outside seeped into his soul. He couldn't become that person again. He'd hated himself back then.

Jarret decided. He had to break up with her.

Lights flashed in the side and rearview mirrors, reminding him of the flash of light he'd seen before slugging C.W. But these lights were red and blue.

Stomach sinking, Jarret lifted his foot from the gas and tapped the brakes. He pulled off the road and into the strip of grass, coming close to a little wooden fence he hadn't seen at first glance.

With a heavy sigh, he dug his wallet out of his back pocket.

An officer with a flashlight marched up beside the car and tapped on the window.

Jarret lowered the window and held up his license, insurance card, and registration while raindrops sprinkled his face and arm. This was getting old.

"Well, hello there, Jarret West. We meet again." Officer O'Brien smiled down at him. The same officer that had talked to him two weeks ago and given him his first speeding ticket over the summer.

~ ~ ~

Jarret stopped grinding his teeth and shoved his speeding ticket into the glove compartment. For the past twenty minutes, he hadn't stopped thinking about Officer O'Brien. Chantelle hadn't stopped talking about every person she knew who had gotten a speeding ticket. And Roland had been peering out the windows, as if worried Jarret would take a wrong turn.

"There! That's his car." Roland pointed to the front windshield, his arm sticking between Jarret and Chantelle. As soon as Jarret had turned down this road on the outskirts of town, Roland had scooted to the edge of his seat. He'd been peering through the relentless rain and thumping windshield wipers with bated breath ever since.

Worried that the car would hydroplane on the saturated road, Jarret gripped the steering wheel and tried to stay focused. The darkness and hard rain kept him from getting a good look at the neighborhood. The Chrysler's high beams revealed houses set back at random distances from the road. Jarret caught an occasional address on the closer houses. This area must've been a pizza delivery guy's nightmare. Jarret's nightmare too, tonight. Rickety fence here, abandoned car there—

"Stop! Stop!" Roland turned in his seat and stared out a side window.

Oh, so the abandoned car must've been Peter's Durango. Anyway, the entire street seemed old and uncivilized.

Foot to the brake pedal, Jarret eased to a stop and then threw the car in reverse. He grabbed Chantelle's seatback and peered over his shoulder through streams of rain rushing down a blurry back window. He backed onto the wide muddy berm of the road, getting as close to Peter's car as he dared. His taillights shined on the Durango, showing no one inside.

"So where are they?" Jarret glanced about for the nearest house.

Roland dug his phone from a jacket pocket. "I'll find out."

Chantelle dropped the visor and inspected her face in the lighted mirror, tilting her head left and right. After wiping under one eye, she flipped it back up and turned to Jarret. "Pretty tense trip."

He nodded, giving a wide-eyed look to show that he seriously agreed. "Ain't over yet. As soon as we drop off the battery, we have to do it all again."

"Maybe we can stop for coffee and wait for the rain to pass."

"Maybe." He liked her attitude. Since picking up Roland, she hadn't complained once. He'd enjoyed talking to her. And she seemed willing and able to turn a hacked-up night into something kind of fun. Maybe he shouldn't break up with her.

"Are we dropping him off?" Chantelle indicated Roland with a glance as she rubbed a hand over Jarret's thigh.

Irritation shooting through him, Jarret flung her hand off his leg. "No, we're not dropping him off. In this mess? We're gonna drop the battery off."

Phone to his ear, Roland scooted from the middle of the backseat to the seat behind Jarret. He peered out the window. "No, I don't see it. But we'll find it. See you in a minute."

Jarret turned around in his seat to face him. "So where is he?"

Roland pointed out his window, over a patch of condensation. "First house up that street."

"Okay. We'll drop his tools and battery off and head home." Glad to have reached their destination in one piece, Jarret straightened and shifted into drive.

"No, you can drop me off too." Roland faced his window as he spoke.

A truck passed by, blinding Jarret as it drew near. Jarret stepped up the speed of the windshield wipers, though he hated the sound of it thumping so quickly, and he pulled onto the road. "No way am I leaving you out here."

"Peter can take me home."

Jarret turned the Chrysler onto the dark street Roland had indicated and watched for the first driveway. "I'm not that confident in Peter's skills. What if he doesn't get his car working?"

"He just needs a new battery."

The road turned, a guardrail on one side and a slope on the other. Then the road straightened and old wooden fencing and a dirt driveway came into view. Trees and bushes shrouded any house that lay behind them.

"Here?" Jarret slowed and turned onto the driveway, the headlamps giving the only light.

"I think so."

Raindrops glistening in the headlights, Jarret followed the driveway to the attached garage of a dark ranch house with a covered stoop and overgrown landscaping. A cement path led from the driveway to the front door in the middle of the house. The front door looked especially dark. A closer look told Jarret that the front door was open with only the storm door closed.

"If they're in the house, why is it so dark?" Chantelle said.

"I don't know, but this is where they are." Roland zipped up his jacket, lifted the hood, and took a deep breath. "Thanks for the ride, Jarret. I know you didn't want to do this, but I really appreciate your help. And sorry for messing up your date."

Peeved, Jarret shifted into park and turned to face Roland. "Oh no you don't. I am not leaving you here. We're an hour from home. It's pouring rain, and I don't trust Peter behind the wheel of a car. Or anywhere else."

Roland rolled his eyes. "Jarret, don't worry. I told Papa what I was doing. He doesn't have a problem with it. And Peter can't change the battery until the rain stops, so we won't be driving in the rain."

"No." Jarret turned around again, shifted into drive, and turfed the front yard. He jerked to a stop by the front door and tapped the button to pop open the trunk.

"What are you doing?" Chantelle held onto the front dash.

"Get Peter's crap out of the trunk and get back in the car." Meaning business, Jarret glared at Roland through the rearview mirror.

"No, I'm staying with him."

Gritting his teeth, Jarret sucked in a breath. He couldn't control Roland. He couldn't even control himself. "All right. Fine. We'll all stay. Chantelle, you can run into the house and I'll park in the driveway."

"What? No." Chantelle opened her mouth and her brows crinkled with a look of horror. "I'm not going in there. We're just going to hang out in a dark house? No way. Let's drop Roland off and go home."

"I'm not leaving Roland here."

"I'll be fine. And if I'm not, I'll call." Roland tugged the door handle and the interior lights flicked on.

Squeezing the steering wheel, Jarret continued to peer through the mirror. "Oh, and I'm supposed to turn around and come get you then?"

"Forget it. I'll find a taxi. Maybe that's what I should've done." Expression neutral, Roland swung open the car door and jumped out.

"You, little—" Jarret cut off the last word, regretting what had come out of his mouth. Then he flung his hands up in resignation. "All right. Have it your way."

Roland slammed the car door and raced to the trunk.

Harsh words and remorse bounced around Jarret's head as he watched Roland through the rain. Two seconds later, Roland slammed the trunk and raced for the front door. The door opened as he drew near, Peter holding it for him. Peter waved.

Resisting the urge to make a rude gesture, Jarret shifted into gear. Before he stepped on the gas, he glimpsed movement by the door.

One hand to his hood, Roland jogged to the driver-side window.

Jarret lowered his window, rain sprinkling his face. "What is it now?"

"Sorry I said that. I totally appreciate this."

Repentance overcoming him, hating the control freak he'd become, Jarret gave a nod. "Me too."

Roland gave the hint of a smile. "I'll call you when we get on the road." He took off, Peter welcoming him into the pitch-black house.

"Can we go home now?" Chantelle asked with a sigh.

"Yeah." Jarret turfed the yard again, circling around to the dirt driveway. "We're going home."

~ ~ ~

Numb from all that he'd experienced in one night, Jarret clutched the steering wheel in stiff hands and drove down Forest Road toward Chantelle's neighborhood. He stared at the section of road illuminated by the headlights. A sprinkle of raindrops fell diagonally in the light. The night hadn't turned out as expected. At all.

Jarret's gaze drifted to Chantelle, who lay curled up in the front passenger seat. He'd been flip-flopping all night over whether to continue seeing her or break up. But the ride home had given him time to think. He would need to talk to her tonight and say a few things he really didn't want to say. He'd probably damage his image from this. But his conscience told him that he had no choice.

Jarret flicked the wipers on and off. As soon as they'd headed for home, the storm had grown in intensity. Half an hour later, it subsided. Not long after that, Roland called to say that they were on the road. And Jarret had finally relaxed.

He'd had to reject Chantelle's advances once again. "Trying to drive," he'd said, removing her hand from his chest. She sulked and then curled up and closed her eyes.

Jarret pulled into Chantelle's driveway, shifted into park, and shut off the wipers. The light over the garage and the porch light shone. But no light showed through any windows. Was anyone home? He'd expected to see Tyrone in the window or on the porch.

He rubbed his chest to ease the tension that had been building since turning onto her street. Tiny drops of rain gathered on the windshield.

"Hey, Chantelle, you're home."

"Hmm?" Sleepily, she uncurled her legs and arms and stretched in a way that emphasized her feminine figure.

Jarret turned away and breathed. "Hey, before you go, I need to tell you something."

"Hmm, what?" She leaned on his shoulder and moved her hand toward his chest.

Part of him wanted her touch and wanted to kiss her goodnight. He could even see himself doing it and not going through with his new intention. An instant before she made contact, Jarret grabbed her hand and eased her back, getting a few inches of space between them.

"Hey, listen." He waited until she turned her eyes to him, dark eyes with enormous pupils. "I don't want to go out anymore. Okay?" It wasn't the smoothest breakup, but he couldn't think of a nicer way to put it. He didn't want to make excuses or lead up to it with a bunch of explanations.

She froze. Shock and then anger flashed in her aqua blue eyes. Fury transforming her posture and face, she tensed and jerked back. "You're breaking up with me?"

He wanted to remind her that this was their first actual date and that they hadn't been "seeing" each other for more than a week. Okay, so they'd messaged each other a week before that, but still.

"Sorry. I like you, but this isn't what I want right now."

She huffed. "You just don't want to be committed to one girl. I see how you flirt. You want every girl."

"What?" No other response came to mind. Why would she say that? He hadn't even tried to mess with her.

She wrestled with her purse strap and flung the car door open. "You're not going to get what you want." She slammed the door to his Chrysler 300, making him wince, and stomped to the front porch.

Dumbstruck, he watched her climb the steps and unlock the front door to her house.

Once she stepped inside, relief washed over him and he exhaled. Then he threw the car in reverse and backed out of the driveway.

CHAPTER 31

Keefe drove down a dark residential street for the third time, peering at house numbers. Tidy little houses lined both sides of the road, a street lamp here or there. As he tried to make out the numbers on a bungalow, a big drop of water landed on the windshield, coming from soggy leaves overhead. The rain had stopped some time ago.

Flipping the wipers on and off, Keefe peered again. Not the address he wanted.

Did the Franciscans live in a house? He'd passed a church with a brick building next door. Could've been a school, but maybe it wasn't. Did the Franciscans live there?

The excitement that had raced through him at the start of his trip had gone, a queasy uncertainty replacing it. Did he dare knock on their door so late? He still wasn't sure if this was God's will for him.

Keefe took a deep breath and released it. Whatever else God wanted, He must've wanted Keefe to come to Piper's aid. Without Keefe's help, would she have continued her journey toward reconciliation with her father? Or would she have gone home? She'd taken the flat tire as a sign to give up, Keefe's help as a sign to follow through. Maybe God had only wanted him to be an instrument in Piper's journey.

And maybe God had wanted him to learn to let his light shine, instead of hiding it. What kind of Christian was he if he felt too uncomfortable to pray in public or tell another of his desire to join the Franciscans? No matter his vocation, he should never be ashamed of the Gospel or scandalized in Jesus Christ.

Keefe turned the wheel with sweaty, jittery hands, pulling into an empty driveway. He backed up and headed in the opposite direction. The brick building must've been the friary. He'd give it a try.

Still scanning the dark houses on either side, he crept down the road.

And what about Roland's call for help? If Keefe had been home, he could've driven Roland himself. Or he could've talked Jarret into helping him. Keefe wished he could've called Jarret back, but his phone had died after the call. And of course he only brought a charger that plugs into an outlet. Had Jarret decided to help Roland anyway? And what about Chantelle? Had he taken her home first or would they be out late together? She wouldn't be his downfall, would she?

The church and the brick building came into view. Keefe found an empty spot behind a compact car and parallel parked. A cross on the side of the building and a Blessed Mother statue in the yard gave him the feeling that he'd found the place. Soft yellow light illuminated a few second story windows, but the first-floor windows were all dark.

Keefe slumped back in the seat and took a deep breath, willing his body to relax. Should he be here at all? Was 8:42 p.m. too late to bother them? If his phone hadn't died, he at least could have called.

Heart rate kicking up and palms getting even sweatier, Keefe shut off the engine and opened the door. He reached behind the seat and pulled out his overnight bag. Of course the friars would let him in. He could explain why he was late. No problem.

Keefe exited the truck and cut through wet grass to a sidewalk. Another sidewalk led to the door. Standing under an overhang, a yellow light glowing above the door to the friary, he curled his fingers into a fist and knocked.

To avoid appearing anxious, he turned and glanced back at the street. The evening air cooled his sweaty neck and face. The long drive had thoroughly drained him, threw him off kilter and made all his muscles stiff. A minute passed. He knocked again, then stretched the arm that didn't hold his bag.

His heart rate slowed as the minutes ticked by. They weren't expecting guests at this hour. They'd likely given up on him. He should find a hotel room and come back in the morning. He could always sleep in the truck. Or he could rest a while and head back home, maybe stop at a diner to charge his phone. Or stop at a store and pick up a phone charger for the truck. He could call and see what Jarret had decided to do. Maybe Jarret needed him tonight.

Five, six, seven minutes... Keefe knocked one last time, counted to thirty, and turned to go. He'd been asking for signs and getting them left and right. He hoped God found his thick head more amusing than annoying.

"Sorry, Lord." Keefe slung the strap of his canvas travel bag over his shoulder and strode back toward the truck. He found a hint of peace in accepting defeat. He'd have to reevaluate a few things and start over. "I know you tried to tell me. I guess I misread your signs."

A soft sound came from behind—a door creaking open— followed by a voice. "Hello, there."

Keefe stopped and turned around.

"Were you knocking at the door?" A chubby man in a dark robe with a white cord for a belt shuffled down the sidewalk. "We were at Night Prayer when I thought I heard a noise. Our house makes all kind of noise so I wasn't sure."

"Uh, yeah." Keefe met him halfway, hope shooting through him. He still had a chance. "That was me."

"You wouldn't happen to be Keefe West, would you?" The brother's smile lit up his entire face.

"Yeah. I... I'm sorry I'm late."

"We were worried about you, called your house. Your father said you'd be late."

"You spoke with my father? How'd he know?" Keefe realized he hadn't called anyone to tell them of his delays.

"I guess he spoke with your brother." He motioned toward the friary. "Come on in. I bet you're tired. Were you knocking long?"

A pair of sandals lay on a throw rug to one side of the door. As Keefe crossed the threshold, an unfamiliar feeling zipped through him, a juxtaposition of peace and excitement, of comfort and apprehension. It started now.

"I'll show you to your room." The brother shuffled down a clean and simple hallway with hardwood flooring, white walls, and a single picture of Saint Pope John Paul II in the arms of the Blessed Mother. "Our chapel is that-a-way." He pointed one way and turned another, leading Keefe through a living room with bookshelves and simple chairs. "Are you hungry?"

"Starved." Keefe's hand shot to his stomach, which growled at the question, and his thoughts turned to the snacks he'd left in the truck.

"After you're settled in your room, I'll get you something to eat. We have plenty of leftovers, unless Brother Damien got to them." He chuckled. Then he twisted around, walking sideways a few steps to look at Keefe. Concern showed in small but jovial eyes behind his wire-framed glasses. A strip of white hair circled around the back of his balding head. His nose, like an arrow, seemed to point out his smiling mouth. "And then we'll talk more tomorrow, okay? We observe the spirit of silence after nine, but if you have any questions, let me know. Oh, maybe I didn't tell you. I got your name and never gave mine. I'm Brother Simon." He offered his hand.

Holding the strap of his bag in place over his shoulder, Keefe wiped his other hand on his jeans and then shook the friar's hand.

Brother Simon turned face forward as he led Keefe up a hardwood staircase. "Glad you made it in one piece. We were worried about you. Maybe that's not the right word. Pray, hope, and don't worry." At the top of the stairs he looked back. "You know who said that?"

Keefe shook his head. The conflicting feelings still raced inside him, leaving him too confused to really speak.

"Padre Pio. He's a wonderful saint. If you don't know him yet, you will— Oh, which reminds me." He paused in the middle of a long hallway with doors on either side and patted the sides of his robe, as if searching for something in a pocket. "No, I don't have it. But I don't need it. I remember."

Keefe shook his head, not understanding.

Brother Simon smiled and shuffled to a nearby door. Twisting the knob, he opened it and motioned Keefe into the room. "John 1:39-41," he mumbled, moving to a simple desk in the corner of the room. He flipped open a Bible, one of two books on the table. "Get settled and I'll bring you something to eat. Later, while you enjoy quiet time before bed, you can read the Come & See verse, John 1:39-41. Because that's what the three days are about." He turned to the door but stopped. "Have you called your father to say that you made it safely?"

"Oh, no, I forgot. Actually, my phone's dead." Keefe withdrew his cellphone and charger from his travel bag and then dropped the bag on the floor.

"I will take care of that, and I'll call your father to let him know you arrived. You are now on retreat." Brother Simon stuck out a hand, palm up. "Unless you feel that you need it, may I have your phone? You won't want it during the retreat."

"I won't?" Keefe handed over the phone and charger. What if Jarret needed him? What if Roland—

Brother Simon left the room and closed the door.

Keefe stood frozen for a moment, forcing himself to trust in God's will. Then he turned and took in the room. In addition to the simple desk in the corner, the room consisted of a neatly-made bed, a little sink, and a lamp on a nightstand. Over the bed hung the same crucifix that Keefe had recently hung in his bedroom, the same crucifix with the image of Christ that had spoken to St. Francis: the San Damiano crucifix. Keefe took a deep breath and exhaled slowly, muscles relaxing and cares slipping away. He knelt by the bed, his gaze on the face of Jesus. "I'm here, Lord."

He waited as if expecting the Lord to reply. A feeling of peace rose inside him, along with a hint of apprehension. Keefe felt a question posed to him, but he didn't understand it yet.

"Did You want me to be here? Is this my calling?"

He allowed silence to stretch out before speaking again. "If it's not, let me down easy, Lord. And show me what to do next."

An ache bloomed in his heart. If this wasn't God's will for his life, what had the inner promptings meant?

He stretched his arms out on the bed and buried his face in the bedspread, praying from the ache in his heart. "I'll be whatever You want me to be, go wherever You want me to go. And if You don't answer me today, I'm okay with that. And if I spend my life searching and wondering where I belong, well, that's okay too. You alone are my answer. Your will is what I want. Let me be in Your will."

CHAPTER 32

A light knock on the door yanked Keefe from dreams of traveling down endless highways.

Then a voice broke the silence, words mumbled in Latin, followed by words he could understand. "Peace and all good."

Longing to return to sleep but also feeling a sense of responsibility and a need to get started, Keefe blinked at unfamiliar surroundings and pushed himself up in bed. The window showed a dark early morning sky and let hazy bluish light into the little room. As Keefe tossed the blankets back, his memories came together and joy rushed into his heart. The Franciscan retreat. He'd made it!

Keefe washed up in the little sink in the corner of the room and threw his clothes on. Brother Simon had told him that the day would begin with Morning Prayer in the chapel at 6:30 am, which was 5:30 am in the time zone back home.

Leaving his room, he joined three other men in the hallway, two friars and one boy about his age. They all exchanged nods and shuffled toward the stairs. Downstairs, two more friars joined in the casual procession, coming from a hallway along the way and exchanging simple greetings or nods.

As Keefe entered the chapel, his gaze skittered over wooden pews and a pale tiled floor to the simple white altar and the cross above it. Keefe's skin prickled at the sight of the San Damiano crucifix high on the wall, the face of Christ glowing under a spotlight.

A friar motioned toward a pew, indicating where Keefe should sit. "You must be Keefe," he whispered.

Keefe nodded, mouthing the word "yes." He sat where directed, next to a friar with a tidy white beard. He counted four other retreatants, each sitting next to a friar with a thick prayer book. Brother Simon, who sat in the row in front of Keefe, glanced back with a smile, his glasses reflecting the yellow light of the overhead lamps as he turned.

After a moment of silence, the bearded friar next to Keefe pointed to a line of text in his prayer book. A minute later, everyone made the Sign of the Cross and the prayers began. "Lord, open my lips," the Brothers on one side of the chapel rang out.

"And my mouth shall declare your praise," the other side replied.

Keefe followed along with a penitential psalm, his gaze drifting to the altar and to the tall windows high in the walls. They revealed the rich blue of the sky at dawn, making Keefe sense something of the uniqueness of this call. While the world slept, the brothers of penance lifted their hearts to God.

Keefe's mind transported him to the first time he'd heard Franciscan friars praying Morning Prayer—Lauds, they'd called it. Last fall, the group that had stayed at the Brandts' Bed & Breakfast had gone out to the woods to pray, having nowhere big or private enough in the house. Keefe had spent the night to learn more about them. And in the morning, he'd followed them into the woods. He'd climbed a tree to watch without them knowing. He should've simply asked to go along. He'd made a spectacle of himself by falling out of the tree. But he wouldn't trade that humiliating experience for anything; it had set him on this journey.

"O God, You are my God, for You I long; for You my soul is thirsting..." The friars prayed different Psalms today but the words from the Psalms he'd heard that day in the fall weaved through his mind and spirit, lifting his soul higher and higher.

After Morning Prayer, they remained quiet for a time and then celebrated Mass, beams of sunlight now streaming in from the high windows on one side of the altar. The high ceiling allowed Keefe's spirit to soar, and he lost himself in the prayers of the Mass, the love of God surrounding him.

~ ~ ~

Didn't want to hurt her. Wish I knew myself better.
Shouldn't have started something with her at all.
She's pretty though. And a cheerleader. So she'll get over it.
She'll have another boyfriend tomorrow. If that's what she wants.
What do I want?

Jarret stuck the pen between pages of the journal and reclined back on the mound of pillows he'd piled against the headboard. His wet hair pressed against his neck and a drop of water rolled down his chest and onto the clean, dry t-shirt he'd put on after a long, hot shower.

The road trip, maybe even the date, had left him feeling grimy. As soon as he got home from dropping Chantelle off, he'd called Roland to make sure he was okay, and then jumped in the shower. Roland said they were almost home. The Durango ran fine with the new battery. Apparently, Peter knew cars. Or maybe Brice Maddox did.

Jarret inhaled a deep breath, slowly filling his chest with air. His muscles relaxed and strange feelings clashed in his mind—Strength? Pride about his spiritual victory? He did it. He broke up with a girl rather than stay in a situation that tempted him. He exhaled slowly and gazed at the ceiling.

With the memories of the canyon fading, fear of failure had grown. Maybe the Lord backed off on purpose so that Jarret could figure out how to handle life himself. He never would've thought it possible, but he could do this. He was on the right track and going to stay there. Nothing would stand in his way. *Thank you, Lord, for today.*

He opened his journal and wrote a few details about the day's trial, temptation, and victory.

Twenty minutes later, footfalls in the stairwell made him stop writing and drop his pen. Even with the cast off, Roland didn't walk as silently as he had before the crutches. A light rapping sounded on the door.

"That you, Roland?"

The door inched open.

The blood drained from Jarret's face as he realized that he held his journal on his thigh. He twisted around and stuffed it between the headboard and a pillow, then twisted back to find Roland in the doorway. And someone behind him. Peter?

"Hey, I wanted to say thanks." Roland swung the door open farther. He'd combed his damp wavy hair back and wore his black jacket, making him look like a greaser from the 1950s.

Peter stepped up beside him, his dirty blond hair flattened to his forehead but sticking out everywhere else. "Yeah, thanks, dude. You're lucky you didn't stick around. We got a few house guests before the storm passed, and everything got wild. A ton of crazy going on out there..." He motioned with his index fingers, making air circles near his head.

Still feeling exposed, Jarret nodded and let out a breathy chuckle. Then he felt stupid for laughing at something Peter said. He had no clue what he meant.

"I'll tell you about it later," Roland said.

Head bowed, Peter took another step into the room, practically standing on top of Roland. "I, uh, know you and I aren't exactly friends. So I really appreciate what you did for me. Totally went out of your way and everything. You know, even after I—"

Roland bumped Peter and threw him a warning glance.

Too late. Fire flared inside and heat crept to Jarret's cheeks. He hated to think that he'd just turned red. "Yeah, well, Peter, now you *really* owe me." He jumped off the bed.

"Well, goodnight." Roland tugged Peter's arm.

"Yeah, goodnight." Peter backed out of the room and turned down the hallway, heading toward Roland's room.

Roland touched the doorknob and started to shut the door.

"Hey." Jarret lunged and grabbed the door up high, stopping Roland from shutting it.

Worry flashed in Roland's eyes, a look Jarret had often seen, but the look soon mellowed to something more like surrender. "Yeah?"

Jarret slid his hand to the knob, maybe needing to feel in control of something. "Why's he here so late?"

"He's staying the night."

"Oh really?" A block of lead settled in his gut. And the flames of the internal fire leaped and twisted. He did not want Peter in his house. All the practical jokes he'd done to Jarret over the past year, all the rude comments...

"We're getting an early start tomorrow. Camping trip, remember?"

He took a breath, forcing the flames down. "Oh."

~ ~ ~

Cool drops of rainwater trickled from the canopy of leaves, striking Jarret's arms, head, and neck and making spots on Desert's creamy buckskin coat. A squirrel jumped from one overhead branch to another, creating a shower where the early morning sunlight stole through the leaves, the raindrops glistening like grace from Heaven.

The rain had stopped late last night or maybe early this morning, leaving nature drippy but fresh and washed clean.

At dawn, Jarret had awoken feeling the same way: clean, free, glad he'd broken it off with Chantelle, and ready for a fresh start. He decided that he wouldn't date for a while. He'd just focus on his last year of high school. Maybe he'd start dating in college, or even after college. If God wanted him to marry, he'd meet his future wife eventually.

How would he know when he found her? *Whatever.* He'd figure that out later.

He may have lost the special awareness of Jesus in his life, but he wasn't giving up. He could do this. He did the right thing last night. And more than once. He didn't have to help Peter, but he did. Granted, he'd only done it for Roland. But he'd done it. He had this game under control.

Jarret rode toward the stables, spotted Mr. Digby by the steps to the veranda, and dismounted.

"Morning," Jarret hollered, leading Desert by the reins.

"Morning, Jarret." Mr. Digby strolled to him at his typical leisurely pace. "You staying home while Roland and your father go camping and Keefe's out of town?"

"Yup. I got plenty to keep me busy."

"Hmm." Mr. Digby reached for the reins. "I'll take care of Desert. Gonna clean the saddles today. You go on in. I believe Nanny is cooking up a nice big breakfast for you boys, what with Roland having a guest."

Jarret's stomach sank and his limbs tensed. He'd forgotten that Peter was over. He strode to the garage that he'd left open, anxious to get back to his bedroom. Who knew what Peter would do in his absence? He'd pulled too many "practical jokes" on Jarret already. One more and Jarret doubted that he'd have the strength to hold back.

Jarret yanked his boots off in the mudroom and walked silently through the house in his socks.

The smell of bacon tempted him as he passed through the great room. Nanny, with her back to the dining room doorway, dug through one of several boxes on the table. Two stacks of folded laundry also sat on the table. Roland and Peter had probably eaten breakfast already, unless she planned to serve them at the bar counter or kitchen table.

Jarret turned to the staircase. As he mounted the stairs, he noticed sunlight streaming from both his and Roland's bedrooms, throwing rectangles of light on the hallway floor. Why was the door to his bedroom open?

His senses heightened.

He reached the top step and stepped into the hallway. His bedroom door hung wide open and a figure moved in his room. Roland would never go into his room without permission.

Jarret clenched his jaw.

The figure stepped into view, rushing to leave. Messy blond hair, a flannel shirt, and jeans.

Peter and Jarret met in the doorway.

Jarret's hackles rose. Suspicion. Anger. Hate? Every muscle in his body tensing, he envisioned slamming Peter into the door.

"Oh, hey, Jarret."

"Why are you in my room?" Jarret prided himself in the heroic amount of self-control he used and his willingness to give Peter a chance. But he'd better have an airtight reason.

"Oh, I..." Peter pointed over his shoulder and stepped aside as if to squeeze past Jarret.

Not having it, Jarret shifted to completely block him from leaving until he spit out an explanation.

"Mrs. Digby... er... Nanny told me to take some things up to your room, clothes and stuff." He looked at the pile on Jarret's bed.

"New clothes, I think." He turned and gave Jarret the once-over, the hint of a smirk on his face. "Did you have Nanny pick out your clothes?"

Jarret looked Peter up and down, arrogance and anger seeping through his pores. "Why didn't she have Roland do it?"

"Uh, he's in the bathroom changing, trying stuff on, I guess." Peter waved his brows and smiled, seeming unduly amused. "Guess she wants to make sure it all fits." He paused and a cocky grin stretched across his face. "She make you do that? Try stuff on?"

Irritation surged through Jarret, but he held back. He slammed Peter to the door in his mind though. Again. How much longer could he fight the impulse?

Remaining in control and ready to answer, he grinned back, but he couldn't keep the threatening look from his eyes. "No. Nanny doesn't *make* me do anything." He stepped toward Peter.

Peter visibly tensed but didn't budge. He looked Jarret over again and cocked a brow, a look of challenge creeping onto his face. His expression and body language almost said, "Do it. I dare ya." But not quite.

"Thought you two were heading out early."

"Oh. Yeah. Roland always has one more thing to do, you know?" He shifted his weight to one leg and propped his hands on his hips, a friendly, casual posture. "Hey, so it's not too late to change your mind. If you decide you want to go. Come up anytime."

"No." In addition to his original reason, he now had Chantelle to think about. He'd hate to see her all weekend at the campground. It would be uncomfortable for them both.

"Okay. Suit yourself."

Disgusted at the tired phrases Peter often used, Jarret sneered and shook his head. Then he hardened his scowl. "Don't go in my room for any reason."

Peter raised his brows and nodded, still with the grin. "Sure thing, Jarret."

Jarret shifted to move out of his way.

Peter squeezed past, his arm grazing Jarret's chest. "Next time I'll set your stuff on the floor."

A rush of animosity struck Jarret, making his eyelids flicker and his hands curl into fists. While all he could think about was grabbing Peter and slamming him into something, he grabbed his door and swung it shut.

Then he took a breath, turned away from the door on the exhale, and sank his hands into his hair. This was another victory. It really was. It just didn't feel like one. It felt like he'd let Peter walk all over him.

His gaze landed on the new clothes on his bed, and his suspicions rose. He glanced about his room, looking for things that Peter may have messed with. His gaze stopped on the scapular he'd tossed onto his dresser after Keefe had given it to him.

How was Keefe's retreat going? He wished he could talk to him. Keefe had a way of putting things into perspective. Jarret would have to handle this one on his own.

Jarret snatched the scapular from the dresser and shoved it into the front pocket of his jeans.

CHAPTER 33

Keefe sat before a plate of scrambled eggs and toast at a long table in the friary dining room.

A brother with a thick silver beard and a serious demeanor led them in the Prayer Before Meals, then he glanced at each of the retreatants, his gaze ending on Keefe. "I'm Brother Giles. I'd like to welcome our new retreatant." The serious expression gave way to a sincere smile. "This is Keefe West. He comes from South Dakota, a good nine-hour drive, right?"

Heat slid up Keefe's neck. Not ready to explain to everyone what made him so late, he only nodded.

"Yesterday, we welcomed the retreatants and invited them to join us at Vespers and Adoration. We got to know each other over dinner and recreation, and we shared a bit about our lifestyle. I believe Brother Simon gave you the 'Come and See' verse to contemplate last night?" Brother Giles' pale eyebrows climbed up his forehead.

Keefe nodded again, realizing he hadn't even looked at the verse. He'd poured out his thanksgiving for having made it here, and then he'd swirled in thoughts of unworthiness—was he really meant for this calling? And he'd made every effort to renew his trust in the Lord's will: he was here for a reason. Sleep had overwhelmed him then, and he'd crawled into bed without another thought.

"So we'll go around the room with introductions for Keefe, and I'll give you a general overview of our day. As much as possible, retreatants follow the pattern of our day, but with a bit more time for discernment." Brother Giles turned to the boy on Keefe's right, a kid with brown skin and a mop of black curls. "Would you like to go first?"

The boy sat hunched over his plate, fidgeting with a napkin. He wiped his mouth and turned to Keefe, now tapping his fingers on the table. "Oh, hey, my name's Wolfgang. I come from a big family. Sort of in the middle of ten brothers and sisters." He gestured with one hand and bounced his leg while he spoke, seeming unable to hold still. "We live here in Minnesota, about three hours away. One of my older sisters is a nun, and one of my brothers is studying for the priesthood." Leg still bouncing, he shut his mouth and smiled.

Keefe nodded.

The boy next to Wolfgang introduced himself, turning his cool green eyes to Keefe. Active in youth ministry and an altar boy, Kieran and his family were good friends with their parish priest. His priest suggested he prayerfully consider that God might be calling him.

"I'm Alex," the next retreatant said, his voice soft and misty like clouds of incense that soon dissipate. "I've been an altar boy since fourth grade, have two brothers and a sister, and I'm homeschooled. I've wanted to be a Franciscan since fourth grade." He glanced at Keefe and a few others, his reserved manner making him seem like the contemplative sort.

Phil, the final retreatant, was homeschooled and active in youth ministry too. He wore a baby blue oxford shirt, neat and crisp as if ready for prep school, and he spoke with a confident air, his hazel eyes conveying inner strength.

Over the course of breakfast, the brothers introduced themselves too: Charles, Bernard, Salvador, Benedict, Leopold,

Paschal. While they all had the brown robes in common, and presumably the desire to follow in the footsteps of St. Francis, their individual personalities shone through as they each spoke. Brother Leopold had a dry sense of humor. Brother Salvador came across as calm and collected. Brother Charles smiled while he spoke, evidently a humorous type. Keefe stopped trying to memorize names and appearances—a shiny bald head, a dark tan, a scraggly black beard, a trim white beard, appears too young for facial hair—and instead concentrated on their brief introductions. Most hinted at the reason they'd felt called.

Running a hand over his beard, Brother Giles explained how he'd known of his vocation since childhood. Brother Salvadore had gone to college and worked two years as an engineer before answering the call. Brother Leopold realized later in life, too, after considering married life. "I grew up in a poor family but we were close." He twisted his scruffy black beard. "I could see myself being a father, raising children. Unfortunately, or perhaps fortunately, every girl I'd ever been interested in had one foot in the convent," he said dryly.

Brothers Benedict and Paschal came from big, devout Catholic families, both of which had always encouraged vocations. Other brothers discovered their calling in their teen years, through prayer or at the suggestion of a priest, relative, or friend. Two had siblings in other religious orders.

Keefe set his fork down, his appetite fading. The more he learned of the others, the louder the voice of insecurity spoke to him.

Still sitting hunched, Wolfgang cleaned his plate and fidgeted with his empty coffee cup. A friar offered to refill it, but Wolfgang put a hand up. "Oh, no thanks." He leaned back in his chair, dropping his hands to his thighs, one leg rapidly bouncing.

Noticing that everyone else had cleaned their plates too, Keefe forced himself to scrape up the last bit of scrambled eggs and shove it into his mouth. A knot formed in his stomach.

After a prayer thanking God for the food, Brother Salvadore assigned the friars and retreatants duties for the day, everyone except for Keefe.

"You'll come with me." Brother Giles touched the rosary that dangled from the white cord around his waist. "We can talk for a bit, and then I'll leave you to prayer. We have our hour of personal prayer now. Then we can talk more."

The friars and retreatants dispersed for the hour of prayer, some going to the courtyard, others to their bedrooms, one to the living room—passing Keefe and Brother Giles on their way out—and most to the chapel. Brother Giles talked with Keefe in the sun-drenched living room, giving him a few thoughts and a scrap of paper with Scripture verses. "We'll meet back here in an hour," he said. Then they parted ways, Brother Giles heading for the front door, Keefe for the chapel.

As he crossed the threshold, his heart flip flopped in his chest and a strange sensation overcame him, making him feel out of sorts. Seeing the others scattered throughout the chapel and wanting to spend his hour alone, Keefe almost drew back. He forced himself to the nearest pew, which was in the back row, and sank to his knees.

His gaze fixed onto the flame in the red sanctuary candleholder suspended from the ceiling. Then he looked to the San Damiano crucifix on the wall behind the candleholder. Natural light crept in through tall, narrow windows that were high on the walls to either side of the solid wall with the crucifix. The only indoor lighting came from the spotlight that illuminated the image of Christ with his arms outstretched on the cross.

Once again, conflicting emotions assaulted Keefe. He didn't belong here. Yet, in a way that didn't make sense, he felt more at home here than anywhere in his life. He wanted to be here. He wanted this life, a balance of prayer and service, with his goal to listen to God's voice and grow in his love for Him, to fulfill the promises he'd made back in Italy. *Lord, I will listen to Your voice. I will live knowing You are with me and that You love me.* He wanted to live the life of a Franciscan, a life of poverty and obedience—

Obedience? Convicted by the truth, Keefe bowed his head and rested them on his clasped hands. He'd lived obedience all his life. He'd lived under Jarret's thumb since he could remember. Was he seeking to trade obedience—*submission*—to Jarret with obedience to a religious order? Life as a friar would be just more of the same. Sure, it would be on a higher level, a more virtuous level; the friars would never ask him to do something against his conscience. But still more of the same. Shouldn't he be his own man, find the strength to stand on his own two feet first?

Make his own decisions, act on his own convictions... Could he do it? Did the thought of doing it frighten him? Was he running away from life, from the possibility of being lonely like Papa, from making mistakes like Jarret? Or maybe he wanted to get away from Jarret altogether. The things Keefe had gone along with...

The knot in Keefe's stomach tightened. He bowed his head lower. If the friars knew his past, they wouldn't want him.

He had to admit that the other boys here had much different upbringings. Half had been homeschooled. They'd all grown up in two-parent families, all surrounded by faith-filled people. Sheltered, protected, safe in enclosed gardens, prepared for a life of humility and self-sacrifice for the Kingdom of God.

Keefe's life had been a wreck... no enclosure whatsoever... a garden overrun with weeds. Mama had died when he was young, and Nanny had raised him for the most part. Papa didn't practice the faith regularly. Jarret had a ton of issues. And even Roland...

His entire family was dysfunctional.

He'd never been an altar server. Shoot, he'd been away from the Church for years. Couldn't remember a lick of the Catechism that Mama had taught him before she died. Being so wrapped up with Jarret's life, he'd never thought about a vocation. No one in his life, whether serious or joking, had ever suggested that he might have a calling. They'd seen nothing special in him.

Little knots formed within the big knot in his gut. Despair threatening to overtake him, Keefe dropped his head into his hands and a deep groan escaped. He hoped no one had heard it, but the acoustics in the chapel magnified everything.

Keefe took a breath and lifted his head. He needed to get off this train of hopelessness and make sense of things. This was a discernment retreat, after all. He needed to get better at discerning.

Let's see... Brother Giles had suggested that Keefe pray to the Holy Spirit and think of the gifts, talents, and interests that God had given him. What was he good at? With his recurve bow, he could hit a target seventy yards away. He could play six different pool games, and win. Though he'd never competed with anyone but family, he wasn't half bad at fencing or marksmanship. He could beat Jarret at any of those games. If he wanted to.

Annoyed by the pride he felt over those worldly accomplishments, he shook his head and his gaze shifted to the carved doors of the golden tabernacle behind the altar. *Jesus, my Lord.* What did any of that matter in the grand scheme of things? What other gifts did he have? He could take care of and look out for others, and follow another's lead. Maybe he needed to face it: he was best as a helper and a follower. Could he be called to family life? Marriage and children. Maybe he wasn't friar material.

Getting up from his knees, Keefe slouched back in the pew. He exhaled, rubbed his face, and gazed at the San Damiano crucifix. Maybe God had only wanted him to prove his willingness to go anywhere and do anything. And he'd done that. He'd come here.

He'd stopped along the way to help someone. And now maybe he should go back home. He wasn't cut out for this.

A hint of relief washed through him. If this wasn't his calling, he could stay with the familiar, his garden overrun with weeds. He wouldn't have to worry about what would become of Jarret, Papa, and Roland. He'd be able to help, encourage, and guide them. Maybe he could pull some weeds and build an enclosure.

Though sadness tinged his mood, Keefe smiled to himself, liking that goal. He could handle that one. He belonged there. Back home. Not here.

One of the brothers climbed to his feet. Keefe realized he'd been kneeling on the floor, off to the side of the altar, facing the tabernacle. Keefe glanced at his watch. Ten more minutes of prayer time. And he still hadn't considered the other things Brother Giles had asked him to think about. "Make a list of the pros and cons of single life, married life, and the consecrated life. You can write them down if that's easiest."

A short time later, while Keefe contemplated this, the other brothers left their pews, genuflected, and padded from the chapel. Moved by their reverence, Keefe remained a moment longer. Then he too slid from the pew and set off to find Brother Giles.

~ ~ ~

Brother Giles stood facing the tall bookshelf in the living room, thumbing through an old book with a green cover. He turned as Keefe strode into the room. "Ah there you are." He ran a hand over his head, flattening an unruly tuft of silver hair.

They returned to the same chairs they'd used earlier, sitting catty-corner from each other, a folder lying on the coffee table.

"Would you like something to drink—water, orange juice?" Brother Giles leaned forward as if ready to bounce back to his feet.

Touched by the brother's humility and eagerness to serve, Keefe shook his head before he could get the reply out. "No thanks."

He didn't want to delay things. Now that he believed he didn't belong here, that he belonged back home, he wanted to get this talk over with. Maybe he'd stay for the rest of the retreat, but maybe he should go. The desire to become a Franciscan had been a dream, but it was time to wake up. He would tell Brother Giles everything: what he liked about the Franciscans, the dysfunctional dynamics of his family, why he wasn't worthy of this calling, and what led him to believe God had called him in the first place.

As he made his resolve, a tingling sensation washed over him and sorrow came to his heart. He didn't want to let the dream go, but he was ready for this.

Settling back in his chair, smiling pleasantly, Brother Giles began. "Do you mind me asking what happened yesterday? You had a pretty long drive. First time you've left the state on your own, your father said. Did you get lost?"

"Lost? No. I..." Keefe cleared his throat, uncomfortable with the thought of retelling it all. "I... I passed a lady with car trouble. And I went back to help her." Keefe described the event, holding nothing back, not even his hesitancy to turn around and help her or his worry over arriving late. "I hope she got to her father before... you know."

"Yes, before her father passes on. We will pray she did. Let's have the brothers pray for them at Adoration this evening. I'm sure she's thanking God for you, regardless. You showed her Christ."

Cheeks burning, Keefe turned away. "I was worried you guys wouldn't take me seriously because of how late I was."

One eye narrowing a bit, Brother Giles gave Keefe a studied look. "Who is your Confirmation saint, Keefe?"

"My Confir..." The blood drained from his face. "...Confirmation saint?" The last nail hammered into the coffin of his Franciscan vocation. He'd never received the sacrament of Confirmation. How had this never occurred to him before? His mother had taught them the faith. They'd been baptized, made their First Confessions, and their First Holy Communions. They'd practiced the faith regularly until she died. After that, overwhelmed by grief, maybe feeling betrayed by God, Papa had stopped taking them to Mass. He'd sent them with the Digbys for a while, but even that had fizzled out. They'd missed Confirmation. All three of them: Keefe, Jarret, and Roland.

Keefe took a deep breath and ran a hand through his hair. Now he had even more to tell Brother Giles. On the road trip here, he'd considered how far he was willing to go and what he'd give up. He'd give it all up and go all the way. Not for what he wanted but for what God wanted.

Jesus, I trust you with this.

Encompassed in a bubble of peace, ready to lay it all out, he opened his mouth to speak.

Stomach growling, Jarret spread mayonnaise on a slice of wheat bread. Not wanting to cross paths with Peter again, he'd stayed in his room until long after he, Roland, and Papa had left for the campground. Jarret stacked lettuce, tomato slices, and bacon strips on two pieces of bread. Then he closed each sandwich with another slice of bread and grabbed an unopened bag of chips from the pantry.

"Did you try on those shirts I got you?" Nanny crossed the kitchen, heading for the laundry room. She carried an armful of clothes, probably Roland's new stuff.

"Yeah, sure." He liked new clothes so he'd tried them on as soon as Peter and Roland had left. She'd gotten him two pairs of jeans with a comfortable fit, two button-front shirts, and a slim-cut t-shirt. "They fit fine. Thanks for getting them."

"Oh, that's good. I'll need to have them back, soon as you can, so I can wash them." She paused in the middle of the kitchen.

"But they're not dirty yet." Mouth watering, Jarret bowed his head and blessed his food. Unable to wait another second, he took a bite.

"Sure they are. You can't wear something straight from the manufacturer. They have chemicals and who knows what. I once read a special report about that—"

"Okay, okay. I'll get them after I eat." He considered getting a plate and sitting down, but he'd waited too long to eat and his stomach said, "Eat now."

Still mumbling about the special report she'd heard, Nanny shuffled into the laundry room.

Jarret took another too-large bite, loving the taste of bacon and tomato.

What was he going to do today? He missed Keefe, but he liked that Peter, Roland, and Papa had gone. He'd have the house to himself for the weekend. What was Keefe doing now? Even if he couldn't call, maybe he could text.

He slipped his phone from his back pocket to see if Keefe had left him a message. Nope. But someone else had. Kyle?

Jarret took another bite and read the message: *Yo bro I cannot believe what you did to Chantelle.*

Amazed that Kyle knew already, Jarret shook his head. Chewing his sandwich, he typed a reply with his thumbs. *Like you never broke up with a girl before?*

Kyle's reply came a few seconds later. *Not like that man.*

Jarret squinted at his phone. *Not like what?*

Like what you did last night.

Jarret revisited their date in his mind. Okay, so they'd walked out of a movie, and he took her on a long, boring ride. He'd offered to take her home first.

Who told you about last night?

Everyone knows about it.

How? From who? He'd told no one, not even Keefe. Not Roland. Roland wouldn't have even guessed it.

Heard it at the campground. You know she is here.

Staring at his phone, Jarret shoved his second sandwich away. Chantelle told Kyle something? No, way. They barely spoke to each other at school. Jarret's thumb hovered over the keypad. Kyle frustrated him to no end sometimes. Jarret tapped the phone to call Kyle. Forget texting. He needed answers.

"Yo, bro. So, wow, you're actually calling me." Voices sounded in the background, laughter and shouting.

"Right. That's what a phone's for. Now tell me straight. What supposedly happened last night?"

Kyle laughed. "You were there. You don't know? You can tell me about it later. I expect details."

"I don't get what you're talking about," Jarret shouted.

"Okay, chill, brother."

"Where is she now?"

"She's sulking with her girlfriends. Don't think her brother knows, but when he does, you'd better watch out. And if Chantelle ends up like Zoe..."

"Wait. You think we... We didn't do anything." He hated that he'd just sounded whiny and freaked.

"That's not what she's saying. She's saying you tried for a home run, she called foul ball and game over, and then you dumped her."

Jarret pulled the phone from his ear and looked at it. Why would she lie? Why would she want people to think something like that had happened?

His phone buzzed, receiving another text. Jarret ended his phone call without saying goodbye and checked the message.

Another one of his friends. *Man, you are low. Can't believe you did that.*

He messaged back, *It's a lie. I didn't do anything.* As soon as he hit send, he wished he hadn't. The message made him sound pathetic.

Wow, talk about ruining his image in one day. Why was she lying?

Wishing the day back to normal, Jarret wrapped his second sandwich in a paper towel and put it in the refrigerator. Then he stomped up to his bedroom. He sat down to check his emails and found three about her lie.

Frustrated, he shut off the laptop and paced around his bedroom. He walked into the bright beams of warm sunlight that streamed through the windows, and he felt a whisper in his soul.

"Why are You letting this happen to me?" he said aloud. "I'm trying. You know I'm trying."

Still in the light from the window, he dropped to his knees and squeezed his eyes shut, willing the memory of the canyon to return to him. The dark night. The gentle breeze. The fire he'd made for Roland. No, that came after. He'd seen the Lord first.

"Jesus, where are You?" Anguish overwhelmed his soul. "Why can't I remember anymore? Did I imagine the whole thing?"

Heart aching with the pain of abandonment, he shoved his fingers into his hair and doubled over. The faintest impression lingered, a figure drawing near, then gone. The terrible things he'd said, the repentance, waking face down on the canyon floor. It all seemed like a dream that he'd lose in a few hours. No vivid impressions remained. Nothing. Had it all been a figment of his distraught mind? Had it never really happened at all?

"Don't leave me," he whispered, drained of all strength. How could he do this on his own? He couldn't.

Wanting to write down a prayer, needing to keep something of the memory, Jarret crawled to his bed and shoved his hand between the cool mattresses. He moved his hand left and right, finding nothing. Then he reached farther to each side. Nothing.

Jarret froze, suspicion dawning on him.

His journal was gone and only one person would've taken it. Not Roland. Never Keefe. Nanny and Papa rarely set foot in his room.

Peter's pink face, tousled hair, and cocky grin appeared in Jarret's mind. Peter Brandt. They'd nearly ran into each other as

Peter had tried leaving his room. He must've taken it this morning before heading out. Did Peter have his journal with him at the campground?

Dread drained the blood from his face. Dragging his hand back out from the mattresses, Jarret rose to his feet. Peter had known about it because he'd seen him hide it last night.

Something harder and colder than anger swelled inside Jarret.

As he turned to his closet to get his boots, his phone buzzed. Mindlessly, he slid the phone out and checked the message.

I warned you. Now I'm coming for you. ~Tyrone

This came from the same number as all the anonymous messages. Had it been Tyrone all along?

Undaunted, Jarret grabbed his boots from the closet. He was going to the campground.

Now I can barely remember the words,

Your words, my words.

You said something about my misery attracting your mercy.

But I don't remember for sure.

And I don't remember the sound of your voice

or how it struck me.

It seems like an old memory that I'll lose in a few hours.

No vivid impression remains.

Had it really happened at all?

Or had it only been a dream?

CHAPTER 35

Keefe stood next to Brother Leopold, the one brother he felt least comfortable around—as if he needed another sign that he wasn't called to this life—while Kieran and Alex merged into the group of friars going to visit a nursing home. Wolfgang and Phil had left immediately after lunch, with another group of friars for street evangelization. After pouring his heart out to Brother Giles, Keefe decided to stay for the rest of the retreat, and he was looking forward to participating in the work of the Apostolate. He'd had to hear his assignment twice before he believed it. Housekeeping.

The front door clicked shut and the muffled voices of Kieran, Alex, and the friars faded.

Brother Leopold pushed off the wall in the hallway. "So..."

"So?" Keefe took a breath, ready to throw himself into the job. He could learn the value of hard and boring work today. Maybe tomorrow he'd get to do something interesting.

"So you get to explore the friary," Brother Leopold said, "with a broom and dust rag."

Struggling to keep disappointment from showing, Keefe forced a smile. "Yeah. It's gotta be done, right?"

"And we'll keep an ear out for the doorbell, be Christ to any surprise visitors we should happen to get, like those saintly porters of the Franciscan order." He motioned for Keefe to follow and turned down the hall. "Friday is a big cleaning day around here. I like to start with the laundry. Having to check it every half hour keeps me from daydreaming."

"Oh." Keefe blinked, wondering if Brother Leopold had a problem with concentration.

Brother Leopold led Keefe into a little sunlit room with a white washer and dryer, a deep sink, and an old wooden table. He lifted a basket of brown robes to the table and grabbed one of them. "Always check pockets. Wouldn't want to wash anyone's pack of cigarettes or lottery tickets."

"Cigarettes? Lottery tickets?" Keefe hesitated and then reached into the basket.

"And you really have to balance the washer or you might as well put on some music."

"Huh?" Keefe pulled a scrap of paper from a robe, set it on the table, and glanced around for the radio.

"That old thing can dance clear across the floor."

Not understanding in the least, Keefe studied the washing machine. What did he mean by "dance"?

Brother Leopold caught him staring at it. "Let me guess, you've never done a load of laundry in your life."

"Uh..." Keefe swallowed his Adam's apple. "We have a live-in maid."

Seconds ticked by as Brother Leopold stared at Keefe. Then his mouth curled up on one side. "Nice. Well, you're gonna learn today."

Once they got the washing machine chugging, Brother Leopold shoved a broom into Keefe's hands. "You can take the living room, dining room, hallways, and kitchen. I'll take... a break."

"Huh?" Keefe tried to understand the fairness. Maybe he'd get a break after the sweeping, while Brother Leopold worked.

"It's a joke." Brother Leopold quirked a grin, the rest of his expression remaining serious.

"Oh." Keefe exhaled.

"But you still have to sweep those rooms. I'll take the upstairs and we'll meet in the chapel." He turned halfway around and glanced back. "When you return the broom to the closet, make sure it's secure against the wall."

"Yeah. Sure."

Brother Leopold turned to go. "Nothing worse than stumbling on a broom handle when you're trying to hide."

Keefe stared in disbelief. What did he mean by that? Did he think Keefe would try to get out of work? Or was he saying that he hides in the broom closet? Or...

Strolling down the hall, into and out of patches of sunlight that snuck in here and there, Brother Leopold lifted a hand in the air and waved.

Keefe continued to stare until the brother turned a corner. He was kidding, right?

~ ~ ~

After sweeping the floors, taking care of more laundry, scrubbing the kitchen, and dusting and rearranging furniture, Brother Leopold and Keefe squatted by a pew in the chapel. Brother Leopold stroked his long wiry beard. "When you clean, you need to focus on cracks and corners. I noticed dirt in some of the corners of the rooms you swept."

"Oh. I thought I..." Overwhelmed and worried that he wouldn't get done in time, Keefe had swept quickly, but he thought he'd swept well. "I'll go back and fix that. The corners of every room?"

Brother Leopold's gray eyes flickered. Then he smiled. "Just focus on this job. I'll dust the statues and icons. And you can wipe down the pews with the wood cleaner and sweep under them, especially by the feet of the pews." He pointed to dirt that gathered in the crack between the pew and the floor. "You can use the dustpan and brush for that."

Keefe nodded and grabbed the dustpan and brush from a bucket of cleaning supplies.

Brother Leopold straightened and shuffled back a few steps, his gaze bouncing from Keefe to the floor and back to Keefe again. Whatever he had on his mind, he didn't share it. He turned and grabbed a long-handled duster.

Determined to get it right, Keefe got on all fours and shoved the brush into the crack. After sweeping under the pew thoroughly, he grabbed the bottle of homemade furniture polish and poured the lemony-scented oil onto his cleaning rag. Pew by pew, he worked, wiping and wiping—careful to get the corners—and sweeping underneath, careful to get around the feet. The monotony of the chore sent his mind wandering. He recited a few prayers that he'd memorized without trying, St. Francis' Peace Prayer and the Act of Contrition. Then his thoughts turned to a story he'd read from the *Little Flowers of St. Francis*, only his mind gave it a twist, throwing him into the story. Keefe smiled as his imagination took over...

~ ~ ~

Keefe's legs and feet ached. Nearing the end of the three-and-a-half-hour walk from Perugia to St. Mary of the Angels, otherwise known as the Portiuncula, he slowed to a zombie's pace. He fixed his weary eyes on the rolling hills on the horizon as he trudged down a muddy road between a dormant vineyard and a field. A few snowflakes spiraled down from an icy gray sky, one landing directly on his nose. The cold burned for an instant. Keefe considered sliding a numb hand from his sleeve to brush his nose, debating whether or not the action would actually lessen his discomfort.

"Ah, it is good to be so close to home." Brother Francis, who had been walking behind a few yards, traipsed up alongside him. He too walked with his hands stuffed up his sleeves. Despite the bitter cold, his face held a serene look of joy.

"Yeah, that's good." Keefe couldn't wait to finally get there, to step inside to the warmth of the brothers' little place and to take a bite of

whatever meal they set before him. His stomach had long since stopped growling and had started eating itself. "Hey, did you hear? One of the friars, a Friar Minor, healed a blind man. He prayed over him and suddenly the man could see."

"Is that so, Brother Keefe?" Brother Francis smiled at him with a childlike look, despite a week of stubble on his jaw and too many sleepless nights. "Would it make you happy to be able to heal the sick?"

"Sure. That'd be awesome." Keefe matched Brother Francis' pace, happy for the conversation. He almost didn't care that a cold breeze had blown the cowl off his head. "Or even if I knew the Scriptures better. Then I could have the right verse at the right time and preach with power."

"Or with the voice of an angel," Brother Francis added.

Keefe smiled, encouraged, and continued to elaborate. "Right, and then I could touch hearts the way some of the other brothers do, the way you do."

"Oh, yes. And it would be wonderful to speak many languages," Brother Francis added. "Or to prophesy or have great knowledge of stars and herbs..." He leaped forward and flung his arms into the air, his voice rising. "...and to know all about the treasures in the earth."

"Huh?" Keefe smiled, amused by Francis' sudden jovial spirit. "What treasures?"

Brother Francis turned in a circle as he spoke, still moving forward down the muddy road. "And the qualities of birds and fishes, animals and humans, roots and trees and rocks and water!"

"Or better yet..." Happy thoughts renewing his strength and even taking the edge off the cold, Keefe jogged a few steps to keep up.

"Better yet?" Brother Francis faced him, walking backwards, his brown eyes beaming with joy. "What do you think is better than all that?"

"Well, what if we could preach so that everyone in the world converted to the faith of Christ? Don't you agree? That would totally rock!"

"It certainly would!"

Another snowflake landed on Keefe's face, melting instantly. A drop of freezing rain followed.

"Oh." Brother Francis held up a palm and peered upward. "Maybe we should run." He pulled his cowl over his head.

"Yeah, run!" Keefe took off, stomping down the muddy path with frozen feet, the straps of his sandals cutting him.

Brother Francis sprinted too, laughing and panting, his sandals slapping the ground even louder than Keefe's.

The cross and steeple atop the Portiuncula soon came into view. The freezing rain fell harder, soaking through their rough tunics. A few more yards and they would reach the gate of the stone fence that surrounded the Portiuncula.

Sucking in ice cold breaths and making little clouds on every exhale, Keefe pushed himself the last few yards. But then his sandal bumped a rock, and he sailed to the ground.

Riddled with pain and frustration, he moaned.

Then Brother Francis' smiling face appeared over him. "You've gotten yourself all muddy, dear Brother." He wrapped icy fingers around Keefe's arm and yanked him up.

As Keefe climbed to his feet, he glimpsed mud on Brother Francis' tunic and realized he'd dropped onto his knees in the mud to help Keefe. A lump formed in his throat as he contemplated that act of kindness.

Lifting his cowl over his head, Brother Francis pulled the cord that hung before the gate. A loud bell clanged, reminding Keefe of a cow bell.

Keefe and Brother Francis huddled together, waiting.

A long moment later, the arched door of the Portiuncula opened and warm yellow light spilled out into the dreary evening. The brother who greets guest, the Brother Porter, stomped to the gate. He crossed his arms over his chest. "Who is it?"

Keefe shrunk back, startled at the gruffness of his voice.

"We are two of your brothers," Brother Francis answered, cheerful as ever.

"You lie. I know who you are. You're thieves who go around deceiving people and stealing what they give to the poor. Get out of here!" And he stomped back to the Portiuncula and closed the arched door, taking the last bit of warm yellow light from the cold evening.

"Uh, wow." Keefe stared, dumbfounded. "He didn't recognize us." An icy breeze blew. He adjusted his cowl, trying to cover his frozen ears better, and then he stuffed his hands back into his sleeves.

Brother Francis turned toward Keefe with a blank stare. His eyes widened as if he had an idea. Then he pulled the cord at the gate again and stood smiling at the Portiuncula.

"But he said he doesn't know us." Keefe glanced at Brother Francis and then took in their surroundings, hoping to find anything that could serve as shelter from the freezing rain.

The arched door to the Portiuncula opened and the Brother Porter stomped to the gate, shouting and waving his arms.

Keefe stared in disbelief. Once the Brother Porter drew near enough for Keefe to make out his bad language, Keefe's mouth fell open. He tugged on Brother Francis' sleeve. "Did you hear what he called us? Do you hear what he's saying about us?"

The Brother Porter unlatched the gate. "Get away from here, you dirty thieves. You won't get anything from us. In fact, if I get my hands on you..." The gate creaked open.

Breath catching, Keefe latched onto Brother Francis' arm and staggered back. "He, he must have no idea who we are."

Brother Francis allowed Keefe to drag him back a few feet.

The angry Brother Porter hollered one last insult before slamming and locking the gate. "Go to the hospital," he shouted as he headed back to the little church.

Face radiant with joy, Brother Francis turned to Keefe and grabbed his shoulders. "Bear it patiently, my brother. Don't you see? He knows exactly who we are. And God has allowed him to speak against us so that we may have something more wonderful than all the treasures of the world."

"What are you talking about?" Cold and anxiety rattled him to the bone, causing Keefe to shiver out of control.

"Above all the graces and gifts of the Holy Spirit which Christ gives to His friends is that of conquering oneself and willingly enduring sufferings, insults, humiliations, and hardships for the love of Christ. So if we bear it patiently and take the insults with joy and love in our hearts, oh, Brother Keefe..." His eyes turned heavenward. "...we have found perfect joy!"

Keefe shook his head, not understanding.

Brother Francis released his hold of Keefe's shoulders and ran back to the gate.

"Stop!" Panic making him shake all the harder, Keefe shouted after him. "What are you doing?"

Like a child playing a game, Brother Francis gripped the cord with two hands and rang the bell once, twice, three times. Then he turned to Keefe, a big smile on his face.

The door to the Portiuncula flung open and the Brother Porter came out with a club....

~ ~ ~

A hand landed on Keefe's back, yanking him back to reality. He sucked in a breath and jerked back, dropping the brush and dustpan. Sitting in an awkward position on the floor, Keefe lifted his gaze.

"Looks great, Keefe, really." Brother Leopold backed up, hands in the air, concern in his eyes. "I think we're done here."

"Oh, okay." He composed himself and picked up the dustpan and brush. "Time for the bathrooms?"

"No, I think we'll skip those today. The Brothers will be coming for Vespers soon. Let's get cleaned up."

Keefe gathered the cleaning tools and followed Brother Leopold from the chapel, still contemplating the perfect joy of Saint Francis. It reminded him of the Gospel tenet that "the last shall be first, and the first shall last." And now he got it! He didn't need to become a Franciscan to find perfect joy. As long as he gave everything his best, he could accept whatever came his way as God's will. If God allowed something to happen to him, it would be for his good.

"Jesus, I trust you!" he said in his heart.

CHAPTER 36

With a white-knuckled grip of the steering wheel, Jarret raced down Forest Road. The pungent aroma of Limburger cheese burned the back of his throat. In his haste to get to the campground—to get to Peter—he'd pulled out of the garage without first lowering the windows of his car.

He pressed the control to lower the windows. A humid breeze rushed in, whipping a loose lock of hair across his face.

Cuss words slammed through his mind, along with memories of everything that Peter had ever done against him, everything he hated about Peter. This was the worst though. Peter had taken his journal. All his personal thoughts laid bare.

His skin crawled and stomach twisted. He imagined himself half naked, hands tied to the overhead branch of the sole tree in a field, standing vulnerable, soul exposed, before Peter and—the way Peter and his friends gossiped—every kid from River Run High.

Jarret rubbed a hand across his chest and pressed the gas pedal to the floor.

Gray clouds raced through a blue sky, hiding and revealing the sun every few seconds, creating a turbulence above that matched the turbulence inside him.

Had Peter already read it? Had he shared it with Dominic the Gossip? Were they reading it right now?

Jarret clenched his jaw, a surreal feeling overtaking him as he sped past a farming supply store on his left and neared a gas station on his right. He would teach Peter a lesson. Should've done it sooner. He shouldn't have let Keefe hold him back the day he'd found the Limburger cheese. No more struggling to forgive.

A police officer stood talking to a woman in a car parked near the front of the gas station. Officer O'Brien? He lifted his head as Jarret flew by. Then he shook a finger in warning.

Jarret tapped the brakes to slow down, but he wasn't gonna stop. *And I ain't looking back.*

A glance to the dash told him it neared 3:00 p.m. He was about to miss his appointment with Father Carston. *Who cares?* He was done with that. He'd been trying real hard to follow the rules and make the right choices, thinking he'd been scoring a victory here or there, but really he'd been failing. If he wanted to follow the straight and narrow, he shouldn't have had Kyle and the gang over to his house. He'd let them drink in the house and did nothing to stop it. He'd even caved in and smoked a cigarette. And he'd done nothing to control his outrage over the prank that C.W. pulled on Roland. Nothing to control his temper. He could've hurt him worse than he did. He'd had nothing inside telling him to stop. And then Chantelle...

Jarret took in a sharp breath. Sure he'd broken it off but not before having his hands all over her. He was no different than before. Without the special grace of an awareness of the presence of the Lord, he couldn't do this.

Within a few minutes or seconds—time made no sense now— Jarret passed the weathered campground sign and cranked the steering wheel. Paying no mind to the speed limit signs, he wound his way back to the camping area.

His eyes narrowed and jaw tightened as he pulled into an overflowing parking lot. Shadow and light darted along chrome and paint as the clouds shifted with rage. Another car pulled in from the opposite direction, on the far side of the parking lot. A teenage boy got out.

Jacked up with anger, Jarret flung open the driver-side door and jumped out. He scanned the parking lot and the camping sites beyond them. He'd probably find Peter near the same sites they'd had last year.

A glimpse at the teenage boy across the parking lot made him pause. A flicker of sunlight illuminated his sandy blond hair. Then clouds brought shadows over him, not hiding his quarterback build and slumped shoulders. Was it... ? It was. Tyrone. After hearing Chantelle's lie, he'd probably searched the park for Jarret, assuming Jarret had come camping with Roland and Papa.

Car keys dangling from a finger, Jarret strode toward the camping sites. He'd deal with Tyrone later.

As he strode nearer, he made out figures and faces, people setting up tents or standing in groups. Kyle and the gang, including Trent, Conner, and C.W., sat on picnic tables. Nate looked out, maybe saw Jarret approaching.

Jarret's gaze raked over them and other kids from school until it landed on Roland. And Peter.

Fist clenching, he inhaled a deep breath and quickened his pace.

The length of a football field stood between them. Peter didn't see him yet. But then he turned, and he and Roland spotted Jarret at the same time.

Jarret gave a hostile glare and jabbed a finger in the air, pointing at Peter to let him know that he was coming for him. Like a tide rushing to the shore, he was coming for him.

Peter exchanged a look with Roland, his expression saying he didn't understand. As soon as Jarret reached him, he would understand.

A few steps later a brick wall rose up in his mind, high and strong, his conscience warning him louder than ever before. He'd heard the voice of conscience so faintly in the past that he almost hadn't recognized it. It had spoken in whispers and made him feel as though he'd simply forgotten something. But it had grown, standing at times like a door that he had to intentionally pass through to do the thing he knew he shouldn't. But today, it stood like a wall. He would have to break through this wall, tear it down brick by brick, to go after Peter. He shouldn't seek revenge. Not even for this. But he didn't care anymore. Peter had gone too far.

This wall was coming down.

With a wave of anger, Jarret pushed through the wall of his conscience. Wanting to free his hands, he shoved his keys into the front pocket of his jeans. His finger bumped something that snagged his thoughts and suspended his mood. He recognized the thick fabric from touch: the scapular that Keefe had told him to wear.

Jarret slowed his pace and pulled the scapular out. He dangled it in front of himself and gazed at the image on the brown square of cloth: Simon of Stock kneeling before Our Lady of Mount Carmel. The words "Behold the sign of salvation" curved over the figures.

A feminine voice spoke in his mind. *If you had come to me, you would not have run into such spiritual danger.*

The hair on his arms and neck stood up. A prickling sensation ran over his skin. If he had come to her...

He understood. This cloth was the Blessed Mother's mantle of protection for her children. If he asked, if he trusted, if he believed like a little child, she would help him do what he couldn't by himself.

Out of the corner of his eye, he saw Tyrone drawing near, another tide rushing in with nothing to stop it, nothing to break the waves. If Jarret kept moving, he'd reach Peter first. But Tyrone would be on him in seconds.

Utterly aware that he was on autopilot and about to do something he might regret but powerless to stop himself, Jarret lifted the scapular over his head and stopped walking.

Peter stood about sixty feet away, staring at Jarret with his head cocked to one side and his eyebrows screwed up.

The blur of Tyrone's moving body came into Jarret's peripheral vision. He would reach Jarret in a few seconds.

The urge to thrash Peter rose up like a powerful current, wanting to pull Jarret along like sand in a rip tide. But he couldn't give in. One hand on the brown cloth of the scapular, Jarret stood his ground. The promises of the scapular whispered in his mind. A protection in danger and a pledge of peace.

"There you are, you—" Tyrone drew near spewing curses and flailing his arms, his face red with rage.

Roland, followed by Peter, marched toward Jarret too.

Jarret held Peter's gaze, the heat of revenge still flowing through him. He couldn't do this on his own, couldn't rely on his own strength. He needed to surrender. He closed his eyes for a moment and pictured the Blessed Virgin. "So, uh, you gonna help me?"

It dawned on him. No one but the humble would believe in this little way. He'd been thinking that he had to be strong, do it all himself, get the help of God directly. But now... Jarret surrendered to the humble handmaiden. Then he opened his eyes.

"I've got a brother like you." Tyrone shoved Jarret's shoulder.

Stepping back to keep his balance, Jarret glanced but returned his attention to Peter. He wasn't going to thrash him. He wasn't going to seek revenge. He was going to forgive the way Roland had forgiven him, the way Jesus—

A rush of longing and emotion cut off his thought.

Then Tyrone's fist smacked his cheek with a jolt of pain, and he staggered to the side. Jarret straightened, rejecting the urge to touch his throbbing cheek. He lifted his gaze to Peter again, who was now running with Roland toward him.

"My brother ain't at home now, thank God," Tyrone said with anger accentuating every word. "He's off at college. I knew you were just like him before I ever met you, when Chantelle came home with your number on her arm..." He stepped closer and grabbed Jarret by the shirt.

Indignation wrestling with resignation, Jarret struggled to win on his own battlefront.

Tyrone grimaced. He locked hate-filled eyes onto Jarret's and continued ranting. "He wrote on my arm all the time, in permanent ink, some dorky name he had for me. I'd rub my arm raw trying to wash it off. Just like you, thinking you're the man, wanting everyone to respect you. You just bring trouble to everyone."

As Tyrone drew back and let fly, Jarret resisted the impulse to block the fist headed for his gut. A burst of pain. Then the air left his lungs and he doubled over. But he didn't fall. Another punch and a sharp pain on his jaw.

Jarret forced his mind back to the canyon and pictured the hand of Jesus open in invitation, and the wound. He did not deserve that. But Jarret did deserve this. Maybe it could make up for beating C.W.

Tyrone threw punch after punch, jerking Jarret in one direction and then the other. He deserved it for all the punches he'd thrown over the years. Jarret's fists had been like the fists of the soldiers beating the Savior. *And the Savior opened not his mouth.*

"Are you crazy?" a boy shrieked. It kind of sounded like Peter. "Get off him, you freak."

The pounding stopped. Jarret lay on the pavement, shielding his face. He lowered his arm, lifted his head, and glimpsed a crowd through his swollen eyes. Kyle, Sherman, and the cheerleaders stood in a circle around him, Nate and a few others with cellphones out. Recording it all. A policeman ran toward them. Officer O'Brien. And then Mr. Brandt and Papa without his hat.

"What in the Sam Hill? You little punk…" Papa had a few more choice words.

Roland and Peter wrestled Tyrone back and were saying something to him. He slipped free and lunged for Jarret. But Roland's fist shot out and landed on his chin.

While Tyrone regained his balance, everyone stopped talking and time stood still, all eyes on Roland. Roland shook his fist out and tossed a shy glance at Papa.

Papa broke the silence. "Well, if he hadn't done it… That boy was about to get a heap of trouble from me." His gaze caught the approaching officer. "And I'd be on my way to the slammer for assaulting a minor." He jerked a hand out at Tyrone. "Beat it on outta here."

Tyrone lifted his arms and mumbled something under his breath. Then he spit out a bad name for Jarret and stomped away.

Roland dropped onto his knees by Jarret. "You okay?"

Aching all over, Jarret pushed himself up more.

Roland and Peter each grabbed an arm to help him. Papa had squatted before him but straightened, stumbling back, a beam of sunlight catching his piercing blue eyes.

"Man, did you lose your mind or what?" Peter said. "Why didn't you fight back?"

Roland said nothing, only stared with a bewildered look.

"I shouldn't have told you to turn the other cheek." Papa brushed off Jarret's shirt and touched his chin, a mix of concern and "fired-up" on his face. "Didn't think you'd listen. Didn't think you'd ever…" He turned his head in the direction of Tyrone, who now stood at a distance with Chantelle and a few other girls.

"Naw, you were right." Mouth aching, Jarret forced the words out. Flooded with immense joy, despite his face throbbing with pain, Jarret met Papa's gaze and laughed. His ribs screamed, cutting the laugh short but not diminishing the joy.

Papa's brows drew together over his squinting eyes, his crow's feet and forehead creases deepening with his confused look.

The hint of a smile passed Roland's lips. The look in his cool gray eyes made Jarret think he understood.

"Help him to my truck," Papa commanded. "I'll take him home. And find my hat."

Peter dragged Jarret's arm over his shoulders and wrapped his own arm around his waist, making eye contact for a split second.

Jarret smiled inside, touched and amused by this act of kindness from the kid he'd intended to pound.

Roland did the same on the other side, his actions more gentle and secure.

"Won on my own battlefront," Jarret mumbled to Roland.

"Won? You must be drunk. Or high?" Peter leaned forward and peered past Jarret to Roland. "Does Jarret do drugs?"

"No," Roland snapped.

Papa and Mr. Brandt led the way. They'd only taken two steps when a figure in uniform crossed their path. "Well, Jarret, I hate to say... you probably had this coming."

Fire flashed in Papa's eyes. His body tensed as if he were about to make a move he might regret.

Roland flung himself between Papa and Officer O'Brien. And Mr. Brandt grabbed Papa from behind.

Seeing a bit of himself in Papa, Jarret wanted to laugh. But it woulda hurt. So he didn't. Instead, he let his archenemy and his little brother help him to his father's truck.

CHAPTER 37

Dinner over, three Brothers got up from the long table. They carried their dirty plates to Brother Leopold, who had just appeared in the doorway with a tray.

"For me?" Brother Leopold said to one, raising his bushy eyebrows, "Thanks," to another, and "Stop, I have more than enough," to the third.

Keefe scooted his chair back and carried his dirty plate to him too. "Need help with dishes?"

Brother Leopold tilted his head back, his scraggly black beard jutting out. "I haven't scared you off yet, huh?"

Keefe laughed. "Not from all the work."

Brother Leopold, who rarely smiled, smirked as if appreciating Keefe's reply, maybe thinking his dry, sarcastic humor had rubbed off. In reality, it had taken Keefe over five minutes to get some of his jokes.

Keefe took the plate from another friar and stacked it on the others. Even though he would never live here, he had to admit that he had liked getting to see every inch of the friary. He'd especially enjoyed cleaning the chapel, though it had worn him out. He'd never done so much house cleaning in all his life. Nanny took care of everything, except sometimes their bedrooms and the recreation room.

"No, I've got it. Other brothers will clean up the dishes tonight. We get to relax." Brother Leopold set the tray on the table and grabbed more dirty plates. "You should go to the courtyard."

"What's there?"

A strange look passed over his face, then a crooked grin. "You'll see."

Keefe followed one of the other retreatants from the dining room, trying to remember his name. Was it Alex? Rolling with the flow of the friary, they hadn't spoken much. Alex barely spoke anyways and always seemed deep in contemplation. Keefe could picture him as a Trappist monk, taking a vow of silence. Keefe loved the balance of life in the Franciscan brotherhood, the humility it required, the support it offered, working and praying together...

With a sigh, Keefe resigned himself to God's will for his life. The retreat director, Brother Giles, had encouraged him to keep praying, even after Keefe had dumped out the mess of his life before him.

"Don't go home, Keefe. Stay and pray. Continue to ask the Holy Spirit to guide you. Your reason for being here may be different from what you think." Brother Giles referred to Keefe's suggestion that God had only wanted him to help Piper. "Ask your parish priest to be your spiritual director. Frequent the sacraments, especially the Sacrament of Penance. That one is so powerful in helping us to examine our lives and come to know our strengths and weaknesses. Keep the door open, Keefe."

Having voiced all of his doubts, failings, and insecurities—hearing the words aloud—Keefe knew he couldn't possibly have a calling. So he decided to use his time at the friary to see what God did want of him.

Alex held open the door to the courtyard and looked back at Keefe.

"Thanks," Keefe said as he stepped outside to the cool evening air.

If Alex replied, Keefe didn't hear it. His gaze was riveted to the far corner of the grassy courtyard. A homemade archery target stood in the corner, about twenty yards away.

"Hey, Keefe, ever shot a bow?" Brother Damien, the youngest of the friars, stood by three other brothers around a portable table. One of the friars strung a bow, another neatened a stack of aluminum arrows. The third, Brother Paschal, talked about the scores various brothers had made over the week.

Keefe smiled to himself, happy for the opportunity to play a favorite sport.

Alex and Wolfgang drew near, Wolfgang with his hands stuffed in the front pockets of his chinos. The other retreatants and brothers must've gone off to do something else, but they would all know of his skill if he played today. He didn't want to show off. For some reason, he liked the idea of being a nobody, someone they'd never see again. He came here hoping for a vocation, but he'd leave knowing nothing, more blind than ever, simply trusting in God's will for his life. Whatever happened to him would be for the best. Keefe's smile grew as he joined the brothers at the table.

Brother Damien took the bow from the brother who strung it. "Ever try archery?"

"Uh, yeah. I have some experience." Keefe studied the shiny recurve bow in the brother's hands.

"Then I don't need to show you how it's done?" Brother Damien's tone held the hint of a challenge. He arched a brow as he offered the bow to Keefe.

"Nope." Keefe accepted the bow but not the challenge. The target stood a mere twenty yards away. He'd heard the scores of the others from Brother Paschal. He could easily hit a target eighty yards away, but he decided to shoot average shots today and not stand out.

"Okay, stand back everyone. We have a new archer." Brother Damien pointed to where Keefe should stand, the corner opposite the target, then he grabbed a handful of arrows. "Stand sideways, you know, with your body perpendicular to the target." He modeled the pose.

Keefe nodded, amused that Brother Damien felt the need to instruct him. Aware of everyone's eyes on him, Keefe stood tall and relaxed as he nocked an arrow. He held the arrow lightly on the string and turned his gaze to the target, the rings of black, blue, and red around a yellow circle. Ready to disguise his skill, he shifted his focus to the black ring and then lifted and drew the bow.

Blessed is he who takes no offense at me.

The sudden intrusion of the verse into his mind made Keefe suck in a breath. Heart thumping, he lowered the bow and his fingers slipped, sending the arrow into the grass a few feet away.

Laughter filled the courtyard. And words of sympathy. One or two had done the same thing themselves. Another said something about follow-through.

But the verse. What did it mean?

Brother Damien retrieved the arrow for Keefe and offered more advice, one hand to Keefe's shoulder.

Keefe nodded but couldn't hear the advice over his own thoughts. Scandalized in Christ? For trying not to hit the target? For not giving his best? For holding back so others may win and not pushing for the victory himself? He'd had a habit of giving in, giving up, letting others claim the victory. Too worried about Papa's reaction, he'd held back and hoped for other ways of discerning his vocation. A part of him even rejoiced in the thought that he wasn't called because then he wouldn't have to explain himself to Papa again. He wouldn't have to fight to win. He didn't want Papa upset over his life choices. He didn't want to leave Jarret either, especially since he was so new in his faith and so susceptible to temptation. And Roland, the loner, needed him too.

His past, his failings... He'd wanted to believe he wasn't worthy of the calling. He'd been weak all his life, going along with Jarret's bad ideas and making moral compromises. A man of faith didn't do that.

Only one receives the prize. Shoot so as to win.

Hoping to calm the wild beating of his heart, Keefe sucked in a breath. He wiped a sweaty hand on his khakis and re-gripped the bow.

"That's it." Brother Damien slapped Keefe on the shoulder and backed up. "You got it. Go, Keefe."

The other brothers chanted, "Go, Keefe. Go, Keefe."

Keefe nocked the arrow and lifted the bow, three fingers lightly holding the arrow to the string, determination flowing through him in every movement of his body and will. He'd blow all their scores away. Brother Damien had better be ready with more arrows.

Focusing on the yellow circle in the middle of the target, Keefe drew the string toward his chin and peered down the spine of the arrow. "All my best for you, Lord," he prayed as he relaxed his fingers and let the arrow fly.

The arrow hit its mark and everyone cheered.

Keefe took another arrow from Brother Damien, who stared at the target with wide eyes. He nocked the arrow and focused on the center of the target. Allowing his subconscious to guide his movements, he raised and drew the bow in one fluid movement and sent another arrow to the center of the target. And another and another until Brother Damien stood with empty hands and an open mouth and everyone else cheered and clapped.

Feeling a strange mix of humility and pride of accomplishment, Keefe handed the bow back.

"Wow," Brother Damien said. "I guess I need to learn something from you."

Keefe dipped his head and smiled. The brothers and retreatants gathered round, including a few others that Keefe hadn't noticed earlier.

"If you decide to join the friary, you can be on my team." Brother Pascal glanced at another brother and pointed first to Keefe and then himself.

"Yeah, about that." Ever since speaking with Brother Giles and telling him that he didn't think he had a calling, Keefe had felt a bit guilty and fake on the retreat. "I don't think I'm cut out—"

"Hey, Keefe." Brother Giles stepped from the back of a cluster of brothers. "Mind if I tell everyone why you were late?"

"Uh..." A fresh wave of heat assailed him, and for a moment he regretted telling the friar. "I guess not."

The group shifted, everyone forming a circle in the corner of the courtyard.

"Keefe would've been here on time. But he passed a stranger in need. A woman had pulled off the highway because of a flat tire. He wouldn't have been the only one to pass her by, but he was the only one to turn back and help her. Her need became more important to him than his need." He proceeded to retell the story, emphasizing how Keefe had not given up when anyone else may have. He sacrificed his time, money, and even his future to serve Christ in the moment.

Brother Giles paused, his gaze piercing through Keefe's veneer. "When you so willingly stop by the side of the road to help a stranger in need, you are preaching the Gospel. As Our Seraphic Father said, 'The deeds you do may be the only sermon some persons will hear today.'" He paused again, all eyes shifting from him to Keefe now. "If the Lord calls you to this life, we would be honored to call you Brother."

The other friars nodded and voiced their agreement.

Brother Charles spoke next, smiling as he almost always did, but with a sympathetic gleam in his eyes. "Don't think about being unworthy. We're all unworthy. Before his conversion, St. Francis made so many mistakes that he said, 'I have been all things unholy. If God can work through me, He can work through anyone.'"

"I have a confession to make." Brother Leopold stroked his scraggly beard. "Keefe..." Shoulders slumped, he lifted his eyes with a somewhat hangdog expression on his face. "When we worked together cleaning the friary, I got the impression you came from money, probably hadn't worked a day in your life. I'd have bet you never even cleaned your own room. So maybe I threw more at you than I should've." His shoulders bounced up and down, a sheepish shrug. "But you accepted everything with patience, which is something I still struggle to do. And maybe you do come from money, but you're poor in spirit. You're more worthy of this vocation than I am." He nodded at Keefe and bowed his head.

"The Holy Spirit has brought you here," Brother Simon said, his long nose pointing out his childlike smile. "Let him continue to guide you. Which reminds me..." He patted the pockets of his robe. "I have a verse for you." He stuffed his hands into his pockets and pulled them out empty. "Well, never mind. I have it here." He tapped his forehead. "Turn often to Isaiah 41:10. 'Fear not, for I am with you. Be not dismayed, for I am your God. I will strengthen you, I will help you, I will uphold you with my victorious right hand.'"

Overcome with emotion, seeing it himself only now, Keefe covered his teary eyes with his hand. How far would he go to please the Lord? What was he willing to give up?

Everything.

Last fall in Italy, God had opened his eyes to His love and planted a seed in his heart, making him long for a way to return love for love. Heart aching, he'd chosen the Lord over Jarret ever since, losing their close relationship in the process. He was willing to give it all up and go all the way for Christ. He longed for a way to return God's love. Total sacrifice of self seemed the only satisfying way.

Then he'd met the Franciscan friars at the Brandts' Bed & Breakfast. Their joy and life of penance spoke to him. And the seed that had been planted in the fall, sprouted over the summer. And now, this fall, it wanted to grow more. Would he keep a lid on his faith? Would he hide behind his fears? Fear of his faith shining in the darkness for all to see, fear of others suffering if he lived his life for Christ, fear of giving his best, fear of being unworthy of this calling... No. He would not be afraid anymore.

Wherever God called him, he would go.

As if jolted by electricity, the hair on his arms stood up and his skin tingled. The charge traveled deep inside from head to toe and his heart now told him: God called him here.

CHAPTER 38

Absolution tingling through every pore in his body and to the depths of his soul, Jarret swung the oak door of the confessional open and stepped out. He couldn't stop smiling as he strode down the aisle toward the altar. A single light shone on the crucifix that hung over the golden tabernacle, and a red candle burned nearby. The faint scent of incense permeated the cool air. Peace accompanying him, he slid into a pew and knelt to make his penance and thanksgiving. God was so good to him.

When he finally lifted his bowed head, his heart stirred. The eyes of the Blessed Virgin statue gazed down at him. He hadn't realized that he'd knelt on the Mary side of the altar. "Thanks," he whispered, intensely aware that her motherly help and protection had brought him victory.

Ready to go, Jarret glanced over his shoulder to find Papa. On the way home from the campground yesterday, guilt over standing up Father Carston had struck him, and he'd begged Papa to run him by the church. But Papa wouldn't do it. "No, I'm taking you home. We need to get those scrapes cleaned up." Papa had later fetched his cowboy hat from the campground but hadn't stayed the night. And this morning, he'd come up to Jarret in the kitchen, rattling his keys. "I'll take you up to the church now."

Jarret had dropped his fork and nearly lost the scrambled eggs in his mouth. Stunned by Papa's offer and aware of the time—the confession hour—he'd shoved his late breakfast aside and taken him up on it.

Now Papa knelt hunched over in a pew, head bowed, Stetson hanging from his clasped hands over the pew in front of him. Was he going to make a confession? It must've been years for him.

Affording Papa his privacy, Jarret got up and shuffled quietly from the church. He strolled across the strip of grass alongside the church and leaned against the solitary tree. A few yellow leaves peeked out from the thick green foliage on branches that reached in every direction. The approaching autumn hung in the cool air.

A few minutes later, Jarret sat in the grass and leaned against the tree trunk. If Papa did decide to make a confession, he might be in there for a while. Father Carston would go easy on him, the way he had on Jarret. Even today, after he'd stood him up yesterday, Father Carston had been understanding.

Jarret had apologized as soon as he'd entered the confessional. "Hey, I'm sorry I missed my appointment yesterday."

No trace of anger in his voice, Father Carston had simply said, "Not to worry, Jarret. Shall we begin in the name of the Father…"

Peace continued to swirl in Jarret's soul. And thankfulness. Incidentally, when he'd gotten home from the campground, he'd realized that Peter hadn't taken his journal after all. Last time he'd written in it, Jarret had stuffed it between the headboard and pillow, instead of his regular hiding spot between the mattress and the box spring. He'd almost pummeled Peter over nothing.

Watching a squirrel dig in the grass a few yards away, Jarret toyed with the cord of the brown scapular around his neck. Without the consolation he'd experienced after Arizona, he had a feeling he was really going to need this in the years ahead. And the Sacrament of Confession. He couldn't do it all on his own, but he didn't have to. The Blessed Virgin would help him. God called him to surrender and trust. That's where he'd find victory.

Movement by the side of the church drew Jarret's eyes.

The side door flung open and Papa staggered out, seeming in quite the hurry. And looking shaken. A few steps later, he adjusted his Stetson and regained his typical long stride as he crossed the mostly empty parking lot toward his silver Lexus.

~ ~ ~

Keefe rolled into the garage around 8:00 p.m., his head aching from having squinted into the sunset for the last stretch of the long drive home. The sight of Papa's Lexus, Jarret's Chrysler 300, and even the Digby's Crown Victoria in the garage made him take a deep breath and sigh. He liked that he'd find everyone at home.

Silence enveloped him as he stepped into the dark mudroom off the garage, though the echo of the road still rang in his ears. Deciding to talk to Papa before anyone else, he dropped his travel bag to the floor and shuffled to the front hallway. The door to Papa's study stood open, but the only light came from the chandelier in the foyer at the far end of the hallway.

Keefe retraced his steps, grabbed his overnight bag from the floor, and went to the back of the house. Light streamed into the family room through the windows overlooking the veranda. He looked through a window. Someone had left a tray of dishes and condiments on a table. No one was there.

He shuffled through the long, dimly lit living room and into the great room. Light from the kitchen spilled into the formal dining room and side hallway, but he heard no voices.

Weary and ready for a hot shower and bed, Keefe flipped on a light and climbed the stairs. He hit the light switch in his bedroom and his gaze snapped to the San Damiano crucifix in his new prayer corner. Joy sparked at the welcome sight. He liked the new arrangement of furniture, the simplicity; though it was a far cry from the bedroom he'd have at the friary.

Keefe dropped his travel bag onto his bed and dug around for his phone and charger. It had run out of charge an hour ago. He plugged it in by his desk and called Jarret to see where everyone was.

"Hu-hey, Keefe. Welcome home." Then his tone turned serious. "We're out back. Get your butt out here now. Papa's lost his mind."

Keefe laughed. He plugged his phone into the charger and traipsed downstairs.

He left the house through the door in the laundry room. As he neared the backyard, he glimpsed the flames of tiki torches farther back. Planted in the yard, two tiki torches flanked the portable archery target. Two more torches stood fifty or so yards away from it, a group gathered in their flickering light. Papa, Roland, Peter, and… Keefe squinted for a better look, glimpsing red hair. Was that Kyle? Kyle lifted a bow and faced the target.

"Hey, there you are." Jarret came from the shadows, bumping into Keefe, maybe intentionally. He pulled Keefe into a hug and then pushed him back and held him at arm's length.

"So check Papa out." He tilted his chin in Papa's direction and grabbed Keefe's arm, dragging him to a circle of camp chairs around a blazing bonfire. "We really need to have that talk. And since we're all here—"

"What's up with Papa tonight?" Keefe studied his surroundings.

Christmas lights decorated the bushes in the landscaping. Nanny and Mr. Digby stood by an open barbecue grill. Mr. Digby scraped the grill grates with a big spatula while Nanny babbled on to him about something. Cans of pop and bottles of water sat in the grass around the camp chairs, a tray of dirty utensils in one chair.

"Keefe!" Nanny shouted and hurried toward him. "We didn't think you'd get here for another hour."

"Yeah, I left earlier than I thought. Didn't want to get home too late." He opened his arms as she drew near.

Mr. Digby shuffled over as Nanny hugged Keefe. Not one for hugs, he offered his hand. "Welcome back. How's the truck?" He wasn't one for personal or sentimental comments either.

"Fine."

"Are you hungry? We have plenty of leftovers." Nanny clasped her hands and smiled.

"No, not really. Just want to relax."

"Oh, very well. I'll tell your father you're here." Nanny took Mr. Digby by the arm. "Maybe he won't mind if we head in for the night. I'd like to get those dishes washed..." Her voice trailed off as they strolled out toward the archers.

Jarret sat in one of the camp chairs, motioned for Keefe to do the same, and grabbed the can of Coke beside the leg of the chair. "Soon as Papa picked Roland up from camping this afternoon—"

"Wait," Keefe interrupted. "I thought Papa went camping with Roland."

"Right." Jarret took a swig of Coke. "Well, he came home early."

"Why?"

Jarret froze, his look revealing he had something he needed to talk about. "We can chat later, but you're gonna hear some rumors about me at school."

"What rumors?"

A strange look passed over Jarret's face. "Something about me and Chantelle. Just know the rumors aren't true. And I'm gonna have to repair my image or learn to live with it. Anyway..." He flung a hand out to indicate the arrangement of camp chairs. "Papa got home and started setting up all this. Then he told me and Roland to invite our friends for a cookout."

Keefe would've liked to hear about Jarret's dilemma now, but he respected that Jarret wanted to change the subject. "A cookout. That's kind of nice. Right?"

Jarret's eyes bugged. "Not if we have to invite our friends. Who am I gonna invite? They all brought beer last time. So I told Kyle he owed me one and made him come alone. Of course Roland had to invite Peter." He gave another bug-eyed look and a little head shake.

The group cheered, Peter's voice the loudest. And Kyle threw a hand in the air. The Digbys reached Papa. Papa and Roland looked Keefe's way and started over toward the bonfire.

"Don't you think it's dangerous to shoot arrows in the dark?" Keefe said.

Jarret took a swig of his pop. "Eh, what's the worst that can happen?"

"They could shoot each other."

Jarret glanced at Peter and Kyle with a grumpy expression. Then he shrugged. "Eh, who would care?"

Happy to see them, Keefe stood as Papa and Roland drew near. Nanny grabbed the tray of utensils and followed Mr. Digby to the house.

Papa looked Keefe over as he approached, then he gave Keefe a bear hug. "I see you made it in one piece. The truck held out?"

"Sure."

Roland had stopped a few feet away and stood with his arms folded, looking aloof, the way he often did.

"What, no hug?" Keefe smiled.

Roland smiled back and shuffled over. "Welcome back," he said in a low voice as they hugged. "Papa's wearing me out with all this family stuff. I just want to be alone."

Keefe laughed.

Papa, Roland, and Keefe joined Jarret in the circle of camp chairs. Roland folded his arms. Papa sat with his legs stretched out in front of him, ankles crossed.

"So..." Jarret dropped his Coke can into the holder on the arm of his chair. He and Roland exchanged strange looks, the orange light from the flames making shadows on their faces. It almost seemed as if Jarret wanted Roland to say or do something. Roland wasn't having it.

Assuming Jarret wanted to get the family talk started, Keefe leaned forward. "So, Papa, can we talk?"

Looking relaxed in his camp chair and happy for the question, Papa nodded. "Sure."

Keefe cleared his throat, a bit worried about how Papa would take all this. "We're kind of worried about you. You've been acting strange lately."

Papa squinted at him. "Strange, huh? How's that?"

Jarret sat bolt upright, his hands flying about. "Are you kidding? All this." He gestured toward the back of the yard, where Peter and Kyle pulled arrows from the target, and then toward the Christmas lights. "And your bucket list?" He paused, glancing from Keefe to Roland, as if wanting them to chime in, and then back to Papa. "You're dying, ain't ya?"

"Way to ease into it," Keefe mumbled to Jarret.

"Well." Jarret shot back. "You weren't saying anything helpful."

"I was trying."

"What bucket list?" With relaxed movements, Papa reached for the dark bottle—root beer?—next to his boot and twisted the cap. "I don't have a bucket list."

"Right." Jarret shook his head irritably. "Taking us out to dinner, wanting everyone to go camping, horseback riding in the Bad Lands... All that?"

Papa chuckled and stared into the bottle he held. "That's not a bucket list. That's me wanting to do something with my boys. You see a problem with that?"

"So you're not dying?" Roland's voice sounded higher than usual.

Papa smirked and patted Roland's thigh. "No, Roland, I'm not dying. I mean none of us knows the day or the hour. But I don't have any special insight into the day of my death."

"Have you been to a doctor?" Roland said.

"Haven't seen the need."

"So what were you and Miss Meadows talking about on the porch?" Jarret blurted.

Papa squinted at him for a long second, then he opened his mouth and finally an answer came out. "Marriage."

All three brothers' mouths fell open.

Keefe thought maybe he should congratulate him, but he couldn't get his mouth to work.

"We haven't decided anything. But one day…" Papa smiled at the campfire. Flames snapped and a branch crackled. "I mean to marry her."

Papa took a swig of root beer and adjusted his Stetson. "Listen, boys. All the trouble this past year or so, all the changes in you boys, I guess it got me thinking. I realize I haven't been much of a family man, and maybe it's a little late, but I'm making an effort now." He looked at Roland and Jarret and then at Keefe. "You boys grew up so fast. Don't know how long any of you will be around before you go running off to college or the monastery."

A smile forced itself onto Keefe's face. He dipped his head to hide it.

"How'd your time with the monks go?" Papa said.

"They're not monks. They're Franciscan friars, you know, a community of Brothers. And it went fine."

"So you have the calling?"

Keefe nodded, happy. "Yeah, I think so. I mean, I'm pretty sure I do." Then he remembered something from the retreat. "Before that, though, there's something I have to do. Something we all have to do." He glanced at Roland and then held Jarret's gaze. "We have to get confirmed. All three of us."

"Confirmed?" Jarret squinted at him. Then his gaze shifted here and there. "Oh, yeah. I guess we've never done that."

"Okay," Roland said. "So what do we have to do?"

Keefe smiled. He was gonna like this.

#

Scripture References

"Blessed is he who takes no offense at me" (Luke 7:23).

"Jesus said to him: No one who puts his hand to the plough and looks back is fit for the kingdom of God" (Luke 9:62).

"I came to cast fire upon the earth; and would that it were already kindled!" (Luke 12:49).

"He said to them, 'Come and see.' They came and saw where he was staying; and they stayed with him that day, for it was about the tenth hour. One of the two who heard John speak, and followed him, was Andrew, Simon Peter's brother. He first found his brother Simon, and said to him, 'We have found the Messiah' (which means Christ)" (John 1:39-41).

"Fear not, for I am with you, be not dismayed, for I am your God; I will strengthen you, I will help you, I will uphold you with my victorious right hand" (Isaiah 41:10).

"Do you not know that in a race all the runners compete, but only one receives the prize? So run that you may obtain it" (1 Corinthians 9:24)

Bibliography

St. Francis of Assisi: Omnibus of Sources. (3rd ed.). Chicago, IL: Franciscan Herald Press, 1973.

Did you enjoy this book? If so, help others enjoy it, too! Please recommend it to friends and leave a review when possible. Thank you!

Every month I send out a newsletter so that you can keep up with my newest releases and enjoy updates, contests, and more. Visit my website www.theresalinden.com to sign up. And while you're there, check out my book trailers and extras!

Facebook: https://www.facebook.com/theresalindenauthor/
Twitter: https://twitter.com/LindenTheresa

About the Author

Theresa Linden is the author of award-winning *Roland West, Loner* and *Battle for His Soul*, from her series of Catholic teen fiction. An avid reader and writer since grade school, she grew up in a military family. Moving every few years left her with the impression that life is an adventure. Her Catholic faith inspires the  belief that there is no greater adventure than the reality we can't see, the spiritual side of life. She hopes that the richness, depth, and mystery of the Catholic faith will spark her readers' imagination of the invisible realities and the power of faith and grace. A member of the Catholic Writers Guild and the International Writers Association, Theresa lives in northeast Ohio with her husband, three boys, and one dog.

www.ingramcontent.com/pod-product-compliance
Lightning Source LLC
Chambersburg PA
CBHW060940120726
47910CB00002B/425